UNDER THE STORM

UNDER THE STORM

A NOVEL

CHRISTOFFER CARLSSON

Translated from the Swedish by Rachel Willson-Broyles

HOGARTH
NEW YORK

Translation copyright © 2023 by Rachel Willson-Broyles

Published in the United States by Hogarth, an imprint of Random House, a division of Penguin Random House LLC, New York.

HOGARTH is a trademark of the Random House Group Limited, and the H colophon is a trademark of Penguin Random House LLC.

Originally published in Sweden as *Järtecken* by Albert Bonniers Forlag, Stockholm, Sweden. Copyright © 2021 by Christoffer Carlsson. Published by arrangement with Ahlander Agency, Stockholm, Sweden.

LIBRARY OF CONGRESS CATALOGING-IN-PUBLICATION DATA
Names: Carlsson, Christoffer, author. | Willson-Broyles, Rachel, translator.
Title: Under the storm : a novel / by Christoffer Carlsson ;
translated from the Swedish by Rachel Willson-Broyles.
Other titles: Järtecken. English
Description: London ; New York : Hogarth, 2024.
Identifiers: LCCN 2023018622 (print) | LCCN 2023018623 (ebook) |
ISBN 9780593449387 (trade paperback ; acid-free paper) |
ISBN 9780593449394 (ebook)
Subjects: LCGFT: Detective and mystery fiction. | Novels.
Classification: LCC PT9877.13.A75 J3713 2024 (print) |
LCC PT9877.13.A75 (ebook) | DDC 808.83/872—dc23/eng/20230712
LC record available at https://lccn.loc.gov/2023018622
LC ebook record available at https://lccn.loc.gov/2023018623

Printed in the United States of America on acid-free paper

randomhousebooks.com

2 4 6 8 9 7 5 3 1

First U.S. Edition

Title-page art by Adobe Stock/Khawla

To anyone who's ever visited the yellow house
next to Toftasjön, just outside of Marbäck

I used to have secret dreams about making it all add up, so that everything would be accounted for, brought to a close. At last to be able to say: It was like this, it happened this way, this is the whole story.

But that would be contrary to better knowledge.

Per Olov Enquist, *Captain Nemo's Library*,
translated by Anna Paterson

MARBÄCK, HALLAND, SWEDEN

November 1994

1

They say death *takes you*. It's an old expression, from the time back when death was an actual character you could meet in the Marbäck forest or along the road. An ice-cold hand grabs you by the throat; a shadow expands around your body until you can no longer breathe. That's how you picture it when you're a child.

People say other things, too. There's this word, used by old men and women around here. It comes across their lips like sinister smoke when someone is a little mean or nasty, when a place or thing has this unpleasant, uncanny feel to it: *kymig.*

He's kymig, that one. Never liked him.

Don't go there. That house feels so kymig.

I did something kymigt tonight.

That's what people say. And, if you were to suddenly find yourself in some kind of danger, it's not *I don't know what to do* but *I don't know where to put myself.* As if your first instinct is to hide.

Tonight, the flames are reaching for the sky. The weather forecast calls for a downpour, but not a drop of rain is falling. Everything is covered with soot and ash, and the big trees are getting singed. The smell of smoke drifts all the way up to Simlångsdalen, and into Skedala, over a mile away.

It's an event people will remember, a reference point. It creates a before and an after.

Where were you when . . .
Was that before or after . . .

Down in Tolarp, the houses and farms are far apart. Closest to the Markströms' house is Ulrika Antonsson's farm. A big field separates their properties. Ulrika is the one who calls it in.

"There's a fire," she shouts into the phone. "The Markströms' house is fucking burning down! Send the fire department, the police, and ambulance, everything, fast as hell."

She walks out into the November night and captures the fire in a photo. She's not the only one to do so. Later they'll get requests from the newspapers: The local paper's photographers don't arrive until the fire department has begun to fight the flames, so their pictures don't turn out. Almost everyone refuses the offers, but Ulrika needs the money and secretly sells her amateur photos for a handsome price. Soon they're everywhere. Her name is never mentioned in connection with them—they're credited only as "reader photographs"—but everyone knows.

Great tongues of flame lick at the black night. The Markströms' brown house is an old one-story wood-frame home, with small windows and a flat roof. The house has a woodstove and a gas oven, bad wiring and old electrics; its insulation is dry as a bone. Previously, these sorts of details weren't widely known, but soon everyone is aware of them. If there's anything people learn in the days following the Tolarp disaster, it's that just about anything can set a house on fire.

Not everyone wakes up. Little Isak Nyqvist up on Svanåsvägen is fast asleep. His best friend, Theo Bengtsson, is too. Two miles away, in Officer Vidar Jörgensson's front hall, Leo is pacing. The racket he's making forces Vidar up to the surface until he opens his eyes and places the soles of his feet on the chilly floor.

The Labrador is waiting at the front door and barking like he hears an intruder.

"What's wrong with you?" Vidar yawns. "There's no one here."

He opens the door. The dog peers out. The November air is ice-cold. Then Vidar smells it, too. When he walks onto the lawn he can even see the fire: At this distance it's nothing but a glow, an orange dome rising over the tops of the fir trees.

"I see," he says. "Good boy, Leo. Thanks for barking." Leo shakes himself off and gazes at Vidar with big brown eyes.

"Well, let's see." Standing in the frosty grass, Vidar tries to guess how far away the fire is. "Yes, maybe. I'll have to check."

He goes back inside, gets dressed, and slips his feet into his heavy boots. He presses his lips to Leo's soft head and gives him a quick scratch behind the ear, and then he takes off.

But he doesn't have his uniform. He's been wearing it for four years, and in that time he's seen a lot. The uniform is important that way; it's a shield. Or armor. The things you encounter stay within it.

Not everything, obviously. Sometimes you see the sorts of things even the uniform can't protect you from.

Vidar walks along old paths edged by tall forest and open fields, small farms and houses. A little village seven miles east of Halmstad— that's Marbäck. Those who grow up here are told they belong to a fortunate few. It's probably true. Disaster seldom visits here.

The stink of the fire grows worse. The glowing dome expands. In the distance, sirens blare.

He passes the Marbäck farmstead and turns, heading over the small bridge and down to the area known as Tolarp.

There it is, roaring in the night, the Markströms' house, ablaze. His eyes sting. The fire department and ambulance have arrived; so have Vidar's colleagues. His heart beats faster and faster as he approaches the blue-and-white police tape. The incident commander, a stocky fireman whose name Vidar can't remember, is talking to the ambulance crew.

"Is there anyone inside?" Vidar asks.

"It's hard to get in, so we don't know. But we don't think so. The house is engulfed, so all we can do now is let it burn."

"Is there anything I can do?"

"You're a police officer, right?"

Vidar nods. "I live out here."

The incident commander looks at the fire. Flames like living beings. "Help out wherever you can. Just stay away from the fire."

Vidar makes his way to the ambulance and borrows an extra jacket. Over by one of the blue-and-white patrol cars, a colleague gives him a pen and notebook. In the glow of the flames he helps keep order, making sure the cordon isn't breached and talking to the neighbors. Almost everyone is outdoors and looking in the same direction, seeing the same thing.

Ulrika Antonsson's property is to the southwest. They've already spoken to her. To the north is Josefina Fransson's farm. She bought it, livestock and all, from her elderly father a few years before he died. For the price of one thousand kronor. A symbolic amount. She's fifteen or twenty years older than Vidar, but he's always liked the look of her. Her mass of hair is shot through with gray, but her skin is almost smooth. She's wearing jeans and an unbuttoned shirt knotted at her waist over a dark tank top that hides her heavy breasts. Those are his weak point, really. He's aware of it, but there are certain things a person can't quite help.

"I saw Lovisa come home on her bike," Josefina says. "I think it was around five, maybe. You know, she works at Brooktorpsgården in town now, so she usually bikes to the bus stop and then back home again in the afternoon."

All that's left of the bike is a sooty frame.

"Did you see her after that?"

Josefina shakes her head.

"But her mom and dad took off later. I guess someone was turning fifty, so they're at a party."

"So Lovisa was at home?"

"I . . . I think so. But I don't know for sure. I haven't seen her since she got home."

Vidar's back is to the fire, but he can still see it. The flames are reflected in Josefina's shiny eyes.

When he walks along the border created by the police tape, he stops short. There, in the grass, is a work glove. He turns toward the house. The flames aren't as vigorous now, but they never made it over this way. Vidar runs his hand over the frozen grass. It's untouched.

Vidar raises his arm and calls a colleague over.

"Uh-oh," he says.

"Yeah," says Vidar.

"I'll get a marker. Will you stay here?"

Vidar stays put. It's cold without his uniform on. His colleague returns with a numbered marker and carefully pokes it into the ground.

The glove has clearly been singed by the fire. At close range, you can also see the flecks of blood.

It takes some time for the chief inspector to arrive, but suddenly there he is, at the center of the action, leaning over a floor plan someone managed to obtain on the spur of the moment. That's the kind of guy he is. Chief Inspector K-G Öberg is a large man, dressed like a woodsman in heavy boots, a knitted sweater, and pants with many pockets. He's a good boss with a strong voice. His hair is thin and gray, his face round and puffy. His eyes, as they gaze down on Vidar, are candid, warm. Despite his size he can move without making a sound—you seldom hear him coming.

"Young Jörgensson," he says, surprised. "Damn it, that's right—you live out here."

"I do."

"Aren't you on duty soon?"

"In seven and a half hours."

K-G waves a hand. "Go home and get some sleep, for Chrissake. We'll need you tomorrow."

Vidar's eyes are burning and his joints are aching. He's been on duty all day, and by now, half the night. His shoulders are stiff, his back sore. Still, he asks: "Don't you need me here?"

"Oh, yes, I want you here. With seven hours of sleep in you."

Vidar hands over the information he's managed to gather and

takes off the borrowed coat, nodding to his colleagues and heading home. Sunrise is still far off. Behind him, the blue lights rotate in silence, police cars, fire trucks, ambulances.

Not far off, he sees movement from the corner of his eye. In the forest.

Vidar stops and breathes. It's so quiet here.

Then he sees.

"Hey." Vidar turns around and shouts back toward the lights. "Hey! There's someone in here."

Someone who didn't know where to put himself.

2

Isak Nyqvist lives up on Svanåsvägen in the red house by the turn-around. They're all in a row there, the small single-family homes, and Theo lives only three houses away.

This morning, Mom crouches down by his bed to wake Isak up, same as always. He can smell her in his sleep; that's what always reaches him first. She's been up for an hour, getting ready before she heads to work.

"Isak. Isak, honey. It's seven-thirty, time to get up."

The same words every morning, but the words aren't what make him open his eyes—it's how she says them. Mom's voice is different today, sort of absent, as if she were watching an exciting movie at the same time but also not really. There's something else between the words. Mom sounds scared.

"What's that smell?"

She doesn't respond. Her eyes are a little red. They're not usually red.

Isak drags himself out of bed. Why is it so hard to wake up on a school day, when it's so easy on Saturdays and Sundays? It's one of life's great mysteries.

:::

Old people say *pightle* instead of *yard*. Isak has recently noticed this, how old people sometimes talk a little different, using words he's not used to. He likes the way they sound. Edvard often says that words are one of the links we have to those who are no longer with us.

From the kitchen window he can see past the *pightle*, all the way to the *woodhouse* at the edge of the woods, on the other side of the bike path, past the stone wall overgrown with spirea and snowball bushes. He doesn't know who owns the *woodhouse*, but up in its ceiling there are huge numbers of *harvestmen*. Nearby are old trees full of fat red apples and round yellow *cherry plums*, but they're hard to get at because the *brennessels* are too tall and will sting you. After one of the first overnight frosts last year someone had yanked the plants up, as if a large animal with huge jaws had passed by and bit the nettles off. The plum tree was finally accessible, so Isak and Theo climbed up and ate so many they got the *collywobbles*.

He hasn't eaten plums again since; the very memory of that stomach-ache makes him feel nauseated.

Now he sprinkles way too much sugar on his cereal, so it turns into delicious lumps in his milk. Usually his mom protests, but not today. She isn't even sitting by him for his breakfast; instead she's in the living room with Dad. He hasn't left for work yet, even though he usually always drives off around quarter to seven.

"*So did you get any sleep?*" Dad asks.

"*No*," says Mom. "*I'll drive him up today. The school bus passes by there, so it probably won't come. Hell, I don't know what way we should even go.*"

Isak sits by himself at the breakfast table, unsure where to look. It's a new feeling for him, and he wants to go to his mother, but he understands he shouldn't. He pretends the flakes in his bowl are heroes, cowboys or soldiers maybe, and the milk is dangerous lava.

He sees big, heavy shoe prints in the hall. They came from someone else.

There was a visitor last night.

This Monday morning is cold and damp. He sits on the booster seat in back, on his way to school up in Simlångsdalen. Mom is taking a longer route than usual. No snow yet. They pass by the old factory buildings. Beyond the trees, down by Tolarp, Isak can see streaks of gray rising to the white sky.

"What's going on, Mom?"

"What do you mean, honey?"

"You and Dad are acting so weird. And it smells like when we have a fire."

Mom doesn't say anything for a long time. "I don't know exactly what's going on."

That's all she says, and he doesn't ask more. Mom's hands are squeezing the wheel so hard that her knuckles are white. When they arrive, Isak has to dash across the schoolyard so he won't be late.

Something is different at school, too. Isak's teacher Iréne looks like she's lost something important. She's smiling, but the smile never reaches her eyes, and during recess she smokes more than usual.

When school is over, Mom is waiting for him. Her face is hard, as if she's hurting somewhere but is trying to hide it. When they get home, Isak notices a stranger's fresh shoe prints in the hall, and the doormat is in a funny spot.

"Mom, who was here?"

"What do you mean?"

"The doormat is weird. And we don't have any shoes like that."

Mom mutters something, faraway.

Theo rings the doorbell a little while later.

Sometimes Theo acts a little strange at school when they're with the other kids. He sort of pushes Isak away. Snaps at him, or sighs. Isak doesn't really know why, but it only happens when other people, like Torbjörn or Håkan, or Malin and Cecilia, are there. But it's only sometimes, and he and Theo are definitely best friends. They just are. It's almost like a *law of nature*, a phrase they recently learned in their classroom up at Breared School.

"Hi," says Theo.

"Hi."

"Want to do something? Play King's Rock?"

Isak puts on his jacket and runs to the kitchen.

"Mom, can I . . ."

She is standing at the sink and staring out the window, her arms hugging her body like she's freezing. Tears are running down her cheeks. She is startled to see Isak; she wipes her eyes, blinking fast.

"Was that Theo just now? Are you going out?"

Isak stands there with his jacket unbuttoned and a scary feeling in his chest. "Mom, are you sad?"

She smiles and shakes her head, still blinking away tears.

"What's going on, Mom?"

"Why are you asking? Did they say something at school?"

"No, but . . ."

"What?"

It's hard to put into words. But it's *something*.

When he doesn't say anything, she bends down and hugs him tight, whispering that everything is okay, there's nothing to worry about, everything will be fine. "Now go play with Theo."

"But . . ."

"No, everything's fine." She smiles through her tears. "I'm just tired."

"Okay."

"When will you be home?"

"At five."

"And what do you do if something happens?"

"Get a grown-up."

"Good."

She kisses him on the forehead. Isak and Theo go outside.

There's nothing to worry about, everything will be fine.

It almost sounded like a prayer.

3

There's a hidden spot not far from the Markströms' house. An opening in the deep Marbäck forest leads down to a part of the river Fylleån where the current is particularly strong.

Edvard was the one who brought Isak there for the first time. He's actually Isak's very favorite person, probably. Aside from Mom, maybe. But he would never tell anyone that. At least not Dad.

It's not November now but summer, a warm Sunday in August three months earlier. Isak is holding Edvard's hand as they move between the trees.

"Hear that, Isak?" he asks.

"No, what?"

"Listen."

His hair is as dark as Mom's, and he has prominent eyebrows and eyes that are big and brown and warm. The sharp angles make him look almost like a cartoon, as if he had just stepped out of a comic book.

Everyone says Isak and Edvard look alike. He tries to imitate his uncle sometimes, but it's hard. When he tries to walk or move like Edvard, it just looks all stiff and jerky.

Isak gazes at him and listens.

"Hear it now?"

Overhead, the branches of the trees whisk lightly in the breeze, insects are buzzing, Göran Antonsson's old tractor putts in the distance. And something else, too: It has grown louder, a dull rush carpeting the background.

"What is it?"

"Come on, I'll show you."

They hurry on between old stumps and thick roots reaching over the path. The rushing sound expands in Isak's ears, and excitement rises in his chest.

Sometimes Edvard is a little like a dad. Isak has never said so aloud, because he doesn't want to hurt Dad's feelings, but sometimes he thinks it. Dad is gone a lot, often working late because they need the money. Sometimes he's gone over the weekend too; he's an extra mechanic for a guy in town who drives racecars, and the races are almost always on Saturdays or Sundays.

Days with Edvard are the best days. They fill Isak with both a thrill and a sense of security. Walking through the forest with his small hand in Edvard's larger one is the feeling of being home.

"Here," Edvard says at last, pointing. "Look, Isak."

He's never seen anything like it. The water is pouring so hard that it foams white and brown; it strikes and splashes the rocks ferociously on its descent. The waterfall reaches higher than the tallest trees, and you almost have to shout to be heard over the thundering sound.

A line of birds suddenly launches into the sky as if something has scared them up, and Isak jumps. Edvard places a reassuring arm around him.

"Take it easy, kiddo. Isn't it great?"

"It's huge."

"Know what it's called?"

"No."

"Dane Falls."

It's damp all around them; the air is thick. Edvard and Isak sit down on the warm forest floor. Isak can already find his way around here. Edvard and Mom, and even Dad, too, have taught him how you can use nature as a map—as long as you know how to read it. By looking around he can figure out where he is, how far it is to the falls, how far it is home, the closest path to the field up there.

"Have you had a good summer, Isak?"

"Yeah. Have you?"

"Very good."

"I like Lovisa," Isak says. "You should see her more often."

Edvard laughs. "I see her all the time."

"But not when I'm there."

"No, but she and I both have jobs. We don't get summer vacation like you do."

"Is that what happens when you're a grown-up?"

"It is when you're twenty-five, anyway."

"Are you twenty-five now?"

"Does that sound old?"

"Yeah. I'm only seven."

"That's not so *only*."

Isak looks at the high waterfall before them. Nothing bad can happen to him here. As long as he's with Edvard, everything will be fine.

"Why is it called Dane Falls?"

"Well . . . listen to this. It was a long, long time ago," he says, like he's telling a secret. "It was summer, just like now, but way back in the past. Sweden was at war with Denmark. The Swedish king was called Karl XI and the Swedes won an important battle. The Danes, who lost, fled into the deep forest here around Marbäck. They followed the rapids. And then they ended up here. Back then . . ." Edvard continues, pointing at the top of the falls, the highest point, "Do you see the two biggest spruce trees up there, on either side?"

Isak squints at the pale sky.

"Yeah, I see them."

"Once upon a time there was a bridge that hung between those trees, so you could cross the rapids. And the Danes needed to do that. It was very narrow, and it would sway and shake."

Something flutters in Isak's chest. He puts his hand on Edvard's.

"And then, as they're standing in the middle of the bridge,

something happens. The bridge breaks. The soldiers tumble into the water."

They're falling. Isak can see them, their bodies dark against the white waterfall before they plunge through the surface and vanish.

"But"—Edvard raises one clever index finger—"it's no accident. Because the Swedish king and his soldiers have been lying in wait up there, just behind the trees. They had trailed the Danes in secret, and when the moment was right, they came out and cut down the bridge."

"That's scary," Isak whispers, excited, squeezing his uncle's hand.

"They say that afterwards, the Swedish king stood right where we're sitting now and gazed at the water where the Danes fell in. That's why it's called Dane Falls."

"Wow."

"And the biggest rock of all, there, in the middle of the waterfall, do you see it?"

It rises out of the middle of the rapids, the size of a man, shiny and ancient. "Yeah."

"That's King's Rock." He picks up a small rock and stands up. "And now I'm going to show you something my dad taught me and your mom, something his dad taught him once upon a time."

"What is it?"

Edvard smiles. "You'll see."

4

Isak remembers feeling strangely close to something very important that time. It was fantastic to know that the Swedish king had visited Fylleån, their river, and had managed to kill the evil Danes.

Was it true? According to Isak's teacher, King Karl XI had never been here. She says the whole story is *improbable*.

But it could still be true.

Isak and Theo leave their bikes not far from the water. The cold and damp is worse in the shadows of the fir forest, and as they gather rocks Theo's nose and cheeks turn bright red. When they're done, they squint at King's Rock, their noses running and their pockets full.

"You start," Isak says.

"I always start."

"That's because you never manage to say *You start* first."

The rules are simple: You have to hit King's Rock. If you miss, you have to take a step toward the water. If you get a hit, you can stay put. If there are two of you, the game ends when one player isn't brave enough to take another step into the rapids. If there are more than two of you, the game ends when all but one person has given up.

Once one player is in the water, the others have to take two steps if they miss the rock and are still on land. Whoever is already in the water, and dares to keep going, drags the others toward the edge, toward an inevitable end.

The rules are so *incredibly smart,* Isak thinks. It makes you wonder who was smart enough to come up with a game like King's Rock. Not even Edvard is that smart.

Theo throws the first rock. It curves through the air and hits the water. Theo makes a face and takes a big step forward.

"Close, for your first one."

Isak misses, too. Theo hurls another rock, a nice arc through the air. It hits the right side of King's Rock with a satisfying *clack*—one of the best sounds in the world—and bounces into the rapids.

Isak doesn't get a hit that turn, but he does on the next, and they follow each other toward the water.

"Remember when Anton played with us?" Theo asks with a grin, taking his aim and throwing.

Anton is in the other class in their grade, and he lives farther up toward Simlångsdalen. He was already standing in the rapids, and he took aim for the rock but missed by a long shot. He turned to the others, shrugging and smiling, but everyone could see the fear in his eyes.

It looked like an invisible underwater hand grabbed his ankle and yanked. There was a dull thud, like when you stomp on a doormat in boots, as the back of Anton's head hit something hard under the surface.

And then he went perfectly limp.

"Anton," Theo shouted. "Are you okay?"

Anton didn't react. His thick winter gear became waterlogged and heavy. The current began to drag him along, away.

They hurried into the water and grabbed Anton's clothes, working together to drag him back to shore. He was heavy, much heavier than he looked. He lay on his back with his eyes closed, his body slack and passive. Theo looked frightened.

"Is he . . . is he dead?"

Isak shook his head. "He's breathing."

"What should we do?" Theo asked.

At that instant, Anton grimaced and grabbed his neck, trying to sit up.

"It's okay," Theo burst out. "He's okay. Don't tell anyone, or we'll never be allowed to play King's Rock again, okay? You're okay, right?"

"I think so," Anton squeaked.

They walked home, and that's the closest Isak's ever been to a disaster.

Until now, maybe. Hard to say. It's been such a strange day. Mom is upset. There was something wrong with Iréne, too. And those shoe prints on the mat in the hall.

"Why is everyone acting so weird?"

"A house burned down last night," Theo reports in a voice full of authority. He looks the way grown-ups do when something serious has happened.

"Yeah, I know, but . . ."

"You missed, you have to take a step."

The wind is cold. The smoke lingers in the air. Isak steps forward. Theo throws. *A house burned down last night.* It sounds so *kymigt*.

"Whose house?"

"The brown house in Tolarp."

"Who lives there?"

"I don't know," Theo admits. "Dad wouldn't tell me more. I'll ask Jacke when he gets home."

Jacke is Theo's big brother. They keep throwing. Isak misses. He makes it two steps into the black water, but it's so cold he feels like he's about to lose his feet. Ice creeps up his legs. At last he's shaking.

"Call it a tie?"

"Sounds good," Theo chatters through his teeth.

That night, as Isak lies in his bed, he listens to Mom and Dad through the wall.

"*There must be some misunderstanding,*" Mom says.

"*Let's hope so,*" Dad says. "*But, you know . . .* "

"*Know what?*"

"*Oh, nothing, I just . . . I was just thinking about August.*"

"*About Dad?*" Mom sounds almost angry. "*Why?*"

Then silence. Isak can hear his own heartbeat, it's so quiet.

And then there are weird, thick sounds. Sobs and sniffles. It's Mom. He wants to run in and hug her, but he's too scared; sometimes you just know it's best to stay away.

The last thought that goes through Isak's mind before he falls asleep is of his breakfast cereal that morning, his cowboys and soldiers, how they were slowly consumed by the milk, the glowing lava.

5

Vidar Jörgensson's family tree is deeply rooted in the land surrounding Marbäck. He comes from here, just like his father, grandfather, and great-grandfather before him. This is where he feels at home, in a small yellow house with white trim, a fireplace, and a dog his friends take on walks when Vidar has to work overtime.

Police work is part of his inheritance. Vidar's father, Sven, was a policeman. Then he got sick and died. That was three years ago, and these days Vidar must live with a sort of emptiness in his chest, something—how to put it—has congealed.

The night lingers within him. There are many unanswered questions. The burning house has been a topic of discussion on the radio all morning, alongside the news that the citizens of Sweden, in the first general referendum since the one on nuclear power fourteen years ago, have voted to join the European Union. By a tiny margin. Half don't want to join; in Marbäck, hardly anyone voted yes. Debates in the village have been frequent and extensive, bitter.

In light of the fire in Tolarp, the EU issue seems distant and insignificant. Everyone is paralyzed.

This morning he arrives at the station in downtown Halmstad, over by Slottsparken and the courthouse, a gray-and-white six-story building of steel and glass which, from a distance, most closely resembles a mental institution. It rises like a watchful eye over Halmstad, the small city by the coast that has grown considerably.

Vidar changes clothes. And he changes, becomes almost a new person; his exhaustion fades away and is replaced by a sharp feeling of being present. Several of those whose shifts just ended were out in Marbäck overnight but had arrived there only after Vidar had gone back home.

"It wasn't a pretty sight." Markus gets a cup of morning coffee from the machine in the changing room. "When they brought her out, I mean."

Markus Danielsson is the same age as Vidar and comes from Laholm. They did their military service together but didn't hit it off until they were recruits, when they realized they were the only Hallanders in the class. Markus's uniform is stained and sooty from the night.

"You didn't know," Markus says as he looks at Vidar. "I'm sorry, I thought . . ."

"Was it her? Lovisa?"

"Yeah," Markus says. "It was."

Vidar pushes the button for his own cup. A weight on his shoulders, a little stab of pain near his heart. He takes his first sip of the coffee, too hot and bitter.

"Do they know how the fire started?"

Markus shakes his head. "Not yet, apparently. Listen, before I forget. About Sunday, you know . . . I can ask Hanna to bring someone if you want."

"You don't need to."

"Sure?"

"Yeah, I'm sure."

Vidar can hear the sounds from within the station, from out on the street. The smell of uniforms and leather, the lockers opening and closing in the changing room. He looks in the mirror. Even when something awful happens, it's a pleasant feeling, the feeling of belonging.

:::

"EU or no EU." K-G Öberg is standing by the window, his hands in his pockets and his large belly bulging toward the potted plants his secretary has to fight to keep alive. "Nuclear power or no nuclear power. It's always either-or in Sweden, have you ever thought about that? Black or white, up or down. It sounds so simple. But it's not like it makes a lick of goddamn difference." This is the first time Vidar's been in here, even though he's been on the force for four years. As a patrol officer, you do what no one else wants to, or has time for. You patrol the streets, search for patients who have gone astray from the psych ward, deal with tinfoil-hatters, go out on emergency calls, staff the passport office, send drugs to the national crime lab, receive tips from the general public, and take down reports. Visiting the office of chief inspectors is not part of the everyday routine.

"I'm sure it will make some difference," Vidar says. "In time."

"There are still taxes to pay, and we're all going to die sooner or later. The big things in life seldom change."

K-G's office is smaller than Vidar had imagined. A desk and a chair; a String shelf full of blue binders. Lots of papers, a few photographs. A diploma from a leadership course. That's all there is.

"Lovisa Markström," he says. "Her corpse looked fucking horrible."

"Yes, I heard."

The chief inspector turns his head. "Did you know her?"

"I can't say that I did."

"But what do you know about her? You're from there, after all."

"She's twenty-something, or maybe just plain twenty, come to think of it. She works at Brooktorpsgården here in town. A smart, respectable girl. I can't imagine she'd have had any history with us. Lovisa's pretty pulled together. Pretty and friendly, only child. Her parents, Hans and Erika, are good folks, well-liked in the area. Lovisa, too," he adds. "According to those I spoke with, Hans and Erika were at a birthday dinner here in town. They were planning to take a taxi back. But I didn't see them."

"No, we drove them straight to counseling."

The large man turns to the desk and hands Vidar a piece of paper. "There were no soot particulates in her mouth," he says. "Nor in her throat or lungs."

Vidar's eyes skim the paper, the cold, technical words. It's one of the first things they look for; that's why this information has arrived so quickly. Lovisa Markström did not, as it says in the report, "respire near conditions of fire."

Vidar stares at the document. "She was dead when the fire started."

"She was," says K-G.

"Do we know how she died?"

"Blunt force trauma to the head."

"So it's . . ."

"Yes."

K-G observes Vidar with heavily blinking eyes and hands him another piece of paper. "This is what we've put together so far. I just received the list. It was compiled very hastily, based on our initial interviews with people. In the middle of the night, in most cases, so we should probably take it with a grain of salt. But do you know these folks?"

Vidar looks at the list. There are five names. "I think so."

"Are there any names missing?"

It feels like a big deal to be sitting here in front of the chief inspector. He should say something clever now.

"All of these people, as far as I know, are locals. Should we consider whether something else might be going on?"

"As you know, it's almost always someone with a connection to the victim, so that's where we're starting. But what do you mean—are you thinking of anything in particular?"

"No. I don't think it's them and I'm sure you're right—but, for one example, we've got that gang of burglars that have been on a spree through northern Skåne and down by Laholm recently. Not to mention all the refugees pouring into the country. We even got one up in Marbäck, that boy Nali. I'm not saying it's them either, but in any case those are links the newspapers might make. It would be to our advantage if we could dismiss them. Like, for example, by making it public that nothing was missing from the house, if that turns out to be the case."

"All sound ideas, Jörgensson. Very smart. It's hard to say whether anything is missing, considering how much damage there was. There isn't much left, and figuring it out will take time. Time that we don't have right now. I don't care much for Yugoslavians or Serbs or whatever in God's name they are, but what would war refugees be doing up in Marbäck?"

"Could be Swedes, too, though."

"Sure. I guess. Anyway, we haven't spotted those burglars anywhere in our vicinity, so it's probably not them either. But good try." He nods at the list. "Anyone else you think is missing?"

"Yes . . . she was dating Edvard Christensson."

"That's right." K-G runs a meaty hand through his beard. "I forgot to include him. What do you know about Christensson?"

"We were in school together. He's a few years younger than me. He was smart but trouble, as I recall. The whole Christensson family is a little off, at least when it comes to the men. He was quite the troublemaker when he was younger; he's a chip off the old block in that respect."

"What's his dad's name?"

"August. He worked at the factory for years before it was shut down, and I guess he drank a lot in the time before he died. He treated his wife, Sara, pretty . . . harshly, or whatever."

Vidar's father had often told stories about August Christensson. As a child, Vidar himself had seen Sara limping and bruised on more than one occasion, but he didn't understand what this must have meant until much later.

"I suppose August wasn't actually a bad man," Vidar adds. "My own father had some dealings with him, and he agreed. But August had a good deal of rowdiness in him."

K-G chuckles. "Rowdiness, sure, I guess that's what you can call it. Not a bad man, you say? When do you stop being a good person? I've heard some things about him, too. He beat his wife black and blue sometimes. And that sort of thing is often passed down."

Vidar turns red.

"But that's good, Jörgensson, very good. Honesty is important. It could be like you say, I just don't believe it. What is Christensson up to these days? Edvard, I mean."

"I know he works part-time at the nursing home in Simlångsdalen, but I feel like I heard he's got an extra gig as a bartender in town, too, at Billiards and Bowling. I wouldn't be surprised if he's here somewhere in our files, for one thing or another. I'm not so sure he keeps to the straight and narrow, if you get my drift."

"He's got a sister, right?"

"Eva," Vidar nods.

"And what's her story?"

"She lives up there too, but on Svanåsvägen. She works for the public dental service and is married to a car mechanic. They've got one kid, a little boy."

"That's all?"

"Well . . ." Vidar scratches his chin thoughtfully. "Lovisa's dad wasn't exactly a fan of her relationship. He doesn't like Christensson, but I don't know why. It's not hard to guess, though."

K-G isn't taking notes. He never does. Malicious opinion holds that he doesn't care. Other, more respectful voices claim he doesn't need to write things down to remember them. Impossible to say who's right. Maybe one doesn't preclude the other.

"Was that all, then?"

"Well . . ." Vidar says again, searching his mind. "Also, when I was on my way home on Sunday night I found Edvard in the forest near the Markströms', all singed and bloody and messed up."

"Exactly. Maybe that's the only fact that matters."

"Have you spoken with him?"

"He's still too shaken up, he says. But we will." K-G points at the list. "They're all from over that way, so do me a favor and talk to them.

Get their alibis and all the usual, make sure everything's on the up-and-up. But above all, ask what they know about Christensson."

Vidar looks at the list. That's why Christensson isn't on it.

"Would you rather man the passport office, Jörgensson?" K-G chuckles.

It's half joke and half subtle threat.

"No, thanks."

"Good. Now get out of here."

Isak was supposed to spend time with Edvard on Sunday, but it didn't happen. Instead, he, Mom, and Dad went to the Gekås superstore in Ullared to do a big grocery shop. It was kind of a strange thing to do, if you think about it, because it's pretty far away, and gas costs money.

Isak's dad works as a car mechanic, so if Isak has learned anything it's this fact about gas. That's why you should vote conservative, Dad says. The Moderates are the only ones who think you should drive a car. Everyone else wants you to bike or some other idiotic crap.

It's a long way to Ullared. It must take a lot of juice to get there. You don't say "gas," you say *juice*. Maybe Gekås is cheaper—Mom is always walking around oohing and ahhing at bottles of shampoo, dishrags, and candles, but if you add it all up, and then figure in the juice, of course, and the fact that they have to eat at a restaurant that day because Mom never has time to pack a lunch, isn't it still more expensive than shopping at the ICA in Dalen?

Anyway, that's why Isak didn't see his uncle last Sunday, because he was at Gekås. Usually he spends every Sunday with Edvard, so Mom and Dad can have a day to themselves each week.

The first snow is falling, and it makes the world bright and quiet. Isak is bundled up and out in the snow, trying to make a snowball while he waits for Theo and Karl. It works, but it's a little tricky because the snow is still so fluffy.

Suddenly he has to pee, bad. He runs inside again, throwing open the front door. Dad is home; it's starting to get dark. As he sits on the toilet to pee he hears them talking in the kitchen.

Lovisa Markström, they say.

There's no way they can mean Edvard's Lovisa, right? He thinks back to that summer day in the forest with Edvard, when he first heard the story of King's Rock. Warmth fills his chest. That must be what Edvard feels like when he thinks about Lovisa.

When he's done he sneaks out of the bathroom and takes the cordless phone into his room. He dials Edvard's number and waits.

It rings. Edvard doesn't pick up.

There's a creak behind him. Isak turns around, still pressing the phone to his ear.

Dad is standing there.

"Isak, who are you calling?"

"I . . ."

"Isak, give me the phone."

"I just wanted to call," he says weakly.

Dad takes the phone. Mom comes in, her eyes red. "Is something wrong?" she asks.

When she sees the phone number, she purses her lips.

"Is Lovisa dead?" Isak whispers. "Edvard must be really sad, so I just wanted to call and ask how he was doing."

"Sweetie," she says, putting her arms around him, and he is confused.

The doorbell rings.

Theo and Karl are here.

Vidar is parked on the east side of Marbäck. A gentle rain is falling, and he imagines the chaos that must be developing around the crime scene in Tolarp as the technicians scramble to protect the evidence they've found. There are four of them down there, two crime-scene techs and two fire investigators, and as they work the sequence of events becomes clearer.

It all started in the kitchen. That's where the life was beaten out of Lovisa Markström, with her parents' black candelabra. Her skull was crushed somewhere between eleven-thirty and midnight. Afterward the perpetrator went to the garage for a can of gasoline.

Soon the house was burning like a torch—an image that is stuck in Vidar's mind. It's late afternoon. Vidar's had a long day, and most of it was focused on the men in Lovisa Markström's life. No red flags to speak of.

An ex-boyfriend, Jon-Erik Pettersson from Simlångsdalen, couldn't be located at first. Then it came to light that he had been evicted and was crashing with a friend in Halmstad. He'd been fast asleep when the crime was committed, and his friend, having been woken by Jon-Erik's *goddamn snoring*, could confirm this—he'd seen him lying in bed, snug as a bug, just before midnight. Jon-Erik hadn't had much flattering to say about Edvard Christensson; quite the opposite. *That bastard should be locked up. He's dangerous. I saw him beat a man half to death at B&B a year or so ago.*

A coworker at the Team Sportia store had provided Tom Johansson, one of the Brooktorpsgården regulars, with an alibi. Tom hadn't had anything very positive to add on the topic of Christensson either. Or much of anything at all, for that matter: *I don't know, is that the guy Lovisa's with these days?*

Hampus Lundberg had been at a family gathering out in Steninge until after midnight; the trip home took forty-five minutes, so he, too, could be eliminated.

These aren't even really attempts to identify a possible suspect. This is verifying alibis, and in each criminal investigation you go through dozens of them, sometimes hundreds. This is just another batch of those.

Dennis Götmark lives in an old ramshackle house. He's a friend of Billy Oredsson, a man who apparently showed interest in Lovisa Markström a year or two ago. Billy supposedly spent all evening at Dennis's last Sunday; he says he arrived at seven and stayed way past midnight.

Dennis has just gotten home; the driver's door of his car is open and he's hauling two heavy toolboxes toward his house. His work clothes are flecked with white.

"Vidar?" he asks in surprise. "It's been ages."

Once upon a time they were at school together, like just about everyone out here. Vidar recalls that Dennis broke five meters in the long jump. Didn't he win a prize? Yes. Sounds right.

"I won't take up much of your time," Vidar says. "I'm here on official business, as you can see."

It seems strange, like holding someone you know very well at arm's length.

"Is it about the fire?"

"Yes."

"It's terrible." Dennis shakes his head. "Is it true that she was murdered?"

Vidar takes out his notebook.

"I'm not sure. They don't tell us much. What I'm doing right now is gathering people's stories from that day. Maybe someone saw or heard something without thinking it was important, but it might turn out to be useful. We just want to be on the safe side."

Dennis closes the car door.

"Come on in. I'll put on some coffee."

So a little while later, they sit down at the small kitchen table, each with a floral mug before them. Who actually buys mugs like this? Dennis must have gotten them from his mom or something. Vidar pours a splash of milk into his.

"How's work?" Vidar asks.

That constant question. Simple to start with.

"I'm hard up. You know how it is." Dennis's broad shoulders sag. "Just Polish guys, Yugoslavians and shit. All the big construction projects are going to the firms in town. You know, when we were little, there were actually jobs here in the village. Now you have to go up to Dalen. I suppose even those will be gone soon enough. How about you?"

"Well, that's what I'm here about, really," Vidar says, as if to show that he finds the situation awkward. "Can you tell me what you were doing last Sunday? I mean," he clarifies, "Sunday night in particular."

"It was a regular old weekend day, or whatever. I suppose I went out and did some errands, some shopping and so on, during the day before the stores closed. I wouldn't say I saw anything out of the ordinary. Everything was the same as always."

Vidar waits. "And that night?"

"Oh, well, that night I had company."

"Who was that?"

"Billy, you know. Billy Oredsson."

Vidar jots down the name. "When did he get here?"

"Around seven or eight, maybe. We played cards and shot the shit, had a few beers, that kind of thing. He really only came over to drop that off," he adds, pointing at an electric drill lying on the floor in the hall. "He'd borrowed it from me. But then he stayed."

"How long, approximately?"

"Wow, you know, I don't know. Past midnight, anyway."

"Didn't the two of you have to get up for work the next day?"

"Yes." Dennis raises his eyebrows. "Why?"

"I was just thinking that maybe people would head home a little earlier then."

"Right," Dennis says, looking down and shifting a little in his chair. "But we got a few hours of sleep, anyway. No big deal."

"Billy knew Lovisa, didn't he?"

"Yeah, I guess he does."

"I heard he liked her, if you know what I mean."

"Did you talk to him?"

"Yes."

"How is he?"

Vidar considers the question. "Not so good, I don't think."

"I think he liked Lovisa an awful lot. Just like Jon-Erik up in Dalen. He was also pretty low when I saw him this morning. Did you talk to him, too?"

"I did," Vidar says. "I wondered . . . Edvard Christensson. What do you know about him?"

"Not much. Or, you know, of course you know everyone around here, but at the same time you don't really. So I guess I know what everyone else knows."

"And what's that?"

"He's been living up in Skärkered the past few years. Mostly stays up there, I don't see him so often. He works at the nursing home in Dalen and at B&B in town sometimes. He's trouble, gets out of control, just like his old man."

"Have you experienced this personally?"

"No, but I know people who have."

"Is he violent, too?"

"I'm sure." Dennis shrugs. "It wouldn't surprise me. Do you

think . . . I mean, they were together. Right? Everyone's saying it was him."

"Are they? That's more than I know." He takes a last sip of coffee. "Thanks, Dennis. I'll have to drop by sometime. Playing cards and having a few beers doesn't sound like a terrible idea at all."

"If it was him," he says, looking gravely at Vidar, "I hope you shoot the fucker."

There is only sincerity in Dennis's eyes. On the way back to the car, Vidar strikes *Billy Oredsson* from the list.

Just one name left, a lanky man a few years older than Vidar.

Apparently he likes to visit Brooktorpsgården, the café where Lovisa worked, and has acted *kind of strange*. This is as specific as Vidar's info gets. The man's name is Martin Thorsén, and when Vidar rings his doorbell in Skedala, Martin greets him, his arm in a cast.

It doesn't look so good, at first; Vidar almost gets suspicious.

He claims he was visiting his parents in Brogård and was helping them adjust their satellite dish that evening. He says he fell and broke his wrist and was at the emergency room from eight at night to four-thirty the next morning.

Vidar contacts the emergency department of the hospital in town.

"Yes, sure," says the woman he speaks to. "Here he is. Checked in at nineteen-fifty and sent home around four-thirty in the morning."

"Okay. Thanks for your help."

And when Vidar asks Martin about Edvard Christensson, the same response comes back to him, almost like an echo.

"That bastard. I've heard about him. Fuck, man, I hope you get him good."

8

Isak's glasses are thick as Coke bottles. When he looked in the mirror at the optician's on Brogatan and saw his reflection, he was filled with horror, like when you look at the long-legged harvestmen in the woodshed. What he saw was almost gross. He had become totally distorted.

When they play basketball or bandy at recess, his glasses sometimes fall off. They've already broken once. When Isak bent down in shame to pick them up, he heard giggling in the background.

There are so many things he doesn't like about himself. He can't swim either. He's not exactly fat, but sort of. *But it's not like it's worse for him than for anyone else, is it? Everyone gets made fun of at some point, for something.* He's heard Mom and Dad saying this, talking about him.

Sometimes, in school, Isak wears a wig he found or a fake nose, or uses a whoopie cushion. But when they laugh at him other times, they're laughing just because he is who he is. Like with the glasses. It's better when people laugh at you because of something you do, instead of for something you are.

He hasn't shared this with anyone. Not even Edvard.

Still, Isak isn't as bad off as Nali, the weird kid with the mismatched clothes, dark hair, and brown eyes. Who came to school last year and started off in the other class in Isak's grade. He hardly spoke any Swedish, and everyone was told they should stay away from him.

Once he hit a teacher, and another time he threw a rock through a classroom window, making glass rain over the desks. The next day he chased after Torbjörn with a table knife. Plus, he acts really weird every time he hears an airplane.

Nali doesn't have any parents. Compared to Isak, Nali is way worse off. Sure, maybe Isak's dad is away a lot, but at least he exists.

You learn that, too: There's always someone who's got it worse. So you should be grateful no matter what.

Anyway, Isak's used to people looking at him a little funny, but now it's different. Some people seem almost scared. Others look at him like something terrible has happened to him.

He and Theo ride their bikes across the slippery bridge, over the river and down to Tolarp. The water streams below them, and the huge afternoon sun makes all the shadows long.

The area is roped off; you can't even get close.

"Wow," Theo whispers, his hat askew under his bike helmet, his eyes big and round. "Look."

They ride up as close as they dare. All that's left of the house is black wreckage. The frozen grass is gray with ash. Police tape flutters in the breeze. They're alone here, as far as Isak can tell. Maybe everyone has already seen everything they can stand to see.

"It looks creepy," Isak says.

Leaning over their bikes, Isak and Theo stand close to a place where death has actually visited. That might be why Theo's eyes look the way they do, entranced and frightened at the same time.

Wonder what Isak's look like?

"Like, if a house catches on fire," Theo says, "I wonder how long it takes for it to burn down all the way? I think ten seconds. What do you think?"

"A little longer."

"Fifteen?"

Isak's best friend doesn't quite understand time, even though he's eight. But it's hard to know with fire; maybe Theo is right and, in any case, you won't get far.

Seeing the wreckage makes something dark and cold form in his belly. A hole that forces Isak to blink in order to keep from bursting into tears.

"Do you know what's up with Edvard?" Theo asks.

"No."

"Haven't you seen him?"

"I'm going to see him on Sunday."

"Jacke says they're saying weird stuff about him."

"Like what?"

"That he . . ." Theo scrapes one of his Tretorn boots on the ground. "I don't really know. But I think something's wrong."

"Lovisa's dead. He must be really sad."

It must be so terrible to have lost Lovisa. Almost like if Isak lost Edvard.

His throat constricts.

"They're saying things about you, too."

"About me?" Isak turns his head. "What things?"

"Hello, boys."

Someone walks up behind them, and they move to the side. It's Göran Antonsson. He's out for a walk with Elvira, his old, tired-eyed, brown-and-black German shepherd. Rumor has it that his wife, Ulrika, was the first one to notice the fire. "What are you doing here?"

"You can't get by," Isak says, and when Göran looks at him it happens again.

The old man goes stiff and purses his lips, his eyes darting here and there as if to keep from looking at Isak.

"I see," he says. "Okay, yes, I see. Shouldn't you be heading home, boys? Come on, Elvira."

The dog obediently follows Göran along the border made by the police tape.

"I want a dog, too," Theo says.

I never want anyone here to die ever again, Isak thinks.

:::

"I just don't know how we can tell him. His world is going to come crashing down."

It's night now. Isak is lying on his back in bed. Everything is spinning. He can hear Dad's voice from the other side of the door.

"I just don't understand how . . . I mean, if it's even true. My God, Eva, we've let our son spend time with him every weekend. What if—"

"But maybe it isn't true. It can't be."

Isak is out of bed now. He stands by the door to their room and peeks in. The many shadows are long and the whole house feels threatening, as if the walls have shrunk in.

"What did Edvard do?"

They both jump when they hear his voice. Mom gets out of bed. She's wobbly and smells bad.

"There's nothing to worry about." She slurs a little and puts her hands on his shoulders. "There's nothing to worry about."

"Yes, there is."

"Go back to bed, Isak," Mom says.

"Can I sleep in here? I'm . . ."

He doesn't want to say it. You're not supposed to be scared. She hugs him. He tries to slip out of her embrace. Hugs aren't much help, when you stop to think about it. But it doesn't work; she's too strong. He gives up and leans against her shoulder.

"I know he did something bad," Isak whispers. "But I don't understand why."

"Me neither, sweetie," Mom whispers back.

9

Ulrika Antonsson likes it when you get rough. He's got a firm grip on her hair, and his other hand is pressed to the curve of her pale back.

It's been going on for a while now. It's a way to pass time, but he's started to get bored. If it were up to him, he would rather be with Josefina Fransson at the next farm over.

The bed creaks. Ulrika's bottom is red from his palms.

He gets out of bed to sit in the chair in the corner. Her panties are lying there, on top of Vidar's boxers.

Ulrika smiles at him. When she does, she's almost beautiful. And then she settles between his thighs and takes him into her mouth.

He grabs the armrest to have something to hold on to. Thick white globs shoot out of him, landing on his chest and stomach. He growls. The armrest creaks.

Once he's caught his breath, Ulrika takes her blouse from the floor and wipes him off, gently and tenderly.

"Is that such a good idea?" he mumbles drowsily.

"He won't see it. I'm the one who does the laundry."

Afterward he never stays for very long. It's simpler that way. Ulrika and Vidar don't have much to say to each other.

Elvira comes up from downstairs, as if she's been waiting for them to be done. The old German shepherd brushes against Vidar. He pets her, distracted.

Vidar always avoids getting too close to the bedroom window. The risk that someone might see him is low, but it's there. Darkness has fallen. A few hundred yards away, he can make out the bright spotlights, how they shine on the wreckage that is the Markströms' house.

"I was thinking," Vidar says as he gets dressed. "You were the one who called the fire department, right?"

"Me and ten other people," Ulrika says.

"But your call was the first." He get his socks on. "What did you see?"

"Not much. I'd been down in the basement to bring up the laundry. I went into the bathroom and then came up here to go to bed. That's when I noticed that there was like a weird, flickering light in the room. And I smelled it. I went to the window and saw the fire. Göran woke up and I ran down to make the call."

And then she went out with her camera.

He doesn't mention this to her, of course, but it's still there in the hall. Vidar doesn't blame her. You have to do what you have to do to make ends meet.

Vidar contemplates a wet white spot on the floor by the chair. It's probably going to have time to dry.

"You didn't notice anything before that? I mean, for instance, before you went into the basement."

"Like what?"

"I just thought maybe you might have seen or heard something unusual."

Ulrika looks at him with a crooked smile. "I want you again."

Vidar smiles back. He buckles his belt. "Next time," he says, on his way down the stairs.

Ulrika follows him down and gives him a look that's hard to gauge.

"Oh my God, the car."

Vidar stops.

"I saw a car when I looked out the window. It was coming from up by the Markströms' house and went by here. Pretty fast, too, because

I even heard it. There aren't usually many cars on this road, at least not that late. Oh my God, how could I forget that?"

Vidar is still standing on the stairs. "That's normal. What kind of car was it?"

"Like a car-car, not a truck or anything. I could hear it. But that's all I saw."

"Did you mention this to my colleagues?"

"No. I told you I just remembered."

He asks her to call the station to report it. It might be important. Probably isn't, but that's up to them to decide.

"It was him, wasn't it? Wasn't he the one you found in the woods? Christensson."

"Yes," Vidar responds, his chest heavy.

10

The night brought more snow. Isak eats his breakfast in silence. It's Sunday, his day with Edvard. He thinks that if he doesn't say anything, if he just sticks to the usual routine and goes to his room to get dressed and gather his things, maybe everything will be like normal.

He can feel his longing all the way out to his fingertips.

"I don't quite know how to tell you this, Isak, but you can't go see Edvard today." Mom clears her throat and presses her lip into a thin pink line. That's never a good sign. "He doesn't live here anymore."

"What?"

"He moved."

"Where?"

"That's hard to explain."

"Well, I can go there instead."

"No," Dad says stiffly. "You can't."

"But he would never leave without telling me."

Dad gets up from the table and walks off somewhere. He often does this when things get uncomfortable.

"He said you would probably be able to see each other again soon," Mom says, trying. "It's tough. I don't think you understand."

Mom has started to change. It's like she has put on a mask. She seems unnaturally stiff and paler than usual, and she looks haggard.

When she brings her hand to her glass of milk, her fingers shake a little.

Isak jumps up from his chair and walks away, something hot pulsing in his body.

"Isak, I—"

"No!"

He doesn't know what he's saying no to. Maybe all of it, or just the fact that she thinks he doesn't understand, but if there's anything he hates, it's when grown-ups lie.

When Mom comes in to see him, he's on his bed, facing the wall, staring at the pattern on the wallpaper. She puts a hand on his shoulder. He wants to shrug it off, but something stops him. His throat feels weird, like there's a lump in it that won't go away no matter how hard he swallows.

"Isak . . . I know you like Edvard. To you, he's super nice and super sweet. But not everyone thinks of him that way. He has other sides, too."

Isak turns over. "What do you mean?"

Mom strokes his shoulders on autopilot, her thoughts elsewhere. "Nothing, sweetie." She tries to smile. "But you can't see him today. You'll have to wait a little. This thing with Lovisa . . . It's not so simple. Okay?"

Isak knows what she looks like when she doesn't know what to say. It makes him sad. He turns over again.

"You're lying," he whispers, but Mom doesn't hear.

Lone snowflakes float from the sky. Isak is standing in the woods with his hands on the handlebars, out of breath from his ride.

Mom and Dad don't let him ride his bike alone, but they think he's with Theo. Right now, he doesn't care.

Edvard lives in the white house up in Skärkered. It looks like it's sleeping. There's an unfamiliar red-and-yellow sign on the front door.

He leans his bike against a tree and tries the door. It's locked. That's all wrong, it's supposed to be open. It always is. The sign on the door says SEALED—NO TRESPASSING.

Isak stands on his tiptoes to peer in the window. The nail above the sofa is missing its picture, and the sofa cushions are every which way. Someone has emptied the bookshelves. That's probably what hurts the most.

When he walks around the house and presses his face to the other windows, he sees open drawers and cabinets in the kitchen, and a first-aid kit with bandages and other items on the kitchen table. In the bedroom, the mattress is upside down. The rug, which Edvard is always so careful to smooth out and adjust, is scrunched up against one wall.

He makes a few laps of the house. This is all wrong. He was supposed to come sit on Edvard's sofa with *The Hound of the Baskervilles* or *Five Go to Smuggler's Top* and listen to the sounds from the kitchen as Edvard fixes a snack, his voice and his questions about how Isak has been since last Sunday, his curious eyes when Isak tells him about the most recent book he's read, and Edvard's supposed to hug Isak hello and goodbye. That's how it should be.

He squints behind his glasses and looks at the NO TRESPASSING sign one more time, as if it's a riddle and, if only he could solve it, all the question marks would be straightened out.

Nothing happens.

Edvard is gone.

But it's impossible. It doesn't make sense. Edvard is books, games, soccer and bandy, King's Rock, exciting stories, a friend, and almost a dad. A great hole has opened in his life, silent and black and empty. If something like this can happen, then the world must be able to do almost anything to you. Maybe that is how it is. You think that everything makes sense, that's what you're taught—but it doesn't.

On his way back, cold tears run down his cheeks. They drip onto the ground, but they're so small that they vanish.

When he gets back to Svanåsvägen, he wipes his eyes and his face.

He doesn't want to be some little crybaby. Outside the house is a car he doesn't recognize. Isak cautiously puts away his bike and sneaks into the hall.

Four boots on the doormat. Two are heavy and black; the others are slimmer and brown. He picks up one of the black ones and recognizes the pattern of the sole, the damp prints on the floor.

He was here the night of the fire, too.

"It's a little tricky to explain the details," a voice says. "Given that we're still investigating the incident. Or the *incidents*, rather. But yes, we're sure." The voice is dull and calm. "I understand how awful this is. Vidar and I—he's the one who suggested we come on a Sunday so it wouldn't be as . . . Maybe this way people won't be as curious."

"It doesn't matter." Dad sounds frustrated. "Everyone knows anyway. People are already looking at us funny, saying strange things. *We're* innocent, *we* haven't done anything, but still, they—"

"Peter. Please."

It's Mom. She sounds so sad.

"I understand," the dull voice says slowly. "But we want to try to describe it for you, just so you can kind of understand what we're seeing."

"I'm sorry it turned out like this," Vidar chimes in. "There's not much else we can do—I personally checked out the other alibis."

"Right away we found one of his work gloves, the right one, at the farm. He owns a pair just like it but can produce only the left one, and furthermore he himself identified the right one as his when we showed it to him. So it does belong to him. It's slightly singed. This means that the glove all on its own can link him to the fire. And . . . Lovisa's blood is on it."

Isak is frozen in place, afraid they'll hear him and stop talking. He tries to follow what they're saying, but the conversation is moving pretty fast.

"There wasn't much left of the house but even so, a technical investigation will provide some information about what happened— more than most people think, in fact. We know, for one thing, that it was an act of arson. The fire started in the kitchen, around Lovisa's body. In the same room, we found the remains of a jacket. It belonged to him. In our eyes, this puts Edvard in her vicinity around the time of the fire. When it comes to the body . . ."

Isak's belly aches when he hears Edvard's name. He listens for Mom and Dad but can't hear them. Maybe they're holding their breaths.

"Considering that the fire started right next to it, the body is simply—how should I put it?—in too bad a shape. But we discovered Edvard before very much time had passed. Beyond that, we have his fingerprints on the candelabra. The fats and oils from the prints burned, but we managed to save some. And we also have their background, their relationship, Edvard's history of . . . well. He is August's boy, after all. I know that Vidar here, his father had some run-ins with August back in the day. Everything we already talked about on the night of the fire."

"Where is Edvard now?" Dad asks.

"He was taken into custody and was in lockup with us. After the prosecutor's decision he was remanded to jail, so now he's been moved over there."

"How . . ." Mom takes a deep breath. "How is he?"

"He's getting three square meals a day, and eight hours of sleep, exercise, and fresh air if he needs it. Of course jail isn't a very pleasant place, but I'd say that under the circumstances your brother is doing fine."

Jail. A sense of hope grows in his belly. That's where he is. Hard to know where Jail is, of course, and it sounds like a harsh place, not at all like Tofta, Tolarp, or Skärkered, but Isak promises himself to bike there as soon as he can. He loses himself in thoughts of Edvard's house, the mess inside. The empty bookcases.

"My brother," Mom repeats. "My kid brother. My baby brother, I don't understand how he could . . . He was always so kind. I don't understand what went wrong with him. Why this always happens to us, why we . . ."

Her words stop. Deep breaths. Isak hears Dad put his arms around her. "Oh, hi there."

A big, rugged man with a lot of beard is standing in front of Isak, looking down at him with curious eyes. Without a sound he has moved in and overpowered him.

"You're good at sneaking around, little boy," he continues, with a faint smile. "Very impressive."

11

K-G squats down before the boy. Who squats in front of an eight-year-old? Vidar lingers to listen to the parents' apologies about the kid.

"I'm sorry," Eva says, wiping her eyes, quick and embarrassed, "this is . . . He was off with a friend and—"

"We're the ones who should apologize," Vidar says calmly.

He looks at Isak, who is standing in front of K-G, caught red-handed. "He spends time at Edvard's place on occasion, doesn't he?"

"Yes." Eva's eyes are big and brown, just like her brother's. She carries the sour smell of alcohol and is blinking fast. "God, yes," she manages to say in a shaky voice. "He loves his uncle."

"Is it okay if we talk to him for a bit?" K-G glances over his shoulder at Vidar, as if asking for help. "Or if Vidar does, maybe?"

"If Isak wants to," Mom says, sounding steadier now.

"But . . . ." Vidar takes a step toward Eva and lowers his voice. She looks weak, all hollow-eyed and shaky. "Will you be all right?"

"I have to." Her eyes are remarkably vacant. "I don't know what will happen if I don't." She sneaks a look at the boy's father. "He does the best he can, but it's not much help."

"You just let me know if I can . . ." he begins, but Eva sways and for a moment he's afraid she's going to collapse.

"Can I just . . ." Eva blinks. "I just need to get a handle on this. He really did it. My brother."

"Yes. Unfortunately, that looks to be the case."

It pains him to say it. Edvard is a Christensson, that's true, but still, in some way, he's one of their own. That's how it is in small towns. Everyone and everything is connected.

Vidar has seen it before. To a certain extent, it's unthinkable that someone you love and even share blood with could do something so terrible. Her shoulders slump.

"Talk to Isak if you want. But be gentle with him."

"You can be there, too." Vidar thinks for a moment. "Could you tell me, does he have any books? Or movies?"

"Some. Most of them he borrowed from his uncle."

"Could you bring me a few he likes, ones he's seen or read?"

Who can say, after the fact, what it's like to be a child? It's impossible. But you still have to try to understand. Otherwise it won't work.

The parents sit on either side of their son. They're rubbing his back. Vidar sinks into a well-worn dark brown leather chair, the one K-G had been sitting in. It's comfier than it looks.

Vidar and Isak look at each other. He wonders what the boy is thinking. There are books and a few movies on the coffee table. Vidar leans forward and picks one of them up.

"*Jurassic Park*. I haven't seen this one."

"Everyone's seen that."

"Have you?"

"Some of it. Even though I'm not supposed to. I'm too little."

"Can you tell me what it's about?"

"It's about dinosaurs, almost like a zoo. A park, and it's about to open. But then it all goes wrong because there's someone bad who tries to trick everyone else. So the dinosaurs escape, like."

"Do you remember any of the people who are in it?"

The boy seems surprised by the question. "Yeah, sure."

"Like the bad person, for example. Can you tell me about them?"

"What should I tell you?"

"Is it a boy or a girl?"

So the boy tells him, uncertainly at first, but with increasing confidence and detail.

"Sounds exciting," Vidar says when he's done. "I like learning about things I don't know. I was thinking maybe you could tell me more, but about something a little bit different. Is that okay, Isak?"

The boy nods. God, if you ignore the thick glasses, he looks so much like his uncle. Vidar saw *Jurassic Park* in the theater; he went with Markus and Nashwan from work. But kids, especially little kids, always think grown-ups have the right answer. That's what the world looks like to them. Grown-ups know everything and always tell the truth. That's why he asked about the movie, so Isak would realize it's different this time. Right now, he's the one who has to help Vidar.

"Do you hang out with Edvard sometimes?"

"He doesn't live here anymore. And she's dead. The house burned down. We biked over and looked at it."

"Who died?"

"Lovisa."

"That's right," Vidar says slowly.

"Where is Jail?"

Isak asks the question like it's a lake he doesn't know the way to. His mother is sitting up straight, stiff as a board. She gazes vacantly at the coffee table, mechanically stroking her child's back.

"Mom, that hurts."

"Sorry."

"Jail?" Vidar says. "It's in town. Pretty close to where I work. I can show you pictures later, if you want. But I mean, when Edvard still lived here, did you hang out then?"

"Yes. Every Sunday."

"What do you usually talk about?"

"Lots of stuff."

"Isak," his father says, "you have to answer as much as you can . . ."

"It's fine," Vidar interrupts. "Just tell me as much as you want."

They wait. The boy scratches his belly. He's wearing a white T-shirt with Batman's face across the chest.

"Everything. About school and my friends. And books and stuff. And ice cream, what flavor is best. About the house he lives in. It needs a new coat of paint. He was supposed to do it over the summer, but then he didn't. And we talk about the lawn and stuff. Things like that."

"The lawn?"

"Yeah, like if he needs to mow the lawn."

"I see," Vidar says, and waits.

"Lovisa is dead. Murdered."

"Yes," Vidar says. "She is."

"We don't talk about her. Only sometimes."

"What do you say when you do?"

"He likes her." Isak's voice grows very thin. "He says she's smart and funny."

"Did he say anything else about her?"

"Like what?"

"I don't know. Whether they ever had fights, for example?"

"One time she made him sad."

"Did he tell you that?"

Isak nods. "I asked him why he was sad and he said it was just that Lovisa had made him feel a little sad. But it was no big deal. Afterward we played soccer."

"Was that only one time? Or did it happen more? That Edvard was sad about Lovisa, I mean."

The boy doesn't say anything for a long time. His knees are small and hard; his lips are thin and his hands look so soft. Vidar wants to put his hand over them and say that everything will be just fine. But he doesn't. Vidar is careful not to move a muscle as he sits in the easy chair.

"I don't know."

"I understand. That's fine, Isak. You're doing great. The time Lovisa made Edvard sad, do you know why?"

"No. But it was no big deal. He was happy later. It makes him happy to hang out with me, he says."

"I bet it does. Did you ever meet Lovisa?"

"Yeah. But I couldn't see her very often, because they worked all the time. Lovisa even worked on Sundays." The boy looks at him. "Edvard did something bad. Something really bad."

His mother stiffens. His father looks like he wants nothing more than to get out of there. Vidar nods slowly.

"Yes, I'm afraid he did."

"His bookshelves were empty. And the rug was all scrunched up."

"Did you go to his house?"

"I said I was going to Theo's. But I wanted to see Edvard, so I biked there."

Without warning, the boy begins to sob uncontrollably.

12

It was probably considered nice back in the day.

That's what folks say about the police headquarters in Halmstad, by way of explaining why it looks the way it does.

The building has belonged to them since the police authority was nationalized back in the sixties. Vidar's father worked here once upon a time. According to him, if you wanted to get an idea of the Swedish police, there was no more revealing description than this very building. The higher up a person sits, the more important he or she is considered to be.

Accordingly, the first floor houses those who are paid the least but deserve most of the thanks for keeping the wheels turning: the command center and switchboard, the office where crime reports are taken, the traffic unit, the uniforms' offices and locker room, the janitor, and the lockup and intake. The second floor belongs to the detectives and technicians, and on the third floor sit K-G Öberg and the other chiefs, along with the property crimes unit. The fourth floor houses the violent crimes unit and the security police, and above them are the district commissioner, the superintendent, and the bureau staff. At the very top is the cafeteria and, most important, the offices of the economists and administrators.

Food and money. On the force, there is nothing more important.

At least, that's how Vidar's father felt, but he was a smart officer and a man with insights drawn from other spheres of life on earth as well, so he was probably right.

He made it to thirty years on the force. During that time he arrested innumerable hooligans in town, drove thousands of miles in his patrol car, got puked on, pissed on, threatened and mocked, was stabbed on two occasions, and once came close to being shot.

He didn't drink, didn't fight, and never cheated, but starting at the age of fourteen, smoked a pack of Rothmans a day. His lungs were what did him in. He was only fifty-four when COPD took him.

Vidar inherited his career but not his Achilles' heel. The smell of cigarette smoke fills him with both unease and comfort.

Vidar and Markus are changing clothes.

"Thanks for the other day," Markus says, tying one boot.

"You, too."

You can't quite call it a tradition, but they usually try to have dinner together once a month. At first it was just him and Markus. Back then they drank more than they ate and mostly talked shop; that's how it goes, after all. Markus's dad wasn't a cop, but his grandfather was.

Then Markus met Hanna, who works at Åhléns. Once they'd met he mostly talked about her, and sometime later Vidar suggested she could come along if she wanted to. Markus asked, a bit hesitantly, if they could maybe talk about something other than work, for obvious reasons.

Then what are we going to talk about? Vidar wondered, and it was a little awkward and stiff the first time, but after that it was fine. That's how it is when you're seeing someone. They get you to talk about other things, and it often turns out you have more in common than you thought.

"How are things in the village now?" Markus asked, the only time during dinner that they brought up work.

An uneasiness has settled across the whole area. As if the world has shown its true face. *Edvard Christensson sure was a heap of trouble when he was younger, everyone remembers that lad. Maybe you can't grow out of that sort of thing. Just imagine, what some people are capable of.*

"Tense," Vidar responded.

"I bet."

They left it at that. Instead: cribs, strollers, and baby clothes, while Vidar and Markus drank wine and Hanna sipped at her sparkling water.

Hanna was the one who brought it up this time, bringing someone new to their next dinner. After all, Vidar hasn't lived with anyone but Leo for ages. He's dealt with his needs in Ulrika Andersson's bedroom, and the rest of the time he prefers to be alone.

"I'll think about it," Vidar said before they left.

"You think too much," said Markus, giving him a firm hug.

Hanna's hug was gentler. She has small hands, and when she placed them around him her pretty nails touched the back of his neck. Her waist was trim and her hair smelled good. Her little belly nudged against Vidar's.

What is it about women? Their clothes, hair, and skin. Why do they always smell good? There was a strange sensation in Vidar's chest. Was it longing?

Now they get in the car and drive out of the garage. A new shift awaits. The police radio crackles. Vidar finishes the rest of a dry cinnamon bun he got from the cafeteria.

"Hey, by the way," Markus says. "I thought of something, but I didn't want to ask while we were at your place."

"What's that?"

"How's his family? I mean, the ones you talked to, you and K-G."

"Not so good, I don't think. I've heard they're thinking of moving."

"Moving?"

Vidar gazes at the gray town slipping by outside the window. The boy at home in Marbäck, little Isak, with his glasses and an uncle who killed his girlfriend, how he suddenly started sobbing. A shocked but stoic mother, a frustrated father.

"How would you feel if you were from a place like Marbäck and someone in your family had just killed someone like that?"

"Sure, but . . ."

"You know, it's not just this. Edvard Christensson's dad, August, was also a troublemaking bastard who no one liked. He drank like a fish, did bad business, and beat his wife something awful. Dad used to talk about him. When Eva Christensson married Peter Nyqvist, everyone said she wasn't exactly upset about getting rid of her last name, if you know what I mean. You can imagine why."

"What, so no one is surprised?"

"Hell, sure, everyone's surprised. It's not that. But there's always been something unpleasant about them. As if everything they touch falls apart."

"Speaking of." Markus winks and changes lanes, out on Laholmsvägen. "I saw Guggan yesterday. She was up in the cafeteria having coffee."

Pia Gustafsson is sixty-two, and one of their three crime-scene techs. She and a colleague were the ones who performed the crime-scene investigation out in Tolarp.

"I asked her if I could have a seat, it's a snooze sitting up there by yourself. *Sure,* she said. I asked what she was working on right then, you know, and she said she was dealing with the gloves from the fire down in Tolarp. *I haven't found any gasoline on the right glove yet,* she said.

"Okay?"

"In other words, it seems like it's a little messier out there than you'd think. Since they found his prints on the candelabra, he couldn't have been wearing his gloves when he touched it. Then he puts them on and opens the garage, gets a gas can, and empties it out inside. That's why his prints weren't found on, for example, the garage door. He was wearing gloves then. Since he's right-handed he was probably holding the can in that hand, so it's understandable that she didn't find any drops on the left glove. But what about the right one? According to Guggan, if you were wearing a pair of gloves while you poured out a can of gas, it would be unusual not to get any gas on the fabric."

Snow is falling. It's a quiet day, a typical Monday. Less than a month until Christmas.

"Pretty weird," Markus continues.

"Yeah," says Vidar.

"So Guggan wondered if maybe he wasn't alone."

"What, so there were two of them?"

"Yes, potentially."

The traffic rushes past them. Advent lights glow in house windows.

Everything looks peaceful.

"No," Vidar says, more to himself than to his colleague. "No, he was alone down there."

Markus laughs.

"Says the master detective."

"Who would have helped him?"

"Good question."

"And," Vidar goes on, "where would his accomplice have gone?"

"I don't know. But look, let's stop here and grab a bite, huh?"

"Hell yeah. I'm starving."

On paper, the best fast food place in Halmstad is called Nyhem Grill. That's not right. Everyone calls it Fat Greta's, and it's the only place south of the Nissan River where you can get a good burger and a soft drink for a decent price. It's a popular fuel stop for the poor city police officers.

Food and money. That's what makes the world go round.

13

Once upon a time, a rich man was buried under a mound on the shores of Fåglasjön, along with his gold and jewels. That's why you might spot will-o'-the-wisps there at night. They're old spirits watching over the village riches and making sure that grabby children don't wander too far from home after dark.

You can see the will-o'-the-wisps from a distance by their flickering flames, and that's by design. If you get too close you might be snatched and taken away. A punishment and a warning to the village: *Keep your children under control.*

If everyone has been good, if the village has been spared from evil, they sometimes leave small gifts outside your door, as encouragement.

No gifts this winter. But the weather is white and cold. Billowing gray pillars rise from chimneys, and tiny white puffs of steam are exhaled by tired farmers and builders. Isak plays hockey on the ice of Torvsjön and the big pond behind the barn at Ernst Hedman's farm. He rides sleds and snow racers down hills. The pipes freeze at Backlunds' and Göranssons'. They go to Bengtssons' or Jönssons' on Svanåsvägen to fetch buckets of water so they can shower and make coffee. No one visits the Nyqvists much anymore.

Instead they're alone. Isak's dad shovels; Isak and Mom roll giant snowballs out back and bring out a scarf and mittens so the snowman won't look cold. And as they say, everyone is fighting a secret battle you know nothing about. So you have to be kind. That's important.

Isak is all bundled up; he buckles his shoes and scoops snow into his hands the second he's out the door. He runs toward Theo, Torbjörn, and the others, who had beat him outside. There's a snowball fight out on the soccer field, just like every other winter day. Isak loves snowball fights: building forts against the enemies from the other classes, rolling ammunition, and trying to think up clever ambushes and sudden attacks. You have to be a little careful—one time Theo got an ice ball to the face, and his cheek was red and swollen all day. But that's part of the fun, too, the risk of getting hit. You have to be on guard and protect yourself.

There are only days left to Christmas break. The cafeteria smells like fried food; the woodworking shop smells like burned wood. Isak catches up to the others, who are rebuilding the fort wall after it was damaged during morning recess.

Snowballs whiz through the air. He ducks and takes shelter behind Theo. "Help us, Isak," Theo says, piling snowballs in the middle. "We need more snowballs. The first-grade babies are helping the fourth graders. There's a ton of them."

Isak peers out from behind the wall. There he is—the fourth-grade kid. The kid's arms are long, and he throws a snowball that says *crunch* as it hits the fort so hard it leaves a mark. Isak squeezes a snowball in his own hands. He steels himself, holds his breath and stands up, swings his arm, and lets fly.

It's a perfect hit.

Everything stops, falls silent.

There's a *poff* as Isak's snowball hits the boy right in the eye. He falls to the ground, holding his face. His feet kick at the ground. The boy is screeching like a baby and crying for his mom. His friends hurry over.

Everyone is aiming strange looks at Isak.

"Sorry."

The boy blubbers. A friend tries to pull his hand away to see how bad it is. The boy doesn't want to let him. From behind Isak, Torbjörn shouts, "What the hell, Isak, what's wrong with you?"

"I didn't mean to."

"You made an ice ball," Theo says in a low voice. "That's against the rules."

When you hold on to a snowball for too long, it freezes hard as a rock, if it's cold enough outside.

The recess monitor is heading their way, cigarette in hand.

"I didn't mean to, I just held on to it for too long."

Theo takes a step back. "Can you just leave?" he says quietly.

"Get out of here!" shouts the crying boy's friend. "No one wants you guys here anymore! You just ruin everything."

The recess monitor arrives. She has stubbed out her cigarette; she stinks of coffee and smoke and looks mad. Her eyes go from Isak to the boy on the ground. He's going to be fine; he's done screeching and is sitting up, sniffling loudly. The skin around his eye is adorned with red.

"Well," she mutters, taking Isak by the arm. "No surprise there. Come on, we're going inside."

His stomach aches. Nothing is ever going to be the same. Isak looks at the sky. It's so far away.

One day before Christmas break, he comes in after recess and sees the words that have been carved into his desk.

Move

Murderer

Someone put those words there. He hears a poorly muffled giggle behind his back. But it doesn't make sense. Do they mean Edvard? Isak doesn't understand. And no one says anything.

Theo is sitting beside him, staring down at his math book. Isak puts his hand over the words, as if to hide them, full of shame.

:::

Then it's Christmas break, Christmas Eve, and New Year's. It's weird, how in one way everything is exactly the same, but at the same time it's totally different.

Isak gets presents. One of them is from Edvard, Mom says, but he can tell by the way it's wrapped that she did it herself. Mom is good at wrapping presents; it was her first side job. She stood at Domus, wrapping presents for all the department store customers one Christmas-shopping weekend in the midseventies. That's how she met Dad. He came in during his lunch, wearing his Rejmes coveralls, messy with oil and grime. He'd tried to wrap the package himself first. There was oil on the wrapping paper, and the tape was all crooked. It was a birthday present for his mother. He had done such a sorry job that Mom laughed at his attempt and said, *I'll help you, my friend*. Four years later they got married. They look so fancy and happy in their wedding photos, Isak thinks.

The present is a remote-control car. Isak has wanted one ever since Theo got one for Christmas last year. It's big and blue, with tires the size of handballs, and it gleams in its box.

"Do you like it, honey?" Mom asks cautiously.

Isak's heart turns black. He doesn't know what to say. There are no words. He picks up the box and walks to the hall, throws open the front door, and tosses the remote-control car right into the snow.

"Are we going to move, Mom?" he asks when he returns to the tree and looks at her.

"I . . ." Mom blinks at the front door. There's a glass in her hand. It smells strong. "No. Who told you that?"

"No one wants us here anymore. Are we going to move?"

"Isak." Mom tries to put her arms around him, but Isak steps aside. "I just want . . ." She leans toward Dad. "I just want us to cel-ebrate Christmas, not . . . Peter, can you go out and bring in the car?"

Dad gets up tentatively. Isak stays put. Mom blinks.

"We're not moving, honey."

:::

No one tells him much more about Edvard. Just as well. Edvard's ruined everything. It's easier to be angry than to be sad. It feels better. He misses Edvard, of course, sometimes so much that his chest hurts. When Isak and Mom make snowmen, he remembers what it was like last winter, when he was with Edvard. On the way through the woods, down to the falls, he sees the clearing where he and Edvard built a fort when Isak was younger. Even up on Svanåsvägen, where Edvard and Dad taught Isak to ride a bike.

Edvard has always been there. With good-smelling cologne and soft hands, fingers gently running through Isak's hair on nights when Mom and Dad worked late and Isak couldn't sleep.

Now he's just gone.

And yet he's near. Always, like a ghost. Mom and Dad often talk about him when they think Isak can't hear them.

"*Isak's right,*" Dad exclaims. "*No one wants us here anymore. And I don't feel like staying, either.*"

"*But it won't last forever. And he hasn't even been convicted yet.*"

"*Can you just stop saying that over and over? If you take a step back and calm down, you'll see it, too.*"

"*But we—*"

"*Edvard is just like your father.*" He interrupts her in a cold, quiet voice that makes Isak shiver with discomfort in his spot by the laundry room door.

"*But I don't want to move. We're from here. And just like you said to the police, we haven't done anything. Edvard has.*"

"*Then what are we going to do?*"

She's crying now. Her voice sputters and wobbles. Isak leaves.

If you ignore all of this, there haven't been that many disasters. Sure, Karl took a hockey puck to the mouth last fall. His lip split and he bled all over the ice. In December, one of the farmers broke a leg on the icy paths. The bone stuck right out and they could hear him roaring all the way up to Svanåsvägen. Hasse Backlund crashed his tractor a few days into the new year. He was a little drunk and drove straight into his own barn.

But beyond that, Marbäck is a safe place, as long as you watch out for the highway. Commuters drive crazy back and forth from Halmstad, so everyone is extra careful out there. It's simple.

As long as you know what to watch out for, life is pretty simple.

14

In the beginning of time, people made their living fishing. The Fylleån was full of trout, salmon, and eel. That was how people survived, Vidar's grandfather explained when Vidar was a boy. Marbäck's first factory was built in the 1600s, with a mill that made paper out of rags. It was replaced in the 1800s by a newer, more modern version a few hundred meters upstream. The farms appeared, acres upon acres of forest, fields, and crops.

The land is the most important resource there is. Throughout history, it has meant salvation from poverty and starvation, hardship and depressions. As a child, Vidar stood in the Breared School library as the ancient librarian paged through old albums, showing him and his classmates yellowed photographs of stoic workmen standing before heavy skids, waterwheels, iron presses, and drying rooms. The quality of the pictures was too poor to see the men's eyes, but their backs were straight, their shoulders broad. You imagined that they had proud eyes.

The mill burned to the ground in 1881. The cause was never established. It was a great tragedy, but by the next year another paper mill was finished. People had worked day and night to rebuild what the fire had destroyed. That's always been the attitude toward fire in Marbäck: It must be conquered. The whole community helped out. This was before Vidar's grandfather was born, but his great-grandfather was around back then. Carl Jörgensson was a constable and carpenter and one of four workers who together mounted the big sign that said MARBÄCK PULP MILL AB on the main building.

At the same time, the railroad was laid; it made transporting materials to and from the mill much easier. The new station was beautiful, almost stately, with its lovely double doors leading to the platform. Soon freight trains were chugging in and bringing sounds and smells, feelings and dreams from the big world outside.

Then came the hard times. Slowly, things began to decline.

The mill held on, but the big world smothered the small one. Modern society had come to Marbäck. It was obvious from the job titles: Vidar's dad wasn't a constable. He became a *policeman.*

Almost three hundred years after the first paper mill opened its wooden doors, the last one closed its own, these made of steel, for good. The railroad was gone. People moved. The fishing trade that people had once been so proud of—that was where their origins were, really—was only a memory now. The water had been spoiled by the paper industry's poisons.

Marbäck became a place where you lived, but no longer worked. The buildings and factories were still there, and time both froze and didn't: The elegant mill farmstead was sold, the railway station was renovated into a house, and the railroad became a bike trail.

Yet, history doesn't allow itself to be rewritten that easily.

When Vidar played in the woods around Marbäck as a child, years later, the thick, dark logs that had formed the railroad ties were still there, half-buried and devoured by nature. They were treacherous; they could trip you in the dark or when you were in the middle of a game and forgot to watch your step.

Before Vidar learned about Marbäck in school, about the stubborn paper mill and the abandoned railroad and all that, the logs confused him. He didn't understand where they'd come from; he knew only that they didn't belong to nature. The day he sat in class and realized that they had been railroad tracks, that trains had rushed by on the very spot he liked to play, he was filled with a strange sensation he couldn't put into words.

"Vidar. Think of this: There might be more logs nearby. Maybe you can follow them away from here, you know, like in orienteering."

His grandpa had suggested it once, as a game. Vidar wondered if it was true, and where the tracks might take someone who dared to follow, but he was only ten years old then and not brave enough to try.

In the evening, the phone rings. "Hello?"

"Hi."

Vidar turns off the faucet in the kitchen sink.

"Oh, hi there, Isak." Silence. "Are you still up this late?"

"Yes."

"You know my phone number?"

"I found it in the phone book."

"Good thinking."

"They think I'm asleep," Isak says in a quieter voice. "But I can't sleep. Is it fun to be a policeman?"

"Yes, it is. Usually, anyway. But sometimes you have to do boring stuff. I suppose that's true of any job. I've never had any other job, so I don't know."

"If I have a mom or dad who murders someone, does that mean I'm going to be a murderer, too?"

The question catches Vidar off guard for a moment, "Definitely not. Who said that?"

"Don't lie to me," the boys says reprovingly. "I don't like it when people lie."

"Me neither. So I don't lie."

"Are you sure?"

"Yes, I'm sure. But your mom and dad didn't murder anyone."

"My uncle did. We're related, too. And they say so in school."

"They do? About you?"

"I hear what they say. And not just in school. They think I don't notice, but I do."

Vidar sits down at the kitchen table. The risk is higher. But not by that much. They learned this in the police program, that people inherit more than you'd expect. The genetic link for criminality is strongest between parents, children, and siblings, but it shows up between other relatives, too, like cousins. Or between an uncle and his nephew. It's not that you're born a criminal, of course. But you can absorb the environment and certain other traits that increase the risk.

Marbäck is no different—quite the opposite. Here, sons turn out like their fathers; daughters like their mothers. Weaknesses and burdens are passed down, just like in other places. Then again, so are strengths and good traits—but people seldom consider those.

"As long as you're nice to others and you care about them, you'll be just fine."

"But Edvard *is* nice. He's like the nicest person I know."

"Sometimes nice people do bad things. You know, Isak, when someone commits a crime it happens for a lot of reasons. Some of them, you don't really have much control over."

"But can you know? I mean," he says, "how do you know if you have something *kymig* inside you?"

"You don't. It's just part of life, not knowing."

The boy doesn't say anything for a long time. He breathes into Vidar's ear.

It's almost peaceful, really.

"I'm very sorry Edvard did what he did, Isak. I don't want you to have to . . ." he begins, but the words won't come.

"But Grandpa had something in him. I know that. And Edvard has . . . maybe it only gets passed down to boys."

"I don't think it's that simple. But I understand what you mean. Would you like to see your uncle?"

"No," the boy responds harshly.

"Okay," says Vidar. "Okay."

A lengthy silence.

"I don't know if I want to."

"Well, if you do, I might be able to arrange it. Just say the word. You've got my phone number now."

"Okay. Thanks."

Vidar looks at the clean dishes, the water dripping from the rinsed plates and silverware.

"I still think there's something inside me," the boy whispers. "I feel so weird inside."

For the first time, Vidar doesn't know what to say.

So he just keeps listening to Isak's breathing.

Under the bridge in Årnarp, about half a mile from Tolarp, is where the Old Man sleeps. Vidar learned as much as a child. The Old Man is a dead person who haunts the area. Few people who have had the misfortune of encountering him have made it out alive, and those who have are tormented every night by nightmares about a terrifying ghost-corpse.

Ghost-corpses almost always stick to their gravesites, but some can't stand the loss of their beloved, so they go crazy. They don't know what to do and lose their way as they search.

That's what happened to the Old Man. For years he searched for the woman he'd once loved, and eventually he came to the bridge. There he stopped to drink a little water from the Fylleån. He was very tired, and beside himself with sorrow and longing. Once he had slaked his thirst he leaned against the pillar of the bridge and fell asleep out of exhaustion, and there he sleeps to this day.

Love is dangerous. That is the lesson. You have to be careful, or else you will go astray.

Edvard and Lovisa became a couple in May. Six months later, it was over.

"Our understanding is that they had been arguing," says Chief Inspector K-G Öberg, lead investigator in the preliminary investigation against the 25-year-old suspect. "She wanted to leave him, and he was opposed. That was the triggering event. He has a history of impulsive behavior and difficulty controlling his anger."

"Why did she want to leave him?"

"We aren't sure yet. There are a number of possible scenarios. But it's not hard to guess."

So it says in the article published on Monday, February 6, 1995.

She'd biked to Christensson's place after work and spent the evening there. An argument broke out and Lovisa left for home around eleven. He followed her on foot, likely because he had been drinking and couldn't drive. She wanted to leave him; he tried to hold on to her. It didn't work, and in the end his pent-up emotions burst out down in Tolarp. He ended her life and then set the house on fire to destroy the evidence. So this is all about love.

No, not love. That's not right. Love makes you want to *build* houses, not burn them down. That's the sort of thing you do out of hate or rage, or maybe desperation. So goes the reasoning, but who knows.

The same goes for a lot of details of Lovisa Markström and Edvard Christensson's relationship: The story is incomplete. Maybe that's always the case with the worst sort of violence, that you can't predict it. Sometimes, a black hole just opens up inside a person, and anything might come out.

Sure, maybe. But it was long since proven that Edvard had a violent streak, and Lovisa had probably been privy to it any number of times during their time together. That didn't mean anyone could have predicted he was capable of going so far.

Did it?

Edvard Christensson was born at Halmstad Hospital on June 11, 1969, almost thirteen years after his sister, Eva, came into the world.

In fact, he was a mistake. August and Sara Christensson hadn't thought they could have more children. But then, one chilly June morning, he came out, by all appearances a perfectly healthy, bouncing baby boy.

The earliest picture of him is from the day he was brought home from the hospital, at the family's house on the north side of Marbäck. His big sister is carrying the tiny, well-wrapped bundle across the threshold, a gleam of pride in her eye. Vidar gazes at it, feeling melancholy, as he sits in one of the patrol officers' old offices. August must have taken the picture. The colors have yellowed, and in the background is a glimpse of Sara, smiling uncertainly.

As a little boy he read books and played soccer with Simlångsdalens IF, like any other child. He went to Breared School, the same school as Vidar, Isak, and everyone else, and was a well-liked but rambunctious child, a prankster with a bookworm bent, a kid the teachers didn't quite know what to do with.

He's smart as a whip for a nine-year-old, but he's often wound tight as a spring. So begins the very first report from his teacher. In time, problems arose.

In the summer of 1980 he was accused of stealing Elise Karlsson's bike. He denied it. Two weeks later, a yellow women's Monark was discovered in August and Sara's storage shed. Elise's shawl was still in the basket. She elected not to pursue the case; after all, she had her bike back and the boy was only eleven.

Later that same year, the boys of class 5B were caught looking at a pornographic magazine after gym class. It belonged to Christensson. After the school threatened to call August and Sara, he promised he wouldn't do it again, and that he would start to behave himself.

A little later, the winter of that year: a principal's report on a fistfight between John Skogman in 5A and Edvard Christensson in 5B.

And so on. Boys will be boys, general mischief, and an age-old way of solving conflicts, testing boundaries. That was the assessment—possibly a correct one.

Villages have their memories. They have their lives and their

deaths. Many are linked. Vidar is two years older than Edvard Christensson. He recalls him as rowdy but smart. He can picture Edvard,
the boy in the schoolyard with short brown hair and a cryptic gleam
in his eyes. They went to the discos that were held up at Simlångsdalen rec center in the midst of *Saturday Night Fever* hysteria. He was
there, too, Christensson, hanging out in a corner with a few others.
Vidar doesn't remember who. Christensson smoked indoors and was
kicked out after a while. Hard to say what people thought of him back
then—he was just like everyone else.

His fifth-year report card was all over the place. B in Swedish, C
in penmanship, D in math, a B in gym, because the porno magazine
incident brought down his grade.

*Considering the boy's background, his schooling has progressed about as well
as one might have dared to hope,* his teacher noted a few years later, at the
end of the school year in 1984.

The boy's background. Meaning August and Sara.

August had lived a violent and hectic life, at sea among other
places, until he finally got too old and calmed down. He had worked
at the mill until it went under, and later he became a lathe operator at
a carpentry shop in Simlångsdalen. Even back then, there were
rumors: They said he had sold a bad batch of lumber to a man in the
village, a large lot of boards and other materials that were infested
with wood borers. Things like that. *You gotta screw other people over before
they screw you over first.* That was August Christensson's motto and general outlook on life.

He had met Sara and, of course, had two children with her.
August drank heavily even back then, and when he became angry,
well, what happened happened. Seldom was there visual evidence, to
be sure, but sometimes it did go that far. Vidar had once seen Sara
Christensson limping through the village. Not long after he was stand-
ing by the shelf of candy in the Simlångsdalen grocery store when
Sara walked by, dropped her pocketbook, and bent down to pick it up.
As she did so she gave a sudden, sharp hiss and grabbed her ribs.

Everyone saw, and knew. August wasn't the only violent man up in the village; Sara wasn't alone in her occasional need to stay inside because of a black eye.

"*It wasn't . . .*" comes Eva Christensson's tremulous voice as the tape begins to play.

Vidar has been called into K-G's office again. A pale but warming sun is shining onto an old tape recorder that sits between them. The tape is rolling, and there's a whistling background noise that settles beneath the voices.

"*It wasn't something we thought about much, you know? Not at first, anyway. He never hit her in front of us. But we still knew. Edvard, too. And, I mean, I just want to have it said that yeah, my dad was a goddamn idiot. But he wasn't a bad person. He loved Mom. I know that. But the boozing made him stupid. And I'll always blame him that he never stopped drinking.*"

From his seat in front of Vidar, K-G grunts.

"*What about Edvard?*" says the chief inspector's voice.

"*Well, he . . . I guess he had it more or less the same as I did. Or . . . what do you mean?*"

"*I mean, was he ever a witness to that?*"

"*Not that I know of, no.*"

"*But you're not sure.*"

Silence.

"*No. Why do you ask?*"

"*I'm trying,*" K-G says, frustration in his voice, "*to understand your brother, that's all. I can't figure him out. You know he acted violently towards Lovisa, right? I mean, before this. And he has two convictions for assault and battery behind him already.*"

Eva's voice is shocked. "*No. I mean, I knew he had been violent towards other people, but not Lovisa. Who told you that?*"

"*It doesn't matter.*"

"Lovisa's dad," K-G says to Vidar, nodding at the tape. "He said so. It happened when they argued. Or when she tried to leave him, rather. According to him, Lovisa had said that Edvard's eyes would go black. Does that sound familiar to you?"

"I've heard other people say so, yes."

The chief inspector leans forward and presses pause. The tape stops; the background noise vanishes. Vidar raises his eyebrows.

"Was that all?"

"Yes, that's all."

Vidar rises to leave but turns around.

"I was thinking . . ."

"Hmm?"

"What does Christensson have to say? During interrogations, I mean."

"Nothing." All of a sudden K-G looks exhausted. "That bastard won't say a thing."

16

Sara got cancer and died six months after the diagnosis, which took a heavy toll on August. He drank a lot, smoked even more, and slept far too little. As a retiree, he had few expenses, a comfortable pension, and loads of alone time. He was in and out of a few treatment facilities but was found dead in his bed at the age of sixty-nine: a blood clot near his heart. Death had taken him quickly and painlessly, according to the doctor. What he hinted at but didn't say outright was that there had been nothing to suggest that August had tried to call someone, move, or make any effort to stay alive.

Maybe he didn't have time. Or maybe he had just let it happen.

People in the village didn't talk about it much.

With a background like his, it was no surprise that things didn't look so good for Edvard Christensson, but once he turned eighteen and had finished school, he began to work part-time in elder care, first as a cleaner in the nursing home in Simlångsdalen and later as an aide. Oddly enough, he became very popular among both the old folks and his colleagues.

I have yet to see a trace of the problem tendencies I was warned about when I hired Edvard, his boss noted after Christensson's first year on the job.

Perhaps Christensson had *grown into himself,* as they say; perhaps he had calmed down and become a conscientious person. That's one interpretation. Another, more likely explanation has to do with adaptation. In time, he had learned to differentiate between times it was to his advantage to keep his cool, when the straight and narrow was the only alternative, and when he could make use of his rage and impulsive nature to get what he wanted.

He had moved out at eighteen and found a place of his own up in the forest in Skärkered. He had to support himself somehow; the shit he was rumored to do on the side, minor fraud and the like, was only enough for some extra cash. So he moonlighted as a bartender down at B&B on weekends and dated a girl named Annika who came from Årnarp and worked with horses. In early 1995 she is interviewed a few times. Vidar himself conducts the first interview with her, since the usual interrogator had to pick up a puking kid from day care. Annika Mirjamsson is a slightly overweight woman Vidar's age with kind eyes and beautiful features.

"Edvard was perfectly normal," she says. "Or whatever. I was desperately in love with him. He's a really lovable person. Okay, he's a little impulsive and stuff when he's been drinking, that's true. But in a funny way, kind of?"

"What do you mean?"

"Well, like, once he got it into his head that we should climb onto the roof at the stables in Årnarp. And another time he wanted to take a bike ride." She laughs. "I mean, a *long* one. He thought it would be fun. Because it was summer, so we could sleep under the stars. Something like that. I talked him out of it. But he was never impulsive in a way like . . . Oh, how should I put it . . . ?"

"Did he ever get violent?"

"No, no. And definitely not towards me. The only time I saw Edvard get violent, if you could even call it that, was when we were out sometimes. I was twenty pounds lighter and looked pretty damn good, I'll have you know, so guys hit on me pretty often. Sometimes there was trouble when I said no, which I always did. Because I was with Edvard."

"What would happen then?"

"Usually nothing. But sometimes, if they wouldn't give up, he would shove one of them or maybe even punch him in the face. But he was doing it to protect me, obviously. He was never violent. Not once."

The incidents she mentions were never reported to the police. They aren't recorded in the station archives.

"But he was the jealous type?"

"Yeah, I guess he was. But he was never threatening or controlling or any of that. More like . . . well, the way guys usually are."

"Do you think Edvard could have done what he's accused of?"

Annika crosses her arms over her chest. "Well, what do you think? You come from up there, too. You must know him, right?"

"I don't know Edvard. And I'm not really the one who should answer the question, I never dated him."

"Okay." She throws up her hands. "Based on how he was with me? He never could have done that. It's unthinkable. Who the hell even burns down a house like that? And with a person inside? Edvard would never be capable of such a thing. But like I said, that's based on how he was with *me*. You can change so much when you're in love, depending on who you're in love with."

"Still, not everyone," Vidar tries, "would turn to violence to try to protect or defend his girlfriend. I understand what you're saying, but most of us use words for that sort of thing."

"Yeah, sure," Annika says, lowering her gaze to the tabletop between them. "Sure, okay."

So maybe it does mean something, Vidar thinks.

"When did you break up?"

"Let's see, it was . . . the spring of ninety-three. His feelings for me had faded, he said. I was crushed, of course. Just crushed. But I recovered. You know, there are other fish in the sea."

It's a different story when they speak to one of the men who hit on Annika back in the day. Vidar visits him out in Harplinge, at the car dealership where he works. He's leaning over an engine, huffing and puffing in the cold. A stocky little man with a cigarette in the corner of his mouth and a potbelly under his blue coveralls.

"Oh yes," he says. "I remember. Shit. He was psycho. I thought he was going to kill me. He probably would have, too, if the bouncers hadn't dragged him outside. I had a cracked rib and a nosebleed, got a cut above my eye, and I was swollen as hell for a week after."

It's still visible, a thick scar through his eyebrow. It couldn't have been a pretty sight when it was fresh. He replaces a wrench in the tool pouch that's hanging above one of the mudflaps and picks up a screwdriver instead. His hands are dirty; his beard uneven.

"Did you report him?"

The man snorts. Ash flies from his cigarette. "What good would that have done? He moonlighted there. The bouncers were his buddies, and the girl was dating him. Who would have taken my side?"

"But if it there was evidence, I mean, swelling and everything . . ."

He waves a hand dismissively. "I just wanted to forget about it and move on."

"Do you think he could have done what he's suspected of?"

"Killing that girl? Hell, yes. I'm not surprised."

Dusk is falling in Harplinge. In the yard is an old Christmas tree, still with lights blinking sporadically.

"Thanks a lot," Vidar says.

Christensson was twenty-three or twenty-four. Shortly thereafter he was found guilty in two cases of assault and battery.

On one occasion he had allegedly attacked a drunk man who was sitting alone on a bench at Stora Torg one Friday night. Witnesses reported that the man had shouted "Fucking trash" when he saw Christensson. Christensson claimed that a few weeks earlier he had kicked this man out of B&B. A simple "I was furious" was Christensson's explanation. He was fined.

The second incident followed close on the heels of the first. The circumstances are not as clear. Vidar squints at the report. Christensson had supposedly attacked one of the old men in Marbäck after the man accused him of stealing his car. The man is named Backlund;

Vidar knows him well. Even so, he hasn't heard this story. It's weird how you all live together in some small place and imagine that you know everyone, and know everything about them, but no one truly knows anyone at all.

Backlund got a set of black eyes and a ringing in his ears that lasted for a few months. Christensson was sentenced to more fines, even though Backlund claimed that he'd had a knife. There was no proof, and Christensson denied it. That was in March 1994. Two months later, he met Lovisa Markström.

He had been working at B&B that night; she'd been at a house party out in Tylösand. They were taking the same bus back to Marbäck.

"*We're going the same way, huh?*" she said.

"*I think so. You live down in Tolarp, right?*"

"*My name's Lovisa.*"

"*Edvard.*"

"*Christensson?*"

"*Yup.*"

She smiled.

According to witness statements from Lovisa's friends, that was more or less how it began. They stood there shivering at the bus stop across from Åhléns until the bus arrived, and then they sat next to each other.

You can almost picture it, how they ride past Sture High School. The bus goes that way. They're sitting next to each other. It's late spring. Everything is finally alive again. No other season can last for eternity like winter does. The air is so mild. At the community college, the bus takes a hard left toward Östergård and they lean into the seat. His thigh moves against hers. He has just asked if she likes working at Brooktorpsgården.

"*Yes.*"

"*Great.*"

She looks into his eyes. Deep vibrations ring through her; she's a tuning fork.

Vidar reads the printout of the witness testimony. *A tuning fork.*

What a weird phrase. According to one of Lovisa's friends, that's what she said later when she told them how it felt.

Vidar underlines it. The phone rings. It's the boy.

17

Dad almost killed a dwarf once.

His name is Li'l Lennart and he drives a taxi; he usually gets the car serviced at the garage where Dad works. He has special pedals in his taxi so he can reach, but he takes them out when he brings the car to the shop. One time Dad waved him off and said the pedals wouldn't be a problem; he could work on the car with them on. And he was right, up until the point when his foot got caught on the gas pedal when he was driving the car onto the lift. The two chocks at the front flew off and the car crashed ahead onto Li'l Lennart, who always insisted on standing at the front to guide his beloved taxi onto the lift.

And everything was perfectly still and quiet.

Oh my God, Dad thought. *I've killed a dwarf.*

From under the car came a mewl.

Dad grabbed the collar of the taxi uniform and pulled Li'l Lennart to his feet again as he mumbled apology after apology. When it was clear that Li'l Lennart was unharmed—he was so small he had fit under the car—Dad began to clean off the grime, oil, and filth with the pressure hose as the shortest cab driver in Halmstad stood paralyzed with shock. A coworker walked by and saw Li'l Lennart and Dad blowing the crap off him.

You can blow as much air into him as you like, he's not going to get any bigger.

Dad tells it as a funny story now. It's not a nice joke, Isak knows, but he doesn't think of it that way either. There's something else to the story of Li'l Lennart. It's not always the case that the weaknesses you're born into the world with are bad. Quite the opposite.

They can even save your life.

Isak gets the day off school. It feels weird; he's never taken a day off before. Mom had a chat with Isak's teacher, who wanted to check with the school social worker, who in turn had a meeting with the principal.

"What a freakin' mess," Mom says in the car. "I should have just told them you had an appointment with us or something."

With us means the dentist. That's where Mom works. Isak likes his dentist; his name is Ulf and his office has a TV on the ceiling that plays *Tintin*. Isak loves *Tintin*. They're the best adventures ever. And each time he's done he gets a sticker.

It would have been nice to visit Ulf today.

"Are we going to move, Mom?"

"No. You already asked that."

"But Dad said . . ."

"Dad says a lot of things, honey," she mumbles, distracted by traffic. "Or . . . do you want to?"

"No."

"You can tell me, if you do. Do you want to move?"

He shakes his head.

Mom parks outside an old building made of pale brick, with high walls. Vidar is waiting for them. He's not wearing a uniform; he's just got his hands in the pockets of a pair of jeans, and he's squinting into the cold morning sun.

It's been three months. Isak has never before been apart from his uncle for so long. Apparently Edvard has been asking about him. Mom said it was up to Isak. His first inclination was to say no, but then something happened inside him and made him change his mind. It's so hard to put words to how you feel. It's like you don't feel one way, but a thousand.

Now he gazes at the building behind Vidar. *Jail*. It looks stern and ugly, sort of like it sounds.

"Hi, Eva," Vidar says, shaking Mom's hand. "Hi, Isak."

Isak places his hand in Vidar's, which is heavy and soft and warm.

"Here's what we're going to do," the large policeman says in a calm voice. "We'll go in over here. We can hang up our coats there, or else we'll get too warm. There will be a few people in there, but you don't have to worry about them. They're my colleagues. Their names are Janne and Therese and they're nice. They'll need to look in your bags. Then we'll go into another room. That door will be locked, but Janne and Therese have keys. After that, we'll go into a third room, and that's where we'll meet Edvard."

"Are you coming, too?"

"If you want me to. Only if you want me to."

Isak does. At least at first. It would be nice. Vidar looks at him with big green eyes and places a hand on Isak's shoulder.

"Don't worry, Isak. This will be just fine. Your uncle is looking forward to seeing you."

It all happens pretty fast after that. Janne and Therese are nice. Vidar says hello and introduces them. They look at him like everything is normal, none of those weird looks people have been giving him recently, and they treat him like anyone else. For a moment he feels very grown-up.

The room they're going to be in is a family room. That's what Vidar calls it when he talks to Mom. It's a little bit like a home, with simple furniture and rugs in pretty colors, a corner with a toy box, games, and puzzles, a dollhouse. In another corner is a crib with neatly tucked sheets, and on the wall there are pictures with cheerful themes in gentle colors.

Isak doesn't quite know what to do, so he sits down next to the toy box. When he hears his uncle's voice, something quivers in his stomach and he turns around.

Edvard is standing in the doorway. He's wearing gray sweatpants and a long-sleeved shirt. He's neither taller nor shorter than Isak remembers, nor is he thinner or fatter. He looks like in Isak's memories. Of course, maybe there's not enough time to change much in three months. Then again, Isak once went almost a whole summer vacation without seeing Jacke, Theo's big brother. When he saw Jacke again in August, he must have grown a head taller, and he was skinnier and spoke in a deeper voice. So when you think about it, a lot probably can happen in three months.

But not to Edvard. At least not anything visible.

"Hi, Isak. It's been a while."

He's smiling at Isak now. Isak doesn't smile back. Edvard notices, and maybe it makes him sad, because his shoulders sink a little.

He hugs Mom, who pats his back awkwardly.

Edvard walks over to Isak and looks down at him in his spot next to the toy box.

"Do you want to sit here?"

Isak wants to say something, but all he can do is nod. Edvard's voice doesn't sound the way it usually does; it's kind of like he's drawling. As if he were about to fall asleep. There's something about his face, too. Yes, up close like this, Edvard looks sort of different. Grayer and paler.

His uncle sits down with his back to the wall and pulls up his legs, looking down into the toy box.

"I missed you, Isak," he mumbles.

"You sound weird."

"That's probably because I'm a little sleepy."

"Why are you sleepy?"

"I have a hard time relaxing in here. So they give me medicine to help."

Isak hesitates. He really doesn't want anyone else to hear. He lowers his voice. "Why did you do it?"

Mom and Vidar have been shifting in the background; Isak

recognizes those little noises that people make when they're not really doing anything. But now they fall silent.

"You know, Isak . . . everyone does stupid things now and then. Things you regret later on. Same goes for me. There's lots of people I haven't been very nice to. Including Lovisa. But I didn't do it."

Isak has spent a lot of time thinking about what Vidar said. *Sometimes nice people do bad things.* But nice people are nice because they do *nice* things. Not mean things. So it must be complicated.

"You're lying," Isak says, and something cold begins to slither snakelike through his blood.

"Do you think so?" Edvard asks, his voice dragging so much it's uncomfortable.

"Yeah. You're being so weird."

His uncle sighs audibly.

"Like I said, Isak, that's the medicine. I can't help it."

"Okay."

"Edvard," he hears Mom's voice. "Go easy on him."

Edvard leans back again, nodding apologetically, as if he's done something wrong. Isak is stiff with uncertainty.

Edvard asks how school is going, whether he's read any good books recently, and what he got for Christmas. Isak's responses are brief at first, but after a while it almost feels like normal. Like that summer day in the forest when it was just Isak and Edvard and nothing bad could happen as long as he was holding his uncle's hand. Edvard laughs when Isak tells him how Theo was so scared after the first fireworks went off on New Year's that he fell off the roof of the playhouse. It feels good, like it should. Still, after a while, they fall into silence.

"What's it like living here?"

"It's kind of boring. But I won't be here for long."

"So you're coming home?"

"Of course I am."

Suddenly Isak remembers. "It's all messy at your house. Everything. Even the books."

Edvard nods slowly. "A few people were there looking for some things. I suppose they didn't really have time to clean up afterwards, so I can imagine it's a little messy."

"Who was it?"

"Vidar and his colleagues."

Isak turns his head. "You did that?"

"Yes," Vidar says solemnly. "They had to. But they should have cleaned up after themselves. I'll have a talk with them."

Isak looks his uncle in the eye. It's hard to be angry. He leans closer so no one can hear.

"When you come home, there's something I have to tell you."

"What is it?"

"It's a secret. I'll tell you when you get home."

18

"Do you think it was because he got to see him?" Markus asks. "Isak, I mean."

"I don't know. Maybe."

Edvard Christensson has started talking. It happened in one of the last interrogations, a day or two after he met his nephew. Is there a connection? They're not sure. Maybe it doesn't matter.

Vidar and Markus are on Kyrkogatan, enjoying the spring sunshine. It's mid-May. They're on break and each has a plastic mug of coffee in hand and a view of the open square. The shadow cast by the beautiful church spire of St. Nicolai's is long and cool.

Within the walls of the district court, a quarter mile away, the proceedings are underway in the trial against Edvard Christensson in the Lovisa Markström case.

He claims she was at his house. Lovisa headed home around eleven because she had to work the next morning. As she took off on her bicycle, Christensson realized she had forgotten her wallet and set off after her, on foot since he had been drinking. When he got down to Tolarp and entered the house, someone struck him in the head and he dropped the wallet.

When he regained consciousness, the room was on fire and he saw Louisa lying lifeless on the floor. He tried to help her but couldn't, because the fire was too severe, so he left her there and got himself out.

This is a poor version of the tale. The prosecutor has already shot it down: Christensson made no attempt to seek help at any of the nearby farms once he got out. He didn't try to call the emergency number. He did nothing but try to escape.

The blow to his head is a useful detail to emphasize. Christensson was bleeding heavily from a gash on his head when Vidar found him in the woods. According to the crime-scene techs, Lovisa had probably been trying to protect herself and in doing so wounded Christensson with a crude weapon—likely the candelabra.

"Whatever made him talk, it's a good thing for us," Vidar says, sipping his coffee. "It will make everything easier. He's claiming, for instance, that he saw a car parked outside the house when he arrived in Tolarp, but we've checked all the cars that passed by there. They've been struck from suspicion. So it will be easier to shoot his story down."

"A car only he saw, a third person inside the house, again, who only he saw, a wallet no one has found." A smile tugs at Markus's lips. "Considering how long he's been in jail keeping his mouth shut, a person might have expected a better story."

An older man approaches them. He has thin white hair and thick glasses and is too lightly dressed for the weather.

"I'm a little confused," he says.

"That can happen to anyone," Markus says.

"Yes, but look here." The old man scratches his forehead as if he's weighed down by a great dilemma. "I'm sort of on the run."

With one elbow Vidar nudges his partner gently in the side and nods in amusement at the pale blue plastic band around the old man's wrist. He's from the hospital.

"I understand," Markus says, handing Vidar his cup. "Come with me."

"Thanks. Well, you see, I just wanted so badly to take a little walk, and then . . ."

Markus leads the old man to the car, so Vidar doesn't hear the rest.

Vidar stays behind and drinks his coffee. The sun warms his face. It's lunchtime. Brooktorpsgården, where Lovisa Markström worked, is just a stone's throw away. It's a lovely old half-timbered building from the 1700s.

Vidar walks into the café, mostly to see what it looks like inside these days. He's been there before, but it's been a few years.

More or less as he remembers it. The wooden ceiling is low; a few customers are sitting around the old tables having coffee. Behind the counter stands a woman with an apron and short, dark hair. She's small and thin, around Vidar's age, with big brown eyes, and seems relieved to see him. Maybe business isn't going so well. Vidar suddenly feels guilty and glances at what's on offer in the counter display cases; he'll buy something little to take with him. He's aware of how he looks when he comes in: big and tall, broad shouldered and silent. He's dependable and calm, one with his uniform. He can dish out punishment if necessary, and take blows, too, if worse comes to worst.

The woman behind the counter mostly looks annoyed. "So *now* you come by."

"Sorry?"

"We called a while ago."

"When was that?"

"Well, it's been hours."

Whatever the reason for the call, they must have solved the problem themselves. It's quieter in here than a nursing home.

"What were you calling about?"

She hands over an envelope, the kind bills come in. Vidar peeks inside. Sheets of A4 paper, folded double. He cautiously takes them out.

It's a letter of sorts. Three of them, all very short. None of them is dated.

How the hell can you do this? Please, I love you.

That's how the first one starts off. Only a few lines after:

Since you won't answer when I call I have no choice but to write. I'm going to take my own life. I don't know what else to do. You can't do this.

The next one starts the same way:

I love you and if you don't do as I say, I won't know where to put myself.

The words were penned harshly and with passion. They hurt to look at.

You will pay for what you've done. Please, I love you.
You're making me hate you. You should be afraid of me.

"Were these sent to you?"

"Me? No, no. It was Lovisa."

The woman behind the counter is named Patricia. According to her, the letters arrived during the fall. Even though their boss at the time insisted, a police report was never filed. That was at Lovisa's request. Instead, their boss placed them in with the safety manual in the office. In October he had gotten a divorce and moved from town to somewhere in northern Öland. They got a new boss, someone named Anita, and she didn't know about them.

"But you did," Vidar says. "You knew about the letters, I mean."

"Well, I was there when one of them came."

"You were?"

Patricia has deep brown eyes, sharp cheekbones, brown skin. He wonders where she's from. She doesn't have an accent.

"It was right before our shift started, and as she hung up her coat and stuff she noticed she'd gotten some mail. We have mailboxes here, but we don't usually get mail delivered at work, mostly only our pay stubs come here. I realized it made her angry, or maybe scared, I don't know. *Why won't he just leave me alone?* she said, and she took the letter and a few others, older ones, I think she was keeping in her backpack or something. *I'll have to show these to Bosse,* she said."

"And Bosse, that's your old boss?"

"Right. I assumed they were reported to the police, and I guess I just forgot about the whole thing. When I got here today, I wanted to check something about our alarm system, but Anita, our new boss, she wasn't here yet so I went in and looked in the folder with all our safety info. And the envelope fell out. When Anita arrived a little later I just wanted to check and make sure she knew about the letters and that they'd been reported to the police and so on, I mean, since the trial is going on right now. She said she'd never even heard of them. Which I thought was weird. Bosse was a good boss. He cared about us, and he was careful about following rules and laws. And we're actually supposed to report any harassment or threats. So all I can figure is that he wanted to report it, but decided not to and kept it to himself on Lovisa's request."

"Right," Vidar says, looking at the envelope, the letters, the words. "That sounds reasonable. Did anyone come by and talk to you? After the murder, I mean."

"Not to me, I was out of town at the time. But they talked to Anita. More than once, I'm pretty sure. And she didn't know anything, of course."

"Thanks," Vidar says. "I'll find out why it took so long for us to come by."

"They're from him, aren't they?" Patricia says, more a question than a statement.

Vidar looks at the letters again. The words are cruel, dripping with nastiness. The fact that he's from Marbäck makes it extra painful.

"Yes," he says. "Yes, it certainly seems like it."

Closer investigation yields a fairly simple explanation.

The call from Brooktorpsgården had come in at nine-thirty that morning. The caller was one Patricia Chincia. It wasn't clear what she wanted the police to do, other than come by. Two of Vidar's uniformed colleagues got in the car and headed out.

On the way they received a call about a burglary in progress at a nearby car dealership. The owner, Birgesson, has been running the business for as long as Vidar can recall. He's a talkative man with a good sense of humor and a healthy outlook on the world, and he also thoroughly enjoys coffee and police officers. That's probably why the patrol officers are still on-site. In any case, they never arrived at Brooktorpsgården. Vidar calls the café to explain once he and Markus are back at the station after handing the runaway grandpa back over to the hospital staff.

"I see," Patricia says. "Thanks for calling."

She sounds honestly grateful. Vidar pictures her serious face, her eyes fizzling with intelligence and curiousness, her small nose. Her voice is gravelly yet melodious. He feels something flutter behind his sternum, near his heart.

That afternoon he looks at the letters one last time. He wonders if they've gotten a handwriting sample from Edvard Christensson. Probably not; why would they have?

He gives them to K-G Öberg on the third floor. The chief inspector is on the phone, grunting curt answers to questions Vidar can't hear. He slams the receiver down with a bang.

"Evening papers," he snaps. "Goddamn vultures. What do you want, Jörgensson?"

Vidar hands over the envelope.

"What's this?"

Vidar tells him. K-G reads the letters with an inscrutable look on his face.

"Good," he says. "Very good. How did we miss these?"

"The woman you spoke with, Anita Björkman, didn't know about them."

"But this Patricia did."

"Yes. And I was thinking . . ." Vidar adds cautiously, "you haven't already gotten a writing sample from him, have you?"

"I actually don't think we have," K-G says. "But we sure as hell will now. Thank you, Jörgensson. You're a dependable sort. I'll remember that."

19

On Wednesday, the twenty-fourth of May 1995, Edvard Christensson is sentenced to life in prison, an indeterminate sentence with the possibility of applying to have his conviction time-limited after ten years. The court finds the crime to have been so grievous and without regard to life and safety—the fire is included in this consideration, because it easily could have spread to the surrounding farms—that the severe penalty is warranted.

That's the long and short of it.

It's hard to say whether the handwriting sample contributed to a guilty verdict, but Vidar imagines it did. It feels good to have helped. It's almost possible to breathe easy.

20

Maybe it came from Grandpa August, originally. He was very strange before he died. Not even Dad liked Grandpa, and Dad likes almost everyone. Everyone except politicians, bosses, and car owners, anyway. Grandpa was very thirsty and grumpy and often walked around with a glass in his hand. But Grandma was okay, and there's nothing wrong with Mom, so it must be that whatever it is only gets passed down to boys.

Right? Isak thinks about Mom. She's also been sitting around with a glass in hand a lot recently, on the sofa, late at night. Maybe it's in her, too. It just doesn't look the same way as it does in Edvard.

Yeah. That must be the way it is, he thinks.

It always smelled weird at Grandpa's house. Kind of like mushrooms, almost. And it was dark and all the furniture creaked. The photographs were black-and-white. One time Isak and Edvard went there to fix the bathroom sink. As Edvard knelt by the trap, Isak and Grandpa sat in the kitchen, Isak with juice and Grandpa with something clear that smelled bad.

"You drink a lot, Grandpa."

He nodded resolutely. "Correct."

"Why are you so thirsty?"

Grandpa, a thin man with unruly white hair, gazed out the

window where the gloomy outdoors waited. It was fall; everything was gray and brown.

"My gray dog."

Isak raised his eyebrows. "You have a dog, Grandpa?"

He chuckled. "You know, Isak, I don't like standing close to the road when the cars go by. I'd rather stand back. In the old days, when I was at sea, I was always afraid of standing at the prow and looking down at the water. One second could make all the difference, I thought. Between existing and not. Do you understand what I mean?"

Isak drank his juice. "No. But I think the ocean is scary, too."

"I often feel restless in my body. In my head. It's like I can't relax. It's gotten worse since Sara died, God knows." He raised his glass. "That restlessness always follows me around. Some people say it's like a black dog that you have beside you all the time, but I think that sounds so sad. I do have an invisible dog by my side all the time, but she's gray. And she can be a real pain in the ass sometimes, Isak. But as long as I drink, she keeps calm."

Edvard peered out from the bathroom.

"What are you talking about, Dad?"

"Nothing, son. How's it going in there?"

Edvard looked from Grandpa to Isak with uncertainty in his eyes. "Everything okay, Isak?"

"Yeah. We're just having a drink."

Grandpa smiled and raised his glass toward Edvard, who returned to the sink without another word.

"Why do you have three dots on your hand, Grandpa?"

Isak hadn't noticed them before, but there they were, in the skin between Grandpa's index finger and thumb: three dark blue dots, tiny, like birthmarks. "Well, now. I've got these so I can do a little trick." He put down his glass and held out his hand. "Look here." He moved his thumb close to his hand and the dots vanished. "Poof. And now . . ." Grandpa slowly separated them. The dots reappeared. He smiled. "Fun, isn't it?"

"Yeah. Did you paint them there?"

"It's called a tattoo. It's a kind of dye that doesn't go away."

Grandpa was so clever. Isak looked at his own hand. When he got home, he took a marker and drew three dots of his own between his thumb and index finger. But he must have done something wrong, because when he showed Mom she seemed almost angry and made him scrub them off at the sink right way. He scrubbed until his skin was raw and red.

There's a lot about life that's hard to understand, like the way things are in heaven and on earth. You're told that a good life on earth means that when it's over you can travel upward and see everyone you miss. This sounds like a nice but sort of strange reward. And a good life—how do you live one of those? It's both unpleasant and sort of cozy to think about, all at the same time. Grandma and Grandpa are somewhere else now. And where is Lovisa Markström? What was she like on earth? Isak liked her, but mostly only because Edvard did, too. It's not easy to know what people are really like, when you stop and think about it.

An invisible gray dog. An uneasy feeling in your stomach. Sometimes good people do bad things. That's not a good life. Edvard won't go to heaven when he dies. After what he did to Lovisa, he must be punished.

Isak didn't want to tell him the secret while Mom and Vidar could hear there in Jail, but he actually saw Lovisa one time last fall. She wasn't alone at the time—she was with Edvard. He thinks. It was hard to see, because they were so far away. He doesn't quite know what it means, but Lovisa seemed afraid.

It's not called an *omen*. People around here say *token*—an augury. In the olden days, people believed it was a sign of what might happen in the future, a sign from God.

He's lying in bed with the covers up to his chin, surrounded by the early-summer night in the safe house on Svanåsvägen. A gray dog moves at your side, silent and faithful. Flames rising in the darkness. A fire like a roar. It must be horrible to burn up.

Edvard has done something terrible, and now he's paying for it. That's only right. Isak didn't have time to tell him the secret. It doesn't matter.

He can hear them all the time now, the voices. The grown-ups in the village shoot him strange looks and talk about him when they think he can't hear.

How 'bout the kid, what'll happen to that one?

Can't be easy with an uncle like that, sure can't. Oh-ho, poor boy.

There's something in the eyes, that kid. Same as his uncle. And old August's story on top of it, why, there's something about that family.

Isak thinks about the time last Christmas when he hit that boy in the eye with an ice ball. It wasn't on purpose, of course. Or was it? He *had* wanted to hit him, but not hurt him. How do you know? Maybe he should have stopped to think, but there's not always time. Or . . . do other people actually do that? Maybe he *is* different.

Can you just leave?

Isak can see Grandpa's eyes turning into Edvard's eyes turning into his own. Behind his glasses they're so alike. He's scared.

Isak's palm and fingertips search for something in his chest, maybe in his belly or thighs, something small, is all.

What if it can be felt under his skin? It can't be easy to find; it would be strange if it were. He tries to find the spot where the token lives, the piece of him he shares with his uncle, the meanness inside him.

NINE YEARS LATER

Fall 2004

21

On the evening of January 8, 2005, Hurricane Gudrun hits Sweden. It's the night the ancient forest disappears.

Before the weather stations are knocked out, they record gusts of more than ninety-four miles per hour. In Marbäck, the storm picks up Ernst Hedman's barn and drags it across the field. The old playhouse behind Theo's house is smashed to smithereens on Svanåsvägen and the forests are destroyed.

People die.

Gudrun is a monster, and Isak Nyqvist doesn't make it out unscathed. The night leaves its mark on him, as it does to the rest of the village. He's outside and survives only because he finds himself—it sounds strange, but it's impossible to describe it any other way— *underneath* the storm.

Lovisa Markström has brought him there.

It all starts about three months earlier. If you arrange the events, put them in sequence, and trace everything backward, that's more or less where it begins.

Isak isn't exactly sure.

It's hard to put it all in order.

About three months earlier, in any case, he's about to kill himself and Theo in a car crash.

When he gets off the bus and returns home after school, a gleaming white Volvo with a pale brown interior is waiting in the driveway. Not until he gets to his room and spots the keys on the table does he understand.

There's a card from Mom and Dad.

Happy Birthday to our fantastic Isak. We love you so much.

It's his eighteenth birthday and all he wants is a car. Considering how tight money is every month, he can only imagine how long Mom and Dad must have been saving up to be able to afford it. Unless they took out a loan.

It's very tempting to take it out for a test-drive. He passed the theory portion of the driver's test a month ago, but his practical exam isn't until next week.

Driving a car without a license isn't all that unusual in Marbäck. Still, Isak stands in the driveway with the key in hand for a long time. It's unnaturally heavy, as if it were actually a key to something much larger. Mom and Dad aren't home; they won't be back for hours.

"Whoa." Theo is walking down Svanåsvägen. "You got a car?"

"Yeah."

"A little better than my present. Even if mine does come in a bag." He hesitantly holds up a plastic sack. It contains a bottle of vodka. "I thought maybe we could drink it on Friday."

"Thanks. Yeah, let's. Fun."

"Have you taken it out for a test-drive?"

"Not yet."

Isak opens the driver's-side door and adjusts the seat, places his hands on the wheel. Next to him, Theo looks hopeful and sets the plastic bag between his feet. Isak turns the key. The engine purrs beautifully. They exchange smiles.

Then they drive down Svanåsvägen and off through Marbäck. Out there, everything is just like always this time of year—the same drizzle, the same colors, roads, faces, the same life—but here in the car something is different. Isak feels oddly free.

As they make their way down to the old factory buildings, he drives cautiously, but as he's pulling a U-turn in one of the gravel lots, he gives it a little too much gas and the tires hiss against the ground. They kick up gravel behind them.

Theo laughs. They play music. Their speed increases.

The narrow road is edged by a rock face on the left and a shallow ditch on the right. Isak brakes hard to take a corner and the tires squeal joyfully; the back of the car skids. He rounds the corner and a tractor is coming at them like an animal.

It's big and red and appears in the blink of an eye. Isak has time to make out the driver behind the wheel up there, a man with a cap and a beard, and the angry front of the tractor looks like a gaping mouth with no tongue.

Theo screams.

Isak yanks the wheel to the right and the world goes blurry and slow. The asphalt is wet and slippery with fallen leaves, and it's like the steering wheel has a mind of its own.

The roar of the tractor passes somewhere to their left. In the cab, the driver turns his head. It's Göran Antonsson, one of the old farmers in Tolarp.

The car enters a fresh skid on the slippery road. Isak loses control.

Everything goes white with fear and he yanks at the hand brake. The tires screech in panic.

They're spinning. One side lifts slightly off the ground; Isak feels it and holds his breath. Then they fall back to the earth and stop, gasping, finally standing still with the engine churning, idling. Göran Antonsson's tractor chugs around the corner and vanishes from sight.

"Okay," Theo says, his hand on the dashboard and his face blank with shock. "That was a good start." He looks at the bag on the floor and takes out the bottle. "I think I'll have a little drink. Want some?"

"No, thanks."

"No, of course not." Theo laughs. "You're driving."

"Yeah." A giggle bubbles up in Isak. "I'm driving."

It bubbles and bubbles and at last a laugh escapes his lips. And they crack up until they're coughing, because you have to do *something* when you've just outsmarted death.

Theo drinks. Isak rests two shaking hands on the wheel and cautiously drives on, turning onto a forest path that winds between the bare trees. He parks in one of the small clearings and takes a little envelope from the pocket of his jacket. It's a regular sheet of paper that has been folded and taped, the kind you learned to make in school when you were a kid. That's how they come.

"Want to share?" Isak asks.

"Oh." Theo looks delighted. "But it'll smell."

"Not if we air it out."

They open the doors and recline their seats, then light the joint Isak bought behind the library in town. They smoke in silence. A line pops into Isak's head, sailing before his eyes as if it were bobbing on an invisible wave: *The downhill slide goes slowly. At first.*

He's not sure what it's from. Some book or movie, probably.

"Happy birthday, by the way," Theo says lazily. "Eighteen, huh? Now you can go to B&B, buy me cigs, and vote."

"But no alcohol."

Theo raises a serious index finger.

"The state store is more serious than democracy, you know. You have to be twenty to buy there."

Isak giggles. They fall silent again. They finish the joint. Isak makes sure that no one is nearby before he leans back in his seat again and closes his eyes. He can see part of the sky. Clouds are drifting by up there, and birds, small and black, nimble silhouettes, move in patterns; they seem to be searching for someone.

It's going downhill. Which is maybe just as well; how else would it end?

"Interesting, though," Theo says sleepily.

"What?"

"That after all these years, you can still scare the shit out of me."

22

The grass in Marbäck is covered in frost, and steam fog drifts across the waters of Fåglasjön. The everyday grind cloaks the village. In town, the buses huff by on Brogatan, and the sky is white as milk.

"Here, look at this." The owner of the computer-game shop downtown rests an index finger on the screen. "Here he comes. So, this is yesterday."

A gangly figure with baggy pants and the hood of his sweatshirt pulled up steps into the shop. He's the only customer.

"And you didn't notice this?"

"I was in the bathroom. I hadn't had time to take a piss since I opened."

Vidar has been with the property crimes unit for six months now, under Chief Inspector Beate Aronsson. Aronsson is almost sixty, has thirty years' experience on the force, and is a good boss in the sense that she mostly just wants to be left alone, and thus allows Vidar and his colleagues to handle most things on their own. Avoiding the boss makes work only marginally more enjoyable. Vidar spends a lot of time doing exactly this, standing in front of a security camera.

The time stamp in the corner of the image ticks ahead: *03:04:32, 03:04:33, 03:04:34.*

The figure in the shop has short, dark hair and long fingers; he looks pale. "Now," the shop owner says indignantly, waving his finger, "look. Here it comes."

The young man reaches for the shelves. His long fingers take two games.

"That's *GTA San Andreas*. One of our newest, hottest titles."

The thief stuffs them in the kangaroo pocket of his hoodie. Then he leaves the store. The owner freezes the image. The time stamp stops at *03:04:50*.

One copy of the game costs 599 kronor. Two means almost 1,200 kronor, which makes the crime a theft rather than just a shoplifting.

Typically, the property crimes unit investigates more serious crimes, such as vehicle thefts, home burglaries, and jewelry store thefts, but Vidar had had a quiet morning so he headed down to the office where reports were filed to take a look at the catch of the day.

The catch of the day. That's what they call it.

"Has he been here before?"

"I don't think so. But it's hard to say; we have so many customers and most of them are around his age."

It doesn't matter. Vidar recognizes him.

The next day, the Wednesday afternoon sun hangs low over Sannarp School. Vidar waits by his car, wearing civilian clothes, squinting.

Sannarp School is a prep school for smart, ambitious kids, future economists and entrepreneurs. It's the direct descendant of the first school in Halmstad, which dated from the fifteenth century, a fact the principal often points out when he's interviewed in the newspaper. As if today's students were the latest chapter in a venerable, six-hundred-year-old story. Strictly speaking they probably are, but the part of the story that revolves around a certain Isak Nyqvist is hardly venerable.

The teen comes plodding out of the building with a worn black backpack over his shoulder and Theo Bengtsson at his side. They're accompanied by a girl with long blond hair.

"Isak," Vidar says.

"Yeah?" He doesn't stop walking.

"Hey."

Isak stops. The girl looks puzzled. Theo snickers and looks at his shoes, a pair of lightweight black Converse.

"Are you headed home?"

"No."

"Are you sure? I can give you a ride."

Isak sighs. "What's this all about?"

"Cars."

Theo's eyes get huge. Isak's, too. The girl's gaze darts between the two of them. Under her fall jacket she's wearing a black T-shirt that says CHILL, MOTHERFUCKER.

Vidar drives out of Halmstad, past Vallås, and on to Snöstorp. Highway 25 is smooth and black; the white lines look almost fluorescent. It's recently been repaved. Tangled and narrow as a string, it winds its way through eastern Halland and toward central Småland. Isak is quiet and shrunken, his backpack between his feet.

"How are you doing, Isak?"

"What do you want?"

"Open the glove box."

"Why?"

"Take out the folder."

Isak's long fingers pull out the brown folder. Three images from the game store's security camera are waiting inside. He studies them for a long time. They pass Snöstorp, and make it to Brogård and Skedala before Isak closes the folder and puts it back.

"That's not me."

"You've got those same pants on right now."

Isak rolls his eyes and crosses his arms. "Are you doing this to fuck with me or something?"

"It was either this or mail it."

From his jacket pocket, Vidar pulls a folded sheet of paper. Isak takes it. NOTIFICATION OF SUSPICION reads the heading. Vidar turns off the highway at Skedala and drives down the narrow coil of asphalt that runs through Årnarp and Tolarp, and on to Marbäck. This longer route to Svanåsvägen gives him more time with Isak. Isak doesn't protest.

"Given that you are of age, it's up to you what you do with this document. My suggestion is that you show it to your parents."

The gangly teenager's defiance has been replaced by uncertainty. It's strange, really. People seldom understand what they've done before they see it written down on paper.

"Am I going to . . . What . . . ?"

"If you'd taken *one* game, it would have been shoplifting. But you took one for your friend, too, which means the value exceeds the lower limit for theft."

"But am I going to . . ."

"If you confess," Vidar continues calmly, "you'll come down to the station and sign a document. That's called 'an order of summary punishment.' And you'll only have to pay a fine."

"But I don't have any money."

"They'll take that into account, and you'll probably still be able to afford a suit for graduation. Maybe secondhand, though."

"What if I don't confess?"

"Then the prosecutor will file charges and it will go to trial."

Isak gazes at the document with his big brown eyes.

A few years ago, he'd had bad acne and glasses, and he was still chubby in the face. He almost looked goofy. Then something happened. The acne cleared up; he shot up in height over one summer and became a lot slimmer. He must have gotten contacts, because he no longer wears glasses. Now he's a pale sack of skin and bones, and he bears an almost uncanny resemblance to both his uncle and his grandfather as young men.

Vidar and Isak roll into Tolarp, toward the spot where Hans and Erika Markström's one-story house once stood. Now all that's left is a lot full of overgrown weeds and trash. Nearly ten years have passed. All the cards are face up. Vidar opens his mouth to ask Isak about his uncle but changes his mind. What would he say? It's hard to even imagine what it must be like.

"Show it to your parents. How is your mother these days, by the way? I know she . . . that you were all having a rough time there for a while."

Isak turns the paper over, as if he doesn't hear Vidar, and asks, "What is this?"

"My cellphone number." Vidar slows down and drops him off not far from Svanåsvägen. "It's up to you what you do. But you have to decide. And return the games."

Isak doesn't say anything. He opens the passenger door and gets out, slamming the door loudly behind him.

23

It's easy to dream yourself away, but dreaming your way *to* something is much harder. The adult world is so hollow.

The goal in life is to *have goals*.

The purpose is to *have a purpose*.

Still, sometimes Isak wonders who he's going to be, where he'll be living in five years, who he cares about. On occasion he tries to see into the future and catch a glimpse of himself—because somewhere the world must have opened up a little and prepared a place even for him.

But where?

Johanna Fältman is in the international baccalaureate program at Sannarp and lives in Skedala. She has bright blue eyes and the softest lips Isak has ever kissed. Sure, he hasn't kissed *that* many girls, but none of them were like her. During a party at Norre Katts park the week before school ended, they started to make out, and then came a weird week of texts and lingering gazes in the hallways of Sannarp. Until he kissed her the next weekend and she kissed him back.

He likes basically everything about her. The music she listens to, the movies she likes, the clothes she wears, the long glances she shoots him, how good her hair smells, how soft and smooth her skin is around her collarbones and her lower back, how her palm feels when it's resting on his chest, the things she likes to talk about.

Maybe the place made for Isak is with her.

The only thing that's not so great is how she's planning to spend the summer traveling with Nina and Meral, and how she talks about it all the time. But in some ways Isak likes it—she gets so excited whenever she brings it up, and Johanna is awfully cute when she's excited.

He loves her, but he hasn't said so. Hasn't mustered the courage.

Isak cracks the door to her room. She's still wearing her CHILL, MOTHERFUCKER T-shirt.

"Hi," she says, smiling, but there's something uneasy in her eyes today.

Or maybe it's just him. They make out for a while and he touches her cheeks, her hair. The bed creaks. Johanna's walls are covered in band and movie posters. There's a computer in one corner. He can see the case out of the corner of his eye, unopened.

He cautiously pushes her away.

"Could you . . ." He hesitates. "Could you give me back that game, do you think?"

"*San Andreas?*"

Isak strokes her cheek. "If that's okay."

"Yeah, sure. Why, though?"

"I just need it back, is all. I'll explain later."

"But, I mean . . . Look, I told you not to buy it. It's too much money."

"I know, I . . ." He laughs suddenly, worried that he'll sound as uncertain as he feels. "I just didn't think it through, exactly. I really wanted to give it to you."

She ejects the disc from the PlayStation, putting it back in its case. Isak's chest is glowing with shame.

"By the way," she says. "I was thinking maybe we should talk."

"Okay."

She sits down on the edge of the bed. "Do you really like me?"

"Yeah. A lot."

"Okay," she says. As if she'd been hoping he would say no.

"What, why?"

"I . . . well, it's just, I don't know how I feel anymore. And after graduation I'm going on my trip with Nina and Meral, and I have no idea how long I'll be away. I mean, who knows, what if I stay there? No matter what, there's going to be a long time where we won't see each other."

"But that's not until June."

"I don't think I can handle it. It'll just be hard to think about. I think it would be better if we were just, like, friends."

"But I want . . . I . . ." he starts, but when he looks at Johanna there are tears in her eyes, and he runs out of words.

He should have told her he loves her. Or he shouldn't have brought up the game. He shouldn't even have come here today, that's it, he should have just stayed away. There must have been *something* he could have done to keep her with him, so it didn't end up like this.

But it's too late.

It is, in every other way, a perfectly normal Wednesday in October.

Isak takes the game and leaves.

24

Vidar wakes up early. He leans to the side and brings his lips to her cheek, stroking her hair before he gets out of bed.

"No, no," Patricia murmurs, reaching out a hand and grabbing his wrist. "Where are you going? What time is it?"

"Five-thirty. I have to go to the bathroom."

When he returns, she mutters something that isn't words and places a smooth, warm hand on the back of Vidar's neck, tenderly but firmly guiding his head toward her thighs.

"God, I'm so tired," she says in a thick voice. "Wake me up. And cover my mouth if I'm too loud, so she doesn't wake up."

Patricia becomes perfectly shiny. Her skin gleams in the cold light from the window. Vidar presses a hand over her mouth and feels her warm breath on his fingers.

She braces her hips, and as she gives a deep, strained moan from behind his hand the warm, wet saltiness shoots toward his mouth. He swallows greedily, gasps for air, and swallows again. The taste is hypnotizing, almost bewitching.

"You taste so good," he mumbles.

Patricia grabs him by the hair and pulls him up.

"My turn," she gasps.

:::

He messed it up for himself. On the day in question, Ulrika Antonsson was at Vidar's place instead of vice versa. It must have been the summer of 1995. Vidar, bored and restless, had wondered how he could break off what he and Göran's wife were doing. After all, he wasn't really all that interested.

Göran had returned to the farm earlier than usual and had, from a distance, observed his wife setting off on her bicycle. For obvious reasons he had wondered what she was up to. So he and Elvira the dog followed her.

And not long afterward, his face was pressed to Vidar's bedroom window.

At that point, the little farmer returned home with the dog. He hadn't said or done a thing; perhaps he hadn't even thought anything.

When Ulrika got home, he was sitting at the kitchen table and explained what was going to happen. She would tell Vidar that she didn't want to see him anymore; they would keep the whole thing to themselves, and life would go on. If she absolutely had to sleep with someone, it should be someone they could agree on and who could be made aware of a few conditions.

When Ulrika suggested that this person might as well be Vidar, since he was more than well *aware* of what was going on, so to speak, Göran shook his head vehemently. *Absolutely not,* he said. *Not him, the man you cheated on me with. And not with that—*

Huge cock? Ulrika said.

Göran didn't respond.

And that was the end of it.

Just as well, Vidar thought. And he was glad it would stay between the three of them.

It did, for a while, but in the end word got out. He wasn't sure how, but one day a large percentage of the population of Marbäck suddenly knew that for almost a whole year Vidar Jörgensson had provided Ulrika Antonsson with something she neither could nor wanted to get from her old man.

:::

Vidar shares an office with Nashwan. There's not a lot of space up in the property crimes unit, even though police headquarters had relocated less than five years ago to the newly built building on the other side of downtown on account of lack of space in the old six-story station building. They're already talking about an addition.

Their office is small, but it doesn't matter. It's *theirs*. Vidar is thirty-seven, taciturn, and from Marbäck; Nashwan is a thirty-nine-year-old chatterbox from Tehran, with three children. He loves puns, especially ones about the police. His favorite is, "Why did they take the cop to the bakery when he had a heart attack? He was wearing a *donut resuscitate bracelet.*"

Maybe their differences and his bad jokes are the reason they get along so well. They were rookies at the same time, like he and Markus were, and have been on a lot of shifts together. They could be friends, Vidar sometimes thinks, if only they had time outside of work. Trust is a rare thing, but when you feel it, you know.

"Top three events in the police Olympics," Nashwan says when Vidar opens the door. He holds up his fingers. "Three: four hundred meter accidental discharge. Two: eight hundred meter looking the other way. One: immigrant toss."

And he gives a hoarse laugh.

"Those aren't even puns."

"But they're still funny."

Nashwan goes back to reading his incident report, with his index finger tracing the words. Vidar takes off his jacket and hangs it on the hook.

"A call hasn't come in from Isak Nyqvist, has it?"

Nashwan shakes his head.

Shit. Had it been too much to hope for?

If it had been anyone else, Vidar wouldn't have worried, but Isak Nyqvist isn't just anyone. Vidar knows what their life is like there in Marbäck. Although his parents, Eva and Peter, have stuck together all these years, it probably hasn't been easy. Eva drank a lot in the years before the new millennium. In a roundabout way, he's heard that she had to spend a few months drying out in rehab, that she and Peter suffered through months of couples therapy to save their marriage. Vidar sits down at his desk and takes a look at the materials waiting there.

Exhaustion settles over him.

They've been fighting with a massive case recently. Halland, Skåne, and Småland are all cooperating on it. The county Criminal Investigation Department has overarching responsibility for coordination but the local units have been handling the fieldwork.

It's all thanks to a band of thieves.

Two brothers, Božo and Darko Miljanovic, came to Sweden as refugees from the former Yugoslavia. After an extensive series of break-ins in southern Sweden, they were sentenced to prison in the fall of 1995.

Both served their time and were released six years later. Darko was killed in a traffic accident outside Höör in Skåne in the winter of 2003. Božo is still around and appears to be done mourning the loss of his brother, because now he's out causing trouble again. He seems to have learned from his and Darko's old mistakes; it's been very tricky to link him to the burglaries that have struck the three counties in the past six months. All they've managed to turn up are circumstantial evidence, sightings, and indirect links.

Is he even the one they're after?

Probably. Thieves of his caliber are rare. But he's likely not working alone. One name, Josif Marinko, has popped up a number of times.

Marinko is ten years younger than Božo and has a rap sheet, but only for minor crimes, and is listed as living at an address in Ängelholm a few dozen miles south of the border with Skåne, about an hour's drive from Halmstad. Early on the Ängelholm police put him under surveillance, but when he neither broke any law worth the paper it was written on nor was spotted with Božo Miljanovic, the effort was called off.

Marinko appears to be clean as a whistle. Božo seems to have gone up in smoke. The case is at a standstill.

Vidar, Nashwan, and their colleagues to the south are looking through old cases, reading ancient records, and trying to work meticulously. Nashwan has printed out the judgments against Božo and Darko, along with a collection of newspaper articles and written materials from the time period. Vidar sits at his desk, reading through the stack of documents.

Božo and Darko Miljanovic were born in 1965 and 1968, respectively, and came to Sweden sometime in early 1991. Božo had a background as a boat repairman for a firm in Sarajevo; Darko had been a hospital janitor. At Christmastime in 1990, a bomb blew their families to pieces.

They had nothing with them when they arrived. The Migration Agency lost track of them in Malmö. They had cousins in Lund so they made their way there and began to work in construction. Later on the city cracked down on illegal workers after an article in the local paper got a lot of attention. This crackdown left Božo and Darko without employment.

They had a friend who made a living breaking into homes. The two brothers began to help him out, and when their friend was nabbed for receiving stolen goods in early 1994 they picked up where he left off.

Božo and Darko stuck to southern Sweden, selling the stolen goods via Helsingborg and Helsingør. This was before the Øresund Bridge was built, so they crossed to Denmark by boat. They were arrested in March 1995 and convicted in October.

Something clicks in Vidar's mind. Now he remembers: He mentioned the gang once. It was during his first visit to K-G Öberg's office, back when they were working on the Lovisa Markström case.

Vidar raises his eyebrows and turns to Nashwan.

"Is this really true?"

"What?"

Nashwan leans over Vidar's shoulder and looks at the document.

"Yeah, that's right." He returns to his own desk. "Don't you remember? Keep reading, and you'll see."

An indictment lays out the principal crime and any secondary crimes. The principal crime is almost always the most serious and it is considered to "consume" any other crimes listed in the document. The secondary crimes are still listed, however. For instance, you could be convicted of battery in a case that also incorporates the secondary crime of unlawful intimidation, if you had first threatened the person you eventually assaulted.

The conviction of burglars Božo and Darko Miljanovic is confusing, because the principal crime isn't breaking and entering, theft, or trespassing.

It's *attempted homicide* and *arson*.

In March 1995, the two brothers broke into a house on the outskirts of Ljungby, a town in Småland. Complications ensued when a neighbor first contacted the homeowner, who was at a party half a mile away, and then called the police.

The owner arrived before the police did. Not all that unusual, unfortunately. What happened next was beyond reasonable doubt.

The homeowner discovered the two brothers in the process of placing valuables into a black bag, reported *Smålandsposten. A scuffle broke out, and the homeowner was struck unconscious by the younger brother. When the homeowner regained consciousness, he found his surroundings were on fire. In the courtroom, prosecutor Fredrik Milewski claimed that the brothers had been convinced they had killed the homeowner and were trying to destroy the evidence by burning it up.*

"They took what they were after and with uncommon ruthlessness they tried to burn the house to the ground to avoid leaving any traces of their crime," he stated during Friday's closing arguments.

"What is it?" Nashwan asked without glancing up.

Vidar checks the dates of the 1990s burglary spree. *When he regained consciousness, he found his surroundings were on fire.*

A reminder from the past. That's all.

"Nothing," he says.

25

Everyone has heard. It's been only a week, but everyone knows: Isak Nyqvist got dumped. For the first few days after, he doesn't even go to school.

Today he has to go. He's already missed a test, and his English teacher called the house to make sure Isak was planning to be there for the vocab quiz today.

The required STUDENT DRIVER sign shines bright green from the back of the white Volvo, and Mom is in the passenger seat. This is officially the first time Isak has driven his own car, and he's glad it's with her. True, Mom isn't technically allowed to be his accompanying adult, since she failed a Breathalyzer checkpoint three years ago. They took her license. She's got it back by now, but still she doesn't count as a supervisor. It doesn't really matter.

She's mostly quiet, and she doesn't seem to care how the driving is going as long as he's not about to run into anything. She even lets him listen to music. With Dad, usually all he hears is *Be careful here. Watch out for that bump. Remember your turn signal, now. There's no one behind us, is there? Because if there is, you have to . . .*

"I know you've driven this car before, Isak."

He lowers the volume on the stereo.

"What?"

"I ran into Göran at the store yesterday. He said he was out on his tractor last week and suddenly almost ran into a car he didn't recognize. A white Volvo 850 with two lads behind the wheel."

"Lads?"

"The word he used isn't the issue here."

Isak can feel her look of disappointment in his peripheral vision.

"Isak, having a driver's license and a car is a big responsibility. You must never, ever do that again. Understood?"

He brakes for the red light and stops, his cheeks blazing.

"It was you and Theo, wasn't it?"

"No."

"Don't lie to me."

"But it wasn't—"

"Isak!"

He clams up. The heat on his cheeks rises to his ears, spreads to his neck.

"Did you tell Dad?" he asks.

Mom gazes out the windshield and doesn't say anything; she's chewing her lower lip. The light changes. Isak drives toward school.

"No, I didn't."

"Are you going to?"

"What does that matter? Are *you* going to do anything like that again?"

Isak shakes his head.

"And have you done anything else I should know about?"

"No."

She looks at him for a long time. The piece of paper Vidar gave him is burning in his pocket.

"Then I don't know that there's anything to tell Dad," she says. "But you're going to shape up now, you hear me?"

There's something in her tone that awakens his fury. A sudden drop of fire takes shape in Isak's chest.

"At least I don't drive when I'm blitzed. You wanna talk to *me* about being *responsible*?"

It's so quiet. Isak can hear his own heart beating.

"I'm sorry," he says.

"It's okay. You're right."

It was really bad for a while. Bottles everywhere, forgotten glasses. Dad threatened to leave again. That was what he said, leave *again*. As if it had almost happened before.

Isak doesn't really want to know. He's ashamed. Because she just disappeared for a few months, because she had to go to rehab, because everyone knew. And there was no doubt about what had set it all off, either.

To be honest, it didn't surprise him. The world stopped being coherent, stopped making sense a long, long time ago.

Isak stops just inside Sannarp School's large parking lot and turns off the engine. He unbuckles his seatbelt but remains seated. It's easier than getting out. The sight of the school buildings makes him feel nauseated.

"Listen," he says.

"What?"

"I was thinking . . . You know, Edvard . . . Are you ever in touch with him?"

"What do you mean?"

"Oh, nothing, really. I just wondered."

"Is it all the crap in the papers?"

They've already started appearing, articles that remind everyone about the ten-year anniversary. They recap the events. They show old pictures. As if anyone needed that. As if people don't still remember but avoid talking about it.

"I don't know," he says. "Maybe. When did you last talk?"

"Oh, when was it . . . in ninety-eight, maybe."

"What? That long ago? Why?"

"That's just what happened."

"But why?"

Mom shifts in her seat. "It's hard to explain. You were so little back then."

A flare of fire inside Isak. There it is again. *You were so little.* As if that meant all decisions were completely taken away from him. What about now? Now that he's eighteen?

"Hold on," Mom says, as if it's only now dawning on her. "You would want to have contact with him? After what he did?"

A girl Isak sort of knows, she's in the healthcare track, passes by the car. She's wearing giant headphones and clenching her jaw, maybe against the cold but probably for some other reason. She's almost always on her own in the hallways.

"No. I guess I don't."

More silence. Mom shifts in her seat again, turning to him. "Isak, I—"

"Are you going to go to the memorial on the thirteenth?"

"I don't think so. I heard Hans and Erika will be there. I'm sure it would just be . . . it's probably best if we don't go."

Isak's eyes follow the girl from the healthcare track. Today he feels a new, unexpected affinity with her.

"By the way," Mom says, glancing after the girl. "This Johanna, are you still seeing each other?"

"Why?"

"Well, until a week or so ago, you spent all your time with her. I just . . . I wondered if something had happened."

She falls silent, as if this were enough for him to understand what she's asking. And, of course, it is.

He opens the door and grabs his backpack from the back seat. "I have to go. Class starts soon."

He calls during his free period after the English test. He failed miserably—probably he won't get more than ten out of fifty correct. It almost feels like a relief to let go and be left alone. The phone feels remarkably steady in his hand, but maybe that's just the way it is. Each day ends in exhaustion, and by then you're too drained to even shake.

"Vidar Jörgensson."

"This is Isak."

"Isak. Great. Hang on a sec." There's a rustle. "There. Hi."

"Were you serious when you said my parents don't need to know about this?"

"That's up to you."

Isak tries to think, but it's hard. Through the large window he sees Johanna walking by with Meral beside her. They're laughing about something. As if nothing has happened. For them, this is just a normal day.

He turns his back to the window.

"I'll come in."

"Great. When can you be here?"

"Well, uh . . . today?"

Vidar takes a deep breath.

"I really appreciate you making this decision, Isak. It's smart and mature. But unfortunately, it can't happen quite that fast. I have to get the go-ahead from the prosecutor first, and prepare some documents. It's not a lot, but around here it takes time just to get a cup of coffee made. Could we say Monday? After school?"

"What do you mean, the go-ahead from the prosecutor? You said—"

"Don't worry, Isak. It's just paperwork."

"I don't trust you."

"That's not too surprising," Vidar says. "But no worries. Come down on Monday and you'll see."

I don't trust you. Most adults find those words to be unsettling, even provocative. If there's anything Isak has learned, it's that. But not Vidar Jörgensson. He sounds unruffled; as calm as ever. It's annoying.

"I'm done at three on Monday," Isak mumbles.

26

Patricia Chincia's parents came to Halmstad by way of Copenhagen and Stockholm as refugees from the civil war in Nigeria. The year was 1970, and with them they had a little girl who was born at Söder Hospital in Stockholm. Her dad got a job at a firm that opened branches in Småland and Halland, and after three years in their new country they ended up in Halmstad. Patricia attended Andersberg School for primary school and Kattegatt High School afterward, and eventually she started working at Brooktorpsgården. That was where she got to know Lovisa Markström and where she first met Vidar.

A large, stable, white policeman. She had her suspicions about where it might lead.

Maybe it was unavoidable. Sometimes they talk about it like that, like there wasn't really anything they could do. The attraction, if that's the right word, was too strong.

Vidar had been to Mårtensson's nightclub in town with Markus and Nashwan. It was Markus's first weekend off since returning to work after his paternity leave in late 1995. They'd eaten dinner and had a beer each, and then a few more.

He met her at the bar. They ended up next to each other. It was the first time he'd seen her since that day at Brooktorpsgården. She was wearing a white blouse and black jeans, boots that made her a little taller.

Vidar really shouldn't have said a word. Strictly speaking, he had met her while on duty. There was no official rule against it, but Vidar strove to keep his private life and work life separate; a maxim he'd learned from his father. That, and *Coincidence is your enemy; never trust it.*

Both were tipsy, which made for some slightly strange and awkward chitchat at first, but there was something about Patricia's eyes. The same thing she saw in Vidar's, maybe.

Not a coincidence.

Patricia laughed. She placed her hand over his and kept it there for a little too long.

He didn't remember her last name. *Chincia,* she said with a smile.

"What does it mean? Or," he backtracked, suddenly embarrassed, "does it mean anything?"

He had to lean down very close to hear her response. His lips brushed her neck. It was a mistake, but she didn't move. She smelled strongly of perfume and sweat.

"It's Nigerian. It's hard to translate into Swedish. But, like, 'God answers' or 'God hears you,' really."

"As in, 'God hears prayers,' you mean?"

"Not exactly. I mean, if you're Christian then God hears if you pray. I suppose that's the idea. But you have to pray for him or her to listen. *Chincia* doesn't mean that God answers you, but more like, God is always with you, no matter what you do."

For Vidar, who was raised in 1970s Marbäck by two Lutheran parents and a God-fearing teacher, this sounded very beautiful.

"So you pray, too?"

She laughed again. Patricia had nice teeth. "Never. I have God only in my name. You?"

"Sometimes."

He went home with her. She lived in Nyhem, in a nice one-bedroom apartment with large windows. He hadn't known what to expect, and realized he had desires that he hadn't been aware of before. She was half reclining on a large, comfortable sofa. Two glasses of wine stood on the table, untouched. His hands unbuttoned her jeans, his fingertips cool against her skin.

Her white blouse became speckled with sweat. He stepped out of his pants, tugged off his boxers.

Her nails left deep half moons in Vidar's thighs, and a pleasant dull pain rose in his groin.

Soon a knot of burning heat loosened and flowed out of him. Patricia drew it out of him; that was what it felt like. She made him shake. By the time it was over his throat hurt. Patricia kissed his eyelids, which surprised him, and Vidar inhaled the scent of her hair for the first time.

"I'm going to be perfectly honest," he said sometime later. "I fell for you because you're fantastic. But the first time I went home with you, it was because I was drawn to you. Because . . ."

"Because why?"

"Because there was something about you. I don't know. An energy. You were so beautiful. And I think part of it was because . . ."

"Because I'm Black?"

"No, not that. Well, not just that."

Vidar hesitated. He'd never been great with words, much less emotions.

It felt so strange to talk about. Patricia is one of the most Swedish Swedes he's ever met: born and raised in Sweden, educated in Swedish schools, fan of Midsummer, new potatoes, cream in her coffee, and, at Christmastime, Arne Weise and Donald Duck on TV.

"I think sometimes you exoticize me," she said.

"Is that what it's called? I don't mean to."

"It doesn't matter if you mean to or not; you still do it."

"Is that . . . does that make you angry?"

"No. Not anymore. More like tired. That's a weird change for me, and it makes me feel bad. Like, I feel I *should* be angry about that, but I'm not. You know?"

"I think so. Yeah. I'm sorry."

She kissed his cheek. "I exoticize you too. I think . . . I mean, in Sweden we grow up with, like, whiteness as the unspoken ideal. Know what I mean? And maybe it's not just here. I grew up experiencing whiteness as something to aspire to. As something safe. It was subconscious when I was little. But later on I figured out what was going on, that it's because of norms, or whatever. I've basically accepted it now, I think. Just, with an awareness, if you know what I mean?"

He did. At least he thought he did.

She straddled him on the same sofa where they'd sat the first time he came home with her, pressing herself against Vidar, dragging her nails down his chest.

Maybe that was it. She filled a hole inside him that he hadn't even known existed, but he had known he could love her. When he fell, it was almost helplessly.

It all progressed seamlessly, until one day when they were walking hand in hand through Marbäck, and the people who saw them wondered what had drawn Vidar Jörgensson to this woman. Was it pregnancy? An odd sense of pride? Manipulation? They figured it to be everything but plain old love.

27

Isak watches Johanna cross Storgatan in downtown Halmstad, hand in hand with a guy from Sture High School, laughing at something he just said.

The last thing Isak catches before he averts his eyes is how the guy leans toward Johanna and how she mirrors him, smiling, placing her free hand to his cheek an instant before they kiss.

He's just left a house party over by Norre Port. Walking to the bus, alone, pretty drunk, finishing the last few gulps of the beer he took to go. That's when he sees them.

I don't know what I feel anymore.

I don't think I can do this. It's just too hard.

I think it would be better if we were just, like, friends.

Isak wants to shout. He can't. He just walks.

It's cold, but there are lots of people out. When he turns the corner on his way to the bus stop at Stora Torg, he runs into two guys.

One is named Jesper and lives in Skedala. He doesn't remember the other one's name. They were two years ahead of him in school. They locked him in the changing room after gym once and broke into his locker and threw all his books, papers, and belongings on the floor. They wrote FAG GET OUT on the door of the locker before they left.

"Shit, watch where you're going," Jesper bellows. "You blind or something? Left your glasses at home?"

They've already passed him. Something sparks in his hands and heart, but Isak doesn't say anything, doesn't do anything.

"Just as pathetic as his sick-fuck uncle. You know that story, right? Everyone out in Skedala knows."

The other guy laughs in agreement. Isak keeps walking, but then something strange happens. He turns around and sees their backs.

He's heard it so many times by now. It hurts every time, as if someone is poking at the most tender part of his soul. In the school-yard, on the bus, in town, down by the waterfall—he has been forced to recall his worst fear wherever he goes. He has reacted with rage just about every time; his first impulse is to respond by saying *Yes, exactly, I'm about to show you why you should have watched yourself and kept your fucking mouth shut.* To use what he has inherited from his uncle as a weapon. Might as well use it for *something.* Better to be mean than to be nothing at all.

But he has stopped himself every time, more for his own sake than for others'. Despite all the bullshit, all the rumors and pointed gazes and all the times he wanted nothing but to have a sudden outburst, he has held back as if to say *No, that's not who I am. I don't have it in me.* And that in itself is probably some sort of survival tactic. Internal resistance. But this time, everything is reeling.

"Hey," Isak shouts. "You little pussy! *Hey!*"

Jesper from Skedala turns around. He looks surprised.

Isak hurtles the empty beer bottle at him.

It's just like King's Rock: You know whether or not you'll hit the target. Something about how the arc of your arm feels. The bottle rotates slowly and peacefully up in the air, on its way down.

It hits Jesper between the eyes, and he falls to the ground. His stupid fuckwad of a friend is dumbfounded as his eyes dart from Jesper on the ground to Isak, who's sauntering down the street toward them.

"You want something with me?" Isak roars. "Huh?"

The friend turns tail. Jesper is still lying there motionless. Isak's body sings with satisfaction. It felt so good to give in.

Then comes the panic. *People are staring.* Shit.

Isak's first thought is escape. That surprises him. Although, really, doesn't he expect it? People say *I didn't know where to put myself.* The first impulse is to flee.

Not all monsters are imaginary. Maybe the future isn't empty at all.

Isak runs. Dashes through the city, his heart pounding.

28

The spree began, as far as anyone knows, on July 2, 1994, with a home burglary in Genarp, east of Malmö. A retired couple lost a nice TV, some china, heirloom jewelry, and a painting that was worth basically nothing. The Carl Larsson painting beside it was untouched. The Miljanovic brothers knew nothing about art. This resulted in a mildly humorous item in the local paper. The next month it happened again. On August 18, they broke into a single-family home in Södra Sandby outside Lund. It seems to have been a case of simple theft. The family was out of town; the house was deserted; no witnesses. They got away but were later linked to the crime because of their car, a dark gray Nissan Primera. It was used in connection with the next break-in, in Veinge one month later. The same car had been observed near the house in Södra Sandby.

The brothers spent 1994 and 1995 traveling through northern Skåne, up the west coast, into Halland, then on to Småland. They hit one or two targets each month, typically a house in the countryside where the risk of being caught in the act was low.

Hoping to form an overview of the spree, Vidar has obtained an old map of Sweden and tacked it up on the wall; on it he has placed small labels to note dates and place names. They form a track through southern Sweden, from Genarp in July 1994 to the arson and attempted homicide in Ljungby almost nine months later.

July 2, 1994. Genarp.

August 18, 1994. Södra Sandby.

September 10, 1994. Ängelholm.

September 27, 1994. Veinge.

October 15, 1994. Skogaby.

October 29, 1994. Karsefors, Laholm.

January 15, 1995. Skrea, Falkenberg.

February 4, 1995. Tvååker.

March 7, 1995. Björketorp.

March 26, 1995. Ljungby.

It's Sunday, and the building is almost empty. The only sounds are the buzzing of all the electronics and the faint hum of the HVAC in the walls. Vidar steps forward to study the map. Two brothers. One will survive; one will die.

In October of 1994 you're in Laholm. January 1995, in Falkenberg. There's an unusual gap in between. Why? What were you doing during that time?

He makes himself a cup of coffee and steps into the elevator, which carries him down to the deep archive. Fluorescent lights flicker, cold light from the low ceiling. The heavy shelves can be rolled back and forth with a crank. He stops at *1995* and steps in.

It's cool and quiet down here, just Vidar and the innumerable tales of crimes packed into identical boxes, case numbers labeled with black marker. The boxes that involve the Miljanovic brothers are easy to identify, since Nashwan has recently been down here to dig up parts of the old material. He left them a little crooked, maybe to make them easier to find again when it's time to put everything back.

Vidar pulls out one of the boxes and opens it. It smells old. The slush file on the Miljanovic brothers—that's what he's after.

No, not here. He pushes the box back into place and moves on.

He has already passed the first box when he catches a glimpse of something familiar, on one of the shelves on the other side of the aisle: a case number. *Isn't that . . . ?*

He backs up. The chilly air makes him shiver. When he touches the box, it feels surprisingly warm.

Almost ten years now. All the cards are face up, and yet there's a sense of discomfort.

He looks around to make sure he's alone.

He lifts the box down. Binders, folders, copies, old cassette tapes. They're marked *PI-1*—preliminary investigation—*PI-2, PI-3, Slush, TI.* He takes out a binder and flips through it. The pages smell the way he remembers. He finds his own contributions: running across Edvard Christensson in the forest, checking alibis, his conversations with Billy Oredsson and Dennis Götmark, Jon-Erik Pettersson and the others. The three cars that drove through Tolarp around the same time as the crime was committed, all followed up on and struck from the list. Lots of this material was done on typewriters—they'd started to use computers by then, but it wasn't like today at all. These documents feel so different. In the corner of each piece of paper, or sheaf of papers, is the same case number and a date stamp.

He puts the first binder aside and picks up another, then a third and a fourth. At the bottom of the box is a yellowed plastic sleeve with lightweight contents. Vidar recognizes it. The threatening letters from Christensson.

He personally handed them over to K-G Öberg in the spring of 1995, on the same day he met Patricia. The memory feels warm in his chest.

It starts as a feeling more than a realization, and he can't quite figure out what he's looking at. Then it registers.

He pulls the box into the light and peers inside, lifting another folder at random; he opens it and finds copies of the plans for the Markströms' house. Marks added where the body was found. Date stamp and case number in the corner. Everything is in order.

He opens yet another binder, browsing faster now. The pages pat softly against his fingertips. Stamp, stamp, stamp, case number, case number, case number . . . it's all in perfect order.

He looks at the yellow plastic sleeve again. Date stamp. Case number.

They're both missing.

It must be a mistake. I brought it in to K-G at the last second, so I assume they were added late. That has to be it. They were added late.

The inventory, he realizes. He can check there. Before a case is brought to trial, an inventory of the evidence that will be used must be compiled. If new evidence comes to light during the hearings, it is inserted as an addendum.

Vidar opens another binder. It should be there somewhere, at the back.

Here. Here it is. This is where the threatening letters should be noted.

He rests his finger against the document.

Because they were included.

He stands in silence, breathing.

Weren't they included?

29

Monday arrives with cold and rain. Isak steps into the lobby and announces himself. He gives his name. Should he show them the games now? Or later?

Later. Not now, probably, it would just be weird if he—

"Who are you here to see?"

"Uh. Vidar. Vidar . . ." Whatever his name is.

"Vidar Jörgensson?" the receptionist suggests.

"Right."

"You can have a seat while you wait. He'll come down."

Soon Vidar is standing there and holding the door open for him. He looks a little tired, but he smiles as he takes Isak's hand.

"I'm glad you could come."

The whole thing takes no more than ten minutes. The prosecutor is a sullen woman with gray hair and stern eyes. She's wearing a blazer and has a heavy silver chain around one wrist. They sit at a desk in a pale room with tiny windows. On the table is a series of documents and forms. They look important.

Vidar seems a little distracted, but he explains what each document means before Isak signs his name. He doesn't know how many he signs; he loses count after a while.

Then the prosecutor thanks them and shakes Isak's hand.

"Pay on time and behave yourself, now."

That's all she says, like an exhausted mom of little kids. She opens the door and leaves. The bag with the two games inside is on the table.

Isak remains seated. The chair is uncomfortable. Maybe that's on purpose. Probably, in a room like this, you're not supposed to be able to relax.

"Well. That's that, then, Isak. Unless there's anything else?"

"Last weekend in town I saw a guy from Skedala take a bottle to the head." He looks at his hands. "I just wondered if he was okay. If anyone called the police."

Vidar raises his eyebrows. "You know, I don't know."

"Can you check?"

"What was his name?"

"Jesper Johansson."

Vidar notes the name on a scrap of paper and picks up the receiver of an old desk phone. It rings on the other end.

"I'd like to check," he says, "on a person who supposedly got checked in this weekend. It's about a battery." He reads from the scrap of paper and waits. "Thanks." Vidar frowns. "Okay, that sounds like a mess. Yes. Yes, I see. Okay, so he did. And when was he discharged?"

A wave of relief goes through Isak. He almost wants to laugh; it's so good to know that idiot is still alive. Vidar hangs up.

"So he's okay?"

"He was discharged yesterday. When he came in he was delirious and saying someone had thrown a bottle at him. By the time he was released the story had changed, and apparently he claimed it was an accident. That he had fallen down some stairs. But," Vidar continues, leaning forward, "something tells me that's not quite true. A bottle to the head." He repeats the words thoughtfully and tilts his head. "Is there anything you'd like to tell me before you go?"

He didn't mean to say anything. It would have been unthinkable when he stepped into the room, but it's like some invisible force drags the words from Isak's mouth. Maybe it's the room, or just something about the remarkably calm officer from his own streets.

"I don't know . . . I don't know what it is with me. I can't . . . sometimes it just happens."

"What just happened?"

"They walked past me in town. They were taunting me." He swallows. "Saying a bunch of shit. And I had a bottle in my hand. I just . . . I threw it."

Vidar doesn't do anything, doesn't say anything. He just sits there gazing at him.

"I didn't mean to . . . I was just so mad."

"I understand. But battery falls under public prosecution. That means that as a police officer, I have to forward your confession onward and a prosecutor will bring charges against you whether Jesper wants it or not."

Isak blinks. "What happens after that?"

"You'll be called in for questioning. We'll also speak with the victim and any witnesses."

The room has shrunk. Isak's palms are slippery. When he grips the armrests, they nearly slip off. He threw a bottle at Jesper's head. It felt so good. He shouldn't have felt like that. This is fair. He deserves it. Maybe it's just as well.

The downhill slide goes slowly. At first.

"Isak. Did you hear what I said?"

Vidar was still talking. Isak could see his mouth moving, but he hadn't heard the words.

"What?"

"I said it seems like there's an awful lot going on in your life right now. I'm going to get in touch with the social worker at your school and recommend you start seeing a psychologist. And I suggest you keep away from Skedala for the time being. I know how conflicts are solved up there."

He wants to say something about Johanna and what happened, the guy who kissed her. It's an explanation of sorts, but he's too ashamed. And it felt so good to hurt someone. To finally stop holding back. How can he explain that?

And what will happen next time?

"One last thing," Vidar says, with an uncertainty in his eyes.

Isak's voice sounds as weak as it feels. "What?"

"I think I need your help."

"My help? For what?"

They're walking down a long hallway. Isak concentrates on reading signs, registering names: TECHNICAL UNIT, INVESTIGATION UNIT, LOST AND FOUND, RECEPTION, ETHICS, PROPERTY CRIMES.

Soon he's standing at the threshold of a messy little office with two desks arranged in an *L* shape along the walls. They're covered in documents and folders, coffee mugs, binders, a computer each.

Isak is wrapped in a veil of smoke. Everything feels like a dream. He is present, but his body and mind are numb. *Public prosecution. Questioning. Trial.* There's something about those words, so technical and cold.

A moment ago he thought it was fair. But is it?

They're not on his side. Jesper Johansson picked on Isak constantly for years. And what kind of punishment did he get? Nothing. Isak fights back one time and ends up here. There's no such thing as fair. It should have been Jesper facing questioning and a trial, not Isak. Suspicion spreads through his body like poison.

There's a group photo on one wall of the office. Vidar is standing next to a man with a big beard. They're embracing each other and smiling at the camera, with medals around their necks. BEST TEAM-WORK, PENTATHLON 2003.

"Come in, Isak."

"Why?"

"Come in and have a seat."

He remains standing on the threshold. Vidar looks surprised, as if this were the first time someone refused to do as he said.

"Okay. Stand there, then." Vidar opens a desk drawer and takes out a thin packet of papers. "I want you to look at these."

Handwritten letters on lined paper. No, copies of letters. All the lines are unnaturally dark and a little crooked. They look old.

Isak reads *You will pay for what you've done.*

He reads *Please, I love you.*

You're making me hate you. You should be afraid of me.

A new kind of fear takes root in his belly. Something's wrong. "I didn't write those. I've never even seen them before."

"I know you didn't. But do you recognize the handwriting?"

"No."

"Look again. Are you sure?"

Isak reads them again. The words are creepy; they sting his eyes.

"No, I don't recognize the handwriting."

Vidar shows him another piece of paper; it, too, is a letter. Or maybe it's just words. The handwriting is different. The first kind was sharp and pointy; this one is more leaning and has more rounded edges.

"Whose handwriting is this?"

Something moves inside Isak. A *clang* seems to creep down his spine, echoing through him. He's gotten entangled in something that has nothing to do with him.

"I think it's my uncle's."

Vidar inspects the paper. It's impossible to say what he's thinking.

"What does he have to do with this?"

"I don't quite know," Vidar murmurs, switching back to one of the first sheets he'd shown to Isak.

"What about this?"

You're making me hate you. You should be afraid of me.

"I told you, I don't recognize it. What is it?"

Vidar folds the papers and places them on the desk. Suddenly there's a trace of worry in his eyes.

"Thank you, Isak. You've been a big help."

Vidar tries to place a hand on his shoulder.

Isak backs away. *You are the enemy.*

30

Question marks. Question marks in the gloomy light. It's early morning in the kitchen at home in Marbäck. Outside, day is slowly pushing out the darkness.

Before coming home on Sunday, he stood in the copy room with selections from the investigation materials in his hands. He carries them in a separate folder. It's open on the table, in the warm light from the kitchen fixture.

October 1994 to January 1995, a gap in the map. A deviation from the pattern. The Miljanovic brothers take an inexplicable break.

Threatening letters, a handwriting sample that doesn't match and was never registered.

Maybe it's nothing.

Vidar considers the documents before him. They are ten years old. One has to do with a missing diary, the other, a right glove.

But this?

He hesitates one last time before he takes the folder, stands up, and walks out.

The old chief inspector is sitting at a window table, gazing out at a frozen park. No snow yet. When Vidar's grandmother spent her final years here in the late nineties, it was called a nursing home. Now it's called "senior living." Old concepts get new names—but that's about it. The walls are still pale, the staff harried, their shifts too long; visits from relatives are just as rare and the food is hardly better than what you'd be served in prison.

But K-G Öberg likes it here, according to the staff. He's lived here ever since his Margareta died a few years after retirement.

"Young Jörgensson." He chuckles. "I'll be damned. Take a load off, will ya? I had no idea you were coming."

K-G is no longer allowed to drink coffee; instead there's a half-full cup of tea in front of him. He isn't paying much attention to it. Vidar places the folder on the table, pulls out a chair, and sits.

"Didn't they tell you I was stopping by for a visit?"

"Oh, sure." The chief inspector waves a hand. "I'm sure they did. Sometimes I forget."

He's aged considerably. He's thinner and wrinklier, and his beard is sparse. His hand, when he waves it, looks almost bony. A pair of narrow, steel-colored glasses perch on his nose, and behind them blink two unusually absent-looking eyes. He looks . . . well, hollow. It's a feeling Vidar finds very familiar. He's heard that the years after Margareta's death took a serious toll on the old chief inspector.

K-G asks whether his old colleagues are still working, what this one or that one is up to now, how it's going for each him or her, and wasn't she still there when Vidar started?

Some of them, Vidar's never heard of. He wonders if they've ever existed. He doesn't mention his doubts.

"Oh yes, oh yes." K-G gazes out the window. "We sure had fun back then. And Margareta was still with us. Now there was a good woman. I miss her an awful lot sometimes. By the way, Aronsson is still there, isn't she?"

"She's my immediate boss."

"There you go, there you go. A splendid woman, that one, and a solid police officer, too. Runs a tight ship. What can I do for you, Jörgensson?"

"It's about an old case. Or two of them, really. I could use your help." Vidar pulls over the folder and opens it. He has prepared meticulously. "Do you remember the Miljanovic brothers?"

K-G squints behind his glasses. "Two good-for-nothing brothers from Skåne. Burglars."

It was one of his last big cases. Vidar takes a list of their crimes from the folder.

"I'm curious about their spree."

"Hmm," the old man says, looking at the paper, mildly interested. "Yes, it's more or less as I remember it."

"There are actually two things I'm wondering," Vidar says. "One is the incident in Ljungby. And the other is the gap, in both time and space, between Laholm in October of 1994 and Falkenberg in January the next year."

"Oh?"

"Yes," Vidar continues calmly. "So let's start there. What I'm getting at is, why didn't they strike anywhere in between?"

"Such as?"

"I'm just wondering if it was something you and your team considered. Whether you explored what was going on in town around the same time. Whether you investigated the brothers' alibis for any crimes. After all, Halmstad seems feasible as a target, considering their general movements."

"I'm sure we did."

"But you don't have any memory of it?"

"I hardly remember how to get to the bathroom in here. No, I don't recall. But as I said, I'm sure we did. Either me, or someone else."

Unfortunately, it had likely never been done. Maybe they'd had enough work as it was. A series of ten break-ins in three counties, the last one crowned with arson and attempted homicide, demands incredible resources from the justice system. Understandable if, in that situation, they were satisfied with what they already had.

"I understand," Vidar says, placing a finger on the list. "The other thing I was thinking about was the incident in Ljungby in March

1995. Their last job, and the one that put them behind bars. Do you remember it?"

"We didn't investigate that one; it was in Småland."

"I know."

Vidar waits. K-G leans back in his chair, crosses his arms, and gazes thoughtfully out the window.

"Yes, I remember, I think. They had a sudden visitor."

"The owner of the house came home and the brothers beat him unconscious. They set the house on fire. It was sheer luck that he woke up and made it out in time."

"Luck or fate."

"Sure, right. Whatever it was, when you read the incident report you are struck by the fact that their actions were very calculating—or at least, I was struck by it. No hesitation, no irrational outbursts. They acted as though they knew exactly what they were doing. It was ruthless, sure, but at the same time very cold and effective."

"Mm-hmm?" K-G says.

"That's not very typical, in my experience, not even if you make your living as a burglar. When something backfires, you panic. So my thought, or my question, really, is whether the team was sure this was in fact the first time someone had caught them in the act."

K-G chuckles. "Beating a man half to death and setting his house on fire sounds pretty panicky to my mind. Wouldn't the most rational option have been to simply take off?"

Vidar considers him for a long moment. The remarkable part isn't what the brothers did, it's *how* they did it.

"Was that all?" K-G asks, blinking wearily.

"One more thing." *Careful now.* "You remember the murder of Lovisa Markström."

K-G stares at him. "Of course I do."

"I'd like to ask you about the threatening letters. Do you recall those?"

"No, I can't say that I do."

"I brought them," Vidar continues, bringing out the photocopies, which were tucked in the back of the folder. "I'm the one who handed them over to you, back in early 1995."

Something happens with K-G's face. He looks uncertain. A pale hand trails its fingertips over the documents.

"That rings a bell," he mumbles. "So I got them from you?"

"It was me, by sheer coincidence," Vidar says.

He doesn't mention that he received them from a woman whom he would later marry and have a child with.

"As I understood it, they were to be included in the preliminary investigation."

"Right."

"But when I looked at the case files, all the letters are missing date stamps and numbers, labels. They were just lying in a separate yellow plastic sleeve, unmarked."

"No, I suppose it's possible we decided not to include them. Our view was that our case still held water."

"But you got a handwriting sample?"

"Yes, I think so."

Vidar takes another document from the folder and sets it before him. A note found at Christensson's home during the search.

"This?"

K-G adjusts his glasses, squints, blinks twice. "Yes, that must be it."

"And would you say they're similar?"

He looks up. "What are you up to, Jörgensson? You know as well as I do what happened down there."

"I was just surprised, since I'm the one who brought these to you."

"Understandable, I suppose. Was that all?"

No hostility, more like exhaustion. Vidar clears his throat and puts the documents back in the folder. K-G rests his fingers on the handle of his teacup.

"I was taking a look at this old case in connection with the Miljanovic brothers, since they overlapped in time, and there was one more thing I wanted to ask."

K-G takes a slow sip of his tea, his eyes on the folder beneath Vidar's hands. "Coincidences like this—the threatening letters, I mean—aren't unusual, you know that. We probably didn't include them because they came to us so late in the process."

"I understand," Vidar says. "But I'm just wondering . . . I saw that in the interrogations of Christensson, when he finally began to talk, he mentioned a diary. Lovisa's diary. Was it ever found?"

K-G shakes his head. "As I recall, the conclusion was that it had been destroyed in the fire."

Nothing wrong with his memory, then. It's true. *According to the mother, she received a type of diary or calendar for Christmas in 1993. She wrote in it now and then during 1994. It has not been found. According to CT1 and CT2, it was likely destroyed in the fire.*

So it says on page 293 of the preliminary investigation. It comes up in other sections as well, among other places on pages 114, 198, and in two of the appendices. CT. The crime-scene techs. Both are in agreement.

So much was destroyed in the fire.

"Why?" the old man asks.

"I just wasn't aware that there had supposedly been a diary. And Christensson suggested we take a look at it. It would explain everything, he claimed." Vidar glances down at the document, a summary of an interrogation from March 1994. "What do you think he meant?"

"No fucking idea. It was pretty hard to make sense of most of what that fellow said."

Long seconds tick by. An aide passes their table discreetly, giving Vidar and the chief inspector a smile and nod. Vidar has more question marks to figure out, but the chief inspector is starting to clam up. It's not a good idea to push his luck.

"Thanks for your time. I'm not up to anything, I should add. I just wondered what was actually done or not done, and what the thought processes were."

"And I think Officer Jörgensson is making a mountain out of a molehill," K-G says. "Which is understandable. You're from up there, after all. But it was a good job we did that time. Like many times before."

"Inspector," Vidar says.

"Sorry?"

"I'm an inspector these days."

K-G smiles, unimpressed. "A ways to go, to chief inspector," he says.

"A ways," Vidar agrees. "But not that far."

As he leaves the senior living facility, darkness falls.

31

The memorial service is beautiful. The whole village is here. Speeches are held. Roses, lilies, and memorial wreaths are placed before a photograph of Lovisa. Tears are shed. A trio plays soft, tentative music. Lovisa's parents stand in the center of it all, their arms around each other. They look grim but brave. Theo's mom and dad, Karl's parents, Anton's . . . everyone is there. Even Vidar Jörgensson. He's standing there with his wife and their kid. Cameras click as the newspaper photographer takes pictures. The pale November light makes all the faces look gray.

Everyone is here but Isak's mom and dad.

Isak stands at the very back, as if he's trying to keep his distance.

A speech concludes. Music takes over, a lament. A few people sing along in low, subdued voices; others move their lips in silence, the familiar psalm like a personal prayer: *Help me then in safety rest, in peace your will be done, dear Lord.*

When he thinks of how everything he sees is Edvard's fault, his uncle's doing, he is ashamed. It's horrible. As if Edvard's guilt is also his own, somehow. Maybe that, too, is inherited.

He can't shield himself from the thought when it comes: another photograph, another family, just a few miles from here—if Jesper had been unlucky. It's sick, feeling glad that someone like him got lucky. It could have been him. It could have been me. It's such a disturbing thought that he squeezes his fists in his pockets to shed the feeling, but it refuses to let him go.

Help me, Lord, come what may, to take from your stalwart father-hand . . .

He's learned one thing, anyway: Vidar Jörgensson tricked him.

Just one day, one moment at a time, until I reach the promised land.

The music ebbs away and the trio takes a step back. A moment of silence follows.

Vidar is observing it all from a distance, his face serious. His eyes sweep across the gathered crowd. His hands are in the pockets of his black coat, and his eyes meet Isak's once; he dips his chin in a discreet nod. Isak doesn't reciprocate.

When the memorial service is over, the crowd is slow to disperse. The Markströms start to leave. Vidar kisses his wife and kid before they go their separate ways, and he rushes off, taking a few hurried strides that make his coat flap behind him.

Isak walks behind them, sunk in dark thoughts. They don't notice him. He hears Vidar share his condolences and say that it was a lovely service.

"Thank you," says Lovisa's dad.

"Yes, it was lovely," her mother agrees mechanically, holding her husband's arm.

"There was something I was wondering about Lovisa. Did she ever mention the threatening letters she received?"

Lovisa's parents exchange glances.

"No," Hans says. "Why do you ask?"

"Are you sure?"

"I think we would have remembered," says her mom.

Her dad's expression is grim. "She received threatening letters from him?"

"I understand if you've moved on. I don't want to reopen old wounds, especially not today, but—"

"Look," her dad says coldly. "We just want to be left alone. So was that all?"

"Do you recall whether anything was missing from the house?"

They stop. The two parents are standing together as if they've been welded at the hip. Maybe that's what sorrow does to people if it doesn't tear them apart.

"Our house burned down," the dad snaps. "Everything burned down. Our daughter was murdered. Our life was ruined. Was something missing? What the hell do you think?"

"Of course," Vidar says. "I understand. I apologize. I was thinking more along the lines of valuables, electronics, jewelry, that sort of thing."

"No."

"Or her diary?"

"It all. Burned. Down. Don't you get it?"

"I was thinking, the diary, what color was it?"

They roll their eyes and walk away.

"Did she write in it often?" Vidar continues, hurrying to follow. "Did she usually carry it with her, in her bag or something?" When they don't respond, he goes on: "The Miljanovic brothers, did she ever mention anything about two brothers from Skåne?"

"No."

"Two burglars from Skåne. They—"

"Jesus Christ!" the dad shouts. "Leave us the hell alone! Are you suggesting our daughter hung out with burglars? How the hell can you be so heartless?"

Vidar stops and gazes after them.

"What a horrible man," Lovisa's mom says tonelessly, walking away with her hand clasping her husband's arm.

Vidar turns around.

"Isak."

They size each other up.

"You tricked me."

Vidar looks surprised. "I tricked you? How so?"

"You know how."

Isak can change his tune as much as he wants. He can retract his confession. He can say the officer was pressuring him. Isak can say just about anything as long as the moron from Skedala continues to claim it was an accident, and he probably will. Isak knows how it works in Skedala, because Skedala is just like Marbäck. Nothing will come of it.

"I didn't throw a bottle at him. I was lying. It was just an accident."

"Okay."

"And I'm not going to a psychologist, either."

"Well, that's certainly up to you, Isak. But I'd still recommend it. For your own sake."

"Go to hell."

32

That Sunday, Vidar returns home with a vague heaviness in his body.

I was lying. It was just an accident.

Of course he would say that. You can con your way through most of life if you have to. There's an unnerving shimmer to Isak Nyqvist.

It all. Burned. Down.

He'd gone too far. Way too far. He had even felt it happen, felt all the questions he'd gathered up pour right out of him. Vidar has been a police officer for almost fifteen years, and if there's anything he's learned it's that reality is messy and complicated, and far too unpredictable for everything to make sense. There will always be question marks, coincidences, and details that are hard to explain. That's just how life works, not least the parts of it that end up in a criminal investigation. He has to accept it. But it's strange.

Vidar thinks about that night in Tolarp: Leo's barking, the odor of fire and smoke, burning wood, how scared everyone was. How he saw movement in the forest on his way home, after trying to lend a hand.

Hey. Hey! There's someone in here.

Vidar himself was the one who led them to Edvard Christensson.

:::

Life is a series of dogs, and for thirteen years Leo was Vidar's most faithful companion. Two years ago he died in his sleep, peacefully, in front of the fireplace with his elderly head resting on Vidar's lap.

How many dogs will a person have by their side in their time on earth? Six, maybe seven or eight? Leo was Vidar's third dog. If statistics are to be trusted, almost half of Vidar's days are behind him. It's a frightening thought, so Vidar has refused to get another dog, even though Amadia has asked for one a number of times.

His little girl is five years old and has her mother's eyes and hair and her father's temperament. She's drawing at the kitchen table when Vidar comes through the door. He kisses her hair.

"Wow," he says. "What a great drawing, sweetie."

"Thanks, Dad."

Amadia is drawing a car with surprisingly accurate proportions and details; it even has a rearview mirror. Patricia has just made herself a cup of tea.

"Want one?"

"No, thanks."

They kiss. His belly flutters.

"It was a nice service," Patricia says, placing a hand on Amadia's shoulder. "Wasn't it, honey?"

The girl nods. Patricia turns to Vidar. "Are you okay?"

"Yeah."

He wants to say more, but where would he start? He doesn't want to dig up the past. Patricia and Lovisa had been coworkers, and Patricia, if anyone, was relieved when it was all over. And furthermore, it was so long ago. Oddly enough, he finds that sort of comforting.

"You seem a little out of it," she continues.

"It's nothing. Just . . ."

It all. Burned. Down. For a moment, he'd feared that Lovisa's father was going to hit him.

"I'm a little distracted, is all."

Patricia nods thoughtfully and rubs his back, her eyes following Amadia's hand as she draws.

The memorial service really had been lovely. He had seen Jon-Erik from Simlångsdalen, who had once dated Lovisa; Billy Oredsson and Dennis Götmark; old man Hedman and his sons; Backlund—everyone had turned up. Jon-Erik had looked grim and stoic, while Dennis stood next to Billy with a supportive hand on his old friend's shoulder the whole time. It looked tender.

Everyone was there but Isak's parents. He doesn't blame them.

It took some time for the rumor to reach Vidar—the rumor that he'd married his wife for some reason other than love. Patricia hadn't yet moved in, but they were thinking about it. She liked the nature in Marbäck, and its houses, the distance from town. Not to mention the summer nights. It felt like a good place for a kid to grow up, when it came time for that.

"But there's not much here anymore," he said. "No stores, no jobs. The people, of course," he added, thinking again of the rumor he'd just heard. "And nature. But . . ."

"And your roots," Patricia said. "Your roots are here."

"But we don't need to take that into account," he objected.

She raised her eyebrows. "I don't have any roots. Not like you do. But if I did, I'd expect you to take them into account. Roots are important to us. They're going to be important for our child."

So Marbäck it was. They moved into Vidar's house, and for the first time, he realized, he was truly happy. He wished his dad could see him now.

The rumor hadn't exactly been put to rest. And he hadn't said anything, either; he was ashamed. Of both himself and the village.

Once he did tell her, Patricia stared at him for a moment before bursting into one of her big, gruff laughs. "That's the stupidest thing I've ever heard. Who do they think I am? Don't they know I speak better Swedish than half the people in this village?"

"Oh, you know, honey, they're . . . they're—"

"They're prejudiced, half-assed racists."

"Yeah. That, too."

"None of them have ever even talked to me."

This fact turned out to be important in an unexpected way. When Patricia finally did get the chance to talk to another citizen of Marbäck, it was Ernst Hedman, who dropped by to borrow some water since his pipes were frozen, and he found himself at a loss for words.

She had the heaviest Halland accent old Ernst Hedman had ever heard. So he said afterward. Not to Vidar's or Patricia's face, of course, but to everyone else—and what Ernst Hedman says is considered of great importance in the village.

Where did she work, by the way? Or, did she work?

"Oh yes, I've been working since I finished school. I used to be at Brooktorpsgården in town. These days I'm a CO up at the prison."

So she kept guard over prisoners?

"Yeah, you could look at it that way," she replied with a smile.

But she was such a tiny person. Could she really handle those goons?

"Well, sure, it's important to stay in shape, but it's really more about technique and teamwork. I have great colleagues. And appearances can be deceiving—I'm stronger than people think. And willpower can get you pretty far."

Yes, right. Ernst Hedman could imagine it did. *How old was she, by the way?*

"I'm twenty-seven."

And where . . . well, where was she originally from?

"Stockholm."

Stockholm, well, sure. But you know . . . where was she born? That was what he meant.

"Stockholm."

Stockholm again, okay. But how about her parents, then, before Stockholm, where . . . ?

"My parents fled the civil war in Nigeria, if that's what you mean."

Nigeria, right, okay. War, how terrible. How lovely that you were so well taken care of in Sweden.

As if Ernst Hedman could determine such a thing. Patricia stared at him. "Uh-huh."

And so he left with a bewildered but almost charmed expression on his wrinkled face, pulling the wagon with the can of water behind him.

Patricia closed the door after him and looked at Vidar.

"We can move," he said.

"The hell we will," she said.

It probably wasn't until Hedman fell and broke his leg the next spring, and Patricia was the one who came to his rescue, that she became a full-fledged part of the village. The bone made a nasty hole where it stuck through his skin, and Hedman hollered and carried on like the devil himself was after him. She knelt beside him on that chilly March morning and called the emergency number, used her own scarf to wrap his leg, and talked to him until the ambulance arrived. She called work to say that she would be late, then accompanied Hedman to the hospital. Only once the doctor had taken over did she let go of his hand.

"Thank you, dear Patricia," he said, so sincerely that he must have meant it. "Thank you so much. You're an angel."

A few days later, an enormous bouquet of flowers arrived at Vidar's house.

To Vidar's Patricia
From Ernst Hedman
(I don't know where she lives)

So it said on the card. When he showed it to Patricia, she smiled.

"Vidar's Patricia," she said. "I like the way that sounds."

33

"What are you reading for?"

It's so cold now, and Isak's car still has its summer tires on, so he has to take the bus to school. He's waiting there, huddled in the bus shelter, a book in hand, when Theo walks up.

"What am I reading *for*?"

Not just "What are you reading?"—it's like Theo is asking him to justify the very act of reading itself.

"Well, for one thing, I read so I can learn how not to ask stupid questions."

Theo's shoulders slump and he looks at his boots instead of at Isak. "I thought maybe we had a test or something."

Isak tries to dog-ear the page but it's too cold; his fingers are too stiff and dry, so he just closes the book and shoves his hands into his pockets.

"Is everything okay?" Theo asks. "You've been acting a little . . ."

"What?"

"Weird. This fall, I mean. I get it if things were rough with Johanna, but, like . . . did something else happen?"

"No."

"Okay." Theo looks perplexed. "So why is Jesper from Skedala gonna kick your ass?"

"Where'd you hear that?"

"On the bus yesterday."

"From who?"

"What's your deal?"

Isak snorts, but it sounds less convincing than he meant it to. He really should say something. Theo would understand; that's the great thing about him. Even so, Isak's tongue seems to lock itself up in his mouth.

"I thought maybe we could . . . uh, go to a party," Theo says instead, as if to cheer him up.

"When?"

"On Friday. It's some house party in Söndrum, I don't know the guy's name but Karl says he knows him. If you want to, I mean."

"Yeah, that sounds fun."

The bus arrives, puffing and gray beneath the equally gray sky. They sit at the back.

"So how was it, anyway?"

"How was what?"

"The memorial."

"That was like a week ago already."

"Yeah, I know, but I didn't ask yet."

"You weren't there, were you?"

Theo shakes his head. "No, I didn't want to go. My parents were there, though."

"I know. I saw them." Isak puts his book in his bag. "How was it . . . I don't know. Mostly sucky, I guess."

A rainy Marbäck goes by outside the window.

"You don't have any contact with Edvard, right?"

"I haven't seen him since I was little."

"Why not?"

"Well, he murdered someone. Isn't that enough?"

Theo doesn't say anything for a long time. The bus stops in Skedala. Isak watches the stop, studying those who get on. No Jesper. Hail is hammering the windows. Snow is just days away; you can feel it in the air.

"Isak?"

Isak turns his head.

"Sorry, what did you say?"

Theo clears his throat. "I just said, but you went anyway. To the service."

"Oh. Yeah."

"Why?"

"I don't know. It was actually really shitty, being reminded of what he did. But then it felt good afterwards, after all."

"I guess that's how it is with lots of stuff." Theo leans back in his seat, his eyes closed. "It feels awful at the time, but pretty okay once it's over."

Once it's over, Isak thinks.

When is it really over?

34

Vidar studies the map of Sweden on the wall in his and Nashwan's office, moving his finger along the line that shows the Miljanovic brothers' path through the country.

"Hey, Vidar."

"Hmm?"

Nashwan is at his desk, behind Vidar, typing at his computer. "What happens when we go to bed at night?"

"I don't know."

"Sure you do. We go undercover." And then he laughs.

"Hilarious. We don't have a handwriting sample from Božo Miljanovic, do we?"

"No, I don't think so. Listen, speaking of. Are you planning to look into the Marbäck murder again?"

Vidar turns around. "Why do you ask?"

"I heard you paid a visit to K-G."

"How'd you hear that?"

Nashwan nods toward the hallway. "He still has friends here. Above all, Aronsson, of course. K-G called to see what was up."

"I'm not looking at the Marbäck murder. It just popped into my head when I saw the Miljanovic brothers' background."

"If you say so." Nashwan goes back to typing at his computer with two bony index fingers. "Aronsson will probably let you stick with it for a little longer; she never likes to get involved. But, just so you know."

"She doesn't have any *reason* to get involved."

No news on the latest rash of break-ins, on Josif Marinko or any other potential partners in crime. Božo still hasn't turned up and Darko's still dead. The case is at a standstill.

"Hold on, what are people saying in the hallways?"

The clattering of Nashwan's keyboard stops. "Well, that you were questioning the investigation."

"I did not. I would never do that."

"*I* know that, but everyone else doesn't." He glances anxiously at Vidar. "Just be careful. Okay?"

It's not a good look, calling your own colleagues' work into question; you risk being reprimanded. Not formally, of course; that would be improper, but cops are cops. It wouldn't be unusual to find that there are some details that don't add up in the Lovisa Markström case, really, but if it came out that a single officer was digging around, it wouldn't look good.

Vidar throws up his hands with a weak smile. "When have I ever not been careful?"

They go back to work. Vidar considers his notes. "Nashwan."

"Hmm?"

But he changes his mind. He doesn't say anything.

From the top of Galgberget you can see past the colossal structures of the harbor and all the way to the sea. The snow should have come already, but it's held off so far. Instead, a cold fall sun glints off the endless roofs and the cars moving on the streets below.

In the old days, people were executed here. A map from the 1600s marks the hill with a little drawing of a gallows. Vidar sits on a bench and gazes out at the city. The gravel crunches as a man approaches.

"It's been a while," Markus says with a smile, sitting down next to him.

"Yeah, you know how it is." Vidar is holding two plastic cups of coffee. He gives one to Markus and sips the other. "Are you still enjoying patrol?"

"I actually like it more and more."

"I can imagine."

"How about you?"

Vidar sips his coffee and squints at the sun. The sky is as clear and blue as a summer morning. "I miss it."

"Why?"

"It was just more fun."

"Did something happen?"

"Why do you ask?"

Markus nods toward police headquarters; glimpses of the formidable brick building are visible down below.

"You used to come here when you wanted a little break from work, as I recall. But it's November—it's freezing out here." He smiles crookedly at Vidar and drinks his coffee. "So I assumed you didn't want to see me just to reminisce."

It's nice to see him, that specific way you're almost always happy to see the person you spent countless hours sitting in a car with during your first years in uniform.

"In some sense that's true," Vidar says slowly. "Do you remember Lovisa Markström?"

"God, yes. I read about the memorial in the paper. Did you go?"

Vidar nods. "I came across something I don't quite know how to interpret."

Markus listens intently as Vidar tells him about the threatening letters. He suddenly remembers his cup and drinks a little more, then goes back to watching Vidar with his calm, clear gaze. "So the letters and the handwriting sample don't match, and they were never entered into the PI file. Okay. That's unfortunate. But . . ."

"That's not all." Vidar shifts on the bench, crossing one leg over the other. A cold wind blows across the hill.

Markus pulls his coat tighter and sips his coffee.

"I went a little too far after the service. Hans and Erika were there, of course, and I had some questions for them, questions I probably shouldn't have asked. But, I don't know, these details just give me a weird gut feeling. I've tried to let it go, but . . ."

"You have a hard time," Markus says when Vidar doesn't know what to say. "Letting things go."

Vidar smiles wanly. "Yeah."

"So what was it, then?"

"The right glove."

"The one that didn't have gasoline on it. I remember. But it all made sense later on."

"No, as far as I can tell, no one ever found an explanation. That's what I wanted to ask you—whether you ever heard more about it. You're the one who talked to Guggan, after all."

Markus frowns. "No, I would have remembered. You're saying it's not in the PI file?"

"The glove is definitely mentioned. But I can't find any explanation. The court didn't attach any significance to it, either."

"Which isn't all that strange," Markus points out. "It doesn't mean much, on its own."

"But taken along with the rest?"

It's a genuine question. Doubt gnaws at him.

Markus is smart and distanced. He's got a good eye for this stuff. "I understand what you're thinking. But how come you're dealing with this right now?"

"We've got a series of thefts on our desks. They could be linked to the Miljanovic brothers, if you remember them?"

"Two burglars. But I seem to recall one died."

"Right. So really we're only interested in one of them, Božo." Vidar takes a deep breath. "There's a gap in their travels, right around the same time as the Marbäck murder, and what's more, that murder was eerily similar to one of the crimes they were convicted of later on, in Ljungby. That's how it all started."

"So you think . . ."

"No, I don't think anything. I just want to know we got it right back then."

Markus looks at him for a long time.

"I understand. Just be careful."

35

Isak doesn't like Söndrum. All the families here have houses with nice lawns, two cars, and parents who are realtors or shop owners. Makes you feel out of place. On this particular night it doesn't matter much, because the fact that everyone's drunk tends to even most stuff out. He hears shouting and laughter in the distance. There's the house, lights on and the front door wide open. People are on the lawn, smoking and drinking without outerwear in this cold. Someone is on the ground puking nearby; music is streaming from inside the house, and everything is just like normal.

Theo and Isak share a small joint. A pleasant dullness grows in his temples. He goes inside and vanishes in the sea of people, gets drunk, and is almost happy for a while.

Several hours later he goes to the second floor and ends up on a cushy sofa. He tries to convince Theo to keep drinking.

"But I'm tired," Theo mumbles, leaning against one of the armrests.

"That can be fixed," Isak urges him, "by having more to drink."

"How are you so awake? I'm thinking about going to the bedroom and resting for a while."

A moan comes from the other side of the bedroom door. A bed creaks.

"The bedroom is occupied."

"But . . ."

"No buts. Here." Isak hands him the bottle of Zaranoff. "You can have some of mine."

"Shit, Isak." Theo loosely grips the neck of the bottle, brings it to his mouth, and takes a sip of the vodka. "It tastes like gasoline."

"It does not."

Then someone falls up the stairs. At least, that's what it looks like. She must have tripped or something, and she does a half somersault up the last two steps, a bottle of beer in hand. Her dark mass of hair becomes a tangle of curls and coils.

"Shit, stairs are so dumb." She grunts, inspecting her beer and cheering up instantly. "Oh. *This* survived, at least."

"I don't think I've ever seen a girl fall *up* the stairs before," Isak says.

The girl turns her head. "How about a guy?"

"Nope, that either."

Theo cracks up but all of a sudden his face is white and blank; he puts down the bottle. "I'm gonna puke."

He leaps up and staggers to the bathroom. The girl steadies herself against the wall and gets to her feet, looking straight at Isak.

"Hi."

"Hi."

She hobbles to the sofa. For a second, as she sits down, her knee brushes Isak's. "I'm always so fucking clumsy."

"I thought you had a certain amount of grace."

She bursts out laughing. It sounds nice. Something breaks downstairs, a glass or a vase. Theo retches in the bathroom and groans loudly.

"I'm Karin," she says.

"I'm Isak," says Isak.

Her eyes get big and round. "A guy downstairs is walking around saying he's going to beat up someone named Isak. Is that you?"

"Was his name Jesper?"

"Probably. He looked like a Jesper."

The alcohol is making Isak pleasantly numb. Maybe he might as well track down that idiot from Skedala and get it over with.

Karin drinks her beer. "Why is he going to beat you up?"

"I don't know."

Karin changes position on the sofa. Her leg touches Isak's again, and he wants to rest a hand on her thigh—it looks so soft—but he doesn't dare to. There's something about her eyes. It's like you want to experience them up close.

It happens sometimes, that you just know. Tonight, maybe never again but *tonight,* it's him and her. Isak struggles to listen to what she's saying, but all he can think about is how pretty Karin is, what nice shoulders she has, how it sounds when she laughs, how smart and funny and confident she seems.

Karin lives behind Brunnåker School in town and is in her third year of the hospitality program at Sture. Tonight she's wearing black jeans and a David Bowie tank with spaghetti straps. Her skin is pale, and when she leans toward Isak a little later one of her soft breasts brushes against his ribs.

When he kisses her she tastes like beer and lip gloss. Karin's mouth is so soft, and when her hair falls in his face she giggles and tucks it behind her ear. She has big dimples.

"I just have to go to the bathroom," she whispers after a while.

"Go downstairs. Theo's in there. He's the one you can hear puking every so often."

"Who's Theo?"

"My buddy."

Karin giggles and gets up. "See you soon."

"Walk carefully."

Karin laughs and heads down the stairs, one hand exaggeratedly grabbing the railing. Isak finds himself just sitting there, dreamy and drunk. Theo groans again from the bathroom.

"Hello."

He's yanked back to reality by a familiar voice. He turns his head, confused, and sees someone on the stairs.

It's Jesper from Skedala.

He's half a head taller than Isak, in jeans and a gray hoodie, and has an ugly cap on his head, maybe to hide the bandage. If he still has it.

Isak sticks his hand in his pocket and closes his fingers around his keys. They're all he's got, but they should be able to do more damage than his hand on its own.

"You and I need to talk," Jesper growls.

"Go ahead, talk."

The idiot from Skedala stares at him, his eyes drunk and empty. He blinks lethargically. Theo has gone silent behind the bathroom door. The creaking from the bedroom has stopped. Suddenly everything is very quiet. The impulse swells inside Isak again. His first reaction is rage.

"You threw a bottle at my head."

"You were saying stuff about me."

"You think you can chuck a bottle at me just for that?"

"Then stop talking shit about stuff you don't have a clue about."

"You better watch yourself."

Isak is squeezing the keys so hard that they're hurting his palm. He wants to—and at the same he doesn't. He decides to leave it up to Jesper. He puts down the bottle and gets up.

"Are you going to hit me or what? If you are, let's get it over with. I don't feel like standing here talking to you."

Something flashes in those moronic eyes. Long seconds tick by.

"I just don't get what your problem is," Jesper says in a quieter voice. "It's true. Everyone knows it."

"Knows what?"

"That you're like him."

"I am not."

"You beat up someone in my class last year," Jesper says. "Because you thought he said something."

"He did. And I didn't beat him up, I shoved him because he was messing with me. He fell by accident."

"So that bottle hit me in the head *by accident*, huh? You can't do stuff like that."

"You're gonna tell me what I can and can't do? After the shit you did to me?"

All the anger seems to drain from Jesper. He stands there wavering, then casts his eyes down and looks at the floor between his feet. He takes a sip of beer.

"If you're going to hit me, just do it," says Isak. "Otherwise, get out of here and leave me alone."

Jesper raises a hand toward him. "Watch yourself. Got it?"

Isak rolls his eyes.

Then Jesper leaves. Isak exhales. Is that disappointment he feels? It would have felt good to give in again.

Words like an echo, a foreboding.

It's true. Everyone knows it. That you're like him.

36

"It was a heck of a nice service." Sweat stains spreading under his arms, Jon-Erik Pettersson loads winter tires into the trunk. "I thought Hans and Erika looked awfully, how should I put it, brave." He stops what he's doing. "But wasn't it kind of strange to hold the memorial service *there?*"

"Yes," Vidar says. "Apparently there had been discussions earlier in the fall. But where else would they have held it? And everyone wanted a memorial service."

Jon-Erik shrugs. "Fair enough. It just seemed odd."

He lives in the house across from the outdoor equipment store up here in Simlångsdalen. It's a nice little house on a huge lot, and it suits his interests: rebuilding old cars. A handful of rusty, half-finished vehicles are scattered around them.

"I wanted to ask you," Vidar says, "the two of you were together, weren't you? You and Lovisa."

"For a little bit, yeah."

"In early 1992. Is that right?"

"Yes." Jon-Erik leans against the only working car he has. "We were in school together. We were each other's high school sweethearts. But school years are so short." He smiles suggestively. "It didn't last more than six months."

"Why was that?"

Jon-Erik shrugs. "I found out she had been making out with a buddy. Pretty seriously, too, like, I mean, more than once."

"And that was . . ." Vidar glances down at his notebook. "Hampus Lundberg?"

"Right. But things were fine after that, both between me and Hampe and me and Lovisa. I mean, nothing major. Just kid stuff, you know." He chuckles. "But back *then*, I mean, I was hurt and I guess I just felt like I didn't want to be with someone who messed around with other guys, like we used to say."

Vidar considers this. "She didn't know Edvard back then."

"I guess you know that better than I do, but as I recall they got to know each other later. By then Lovisa and I weren't in touch at all. I'd already met Maria, and I was fighting to make enough money to keep from being evicted."

"Which you were anyway, right?"

"Yeah, I was, in the end. And I couldn't stay with Maria because there wasn't room. So I slept at my buddy's place. I think that's where I was, the night she died."

Ten years between conversations, but his story's the same. Vidar was the one who talked to him back then. "Yes, that's what you said."

"What's going on?" Jon-Erik asks, as if he can see it on Vidar's face.

"I saw you at the service and just wanted to ask a few questions, now that some time has passed. Time can make a person remember more details or want to tell more."

Jon-Erik looks puzzled. "Ten years is a long time. And I told you everything I knew back then. I had nothing to hide, I told you that right away. I know the drill—when girls die, you look at their boyfriends. So I made sure to tell you everything I knew."

"And we appreciated that. That's not what I was getting at. What I had in mind was more, who was around her during those last days, who did she know and hang out with and so on."

Jon-Erik shakes his head. "By the end we had gone very separate ways. All I know was that her and Billy, you know, Billy Oredsson, hung out. And Hampe, back then, he was pretty damn hot for Lovisa during our last year of school, in ninety-two. And Edvard, of course. I didn't know him but you saw them around together sometimes. Everyone knew they were a couple, everyone but the parents, probably."

"Yes," Vidar says, searching, "that was the case, wasn't it?"

"It was." Jon-Erik nods. "It was her dad, Hans, above all, he was the one who didn't like Edvard."

"Do you know why?"

"Well, I remember there were rumors going around. Someone had seen Edvard kick him out of B&B. He worked there," he adds, "as a bartender. But I don't know if that was it."

"Is it true that Lovisa kept a diary?"

Jon-Erik frowns. "Yeah, sure. She'd been doing it since she was fifteen or so. She had, like, this little hardback book. She didn't write in it all that often, I don't think, just every now and then. That was true when I knew her, at least, but I don't know if she kept writing after that."

"Were they usually the same? I mean, do you know if she tended to buy different kinds of books?"

Jon-Erik leans against the car, more perplexed now. "You know, I don't actually recall. Why?"

"There was something else I wanted to ask about, as long as I'm here. Two brothers, Božo and Darko Miljanovic. Have you heard those names?"

"Who are they?"

"So the names don't sound familiar? She didn't know them?"

"No. Not when I knew her. But check with Billy and Hampe, maybe they know."

"Hmm," Vidar says thoughtfully.

"What?"

"I was just thinking. You said you weren't close there toward the end. And yet you attended the service the other day."

Jon-Erik crosses his arms. "Everyone was there. I wanted to show my, I don't know, that I cared. Nothing strange about that, is there? It was awful, what happened. What a fucking story. Shit. I mean, Lovisa. Everyone liked her. Including me, even though she had messed around with Hampe."

Vidar waits for him to go on. He doesn't.

Jon-Erik shoots Vidar a challenging look.

Vidar helps him load the last of the winter tires and thanks him for his time.

His talk with Billy Oredsson doesn't start any better. He meets him at a café in Åled about seven miles from Marbäck, since that's where Billy is working at the moment.

"I'm repairing a bunch of washing machines for Anki," he explains, nodding toward a colorless building across the street, where a sign that reads LAUNDRY AND DRY CLEANING hangs low above the door.

"But you live down by Toftasjön?"

"Yup. I'll probably be there 'til the day I die."

"You like it there?"

"Well, I grew up with my pa, you know, and he didn't like the village. Thought it was too small. He probably would have moved if he could. But I bought the house by Tofta seven or eight years ago, and I've never been better."

Billy Oredsson has a drawl to his speech. He doesn't say "Dad," he says "Pa." Billy's thin and sinewy, the skin of his hands ingrained with motor oil and gunk from the day's work. He drinks a cup of coffee and takes in Vidar and his notebook with a look of skepticism. "What do you want with me, Officer?"

"You knew Lovisa Markström, right?"

"Yes and no," he says. "I guess I wouldn't say I did. Why?"

"I don't know if you recall, but you and I met once before, a—"

"I remember. It was right after."

Vidar repeats what he told Jon-Erik: *I just have a few questions. Time may have helped you remember.*

"Okay. But why?"

He sips his coffee. "We're working on a big case that involves a number of burglars," Vidar says. "There's a chance they came through Marbäck around the time of the murder."

Billy's eyes get big. "Okay."

"You said 'Yes and no,'" Vidar continues, "when I asked if you knew Lovisa. What does that mean?"

"You know," Billy says, shifting slightly, "once upon a time I guess we knew each other a little. But in the end she was just with Edvard."

"Did you know him?"

"I knew who he was, obviously. I was a few years behind him at Breared. But we didn't hang out."

"And you and Lovisa didn't either?"

"It was her ex who gave you my name, I think. Jon-Erik. I got to know Lovisa not long after they had broken up, towards the end of our school years. I guess we hung out a few times. I thought maybe there could be something between us, but it never happened. Then we went our separate ways, she met Edvard, and I fell in love with the office girl at my job." He laughs. "I always fall in love with the wrong girls."

Vidar laughs along. "Same here. Believe me."

"You're the one who's with, what's her name . . ."

"Patricia."

"Right."

The bell on the door tinkles. A new guest enters the café, and Vidar sinks into his chair. *Fuck, that's right. She lives out here.*

The woman is tall and lanky, with a wide mouth and small gray eyes, a stern face. She was probably beautiful once, but a life working for the authorities can wear away just about any beauty in this world. It's his boss, Beate Aronsson. She cheerfully greets the owner behind the counter and orders a cup of tea.

She and her husband, whatever his name is, sold their apartment in Halmstad and bought a house out here once the kids had moved out. It sounds backward, but Aronsson explained it to him once: *Who*

*the hell wants to raise kids in a house, where they can sneak in and out however they
please, and have house parties and organized fights and God only knows what all?
Oh, no. Better to live in a cramped apartment so you know where the kids are and
can keep an eye on them. Later, once they've flown the coop—that's when you can
move.*

Aronsson sits down at a table with her back to Vidar and opens a
newspaper, taking small sips of her tea. Vidar goes on in a lower voice.

"What I want to ask you about is the Miljanovic brothers. Does
that name sound familiar?"

Billy looks at him for a long time, his forehead creased.

"Yeah . . . Yeah, I think I recognize it."

Vidar leans forward. "In what context?"

"I don't quite remember, but I think I heard it around then,
around the same time."

"As when Lovisa was murdered?"

Billy nods slowly. He drinks his coffee as he tries to remember.
"Yeah, I think that was it."

From the corner of his eye, Vidar can see Aronsson turning the
page, sipping at her cup. She seems relaxed in a way Vidar has never
seen her before.

"Did she mention them? Like, that she knew them?"

"We had drifted apart by then," Billy reminds him. "So probably
not then. It would have been earlier."

"In ninety-four?"

"More like ninety-three."

It's something, at least. "Tell me more."

"I don't know what more I can tell you," Billy says evasively, his
gaze slipping back toward LAUNDRY AND DRY CLEANING.

Vidar recognizes the behavior—it's typical of witnesses. Billy is
about to start making guesses and assumptions.

"I think it might have been ninety-three, like I said. But I don't
remember the context, just that I recognize the name. Maybe she
mentioned it."

"Their first names?"

"I don't know. Something that started with D, maybe."

"Darko?"

"Maybe. I don't know."

"And you don't remember the context?"

He shakes his head and stands up. "I just need to go to the bathroom."

Billy walks away. He passes Aronsson, who looks up from her paper. She checks her watch, folds the paper, and takes one last gulp of tea. Then she stands up and leaves.

Vidar makes a note in his book: *LM may have mentioned the M brothers to Billy.*

That's all, really. Far too vague to do anything about it.

Sometimes that's all you get. At least it's something.

Billy returns.

"I was thinking," Vidar starts, "I don't suppose Lovisa kept a diary or anything?"

"Yeah, she did. At least when I knew her."

Billy says he doesn't really remember what it looked like. But it was hardcover and dark. Maybe blue or black.

"But I don't know if she was still writing at . . . you know, at the end. Or whatever."

"No," Vidar says calmly. "I understand. I was thinking, speaking of that—you said you weren't in touch toward the end. But you still went to the service just now?"

"Yeah, I did. Although I went back and forth on it for a long time. But I'm from the village, after all, and I'd heard that basically everyone would be there. I went with Dennis, who I was with that night. It was actually . . . well, it was heavier than I was expecting. You know, Lovisa was a damn good person. She wasn't always easy to deal with, but there wasn't a bad bone in her body. She liked people. I was so goddamn sad and angry afterwards, once I realized what had happened. So I went, to show my support."

Just like me, Vidar thinks. *Just like everyone else.*

37

December comes. Advent candelabras shine in the darkness. The first snow falls. Patricia pulls a laughing Amadia across the field on a sled, while Vidar captures the moment for posterity with the family's new digital camera. Amadia orders her mother to sit on the sled, hands the string to her dad, and takes over the camera herself. She manages to take two pictures before the camera slips through her slippery mittens and falls into the snow.

Across the field, a surprisingly cheerful Isak Nyqvist is walking with a girl by his side. Vidar watches them, curious about who she is. She's not from Marbäck, anyway.

The day after St. Lucia's Day, Vidar is heading into the hallway to grab an interrogation report he's printed out when his desk phone rings. He answers distractedly. On the other end is a woman with a bright, agreeable voice.

"Yes, hi, my name is Clara Nikander from Carlsson and Ericsson. You had tried to reach us."

"That's right. But I was trying to reach Dana Malmberg."

"What is this in regards to?"

"A case she defended."

"Which one?"

Vidar's colleagues are moving around in the hallway. He lets the printout be and closes the door to his office.

"She defended Edvard Christensson."

"She did. But I'm afraid it's going to be a little tough to talk to her, unless you turn to the spirit world, if you're into that. Dana died of a heart attack, let's see, almost five years ago."

"She did?"

"Yes, I'm sorry to say. We miss her an awful lot around here. What did you need to know?"

The radio in the window is playing peaceful Lucia hymns. *The spirit world.* Who says that? He turns down the volume and explains what he's looking for.

"Okay," she says, with a different sort of gravity to her voice now. "I don't suppose you could come over here, could you?"

Lovisa Markström, dead. Darko Miljanovic, dead. Dana Malmberg, dead.

K-G Öberg, more or less dying.

As if everything were cursed.

Large windows face the Nissan neighborhood, Picasso Park, and the Österskans bus terminal. The lawyers of Halmstad have a much better view than the police. More space, too; Clara Nikander's office is spacious and bright, with a massive desk in one corner and three comfortable chairs around a table made of warm wood in the other. Clara sets two cups on the table and sits down, crossing one leg over the other. She's short and small but carries herself as if she's used to getting her way. Her attire is unexpected: well-worn, high-waisted black jeans and a white T-shirt with the dark red Levi's logo on the chest.

"I don't have to appear in court today," she explains. "You know, if I'm not in court and I still put on a blouse and jacket, it feels like I spend all day getting psyched up for something that never happens."

She's not from here; he can hear it.

"Kalmar," she says when Vidar asks. "I moved here seven years ago, when I needed a fresh start in life."

"So you weren't around when it happened."

"No. I've only heard about it. Mostly from Dana, of course, but from others, too. And I have access to the material, or what's left of it."

"That was partly what I wanted to talk about. The material, I mean. I'm wondering if I can take a look at it."

"What else?"

"I'd like to inquire about the possibility of getting in contact with him."

Clara raises one thin eyebrow. "Your first request will probably be difficult. The material is marked confidential, and you know it. But why would you need our help getting in touch with him?"

"I'd like to avoid it getting out at work."

He hesitates one last time. Then he hands the documents to Clara. "What's this?"

"Letters that were written to Lovisa. And a handwriting comparison."

Clara places the sheets of paper beside each other to read and compare.

He's heard about Clara Nikander. She's not exactly just your average person. She's young and hungry, a sharp intellect crowned by modern legal acuity. Thanks to her, many people who ought to be behind lock and key are out on the streets that Vidar and his colleagues try to keep safe and secure.

She pushes away the documents. Leaning back, she drinks her coffee. For once Vidar feels inferior. Her education fascinates him. He never considered becoming a lawyer, not seriously, but the thought was always there as a potential option. He could have been someone else today.

"Interesting," she says.

"There's another thing. I also wanted to ask . . ."

"Mm-hmm?"

Clara Nikander looks almost amused. He, too, is aware of how this looks, the conclusions that would be drawn if it got out. *Vidar Jörgensson has defected to the other side.*

"I didn't attend the trial, but I've read the verdict. The court bought the prosecutor's argument completely."

"They didn't have much else to go on. It was the narrative that made sense. The only thing that backed him up was his own version, and that was hard to support with evidence."

"But he talked about a car," Vidar says, leaning forward. "Right? Or, well, a *fourth* car in that case. It was allegedly parked down in Tolarp when he arrived. A dark car, maybe black, a sedan."

"If you say so, I believe you. But I don't know—like I said, this was Dana's case. Didn't anyone check up on the cars in the area?"

"Yes. Before he started to talk. At first he wouldn't say anything, you know. That was when the checks were done, and they came up with three cars, based on reports from witnesses and people in the area."

"But is it very likely he saw a car no one else saw?"

Vidar doesn't respond right away. "No. But unfortunately, it isn't impossible."

Clara tilts her head.

"What are you really after here?"

It's a difficult, dangerous question disguised as a very simple one.

"I want . . ." He searches for the right words. "I just want to know we got it right back then."

"So you're not convinced you did?"

"What I'm most interested in," he continues, with as much certainty as he can muster to hide his doubt, "is the content of any conversations that took place between him and you all. Post-conviction, I mean."

Clara looks at him for a long time before shaking her head. "Conversations between a client and his counsel are bound by attorney-client privilege. You know that. What I can tell you is that there's not much."

The conviction was appealed, but the court of appeals—although nonunanimous—affirmed the county court's finding. As Christensson's counsel, Dana Malmberg was the only one who was in contact with him, and according to Clara, that contact became more and more sporadic over the years, not least because Christensson sank into a fairly serious addiction to smuggled-in opioids. It began during the months he spent in jail and continued for a number of years, until it was discovered during a health checkup and cell search. By that point Christensson had been in such poor shape that he almost didn't make it. It might have been a type of self-medication, but even that can sap one's health. This was probably what Vidar had seen hints of when he was there during Isak Nyqvist's sole visit to his uncle in early 1995.

"I've heard about that," Vidar says.

"He recovered, apparently, although he still bears physical traces of it. Not outwardly, I mean, but on the inside. That's what Dana said. They had slightly more contact later on, but since her death there really hasn't been much in the way of direct contact between us." They will, however, have to meet again quite soon, since his sentence will be converted to time-limited this spring.

"I'd like to speak with him before that," Vidar says.

Clara looks at him. The nail of her index finger taps thoughtfully against her china cup.

"What I can do is forward your inquiry to him."

He puts down his cup and looks at the documents before Clara. He pulls them across the table, folds them, and puts them in his inner pocket. Regret suddenly settles over his shoulders like a cloak. This is wrong. He shouldn't have done it. He can't.

"If you want me to, that is," she clarifies.

Vidar forces himself to smile.

"Please do."

38

Isak Nyqvist feels like he's in a kind of heaven, dizzy and overwhelmed. Karin runs a finger along the corner of her mouth.

"You need to get one thing straight," she says softly, lying down on the bed beside him and taking off her panties. "No girl likes how it tastes." She spreads her legs. "Anyone who says she does is lying."

"But you said . . ."

"I like how it feels. And most of all," she says, helping Isak put two fingers inside her, "I like the look y'all get in your eyes. So it's worth it."

Karin's skin is so pale, so soft. Her eyes are so brown. Wet warmth enfolds his fingers. When he moves them she makes a weird face.

"Not quite like that. Try like this instead."

He feels awkward, inexperienced. It's kind of embarrassing.

"Yeah, there. Better. That's nice."

Karin is breathing hard. He stares at her, a goofy smile on his face.

"Again," she says. "A little gentler."

It's December sixteenth. Marbäck is covered in peaceful, white snow. How do you know when you're a couple? He and Karin haven't exactly said anything out loud. It just happened. Maybe that's how it goes with lots of stuff. Most things in life just happen.

After much hesitation, he bought her a watch for Christmas. She likes wearing a watch, she's said, and she's disappointed that her old one broke.

All fall she meant to bring it in to get fixed but never got around to it. As Isak walked toward the bus he anxiously squeezed the box in his pocket; to him it's worth much more than the four hundred kronor he paid for it. He wonders if she'll like it. It's sort of like her old one, but not identical.

"Get out a condom."

Isak is stunned. They haven't had sex yet. Not real sex, or whatever. This is the first time. Once she's on top of him, sinking down, it feels like Isak is sinking, too. Karin props herself up with her hands on his chest.

"No, wait," he whispers.

"What? Is something wrong?"

Nothing's wrong. It's too good. His hands squeeze Karin's thighs. She smiles and moves faster.

"Karin, wait, I . . ."

That's as far as he makes it. She laughs and kisses him for a long time.

"You're great," she says. "Really great."

Afterward they lie next to each other, looking up at the ceiling. The same ceiling, Isak thinks, that he's looked up at almost every night in his eighteen years of life.

They're home alone. This is the third time she's come to his place in Marbäck. He likes to watch her moving around the house, the way she stops at photographs and asks questions. There are no pictures of Edvard. It's almost four in the afternoon, and darkness is falling outside.

Out in the living room, the phone rings.

"It's probably Mom. She's done with work now, so she probably wants to know if she needs to pick anything up on the way home."

"More condoms would be nice," Karin says, looking for her

panties. Laughing, Isak goes to the living room and picks up the phone.

"Hello," says a voice. It's not Mom. "Is this . . ." There's a sudden racket in the background, a heavy door opening and closing. "Is this Isak?"

"Yes. Who is this?" Isak asks, although he knows.

Nervous laughter. "Well, it's Edvard."

39

Monday, December 20, 2004, is cold and gray. The snow that had blanketed the southern parts of the country has melted away. Isak takes in the wall, the gate, the tall fence, and the coils of barbed wire. Low buildings, like factories. Almost like a school.

Isak steps out of the car. Clouds sweep past in the sky, ragged and hurried. He thinks of the paper full of questions in his pocket. He tried to memorize them so he could leave the piece of paper where it is; he doesn't want to take it out while they're together.

"My name is Isak Nyqvist," he says to the speaker in the gate intercom. "I'm here to see my uncle."

It feels strange to say it out loud.

"What is your uncle's name?"

"Edvard." Isak hesitates. He hasn't changed his name, has he? "Edvard Christensson."

The gate makes a heavy *clunk* and opens. A correctional officer comes out and escorts him to one of the buildings. Isak gives him his form and ID, and the man inspects them closely as his colleague leads Isak through the security checkpoint.

"Do you have anything with you?" he asks.

"Like what?"

"Well, like a present, a Christmas present or something. If you do, I have to take a look at it first."

"Am I supposed to have one?"

"No, no, it varies. But this is your first time, right?"

"Do people usually bring presents?"

The man shrugs. He's loud, broad shouldered, and tall, but his eyes are warm and smiling. "Some people do, others don't. I just wondered." He places a hand on Isak's shoulder. "Don't worry. Everything will be fine. Your uncle is really looking forward to seeing you."

I should have brought a present, Isak thinks.

Everything seems vaguely familiar, like visiting a place you've seen before in your dreams. He was here a long time ago. Or, well, not *here*. But a place *like* here. And the time that has passed hasn't made much of a difference: Suddenly he is small and uncertain. A boy being led into a visiting room, where a murderer awaits.

"Hi, Isak."

There's no preparing for it. Maybe it would have been impossible, but Isak is almost angry that no one, not anyone from school or at home or anywhere else, has tried to help him. He should have said something to someone. Everyone needs help.

Edvard is so skinny. And there are lots of wrinkles around his eyes now; the hair at his temples is streaked with gray. He has a small cardboard box in his hands, like a shoebox. He sets it on the table.

"Hi."

Inside the room, a table with a thermos of coffee and plastic cups waits for them. They sit down and pour the coffee. It's the darkest time of year, and dusk is already falling.

"It's been . . . it's been a long time. You're basically grown up." Edvard looks at Isak's cup. "When did you start drinking coffee?"

Isak remembers the smell of smoke on a November morning ten years ago, a feeling of uncertainty. They knew something had happened, but never could have guessed how bad it was. Sometime later—was it a week?—he had stood in front of a deserted house, the one that had belonged to his uncle. Police tape flapped in the wind. Wasn't that right? Or was he misremembering? Was there really police tape? Wasn't it just a sign? The police tape must have been down in Tolarp.

Isak stares at his uncle. "Do you have any idea how much you ruined?"

Something happens to Edvard. Until now his face has shown a warmth that matches his voice, but now it's like a black hole opens up inside him and sucks that expression away.

"Yes."

"And then you just disappeared."

"I didn't exactly have a choice."

"There's always a choice between calling or not calling, for example."

"Would you even have wanted me to?"

"What do you mean?"

"After all the shit that happened?"

"I don't know."

"So in that case, why didn't you get in touch with me?"

"I was eight. You can't put that kind of responsibility on a little kid."

"I'm not, I . . ." Edvard's face hints that this is starting off as badly as he feared. "Okay, here's the deal. Your dad wanted to move. But your mom wanted to stay in Marbäck. You had Theo there, and Karl and them. The only way for that to work was to break off all contact between us."

"Why?"

"Well, what do you think?"

Isak crosses his arms. "So, it was for my sake?"

"Not only yours. But part of it was, yeah. We measure time differently in here. At first I thought I would let it go on for a week. Then a month. Then six months. A year. Two years. And it got harder and harder, too. I assumed you would rather forget I existed."

"But *ten years*. Without a single word, a single happy birthday, a single . . ."

Isak looks at his uncle. For a moment—almost like an illusion—he looks like he did ten years ago. Forget he existed? How would that even be possible? Isak looks at his uncle's hands, their gentle grip on the cup of coffee. He can see them turning pages in a book or peeling a tangerine, helping him put on his jacket and his backpack when it was time for Isak to go. They were once among the safest hands he knew. Those hands that destroyed so much.

Edvard's eyes slide to the cardboard box on the table.

"I haven't kept in touch with many people." He rises to get the box, places it on their table, sits down again. "But . . ."

He pushes the box across to Isak, who opens it. Inside is a stack of cards. Christmas cards, birthday cards, postcards. Isak turns them over and recognizes the handwriting. They're from Mom. The oldest one Isak finds is dated 1997.

"Your dad doesn't know," Edvard says quietly. "But after a few years she started to get in touch. Not often, but for my birthday and Christmas and stuff."

Isak reads them carefully. She wrote short messages in them. Here and there, he finds a line about him. *Isak turned fifteen this fall. He had lots of fun on his birthday,* one says. *Isak has his learner's permit,* she mentions in another. *He's a good driver.* That sort of thing.

"Do you write back?"

"I wasn't doing so well the first few years. I wasn't really myself. But after that I started to write back, not every time, but sometimes. It's hard, though, I . . ." Edvard scratches his chin. "It's a long story, we can talk about it another time. I . . . I heard things have been a little rough for you." Edvard looks dismayed. Not with Isak, but more with himself, as if he regrets bringing it up, or regrets the way he brought it up.

"What, did Mom tell you that or something?"

"No, no. Do you remember Vidar Jörgensson?"

A sudden fall, no, *drop,* in his belly, like when you're taking off on an airplane or turning a sharp corner on a roller coaster at Liseberg. So *that's* how this happened.

"You talked to him."

"More like he contacted me. He said you . . . well, that you were having a rough time."

"And what are *you* supposed to do about it?" Isak says, his words crueler than he'd intended.

"I said the same thing. What am I supposed to do about it? But he thought this would be good."

"Like you're such a great role model?"

"No, but . . . Isak, I mean, if I've understood correctly, some of what you've done is pretty serious. Throwing bottles at people's heads, for example, believe me, that's not a good—"

"Well, at least it's not murder," Isak snaps.

Silence. The instant of satisfaction is replaced with deep shame. As if Isak is cheating, hitting below the belt. He turns away. You would have thought the window would have bars on it or something, but it doesn't. Outside it is the courtyard, a little piece of nature, and beyond that he can see the highway. It must be weird to watch the cars go by on their way here or there every day.

A lump grows in Isak's chest. You should *really* get some sort of help before doing this kind of thing. "I almost fell asleep one day in class last year. I didn't think I would like it, but I did."

"Huh?"

"You asked when I started drinking coffee."

"Oh." Edvard chuckles uncertainly. "Do you like school?"

"I guess so. It's okay. I used to skip a lot, but I'm trying to shape up."

"What subjects do you like?"

They take turns asking questions. Isak wonders if Edvard gets visitors (yes, if he wants to, but he usually doesn't have any), if the food is good (no), whether he can listen to music and watch movies (sometimes), whether they get to choose the movies themselves (on weekends, but they can't see just any movie, their selections have to be approved). Whether he likes the people in the other cells (yes, but they say *rooms*, or at least the staff do, probably to make it feel better).

"Does it work? Does it feel better?"

"No."

Edvard knows them pretty well, he goes on, the people around him. Lots of them are good people, really, they just ended up here because something went wrong. Sometimes it's something major, like their whole childhood, and other times it's something very specific, like a fight that got out of hand.

"It doesn't take much for things to go wrong," Edvard says, a new look in his eyes, something almost like worry.

What was it in your case? Isak wants to ask, but he doesn't have the guts. He takes a deep breath.

The questions. The paper in his pocket.

"I was thinking . . ." he begins. "Božo and Darko Miljanovic. Do you know who they are?"

He says the names a little uncertainly. More or less as Vidar pronounced them. Yesterday he'd contacted Isak to say he'd heard he was going to visit Edvard. *I have a friend at the Borås prison*, he said. *She noticed your name and called me. I thought I would take the opportunity to . . . This might sound a little strange, but I want to ask you a favor.*

He made it sound like a coincidence, happenstance that presented him with an unexpected opportunity.

Vidar had a question he wanted to pose to Edvard, and wondered whether Isak, as long as he was going to visit Edvard, could ask it in his place. Isak should have been suspicious. But he was still in mild shock over having just spoken to his uncle for the first time in ten years, and he said yes to the crafty goddamn cop, without thinking it over.

Edvard raises his eyebrows. "What were their names, did you say?"

"Never mind. Forget it."

"No, what did you say?"

"Forget it."

"Tell me."

White noise in Isak's brain. Everything has disappeared. He works the paper out of his pants pocket and unfolds it, reading.

"Božo and Darko Miljanovic."

"No. No, who are they?"

"Do you know if Lovisa knew anyone by those names?"

Edvard shakes his head and looks at the wrinkled paper in Isak's hands.

"What's that?"

"Vidar Jörgensson," Isak says, his head hanging as if he's confessing to bad behavior. "He wanted me to ask. He showed me some papers with handwriting on them. One of them was yours, I recognized it. The other belonged to someone else."

"Isak."

"Yeah?"

Edvard looks at him. "I didn't kill Lovisa. I told you that once. Do you remember?"

"Yeah."

"Do you believe me?"

"No. I mean, you . . . you were there."

"I was there," Edvard says. "That's true. But the rest of it is wrong."

"I don't really know what happened," Edvard says. "That's the weird thing. If I had known maybe I could have . . . I probably wouldn't be in here. But it was . . . it was a perfectly normal day. I called her that morning. She sounded happy then. It made me feel kind of relieved, because we hadn't seen each other for a few days. The last time didn't end well. She said she missed me. Or she whispered it, anyway."

"Why?"

"So her dad wouldn't hear, I assume. He didn't like me." Edvard gives a crooked smile, and his real-life face matches the one in Isak's memories. "We decided to meet up that night, and when she got home from work she biked up to my place. I was out chopping wood; the pipes were old so I had to have a fire pretty often or else they would start to clank. Do you remember that?"

Isak does.

"We went in and made supper, but we didn't eat until later. It must have been . . . I'm not sure what time, but we just relaxed and had some wine, watched a movie for a while. But eventually it was around eleven and she had to go home, because she had to work the next morning. But she forgot her wallet. It was on the kitchen table."

He's speaking mechanically, as if the events he's describing have nothing to do with him. As if he's just reading someone else's words. It's unnerving.

"Me and Lovisa, we . . . we had good days and bad days. And I treated her really badly a few times, especially when I got mad. Our relationship was stormy, even if you never noticed it. We wanted different things, and . . . well, sometimes we were really mean to each other."

"Did you hit her?"

"It's not that simple . . . She hit me, too. But we had lots of good times. And that night was one of them."

"That's not the version I heard."

"What did you hear?"

"That you started fighting. She wanted to leave you, but you weren't going to let her. At last she ran off."

"That's not what happened."

"She didn't want to leave you?"

"I . . ." Edvard begins, but he can't find the words. "Yes. But not that night. I'd been drinking wine so I couldn't drive, and my bike had a flat tire. So I put on a jacket and my gloves and took off after her. I didn't have much choice—she needed her wallet. Bus pass and ID, money, all her stuff was in it. I thought I would catch up with her if I went fast."

"Did you?"

He hesitates to answer, as if he isn't quite sure about this part.

"No. And I was confused when I got to Tolarp. There was a car stopped on the road."

"What kind of car?"

"Not a station wagon, the other kind . . ."

"A sedan?"

"Right. I don't know what kind of car it was. All the lights were off in the house so I assumed she hadn't made it in yet. I stood there with her wallet in one hand, staring like an idiot. Then I realized the door was open, so I walked up to the house. I called her name, you know, like you do when you're wondering if someone is home. And then . . ." He frowns. "I was standing in the hall, but I didn't have time to turn around before a horse kicked me in the back of the head. That's what it felt like. I know I dropped the wallet. Then everything went black. I think someone was standing behind the door there, near the hall. They must have hit me with the candelabra." His voice is very thin. "The same one they used on Lovisa. Then, well . . . I'm lying on the floor. When I open my eyes, it's ridiculously bright and for the first few seconds or so, I don't know how long, my ears are ringing so I can't hear anything. When it fades away a little I hear crackling and snapping. And then I smell it. Smoke. Something nearby is burning. I realize, oh my God, the house is on fire. I could see her through the flames, she was lying halfway in the kitchen and it . . . she had . . . I saw blood, there was blood everywhere. Around her head, I could see it. The flames were touching her, her clothes were on fire, and her hair, but she wasn't reacting. I took off my jacket and used it as protection, or whatever. I went over to her and . . . I tried to put out her hair and her clothes with the jacket but I couldn't. Her shoes were burning. The rubber was starting to melt. I got her blood on me, on my knees and my hands. Everywhere. I grabbed her and tried to lift her up but I just fell backwards. I tried again but she was totally limp, I realized she wasn't . . . whatever had happened, it was too late to stop it. So I left her there. I left her."

He stares vacantly ahead. Then he starts, as if an invisible hand has yanked him back to the present.

"That's what happened. Or, well, it's my version of what happened." Edvard looks at him almost beseechingly.

Isak stares back. "I . . ." he begins.

But he's interrupted when the door opens. A correctional officer gives Edvard a pointed look.

"Are you wrapping things up here?"

Edvard's remarkably empty eyes sweep from Isak to the officer.

"No," Edvard says, a strange tone in his voice. "Can we have five more minutes?"

The officer shakes his head. "I'll have to ask you to finish up."

Edvard turns to Isak.

"I guess we'll have to continue this another time. But do you believe me? I mean, do you trust me?"

"I . . . no, I don't know."

The officer places a hand on Isak's shoulder. It's probably meant to be a comforting gesture, but it just feels heavy.

"Hold on a minute." Edvard takes a small present from his pants pocket. The paper is worn and the ribbon is droopy. "I almost forgot. Merry Christmas."

Isak takes the present. "I didn't . . ."

"You can give me one next time you come. Remember how," Edvard continues as they walk to the door, "you had a secret last time? You said you had a secret you wanted to tell me. Do you remember what it was?"

It rings a bell in the back of Isak's mind, a dull tone of recognition. Yes. That was true. Right? All his feelings and thoughts are bouncing around inside him, striking one another like billiard balls.

"I think so."

"You never told me."

Expectation shimmers in Edvard's face. Isak's chest fills with a strange, almost unreasonable fear of disappointing him.

"I don't remember what it was."

The shimmer vanishes. Edvard forces a smile and places his hand on Isak's shoulder.

"Maybe it was nothing. Or maybe you'll remember for next time."

41

His cellphone is already ringing when Isak gets into his car. He recognizes the number by now. "What the fuck do you think you're doing?" he snaps.

"I apologize, Isak," says the calm policeman. "I—"

"You lied to me *again*. I fucking hate you and your goddamn games."

Isak's fury has pushed the needle of the speedometer up to eighty-six miles per hour. He forces himself to ease up on the gas pedal.

"It's perfectly understandable if you feel that way, Isak," Vidar continues placidly. "Like I said, I apologize. But I have to ask, what did he say? Did he recognize the names Darko or Božo Miljanovic?"

"No."

"And Lovisa . . ."

"No, I said! Leave me alone," he shouts, alone in the car, and hangs up.

The road zooms by. He passes slower trucks. Somehow, his anticipation of seeing Edvard gave him tunnel vision. Isak didn't think, didn't question anything. He just did as Vidar said, like a puppet.

He takes out his phone again, listens to the rings. A click in his ear. "Yes?"

"Why was it so important for me to ask him?"

"I—"

"You don't think it was him, do you?"

"It's not that simple."

"Then tell me. Why didn't you say so from the start?"

"It's . . ." Silence. There's a creak. A door closes. "I can't talk about this right now, Isak."

Sitting in his car, one hand on the wheel and the phone pressed tightly to his ear, Isak searches his memory. The secret Edvard asked about. What was it? And the cards from Mom. She hadn't cut off all contact with him after all, despite what she said.

"But why . . . He told me he didn't do it. Is that true?"

Too much has happened in a short time. Isak's mind feels stretched, overloaded. A monster lives in his uncle. This is the truth he has lived with. The world is illogical, nothing but a swarm that forms a temporary pattern now and then. He has accepted that. It's all chaos. *He welcomes it.* A gray dog moves at his side; it was once his grandfather August's companion. For Isak, it's the other way around—he's the one who follows the dog.

Vidar's response is slow in coming. "I can't talk about this, Isak. Edvard can only speak for himself." He waits, as if Isak is supposed to understand. "We'll talk soon, okay? I'll be in touch."

The phone clicks.

Over these memories, a shadow. Later on, he will hardly be able to account for his trip home to Marbäck. He stops somewhere along the way to think.

Darkness has fallen; a starless night. It's cold out.

That's all.

42

He has erected a brick wall, cold and protective. On the other side is where Isak stores everything that has to do with Edvard: his uncertainty about what pumps silently through his blood, his rage and sorrow, his confusion, the pleasure he took in finally loosening the reins and throwing that bottle at Jesper from Skedala.

He permits no one through that wall. There's no room for Karin or Theo even, only Isak, and as he sits at home, on the sofa in front of the TV, he is struck by an unexpected wave of loneliness.

That's why he does it. He picks up the remote and starts the old VHS tape. It's the first time. He's thought about it many times, but he's always pushed it aside. It would hurt too much; he would end up feeling angry or sad. But this time he watches it despite all that and catches a glimpse of the past.

The sun is high in the sky, blinding the lens for a moment.

There they are, all of them: Isak, Mom, Edvard, Grandpa, Dad, Grandma. It's Midsummer's Eve.

They're in the pightle. Beyond the white fence you can see Theo's house, a flash of the playhouse roof. Dad is filming. Grandma and Grandpa, Dad's parents, are in the shade, on either side of the bench. Grandma is large and plump, resting her hands on her stomach. Grandpa is thin and sinewy; he has a glass in his hand and says something that makes Grandma laugh. They got along well. Mom walks by with a cake plate, looking stressed, but her face is bright. She has a wreath of flowers in her hair and looks young.

Dad sets the camera on the table, its lens aimed at the lawn.

There they are, in the sun in the middle of the grass. Isak and Edvard. Isak's wreath is a little too big. Edvard had helped him adjust it, but Isak isn't happy; he says it's rubbing.

"*Oh,*" Edvard says. "*Here's the problem. This little twig.*"

He gently lifts the wreath from the boy's head and begins to fix it again.

"*Are you happy, Edvard?*"

"*Why?*"

Isak squints at him. The sun is in his eyes. "*You look happy.*"

"*Well, Midsummer is fun. But mostly I'm happy that I get to see you. And later tonight I'm going to see someone else I like.*"

"*Lovisa?*"

It's so strange to look back through time. From his spot on the sofa, Isak leans toward the screen and studies his uncle. It's June. In less than five months he's going to take her life.

"*There's something you should know, Isak. The best days are the ones we spend with the people we care about the most. All the other days we're just sort of waiting. So, yes. Today I'm very happy. How about you?*"

"*What?*"

"*Well . . .*" He inspects the wreath. "*Are you happy?*"

"*Yes, and I already got ice cream. I like Midsummer, too.*"

Edvard laughs again.

Isak looks at his grandfather's eyes, his uncle's eyes, his own. History is a series of small occurrences that expand and become large ones.

The wreath is ready. Edvard carefully places it on Isak's head.

The clip stops. A new one takes over, from later that same night. They're down at the sports fields—not Isak, he's too little. But Mom and Dad are there, and Edvard and Lovisa, too. The light is bluer and dim; the image is grainier. They're dancing around the Midsummer pole, along with many others. They look happy.

A secret, Isak thinks. Edvard asked about his secret. What could it have been? He can't figure it out.

43

Vidar is standing in the early-morning dark of the garage. He's wearing work gloves and holding a gas can, testing its weight, the feel of its heft. He squeezes his fists. The gloves creak. He walks out into the pightle and starts to pour it out, quickly, harried. The liquid glugs out and splashes the ground. It splashes Vidar's shoes, his face, the patio furniture, the empty flowerpots.

"What are you doing?"

Vidar turns around, squinting. His eyes adjust slowly. Patricia is at the back door, bleary and barefoot in the doorway, her arms crossed and her body wrapped in a blanket.

"I, uh . . ."

She takes a step out. "Is that gas?"

"God, no, it's just water and dish soap." Vidar puts down the can. "I was checking something out."

"What?"

"Nothing."

"Vidar." Patricia's voice is tight with worry. "What's wrong?"

He comes inside again and closes the back door behind him, takes off his shoes and gloves.

"You've been acting weird all fall."

"I'm sorry."

He looks at the wall clock in the kitchen. Almost six-thirty. Half an hour, at the most, before Amadia will wake up.

Lovisa had been Patricia's coworker. They didn't know each other very well, and they hadn't worked together for very long, but—Patricia has told Vidar—when the verdict was handed down, she was relieved. They missed Lovisa at work. She'd always been cheerful, always positive, always had something kind to say about others. She left behind a void. *He really robbed this town of a good thing,* she had said back then. *I'm glad he's behind bars.*

Vidar sets his gloves on the kitchen table and starts to fix a pot of coffee. "What is it?" Patricia asks again.

"Do you remember," he begins, "whether Lovisa ever mentioned two brothers, Božo and Darko Miljanovic?"

Patricia raises her eyebrows. "You mean Lovisa Markström?"

"Yeah."

She leans against the kitchen counter and starts to fold up her blanket. "No, I don't think so."

"You don't recognize the names?"

"No."

"Wait here."

Vidar starts the coffee maker and goes to the hall, where he opens his bag and returns with photographs of the brothers.

"Did you ever see these guys at Brooktorpsgården?"

Patricia hesitantly takes the pictures from his hand. "It's possible. I don't know. We had hundreds of guests every day."

"But it's possible . . ."

"I don't know, Vidar. Sure, maybe."

Between the photographs is a folded piece of paper. Patricia opens it and looks puzzled. "What's this?"

Written in purple crayon are the words *Genarp, Södra Sandby, Ängelholm, Veinge* and so on, the Miljanovic brothers' entire route through Sweden, including an addition with a question mark: *Tolarp?*

"It's just a list."

"When did you write it?"

"I don't know, sometime last week."

"When you were drawing with Amadia."

It's not a question. She sounds surprisingly cold.

"Yes, maybe? I don't remember."

"So you did this while you sat down to color with your daughter for a little bit."

"I . . ."

She picks up Vidar's gloves.

"What were you doing in the yard?"

"I didn't want anyone to see. That's why I had to do it while it was still dark out."

"See what?"

Vidar takes the gloves from her, feels them. They're covered in splashes, stains the size of five-krona coins.

Not just one of them. Both of them.

"When you are with your daughter, you leave this alone. When you're with me, you leave it alone." She looks at the piece of paper again. "This is not fucking okay, Vidar."

For a brief moment, he feels something that scares him: a powerful, powerful rage.

"What is wrong with people, you know? It's Christmas Eve tomorrow, God dammit."

Nashwan is gazing upon the decline of morals, staring at the empty spot on the wall where the new flat-screen TV had once been. Vidar crouches down at the patio door and studies the broken glass. His knees creak as he stands up.

"They unscrewed it," Nashwan says, fingering the small holes in the wall. "Look."

The single-family home on the outskirts of Vallås is airy and bright, inviting. There are two kids' bedrooms upstairs. Both have computers. Vidar turns to Markus, who's standing right next to him.

"Where's the alarm?"

Something went awry when the crime was called in, so not only have Nashwan and Vidar from the property crimes unit been called in, but Markus from the uniformed patrol showed up as well.

He beckons for Vidar to follow him. "Listen." Markus lowers his voice. "I was wondering, how's everything going?"

"Not great."

"What does that mean?"

"Patricia is mad at me."

Markus looks curious. "Okay?"

"You know, she worked with Lovisa."

"Right. Of course."

"She doesn't like that I'm . . ." Vidar doesn't finish his sentence. "I get it. Maybe I should just forget it."

"Yes, maybe you should. You have a tendency to get too absorbed in things."

"I do?"

Markus shrugs. "Sometimes."

"But he still denies it. After ten years. Most guilty people confess after a while—partly because they have a lot to gain once they're in prison, and partly because they don't have the energy to keep up the lie. But he still flat-out denies it."

"Nothing strange about that—he's serving life. If he's ever going to have a chance at a retrial, he has to keep denying it. He has applied for a retrial, hasn't he?"

"Twice, apparently. Both times were rejected."

"Wouldn't have expected any different," Markus says. "Listen."

Vidar meets his gaze. "What?"

"Be careful. Whatever it is you're up to."

"I'm not up to anything."

A smile tugs at Markus's lips. "Anyway, it's up here. The alarm, I mean. And—yup. You can see for yourself."

It's an old alarm, encapsulated in a small metal box. The wires running from it have been cut. The protective case is broken. Vidar takes out a flashlight and shines it on the box—from beneath, from above, from the side.

"Where are the folks who live here?" Vidar asks.

"We took them to the station."

"Make sure we get their prints for comparison."

The burglars had worn gloves, probably very thick ones, given how they had broken the glass of the patio door. But not the whole time. Alarm systems can be tricky even if they're old, the skinny wires difficult to grab hold of. It's possible that at least one of them would have been bare-handed for that stage of the crime.

Vidar aims his flashlight at the side of the box.

"There they are. I'm sure they're on the wires, too. He had to grab the box here so he could brace it when he yanked them out."

Markus leans forward to see. Sure enough: three clear fingerprints.

The analysis isn't finished until late that evening, when Vidar has already left the station to buy one last Christmas present, a piece of jewelry, for his wife.

Bingo.

The fingerprints belong to Božo Miljanovic's known acquaintance, Josif Marinko, thirty-eight, Ängelholm. Burglar, fence, former drug addict. He probably wasn't the sole intruder in the home in Vallås; the shoe prints in the living room suggest more than one perpetrator, but at least it's a start.

If only they could find him.

Isak could have chosen a better time. He thinks so himself, in retro-spect, but it's too late now. About halfway through Christmas Eve dinner, he reveals that he went to see Edvard.

"What are you saying?" Dad asks.

"Oh my," says Mom.

They have questions, of course. Tons of them. He immediately regrets mentioning it, but it's pointless—he would have had to tell them anyway. Isak put the package from Edvard under the Christmas tree in the living room. He wants it there among all the others. Mom has already aimed several curious glances at it.

"Okay." Mom looks at her plate, at the holiday soda in her glass, and slices a meatball down the middle, trying to act normal. "Well, how is he doing?"

"Good. I guess."

"Why didn't you tell us?" Dad asks. "Going to see him is a touchy subject up here, even *talking* about him is, my God, you have to—"

"I didn't say anything," Isak says, his grip on his silverware tight-ening, "because I wanted to avoid this."

Dad goes red in the face and opens his mouth, but Mom jumps in before he can speak.

"Peter."

"He said you had broken off all contact with him. Is that true?"

His parents exchange long, telltale gazes. In the background, the radio plays Christmas music. Everything is quiet.

"We did. We had to."

"Was someone holding a gun to your head or something?"

"Just about," Dad mutters.

"People were talking about us," Mom says. "They were starting to avoid us when we were out shopping. Other parents called to ask if . . . Well, they wondered about you. They knew how much you liked Edvard. There was a risk that we—especially you—would end up being frozen out completely. And your whole life was here. Ours, too. And we have a lot of history here. So we wanted to stay. Or, *I* wanted to stay," she corrects herself.

"But in order to do that," Dad goes on, "we had to show that we were distancing ourselves from Edvard. Completely. So we . . ." He looks at Mom. "So we did."

"Just like that," Isak says.

"No." Mom presses her lips into a pale line. "It wasn't *just like that* at all. It was really hard."

Silence. What is there to say? He could have picked a better time. "But you still sent him cards."

"No, I didn't."

"I saw them."

Mom's eyes are pleading. Dad stares at Isak, then at his wife. "What? Did you?"

"Just a few times."

"Why?"

Mom takes a deep breath and sits up straight, aiming a steely look at Dad. "Because he's my brother."

"For Christ's sake, don't you remember what it was like? And how awful it made you feel, it was—"

"I feel fine now. And it's only a card a year."

"But—"

"He says he's innocent," Isak interrupts. "And Vidar Jörgensson believes him."

They both look surprised.

"He does?" Dad asks.

"Yeah, it seems like it."

Mom drinks her soda. It looks like she wishes it was something stronger. "Edvard has always said that."

"You don't believe him."

"Of course we don't," says Dad. "Edvard is pretty good at hiding the truth when it suits him. Are you going to see him again?"

"What, are you going to *let* me?"

Dad starts to say something, but Mom beats him to it. "We can't stop you."

"What do you mean, he's *good at hiding the truth*?"

Dad heaves a deep sigh. "Just . . . nothing. It was nothing."

"You can't just say that."

"I can say whatever I want."

The conversation comes to nothing. The rest of Christmas Eve is strange. Karin calls to say she loves the watch. Isak's chest fills with warmth—it's the first time he's heard Karin say *love*. The word has a melody of its own when Karin says it. Isak responds that he's so happy—the backpack she got for him is exactly the kind he wanted.

She laughs at him. "Great. See you tomorrow?"

"Definitely."

After their phone call he goes back out with Mom and Dad, who are sitting around the tree, each with a glass of glögg in hand. Only one present is left: Edvard's.

The small package feels unnaturally heavy in Isak's hands.

He opens it: a small wooden box. In it is an intricate bracelet made of delicate silver links. Infinite loops, almost like a skein of yarn. Some parts are braided or tied; other parts appear chaotically linked. Even so, it's not heavy. Small strips of leather are twined around it.

Isak has never seen anything like it. He fastens it around his wrist. "Isn't it nice?" he says.

Mom takes a close look at it. "Really, really nice," she says.

She gives a sob and leaves to blow her nose.

:::

"Hello?"

"Hi, Isak. Can you hear me?"

"Yeah, I can hear you."

"Great. The sound has been kind of bad on this recently; I think they need to get a new phone. It's one of those cordless ones, you know?"

"I'm on a cordless phone, too."

"Are you? It's pretty practical. Like, you can move around more. Even though that's not really necessary here."

"Yeah . . ."

"Did you open your present?"

"Did you make it yourself?"

"Yeah. Does it fit?"

"Yes, it does."

"It's called a Byzantine chain. We make them in the workshop here. But I wanted to make it fancier, so I added a few things, braids and stuff."

"It's super nice, honest. I love it. What did you get? Or, uh, did you get anything?"

"Oh . . . we got Christmas food from the screws. It was actually pretty good. I like Christmas ham."

"Me too. The screws, are those—"

"That's what we call the guards here. Or the COs, we're really supposed to say. I guess the name is because a long time ago guards used thumbscrews to torture the prisoners. It's kind of a derogatory term, like calling us 'cons.' Formally we're inmates or clients."

"Weird."

"Right? As if changing the words can change the reality of it. Some of the guards call us 'bandits,' even though it's not like we all stole stuff. But I almost like 'bandit.' It's kind of mischievous. Don't you think?"

"Yeah."

"Listen, Isak, you mentioned two brothers. What were their names?"

"Miljanovic, I think. But that was only because—"

"I know. I think Vidar meant well. Does he think they might have done it?"

"I don't know. He didn't say much."

"Okay. Anyway, I don't recognize the names. I don't think Lovisa mentioned them, but I guess they could have been customers where she worked or something. An awful lot of people went there. Brook-torpsgården was ridiculously popular back then. So they could have met there."

"Okay."

"Could you . . . Isak, I don't want to be a pain, but it's a little hard for me to . . ."

"Do you want me to tell him that?"

"Yes, if you can. But, I mean, you don't have to."

"It's fine. Whoa, you're coughing a lot."

"It's no big deal, I think I'm coming down with the stomach flu or something. I'm not feeling well; I'm a little dizzy and stuff. But it's no big deal. Hey, something occurred to me."

"What?"

"Well, what I asked you before you left, about the secret. Did you think about it?"

"I can't remember what it was."

"It's fine, Isak. I was just wondering. I have to go now, other people want to call their families for Christmas, too. But let's talk again soon, okay?"

"Okay. Sure."

"Say hi to your mom and dad from me. Merry Christmas, Isak."

"Merry Christmas."

45

Karin has classmates who are on vacation in Phuket, Thailand. She gets a text in the morning, *we're okay*, and that's it. It's like proof that it really happened.

An earthquake in the Indian Ocean caused a tsunami—it's a word that, up to now, has been unfamiliar to basically all of Sweden. A wall of water several yards high comes crashing down on the South Asian coastline, destroying everything in its path. The aftershocks of the earthquake soon reach Marbäck: The Nilssons' house farther down Svanåsvägen is empty. They left for Khao Lak, Thailand, on December 21.

"Dreadful," people say.

"And almost ten years to the day."

That's all anyone needs to say. Since death took Lovisa Markström, the village has managed to avoid great tragedies and sorrows. Now, ten years later, they're facing another trial. That's how they think of it, a period of suffering that must be endured.

People call and visit one another, contact the Ministry for Foreign Affairs and the Swedish Embassy in Thailand, the hotel in Khao Lak, even the media, to ask if they might have heard anything about the Nilsson family. No one has, and the village prepares for the worst.

Even as the search for the Nilssons and the dread of their fate leave their mark on the last days of the long year of 2004, something else happens.

It starts when Isak and Karin are playing video games on the day after Christmas, shortly after the news exploded in Sweden. No one quite understands the extent yet; it almost seems unreal. That's when she asks about his family. It's an ordinary question—there's not really anything in particular behind it. And, slowly, he starts to explain.

Karin listens in silence. Her nimble fingers stop moving; the controller rests in her hands. The character on screen has stopped moving.

"Yikes," she says, as if Isak has spilled something on her. "That's bananas."

"There were . . ." he continues. "I mean, a whole lot of rumors started going around about me. Like that I had threatened some guy in the cafeteria because he was talking smack about Edvard. That I kept huge, framed photos of my uncle in my room. That I had a massive knife collection. Crazy shit like that. I didn't even have any contact with him. But I . . ."

It's so hard to put into words. Almost every time he gets close to expressing something like this in front of another person, it's like his language is on guard and tries to say to him, *Some things you're better off keeping to yourself,* and he stops.

"Since everyone thought I was just like him, I didn't really care what I did. I think that's why I sometimes do things without thinking them through first."

There's more to say, but he doesn't know how.

"Wait, what do you mean?" Karin asks slowly. "Like what?"

"I . . . I just sort of have trouble holding back sometimes. Like that thing with Jesper last fall, if you remember. The guy who was going to beat me up at the party."

"Yeah?"

"I had done something to him before that."

Karin looks uncertain. "What did you do?"

"I know it doesn't sound great," Isak rushes to say, almost

stumbling over his words, "but he said this thing about me. And I got so mad. It was in town and I was on my way home, with a beer bottle in my hand. So I . . ."

He changes his mind. Most of all he wants to keep playing video games, but it's too late.

"I threw it. At him."

"You threw a bottle at him because of something he said?"

"Yeah, but . . ."

"What else have you done?"

"Nothing, I mean, nothing major . . ."

But the words trickle away. This is when she figures it out; Isak can see her putting it all together. He will never, *never* admit how it felt to throw that bottle. He wants to, because it would almost be like confessing—he wouldn't have to carry the knowledge around alone anymore, and he might get *answers*, but he can't say that to Karin. She would never want to see him ever again.

Karin's cellphone rings. It's Elin and Hanna, calling from Phuket.

"I'm sorry," Karin says. "That was just a little . . . I have to take this. And I should be getting home. But I'll call soon, okay?"

She smiles, but it doesn't reach her eyes. The phone is still ringing. She puts it to her ear and leaves.

Isak watches her go.

So much gets ruined. Everything gets ruined. You have to watch yourself.

46

"What did you say, Isak?" Vidar presses the phone closer to his ear. "Okay. He doesn't know them, you say." He sighs inaudibly and listens to the apathetic teen. "To her work? Yes, of course, that's a possibility."

The Miljanovic brothers were moving through southern Sweden that fall. They might have visited Brooktorpsgården to do some recon, to check out possible targets. But why Brooktorpsgården in particular?

He tries to link the letters to the brothers. It's hard—he can't think of a way.

Isak is quiet for a moment. Then comes the question: Was it him?

Vidar hedges. It could have been. Probably? He isn't sure. Maybe he shouldn't have been convicted.

There's a difference between an innocent person being convicted and a wrongful conviction. In the first case, a person is found guilty of something he didn't do. In the latter case, he's convicted of something he might have done, but the prosecutor's argument is too weak to say one way or the other. In such cases, the defendant should not be convicted. Better to let a suspect go free than risk finding an innocent person guilty.

But how can you say this to a sullen, confused teenager? What do these sorts of legal distinctions even mean to regular folks?

He clears his throat. "I was going to ask, Isak, how are you doing? After everything . . ."

Click.

Vidar listens to the static, resigned.

The people in Marbäck have never really given up on God. The signs may be small, but for the ones who know, they are clear as day.

They say death takes you. But not always. Sometimes, the end of life is described as being *called home.* The literal way home is often a journey through thick forest, sometimes over a field or open water, but the implication is the same: We have our time on earth, to love and wound and work, all the big things and all the small ones. Then, when that time is over, you are allowed to return home and rest.

As a child, sitting at his desk at Breared School facing his teacher Frank Niklasson, a Lutheran, Vidar thought this sounded lovely. Breared Church, their teacher informed them, dated back to the Middle Ages. It stands there still today, a façade of plastered gray stone surrounded by a large graveyard called God's Field.

God's Field is a field of memories where the dead are laid to rest after they've finally been called home. So the description reads. Some have been resting there for a very long time; the oldest graves were dug in the thirteenth century.

It's the list of Swedes missing in Thailand that makes Vidar think about God again. The list is the length of a curtain. All these names, bodies, fates no one knows anything about yet. When the wave washes over the children of God, it's meant to be in the form of salvation, not punishment. They learned about it in Christianity lessons: A flood of God's warmth will stream through everyone; inner and outer wounds will be healed by the amazing power of divinity.

So they said.

But then there's this list. It's almost impossible to conceive of. In all the God's Fields all over Sweden, grave after grave will soon be dug. It takes almost half a workday to prepare a grave. If one single person were responsible for all of them, he would have to dig for almost a year.

A bit further down the list, more or less in the middle, are four inconspicuous lines.

Nilsson, Börje

Nilsson, Ann-Charlotte

Nilsson, Frida

Nilsson, Håkan

One family out of hundreds. A family from Marbäck. They've checked with the ID committee up in Stockholm, which is working with the Ministry for Foreign Affairs and Interpol, and all the embassies. Nothing yet.

Maybe it's not just the tsunami, really. When Amadia was born and Patricia's blood pressure dropped immediately afterward, she was pushed down the long hallways of the hospital. Left behind was Vidar, a tiny bundle in his arms, praying to God that everything would be okay. When his father was on his deathbed, Vidar sat at his side, hoping that Sven wouldn't suffer in his last moments. So few, but so crucial, are the times he remembers asking for help from—how should he say it?—*beyond*.

They were also taught about forgiveness. Maybe he can be forgiven for the game he had forced Isak Nyqvist and Edvard Christensson to play, approaching each of them separately but keeping that fact to himself. He had hardly expected not to be found out, but he didn't know another way. He had to be careful.

It's the day before New Year's Eve. The door is opened by Nashwan, who looks surprisingly chipper.

"Listen, this Josif Marinko. I just heard from our friends down in Ängelholm that he was sitting at a café and reading the paper there. They apprehended him and tossed him in the clink," Nashwan says.

"Has he been in Ängelholm this whole time?" Vidar asks.

"I suppose only he and God know that."

Vidar raises an eyebrow. *God?*

"Meaning, he hasn't said a peep yet," Nashwan clarifies.

Vidar takes his winter coat from his chair and grabs the results of the database searches on Josif Marinko. A lot of things have been piling up on his desk since the holidays due to the tsunami disaster.

"Let's go."

Maybe not a flood of God's warmth, exactly, but at least there's a spark to ignite hope. You have to take what you can get; you can't be choosy.

Karin doesn't call. Instead: silence, for days. Isak starts to wonder if he's depressed. He has no desire to either eat or drink.

He's tried talking to his uncle, but with no success. Edvard is sick, they inform him. *Edvard is resting right now. He'll call you when he has telephone time tomorrow.*

He still hasn't called. Maybe he doesn't want to talk to Isak. It might be hard on him. Maybe that's just as well. It would hardly help Karin calm down if she found out he was in regular contact with Edvard.

Maybe she's scared of Isak now. Like he's a monster. How awful.

All that anyone around him is talking about is the tsunami. About the Nilsson family, who're all still missing. Isak's thoughts are elsewhere. In the silence of the telephone that refuses to ring, he tries to recall what his uncle told him. What did he say about . . . ? What happened with . . . ? His questions are piling up.

On the day before New Year's Eve, he sends a text to Karin: *see you tomorrow?* She responds, *yes, im coming. sorry i havent texted . . .*

As if everything is left hanging.

Why do girls always end their texts with three dots?

:::

The New Year's Eve party starts to derail around ten-thirty, when Isak and Theo decide to set off one of the fireworks in the hall.

"I mean," Isak says, raising an index finger as if to assure the frightened Anton that it's going to be fine, "out the door."

"Okay. But why?"

Isak turns to Theo, who's holding the rocket in his hand—it's red and yellow, shaped like a bowling pin, and says LIL' BASTARD down the side. He's looking hopeful.

"You know," Theo says, slowly, "because we can?"

They're in a fancy house up by the military base in Halmstad, the home of a guy whose dad is a major in the air force. Isak and Theo, Anton, Karl, and like a hundred other people.

And Karin. She's here with some school friends. They said hi when she arrived, but they've been keeping their distance even though they will inevitably run into each other sooner or later.

"Everything okay with you two?" Theo slurs.

Isak shrugs. "We'll talk later."

"Better do it now." Theo places a hand on his shoulder. "Before you get too drunk. We can hold off with the fireworks until . . ." He squints at something over Isak's shoulder. "Does that have tits?"

On the shelf is a stuffed fox, looking proud with a puffed-out chest and its gaze fixed in the distance. It's wearing a bright pink party hat and a pair of big, fake breasts from Buttericks novelty store.

"Where'd Anton go?" Theo turns around. "He had a camera. Anton!" He spots Anton across the room and shouts, "Anton, take a picture of me with the fox before we set off the fireworks!"

Isak is alone in the crowd. People pass him, many already shit-faced.

He walks out on the veranda, where he can hear the shouts and cries and laughter from other nearby parties. Even now, fireworks are shooting toward the clear sky. A girl is lying on the ground, puking, while a guy gently holds her hair and strokes her back.

"You have to . . ." Something breaks. "Oops."

Her voice behind his back. He turns around, and there's Karin, her eyes on an overturned, cracked planter. She puts down her beer and tries to right it. A single dead plant is about to fall out; the potting soil is leaking and crumbling on the hardwood floor.

"I'm so clumsy," she mumbles. Isak walks over to help her.

"You have to understand why it's weird," she says. "Your uncle murdered his girlfriend. Everyone says you're so fucking similar, and now I'm *your* girlfriend."

"I get it," Isak says. "I think."

"You have to tell me exactly what you've done. Just so I know."

The plant is beyond saving. They stand up, and each takes a sip of their beer. It's starting to get cold.

"For example," Karin continues, "those rumors about you. Were they true?"

"Which ones?"

"What, some of them were true and others weren't?" Her voice is so cold, so distant.

"No, no. I just wondered which ones you meant."

"Like that you supposedly have a knife collection."

"No. None of them were true."

She gazes at him for a long time. "What's wrong with you, then?"

He's touched upon that question before, in secret, cautiously—the way you test a tender spot by poking at it. A detail, a thought or a memory, sometimes no more than a sound or a smell, can bring him back. *Edvard.* All of a sudden, everything that happened down in Tolarp comes back to Isak and overpowers him. How could he? And how much darkness does Isak have inside?

So Isak always yanks his hand right back, as if something has burned him. He can't be blamed for that.

"It's weird, you know. For a while it felt almost freeing to know that I was the way I was because of him. I guess it's a little like if you don't feel well for a long time, and you've got all these symptoms, and finally a doctor gives you a diagnosis. It was like an explanation, kind of."

"What, so you don't feel that way anymore? Or what do you mean?"

It's hard to say. It's so hard to wrap his mind around the idea that Edvard might not have killed Lovisa. That's the story Isak carries inside. It's like if someone suddenly showed up to say that his parents are actually immigrants, that Mom and Dad have completely different jobs than they do, or that he has a secret sibling. It just can't be true.

From inside the house comes a loud cry of fear and delight, and the next instant a rocket shoots out of the hall like an arrow. It whizzes across the street, trailing a tail of sparks, and explodes between some nearby houses in a shower of colors.

They didn't wait. It doesn't matter.

"Sorry, Isak, but I have to pee. Bad timing, I know, but I just want you to . . ." She bites her lip. "Just, think stuff through from now on. And talk to me."

"Okay."

Karin places her hand against his rib cage. "Promise?"

"I promise."

Everything but how it felt to finally give in. He can feel that memory in his fingertips, how they sting and tingle pleasantly when he thinks about it. Why does it feel like that? He wishes he knew.

Maybe he's just drunk. Even more reason not to say anything.

Karin reels her way inside. Isak looks up at the sky. He wonders if Edvard is looking at the same sky right now, what he's thinking about, how he's feeling. Does he even have a window in his cell? He never asked. *Room.* It's called a room, not a cell.

The girl down on the ground throws up again. The guy strokes her hair and speaks in a low voice.

Around the corner of the house, alongside the stairs that lead to the porch, he hears steps—and there she is with a bottle of wine, or maybe champagne, in her hand. She's wearing a black dress, black tights, an open puffer jacket, and boots, and, unfortunately, she is very, very hot.

"Hi," Johanna says. "I couldn't get in the front door."

"They're, uh, they're shooting off fireworks there."

"Oh."

"Did you come by yourself?"

"I know people inside."

"Where's your boyfriend?"

As if that were some disgusting sort of food. That's how it sounds when Isak says it.

"He . . ." She takes a few steps in his direction. "He's not coming. We broke up."

"Oh."

"*I* broke up with him," she clarifies.

Johanna's an arm's length away from him right now, and her eyes are shining in the light from the party.

"Okay."

Then, almost in a whisper, she adds, "Because I miss you."

"What?"

"I miss you. I realize now that I . . . that it was a mistake."

She takes the bottle out of its bag and unscrews the lid, takes a big gulp.

It's wine. He notices that it's only half full.

"You lied to me" is all he manages to say. "About what you wanted."

"Sorry. I was so confused. I mean, I didn't know what I—"

"I felt so dumb."

"I know. But you're not. I'm the dumb one."

Johanna touches his arm. A warm palm. She has nice hands, and she smells just like the end of summer.

"I know you were mad, Isak, but I can . . . if you give me another chance, I'll show you you're not dumb. You're so great, Isak. You're so fucking great and I miss you so much. I'm not a good person, I know that, but I'm a little better when I'm with you."

She brushes his cheek. He doesn't get why she does it, but it feels good. God, shit, he's too drunk for this, and where's Karin, is everything okay between them or what? He needs to talk to Theo, Jesus, girls are weird. Johanna's breasts are resting against his ribs. He can feel them in his hands already, and how soft her skin is way down on her belly, how the wine tastes on her tongue.

"We can . . . Isak, we can try again. Go slow, if you want."

He gave Johanna a ride through Halmstad on her own bike one summer night, and she said she was in love with him. The memory fills his chest with joy.

"Isak . . ."

"Stop."

"Isak, I lo—"

"No."

He takes a step back, freeing himself from her.

Johanna's eyes get shiny and something happens to her cheeks and mouth, they get sort of twisted, her whole face is suddenly naked and ugly and it almost makes him feel embarrassed.

He walks past her and down the stairs without looking around, turning the corner toward the wide-open front door.

Another rocket whizzes across the street. It's louder than the first one when it explodes. A car alarm goes off.

"One more," someone cheers from inside. "One more time, can I try?"

It's Karin's voice.

48

Josif Marinko is a little hawk of a man with low cheekbones and a cruel mouth; there's an expression of displeasure in his sharp eyes. He's sitting in the oldest of the three interrogation rooms down in Ängelholm, drumming his fingers against the tabletop. Vidar opens the door and sets a binder on the table, then offers his hand.

"Josif," he says. "My name is Vidar."

Marinko stares at his hand in surprise. "What do you want? I didn't do anything."

Just like almost everyone else these days, he wants to wait for his lawyer. It's going to be a while; the officer who met Vidar and Nashwan in the lobby informed them that unfortunately the request had not yet been processed, but that it's finally in the works now.

And then he winked at them. Nashwan stared at him but didn't say anything.

"You know," Vidar said calmly. "Defense attorneys are not the enemy, but one of the basic building blocks of the justice system. It's not a good idea to try to upend that."

The officer looked puzzled.

Now, Vidar opens his binder. Marinko observes his movements with vigilance.

They apprehended him on the spot in the café. He didn't have time to let anyone know, and he still hasn't been allowed to make any calls, so maybe this will work.

"I don't care what you've done," Vidar says. "I just want to know where you've been."

Marinko frowns, his forehead turning into a hostile *M*. "Where I've been? Why?"

"You and Božo Miljanovic lived together in a house at Västra Långgatan 23 in Munka-Ljungby, I know that much. What I'm wondering is whether you also stayed from time to time in an apartment on Ellenbergavägen."

"Ellenbergavägen is only a few blocks away; why would I live there, too?"

"That's what I don't quite understand," Vidar says, looking down at the binder and placing his index finger on the page. "Ellenbergavägen 8A. You haven't been there?"

"No."

Vidar stands up. "Okay. Thank you very much."

Marinko sits there with his mouth agape, confusion all over his face.

Nashwan looks equally confused; he's waiting outside the room with his arms crossed. "You're done already?"

"Yes."

"What about the rest? Aren't you going to ask him about the break-in in—"

"The others can handle that."

A grim sigh from Nashwan. "So this is about Markström."

Vidar looks at him in surprise, but he feels a sudden, searing sensation inside. Just before Christmas he'd crossed over to the other side. He'd made contact. He can certainly be blamed for that.

"No, this is about our job. After all, Miljanovic is one of our suspects in this case."

"I just think all this digging in the Marbäck murder is—"

"I'm not digging."

"I mean, for my part, I think Christensson is best left where he is."

"I think so, too."

Nashwan looks at him imploringly. "Do you really?"

"Yes."

"What would the hypothesis be? That Božo and Darko wrote the threatening letters? That they had a relationship with her?"

"Nashwan." Vidar's tone hardens. "Let it go. I don't have a hypothesis."

Nashwan looks defiant. Vidar stares back. At last Nashwan gives in. His gaze slides toward Marinko.

"Do we think he lived in that apartment, then?"

"No, we don't think so."

"So why did you say that?"

You have to hide your actual objective. That's the trick, simple on paper but more difficult face-to-face, when there's something on the line. You ask a question that's really irrelevant; the important part of the question is in the detail, in what appears to be trivial. By getting an answer to the uninteresting question, you also get what you really want to know.

"Miljanovic obviously doesn't live where he's listed," Vidar says. "So it's within the realm of possibility that he's lying low at one of his friends' places. Marinko's if I were to guess. He didn't correct me when I mentioned Västra Långgatan, which he would have done if I'd guessed wrong. If I recall, we haven't had eyes on that house for a while, so it might be worth checking out."

"So we're going to do a home visit?"

"We are," says Vidar.

"A giant white policeman and an equally giant but non-white policeman. I actually think we'd make a good team on TV."

"I don't watch TV," Vidar says. "Now, come on."

49

With a dark gray Nissan Primera, all the pieces fall into place.

Edvard Christensson claimed that a car was parked outside the Markströms' house when he arrived. It was dismissed as an impossibility. Three cars were identified and cleared. The driver of the last car, an older man in a rust-brown Mazda that was practically just as old, stubbornly insisted that the house wasn't on fire when he passed through Tolarp, saying he would have noticed if it was.

At the same time, Ulrika Antonsson claimed to have seen a car go by immediately *after* the fire started.

One of them was mistaken: Either Ulrika saw the car before the fire started, not after, or else the fire hadn't engulfed the house yet when the driver went by, and so he didn't notice.

That was how the contradiction was interpreted. But that interpretation wasn't necessarily the right one.

There was a fourth car.

Božo and Darko drove it during the fall of 1994. The car was junked in the summer of 2000 and, unfortunately enough, a detailed forensic investigation of the car was never performed even though it had ended up in police possession shortly after the brothers' arrest in the spring of 1995. There is an evidence log sheet, of course, but there are no notes that reference searches for hair, bodily fluids, or other biological traces that might have supported or dismissed the idea that Lovisa Markström had ever been in the car or had any sort of contact with the brothers.

And she probably never did, but that doesn't matter. The pieces fit. When Vidar closes his eyes, he can almost see it:

It's November 1994. A dark gray Nissan Primera drives through Marbäck. In it are two brothers. They hit the Markströms' house. Lovisa comes home and surprises them. They are forced to take drastic measures. They kill Lovisa and try to do the same to Christensson. He manages to get away. She is left behind.

Six months later, it happens again, in Ljungby. The brothers' handling of the situation this time is too goal oriented, too collected. Burglars aren't this rational when they panic; they do things they shouldn't, blunder and fumble, make mistakes. They probably made some back in Marbäck, too, but they got lucky. The fire destroyed every trace of them.

When it's time for Ljungby, they know what to do. They've already done it once.

Evening, Friday, January 7, 2005. Vidar is trying to keep a low profile in the car, which is parked near Västra Långgatan 23 in Munka-Ljungby. His eyes are on the house huddled in the darkness before him. Still nothing. All the lights are out. Nashwan took off an hour ago.

A car goes by. Vidar sinks down in his seat. It's cold. He misses Patricia and Amadia. On the radio they're talking about the aftereffects of the tsunami and an approaching storm.

Late that night he is relieved and heads home. Amadia is lying next to Patricia in the big bed. Vidar strokes his wife's hair and takes Amadia's hand. She squeezes it in her sleep, but Vidar remains awake.

Patricia mumbles in her sleep, places her palm to his cheek, stretches up, and gives him a light kiss on the chin.

"Everything okay, honey?"

"Fine."

"Hmm." Patricia gently taps one finger against his cheek. "Tell me."

"You're sleeping."

"No."

Vidar gazes at the ceiling. Blinks.

"I'm just not totally convinced," he says.

Patricia, likely too tired to resist, turns her head and strokes Amadia's sleeping back, then moves closer to Vidar.

"Because?"

Well. Where to start? He begins to explain in a whisper. Patricia runs her hand over his chest.

"I understand. Or, I don't know if I understand. Do whatever you feel you have to do. But if it involves walking around splashing gasoline all over the yard, give me a heads-up."

Vidar chuckles quietly. "It was only water and dish soap."

She doesn't say anything for a minute. "You know, I have a life, too. I mean, a life outside this family. I want to keep having that. But this winter, it's basically been impossible because of . . ."

"Me?"

"Because of the situation. I didn't say anything because I thought it was only temporary, with the ten-year anniversary and everything. But this isn't going to work. So I just want to have it said. You're basically never home. And I'm not saying that because, like, *be with me instead*. I'm not that kind of person and you know it. I'm saying it because I have a life, too, friends and coworkers, conferences and parties and so on. But I've barely . . ."

"But you never said anything."

It sounds more accusatory than it is.

"Maybe I didn't feel like I could."

But, Patricia, I'm not a mind reader.

That's what he wants to say, even though he knows it would be a bad idea. She never said anything. Should he have realized? Probably. But when? It's hard to learn to live with another person.

He squeezes her hard. "I understand," he whispers, although he's not sure he does. They listen to each other breathing in the dark.

50

Some sort of end is approaching. It's January 8, a Saturday morning that will move toward evening and night. The night the old forest disappears.

Isak and Theo need clothes for graduation. They each received money for suits for Christmas and were urged to buy them now before school starts again, because the parents know their children and are aware that there's a great risk the money will be used for other things.

Isak has never owned a suit. Jackets, stiff shirts, and ties are rare in the Nyqvist household; Dad likes to say that something weird happens to his face as soon as anyone forces him into a suit. It's like he walks around looking miffed the whole time.

Isak wonders if he has inherited this trait. He hopes not. He saw Edvard in a suit once but can't remember the event; maybe it was a birthday or something. He looked great in it and Isak hopes that this, no matter what else, is a trait he has inherited from his uncle.

The shoulders should be straight. He read that somewhere. That's how you know the suit jacket fits. Tough to say whether Edvard's shoulders were straight, but probably they were.

As Isak and Theo cross the square in town, the wind picks up. The stores have only just opened and the city center is still sleepy, as if everyone's still recovering from their Friday-night benders.

Isak stands in front of the fitting room mirror for a long time. He doesn't feel right in the suit, but he supposes he doesn't look that bad, and at least the shoulders are straight.

"This is so unnecessary," Theo says from the other side of the curtain in the fitting room. "I could buy five video games for this."

"Or a whole lot of actual, regular clothes."

"Or beer."

Standing there in the fitting room, Isak considers his reflection. He does look an awful lot like his uncle. But who is he seeing, really? What does Karin see? Or Theo?

They dutifully purchase their suits and leave the store. The wind on the square yanks at their bags.

"We missed the bus." Theo makes a face. "The next one doesn't go for two hours. Fuck, it's so windy."

They take a bus to Brogård and walk the rest of the way. The strong wind makes the wide-open expanses of fields undulate. In the distance, the treetops are bowing down, as if entranced by something no one can see.

"Hey," Theo says as they're finally approaching Marbäck. "Wanna play King's Rock?"

It's been years. Not like Theo to suggest it, but when they get to the falls and hear the familiar roar Isak is surprised to find that he feels very calm.

"Shit, man, it's going to be so cold on our feet," Isak says.

"That's part of the challenge."

They carefully stash the bags with their new suits next to a tree and start to collect rocks. Isak takes up position next to Theo, ready, a rock in hand, and looks at the falls.

"The water's so high. Look at those small boulders there, they're almost totally under water."

"It must be the wind."

It's whipping up the water. But it feels less windy here; Isak and Theo are sheltered by nature.

"Dad said he heard on the radio this morning that the storm isn't supposed to be that bad," Theo says. "So maybe the power won't go out, at least."

No power. A nightmare. The power goes out a lot, in both summer and winter, anytime there's a thunderstorm or strong winds. No power, no *San Andreas*. That's their plan for the evening, to meet up at Karl's place and finish the game. They have only a few tasks left.

Isak tosses the first rock. A miss. He takes a step forward.

Theo misses, too. "Did you hear they found the Nilssons?"

Isak has heard. But they haven't returned yet.

"I guess they'll be back next week," Theo says. "Mom's friend had talked to them on the phone. She said they were still in shock."

"At least they're alive."

Isak throws another rock. He misses again. He takes a step forward. "Yeah."

Theo glances at Isak. "You saw Edvard before Christmas, right? How was it?"

"Fine, I guess."

Theo's turn. Hit. "What did you talk about? If you want to tell me, I mean."

"Sure, it's cool. Kind of everything, really." Isak throws again. *Clack,* it rings out. The hit sings through his body. "I wanted to wish him a happy New Year, and I tried to call, but he hasn't gotten back. Apparently he's sick right now."

"Sick, how do you mean?"

"Stomach flu, I think."

Both Theo and Isak miss. Soon Isak is taking a step into the swift water.

It soaks through his shoes, and the cold is so sharp that he gasps. "Fuck, it never used to be this cold."

"We're just wussier. Or else we have crappier shoes."

"Edvard says he didn't do it."

Theo stops short. "Do what?"

"Kill Lovisa. And this policeman believes him. I think."

"Okay. Who?"

"The one who lives here. Vidar Jörgensson."

"So, what? Do you believe it?"

Above them, the wind blows harder. It whines.

"I don't know. It's just so hard to . . . I don't know. I'm going to start by talking to him when he's better."

Afternoon arrives and the sky darkens. Isak's feet are numb, and Theo's teeth are chattering. On their way back they walk along the old gravel path that borders the farms. The animals typically spend afternoons standing very still and eating, as if it were a holy occasion and you must show respect. Today they're moving back and forth anxiously, going in and out of the big, solid barns. The farmer stands nearby, raising his eyes to the sky.

In hindsight, this is what Isak remembers: He looks toward his best friend's house. Behind it is the red playhouse with its white trim and black door. It's a sturdy and resilient little cottage; it's made it through a lot: storms, heavy rains, blizzards, even accidents and attacks. Throughout the years, they've run into it on their bikes, jumped on its roof while playing war, and used everything from baseball bats to airsoft guns on it since it occasionally played the role of enemy headquarters and therefore had to be demolished.

But the playhouse has held up. Even the time Jonas Persson from Breared lost control of his moped—they say he had been drinking, which he surely had been—and drove straight into the playhouse, it was fine. Not so Jonas Persson, who had to go to the emergency room with blood on his face and his right foot at a funny angle. And they'd had to take the moped to Bernt's workshop down by the factory buildings.

It's three o'clock in the afternoon. In just over eight hours, Hurricane Gudrun's powerful grip—not unlike how you might imagine the hand of God—will tear the playhouse from the ground, carry it over the house, and smash it to kindling on the asphalt of Svanåsvägen.

51

"Hello?"

"Yes, hello. Clara Nikander here."

As Vidar straightens up, his back cracks. He wishes he could recline the driver's seat, but he wouldn't be able to see well enough. He's cold; a hard wind is blowing, catching hold of the car and rocking it.

She asks if she's interrupting anything. "No, not at all."

Luckily enough, he's alone. It's a side effect of deception—the constant feeling that you will soon be caught.

Clara says she has two questions.

"Okay."

"How are things going with Edvard Christensson?"

"I can't really discuss that."

"I know. But how is it going?"

A car stops down the street. A woman steps out. The wind tugs at her hair, her coat; it yanks at her plastic bags. She hurries into her yard.

"What was the other question?" he asks.

"Your boss contacted me over the holidays."

"Aronsson? What did she want?"

"She wondered if you had been in touch with us."

Vidar goes stiff in his seat. "What did you tell her?"

"I said no, of course."

He exhales. "Thanks. Why was she asking?"

"A colleague of hers had apparently seen you leaving our building when you were here. She just wanted to check and make sure everything was on the up-and-up. So, I'm guessing that means she hasn't talked to you? That was my other question."

"No. She hasn't."

"Wasn't she one of K-G's closest allies?"

"Yeah. Or at least, she became one in time."

She had been one of the first female higher-ups at headquarters. K-G avoided her like the plague at first, but once he realized she was an extremely capable police officer and an even more competent manager, he began to give in. By the end, he was very fond of her.

Then it happens. A light comes on in one of the windows.

Nothing has broken the lull around the house on Västra Långgatan; no one has come or gone. But there's definitely a light on.

Vidar squints. He catches a glimpse of a shadow inside. "I have to go," he says.

Vidar gets out of the car and steps into a brisk, sharp wind. It must be close to a full gale. He hunches over as he walks toward the small, yellow one-story house. A neat little pightle of a yard, as unkempt as anyone else's this time of year. The house could use a fresh coat of paint. No car, but there's a bike that's been knocked over by the wind.

Vidar does the nice thing and rights it, leaning it against the wall before stepping onto the narrow stone stairs and pressing his thumb to the doorbell. Movement inside. Steps. Hesitation—Vidar can feel it. *Just open up.* The lock turns and a short man with a familiar face, surprised look, and dark hair that's graying at the temples studies him.

"Božo," Vidar says. "Good evening."

52

As long as Isak and Theo stick to the protected areas between houses it's fine, but there's a shockwave moving down Svanåsvägen. It hits your belly, chest, and face, and muffles your ears, takes your breath away. They pass the bus stop on the way to Karl's place. The pole that holds the old timetable is swaying alarmingly, and rain whips their faces. Then they see it.

Tiles are lifting from rooftops. Sometimes that happens in a strong wind; they loosen and fall to the ground.

"Look," Theo says.

The roofing tiles come loose but just hang in the air for an instant before being carried away; some fly so far you can't see where they land.

"Come on, let's get out of here," Isak says.

Karl's parents are gone for the weekend. He meets them in the hall with a can of beer in one hand and a controller in the other. It's time to finish *San Andreas.*

"There are like five tasks left," he says. "And they're all a real bitch."

"Perfect," Theo says.

The wind is no longer whining. It's not roaring, either. The storm sounds like thunder—a deep, sustained rumble.

The village gets its power from bare-wire lines from the early

1900s. They look like thick, gray ropes; they're not insulated and they are sensitive creatures, mounted on old poles in the forest. The wires in town were upgraded long ago to modern lines, or buried underground. This is how rural people are exploited: Folks in Marbäck, Simlångsdalen, and Tofta pay just as much for their electricity as those in the city, but out here, the second a tree, branch, or twig falls onto the lines, the power goes out.

They've made it through two beers each and have been playing for an hour or so. Two more tasks and they'll be done with *San Andreas*. Suddenly everything goes quiet and black. Theo throws down his controller in the darkness.

"Shit. We were so close."

"Anyone have a lighter?" Karl asks.

Theo hands his over and Karl begins to light candles and tea lights. Isak finishes his beer and walks over to the window.

All of Marbäck has gone dark.

They're not going to get the worst of it. Marbäck suffers extreme damage from Gudrun; when people see pictures of the effects of the storm they are shocked, but there are those who have it even worse. They learn this, too, Theo, Karl, Isak, and everyone else: There's always someone who has it worse.

No matter what, you should be grateful.

"I'm sorry," says the man on the phone. "Edvard actually isn't here. He's receiving care at Södra Älvsborg Hospital."

Isak's stomach clenches. "What? Well, how is he?"

"Listen, I don't know, but he was complaining of a severe migraine."

"You have to go to the hospital for that?"

"No," the correctional officer says uncertainly. "Like I said, I don't know much, but I'm sure he'll be fine."

"But I've been trying to get hold of him for days. It must be really bad if he's too sick to talk on the phone."

"We've been a little understaffed, too, I have to confess, what with Christmas and New Year's. We've been pretty busy just keeping order in the units. That's not supposed to carry over to their relationships with you—their families, I mean—but unfortunately that's just the way of it sometimes. I apologize."

"Can I call them? The hospital, I mean."

"You can," he says. He gives Isak a phone number.

So that's why Edvard hasn't been able to get in touch. It's understandable, and Isak feels a little relieved. He calls Södra Älvsborg Hospital, but there's no answer. This will turn out to have an explanation too: Gudrun has caused a chain-reaction crash on the highway outside Borås. The wounded are brought to Södra Älvsborg and overwhelm the already seriously burdened hospital.

The rain whips at the windowpanes. Karl's house creaks. The electrical outlets are buzzing. Gusts are creeping up through the baseboards. If you hold your palm to the windows, you can feel the pressure on the other side.

"We should probably cover the windows," Isak says.

"What?" Karl says, still lighting tea lights.

When Isak turns to face them he sees fear flicker in their eyes, just as it's flickering in his own chest.

"In case they blow in."

53

Božo Miljanovic stands with one hand on the door handle, looking curiously at Vidar.

"You're a policeman."

"That's right." He offers his hand. "Vidar Jörgensson." Božo gazes at the hand blankly.

"What do you want?"

"To come in. This wind is awful."

Božo's neck is thick. His mouth is small. His eyes are big, brown, and watchful.

"But what are you doing here?"

"I want to talk to you."

"What about?"

"Josif Marinko."

"He's not home. I don't know where he is."

"I want to talk *about* him, not with him." Vidar throws out his hands. "The sooner you let me in, the sooner you'll be rid of me."

Božo glances over Vidar's shoulder.

"I'm alone," Vidar clarifies.

One of the most skillful burglars in Skåne steps to the side.

It smells stuffy. Drooping plants decorate the kitchen windows. "Have you been away?"

"Just over the holidays," Božo says, pulling out a kitchen chair and nodding at Vidar to take a seat on the other side.

"I don't suppose you happened to be in Vallås, in Halmstad, along with Josif Marinko on the day before Christmas Eve?"

Božo shakes his head. "I was in Lund. I have family there."

"Can they corroborate that? If I were to call them up, for example?"

"As long as the phone lines survive the storm, sure."

It's a cozy kitchen. There are small paintings on the walls and old photographs of an extended family, all dressed up: serious men and women. The pictures weren't taken in Sweden. On the table is a checked cloth, and on top of that is what looks to be a handwritten shopping list.

"Do you live here?"

"Yes, I've been here for a little while."

"I want to ask you," Vidar says slowly, "about the fall of 1994."

"Why?"

"Some questions have come up in a case we're working on. I'm curious about what you know."

Božo looks puzzled. It's well played, but you can tell he has guessed what's up. There's a glint to his eyes.

"What I know about what?"

"A woman died in Marbäck, outside of Halmstad, back then. I'd like to ask you about it. I know you and your brother—"

"I don't want to talk about it."

Vidar raises his eyebrows. "Why not?"

"My brother is dead. We had nothing to do with what happened in Tolarp."

Božo stands up.

"Božo, I want—"

"I just need to take a leak. I'll be right back. Stay there."

Vidar doesn't have much choice. He watches Božo go, watches the short, stout man walk into the bathroom. He reaches for the shopping list. *Meat, Red onion, Cream, Thyme, Potatoes* . . . Vidar studies the capital letters, the small curves and angles of the ink.

A number of features of this handwriting look very much like those in the threatening letters. Vidar slips his hand into the inner pocket of his jacket, resting his fingers on the reassuring butt of his service weapon just under his left armpit.

It's the small details that get you.

Tolarp.

Božo knew the name, even though Vidar hadn't used it. As if he knew.

Vidar keeps his hand on the gun. He listens to the man as he moves around the bathroom, trying to tell if any noises are out of the ordinary. A flush. The faucet turns on, then off. The door opens and closes. Plodding steps. Božo sinks down at the table. Slowly, Vidar takes his hand from the weapon.

"Did you write this?"

"I was going to go shopping, but I changed my mind when I saw how windy it was."

"You said you and your brother had nothing to do with what happened in Tolarp."

"We didn't."

"But you said *Tolarp.*"

Božo studies Vidar's hands, how they rest against the tabletop. "That occurred to me too," he says. "Oops."

54

Strange odors arise. The smell of forest and soil and water and winter, but also an acrid, metallic stink. Something that smells like smoke leaks into the house, through the narrow cracks at the baseboards and the windows. Isak and Theo draw back one of the heavy blankets and gaze into the January night.

"Shit, look at that," Theo hisses.

Beyond the silhouette of the forest is a dark shape, the roof of an old barn. As if an invisible, powerful foot has decided to stomp on it, the barn suddenly vanishes.

"I wish we could have some music." Isak turns his back on the window. "It would be nice to hear something other than this fucking wind."

"I think there's an old boom box in the basement," Karl says.

With a flashlight in one hand, he leads them to the basement door. Isak's phone rings. It's Mom.

He sighs. "Go on down. I'll be right there."

Isak puts the phone to his ear. The line crackles and hisses.

You have to be prepared for the worst. That way it will never be as bad as you feared. And yet, it will be. Sooner or later.

Mom's voice is loud and shrill. "Are you all okay over there?"

"Yeah, but I'll probably stay here until it blows over."

"Good. You do that."

"How about there? You sound weird, what's wrong?"

"The power is out here. We heard the telephone lines were knocked out further up so I wanted to call before they came down here, too."

She lowers her voice.

"What did you say?" Isak presses the phone to his ear. "I can't hear you, you have to talk louder."

"I said I just got a phone call from Borås. It's Edvard." The call went to her because she was listed as next of kin.

Yes. Sooner or later, everything turns out to be exactly as bad as you feared.

"What did you say?"

She sounds indifferent. Maybe she is. Isak hears *migraine* and *pain-killers, morphine* and *overdose, declared dead at quarter past seven.*

The open basement door awaits him. Somewhere down in the darkness, a beam of light flickers from the flashlight in Karl's hand.

"But I just talked to them. They said everything was fine."

"The hospital?"

"No, I couldn't get in touch there so I called the prison."

"They probably didn't know."

"Okay." He should say something more. "How are you?"

"I'm sad, of course, he's my brother, but I . . ." Seconds of silence tick by. The sound of the storm increases; the creaks in the house are sharper now, harder. "I shouldn't have told you like this, I just wanted to make it before . . . I thought it would be better if you heard it from me instead of someone at the prison or the hospital."

"It's okay." He adds, "After all, I barely know him."

"But . . ."

At that moment, Gudrun severs the telephone lines and the call drops. Isak stares at the phone.

I barely know him.

He walks to the basement stairs and calls down to Karl and Theo. Either they don't hear him, or else he isn't making a sound.

Impossible to go down there. Unthinkable. Home. Edvard is dead. He has to get home.

Isak staggers into the hall and puts on his coat and shoes. The window nearest him blows in; the sharp pieces slice through the tablecloths and blankets the boys hung up. The storm roars in through the window.

He pictures his uncle. There he is: Midsummer's Eve. He can hear his voice. *The best days are the ones we spend with the people we care about the most. All the other days we're just sort of waiting.*

He looks around one last time.

And then he hurls himself into the dark.

55

He should have brought someone with him. The neighborhood is sleepy. People would rather stay inside than keep an eye on their neighbors, especially on a night like this. Sitting at this table, Vidar is alone and vulnerable.

He leans forward. Although there's no reason to, he lowers his voice. "What happened? That's all I want to know."

"Happened? Nothing happened."

"You and Darko were out on a crime spree in the fall of 1994. In November you hit the Markströms' house in Tolarp, just outside Marbäck. Tell me about that."

Božo crosses his arms; his chair creaks as he leans back.

"We knew about what happened, you know. Me and my brother, we followed it in the newspaper."

"What do you mean, you followed it?"

"You have to keep tabs on what's up in the general area, if you get my drift."

Božo starts to get up again.

"I'd prefer you remain seated, Božo. Until you're done telling your story."

"Talking makes me thirsty." Božo goes to the fridge and grabs its handle. "You want me to tell you? The truth? Then you can decide whether you believe it or not. I know that what I'm about to tell you is true, but you'll have to make up your own mind."

He opens the fridge. Vidar's hands are still but every muscle is tense and his heart is pounding.

"Tell me," he says.

Božo takes out a can of soda pop. He taps the lid before opening it. The can hisses.

Vidar forces himself to relax.

"So," Božo says. "Want me to teach you how it works? If there was a concert in some backwoods town, that was fantastic, because everyone would be there. Empty houses, you know. But in some ways there was a downside, because with lots of people moving around it was easier to be spotted. This was in the nineties; you had to read the papers because that was basically the only place to get any information. So we kept an eye out. That's why we made it as long as we did. And it's true, I mean, yeah, we were moving through Sweden."

He takes a gulp. Burps. Sits back down at the table. It has started to rain.

The storm sends hard drops against the windowpanes.

"Once the media started putting the pieces of the map together, they would figure out our path. We wanted everyone to be afraid, so they would feel like we might strike their house next, but no one would know for sure. That's what we wanted, to be, you know . . ."

"Remembered?"

"Exactly. So stupid, but that's how we felt. So we checked there, too. It's true, we considered the area around Skedala, Marbäck, and what's it called, Simlångsdalen? But we decided to lie low. And then, you know, we kept reading the papers so we would know what was up, so we saw what had happened. To that girl in Tolarp." He shrugs. "That's the truth."

"Why did you decide to lie low?"

Božo offers the can of pop to Vidar. "We can share if you want."

"No, thanks. Why didn't you hit Tolarp?"

He makes a face as if Vidar has reminded him of something

embarrassing. "Oh, you know, we had been a little careless. We got a little too bold. My brother thought someone was watching him. Our cousin in Lund was turning forty right around then, and that's a big deal in our family; we didn't want to be stuck in the slammer and miss it. Plus we were flush with cash at the time. We didn't need to do anything."

Vidar observes Božo's hand, his fingers around the can; he pictures it raising the candelabra toward Lovisa's head.

"What you're saying isn't true," Vidar says. "Where were you on the night of November thirteenth, 1994?"

Božo is staring at him. His expression is suddenly grim. He slowly lets go of the can.

"Get out of here before things turn ugly."

"Unfortunately I can't do that, Božo."

"I want you to leave now."

Vidar remains seated. A strong gust makes the house creak and an instant later, the power goes out. Everything is black and silent. And then he hears Božo slowly rising in the dark.

56

Something cuts through the roar.

It's the trees. The forest whimpers and cries, wailing ahead of its collapse. Isak's heart is in his throat.

Spruce trees bend across the path with their heavy moans, and the ground shakes. Branches tear at him. Downed power lines spark and crackle. The rain is tiny nails against his skin.

Between the fallen trees he makes out a shape. An opening and then a field, a barn that has survived. It's Ernst Hedman's. The heavy wooden doors are open, flapping in the wind. He fights his way over.

By the time he reaches the barn, the door is gone. The entrance is a huge, gaping hole. Then he sees. The storm is dragging the door across the field, its hinges trailing and banging behind it.

Hedman's barn is one of the largest in the village. It houses the farmer's horses and cows, their feed, and what's left of the year's threshed seed. It smells warm, like old wood, hay, and horseshit in here. The animals are stamping in their stalls and corners, mooing and moaning.

Finally inside. Finally. He made it.

The horse closest to him stops and turns its head. Isak has no experience with horses, except for that he and Edvard sometimes used to watch them move around their pastures in the summer.

His legs shaking, he steps into the stall. It's an anxious mare. Isak pats her awkwardly. It doesn't help—kind of the opposite. She isn't even looking at him anymore, just standing there trembling.

Something warm is running down his cheek. Isak wipes it away with the back of his hand and notices a dark streak. His fingers search his face until it stings. The pale lining of his coat is the wrong color. *I'm bleeding. I'm bleeding a lot. Help me.*

At last he dares to put one hand above the horse's muzzle and pets her between the eyes and up on her forehead. She gets a little bloody, but she doesn't seem to care. Instead she takes a step toward Isak and lowers her giant face as if she were about to attack. But she doesn't. Instead she burrows her head against Isak's side, and he thinks he can hear her exhale.

Something catches up with him. He's bleeding. Edvard is dead. How is it possible? It's like . . . well, exactly what it's *like* is kind of hard to say. It's impossible. He's bleeding. He never had time to tell him about the bottle. What that felt like. There's so much Isak will never get to say now.

Later on he'll have trouble remembering exactly what he said to the horse, but he thinks it had to do with Edvard. About what happened. How it sort of doesn't make sense. He might have said *migraine* and *painkillers, declared dead at quarter past seven.*

Isak comforts the mare as best he can. It's a distraction, somehow. Her trembling subsides. She has clear, dark eyes. They glisten like pools, and Isak thinks she must be smart, for a horse.

Then suddenly, as he's standing next to her, everything becomes perfectly, perfectly quiet. Complete silence.

Finally. Finally, time to rest.

"There," he says, placing his hand on the mare's cheek. "Now it's quiet."

The mare whuffles and shakes herself, nudging him away. *There, thanks, I'm fine now.*

Exhausted, he backs out of the stall and sinks to the ground among hay and droppings and other filth. It's nice just to rest for a minute. *We can handle more than we think, but not without limits.* He tries touching his cheek again. The cut is bleeding profusely and, in the last few minutes, or maybe seconds, it's started to throb.

The horses rear.

In an instant, a din rises from the silence and an invisible wave sweeps over the barn. Gudrun returns with a roar and, although Isak rushes to the door, he realizes it's all over.

Gudrun lifts the barn from the earth and sweeps it along.

Afterward, measurements are taken. All in all, the barn moved more than twenty yards. Half a mile away, standing inside the neighboring house with his binoculars, old man Göransson watches Ernst Hedman's barn lift from the ground. Upon landing it stands for a moment, then collapses like a house of cards.

Of the thirty-seven animals inside, twenty-five die on the night of the storm. Another eleven are put down afterward. Only one animal, a mare, survives. How, no one knows.

"We're so happy she made it," Ernst Hedman says to the local paper as he stands on a farm that's gone without electricity and water for a week.

At the height of it, half a million households were without power. But it's not electricity or water that is on everyone's minds. Behind Hedman is a fallen forest; a life's work and fortune has been destroyed overnight. He's only one of thousands of farmers and forest owners in southern Sweden who will go under in the wake of Gudrun.

"We're so happy," he repeats. And then he bursts into tears.

Isak throws himself out of the barn. Behind him, the animals cry out for help or in rage: *You're deserting us.* Then it's quiet.

The barn is crumpled, leaning.

And then, through the whine of the storm, a sign. Someone is whimpering. The entrance is in pieces, so he has to crawl in.

There she is, the nervous one. The mare is lying down as if trying to hide.

She's whining but goes perfectly still when she sees Isak.

He tries to help her up, but she's too heavy. He tells her so. She seems to understand somehow and struggles her way up.

"Careful," Isak says. "Watch your head, you have to bend down."

The buckling roof creaks. As Isak leads her out of the barn it gives way in a wet, cold cloud of debris and dust. All that's left is wreckage.

He leaves her, although it hurts a little. She looks so alone, standing there limp and dazed, the wind tugging at her mane. She scrapes a hoof at the ground and takes a step forward, shaking herself off.

"I'm sorry," he says.

Then he runs across the field. The wind knocks him over, and he scrapes his hands and knees but fights his way to his feet again.

Soon he'll be home. He just has to get through the forest on this side of the field, and then a little ways up to Svanåsvägen.

The forest closes behind him. It's as dark as the bottom of a well, but that doesn't matter. The nature here is a map that has been etched into him, into his feet and his palms. He can feel his way home. He walks quickly into the depths of the forest. The smell of pitch stings his nose.

And then the trees fall. The roar deafens him. He throws himself out of the way, spitting dirt and needles; he gets on his feet again, he has to keep moving.

Isak tries to determine which way to go, and only then does fear overpower him.

There is no greater danger, he has learned, than getting lost. That's why you learn to find your way, to navigate through the forest more by feelings than by senses.

He takes out his phone. It shakes violently in his hand; it's wet and filthy from rain and dirt, brush and crap. He tries to call home but there's no way; the network is down.

The world is transformed. The paths and the roads where he walked and played as a child are no more. He is lost; he staggers on. Blind—that's how he feels. He's starting to get cold and his senses are sluggish; he's tired and weak. Everything hurts. Roots of fallen trees tower, the size of houses, giving off a bad odor.

The forest twists and turns around Isak, or maybe he's dizzy. Sharp branches tear at him, and before he knows it he plants his foot into a huge, dark maw that has formed in the ground.

Weird, Isak thinks. And then he's falling.

57

It's black as a coal cellar in the house on Västra Långgatan. Violence hangs in the air between Vidar and Božo at the kitchen table, like an agreement in the silence.

"I've got candles," Božo's voice says in the darkness.

"How did you know Lovisa Markström?"

"I didn't."

"That's not what I heard."

"What did you hear?" Božo sneers.

"You didn't expect her to come home, did you?"

Something clicks. Vidar draws a breath. *He's armed. Shit.*

A warm, orange flame appears before him. Božo's holding a cigarette lighter and smiling. Vidar hurries to take his hand from the butt of his weapon.

"You said November thirteenth, right? Ninety-four?"

"Yes."

"Then I'm afraid you're mistaken," Božo says.

He leaves the kitchen. The tiny flame is a warm, glowing ball in all the blackness. Beyond the windows, the wind is overturning garbage cans and dragging bicycles across the street.

"You need to talk to me, Božo. Where are we going with this?"

Božo stops at a cabinet in the hallway. His eyes are black in the glow of the flame.

"Božo."

"Calm down."

He pulls out a box of candles. And then a photo album, the old kind, bound in dark leather. He lights a few of the candles and places them in a candelabra. The glow gets a little stronger.

He pages through the album.

Vidar stands in front of him, uncertain.

"You're in luck. It so happens I remember that particular day. Typically it's a little, what's the word, absurd to come around and ask what an innocent man was doing on a particular day ten years ago. Most people hardly remember what they were up to a week ago."

He holds out the album. A photograph. A big family dinner; everyone seems to have gathered for the picture. They're sitting or standing in a row alongside a set table, and they're all smiling at the photographer: men, women, children. Only the large German shepherd in one corner has its attention on the plates instead. Behind them is a large mullioned window, and beyond that is darkness. The two brothers are near the center of the photo.

"I told you," Božo says in the flickering light of the candles. "My cousin was turning forty. The family rented a place in Lund. Here I am, and there's my brother."

In the bottom corner is a date: *13 11 94,* and on the back is a time stamp. "I told you, what I'm saying is the truth. I've got it on video, too, if you want to see it."

All the air goes out of Vidar. *No. It can't be true.*

The picture was taken at 10:54.

It would have been impossible for them to be in Marbäck an hour later. He walks to the window like a sleepwalker. Roof tiles are blowing away.

Trees are falling. He's not going to be able to get home.

"Sit back down," Božo says from behind him. "It's okay. I have more pop in the fridge."

58

It's another time now. Isak is little again. He, Theo, Karl, and a few other boys are running toward the just-frozen pond down on the field with their ice skates, hockey sticks, pucks, and goals in hand. Joy follows in their tracks, the sound of little voices and excited breaths.

Down on the ice they put on their skates, set up the goals, and divide into teams. It's fall. Cold steam rises from their mouths. The world around them is gray and brown.

The kids' skates slice at the uneven ice. Isak passes to Theo, who shoots and misses. The puck slides into the snow, and Karl goes to retrieve it.

Something moves in the corner of his vision. Isak looks at the edge of the forest. There she is, Edvard's Lovisa. She's waiting, her arms crossed as if she's cold.

Behind him, Karl has found the puck. The loud *clack clack clack* as they pass the black rubber disc between them echoes around and around the field. Isak receives it and passes it on, turning toward the forest again. She's still there. For a long, quiet second she and Isak are looking straight at each other.

She's so pretty.

Now someone else is coming. A guy. He's moving toward her through the trees. He's wearing a red cap, a dark jacket, blue jeans. *Oh,* Isak thinks, *it's Edvard.* It's kind of hard to tell, they're so far away.

Lovisa startles when she sees him, and she backs up, starting to move away.

"Isak!"

Isak turns his head. The puck is flying at him. He captures it, feints right, and scratches his skates twice to the left. He's free—he passes to Theo, who misses and hits Karl in the mouth.

A tooth flies onto the ice, a wet tail of blood trailing behind. Karl collapses, wailing. They rush over to him.

When Isak looks back at the forest, they're gone, Lovisa and Edvard. He scared her.

But it's starting to hurt. The ice disappears; the edge of the forest dissolves and it gets dark. Everything hurts; his head is pounding, and his back is aching, but worst of all is his arm. At first the pain is just a small, burning point, like someone is sticking a needle into the crease of his elbow. Then it grows and spreads through his arm until it's so great that the darkness around him dissipates and gives way to a blinding white light.

Karl's cry has become Isak's. He screams himself awake.

Isak is lying on his side in dampness and icy water, a whole lot of slush and debris. He tries to move. Lightning shoots through his arm. He stretches out his other hand. Old, chilly stones. He gets to his feet and follows the stones with his hand. A circle.

Everything is fuzzy. He ran through the forest. He remembers that, and the sensation of falling.

Above him, way up high, a slight brightening. Then he knows.

A long time ago, everyone got their water from wells. Most of them are abandoned these days, but a lot of them still remain. There's an old farm well in the forest behind Hedman's place.

He looks up at the opening. Several yards up.

It's strangely quiet down here. He's *under* the storm.

He doesn't dare to look at his arm.

Instead he tries to take out his phone. It's wet and weird and reacts slowly when he presses the buttons, but it works. It's one in the morning. He tries to make an emergency call, but nothing happens. When he holds the phone to his ear, his hand shakes violently.

He can't move his arm. It's just hanging there, useless, at a strange angle, and it looks so nasty that his stomach turns inside out.

He leans back against the cold wall of the well, bends double, and throws up. Snot and tears mix with his vomit. When the gasping dies down, he looks back up at the mouth of the well. He tries to call for help. All that comes out are hoarse shouts that are drowned out by the roar of the storm, and the wind sweeps pine needles and dust, soil and grit into the hole. It gets into Isak's mouth and he coughs.

The secret.

The one Edvard asked about. The dream from earlier, where he was before he regained consciousness. It's all coming back: the ice and the forest, the puck and Lovisa. He tries to recall it in its entirety, remember the context, but he can't.

As if it matters now.

He's lived with his uncle's guilt for so long. Didn't he expect that everything would one day come to a resolution after all? Hasn't he hoped that it would pass? The thought, like in that one Christmas song he actually likes, that if you can see through time, into the future, then one day they'll all be together, if only fate allows.

It didn't.

Instead: emptiness. Guilt and innocence mean nothing in death.

He's getting sleepy and weak, cold and hungry. He also has to take a piss, and what can he do? He pees into the water where he stands.

One second he's leaning against the wall; the next he's sitting in the cold water with his phone in hand. He fell asleep—he scrambles up, shaking with cold. A gray dog sits quietly at his side, watching him.

Maybe it's necessary, everything that happens. Mom says that about life sometimes, that it's probably *all part of the plan, in the end* when things happen the way they do.

Why does this have to be part of the plan?

59

It was the night the ancient forest disappeared.

That day, when Vidar left Marbäck and headed to Ängelholm, it was there, you could see it clearly. It stood where it had always stood just like always. Then came the night, and now that morning is dawning, it's gone.

No one in Marbäck has power. The village rests in a pale blue dawn light. As Vidar walks over to inspect the damage, he sees that the trees that are still standing move gently. He had to park his car down on the highway. Up here you can only go ten or twenty yards before the road is blocked with trees and debris.

The house survived. The pightle, too, although the birches are lying on the grass, leaving deep wounds in the ground. He hardly recognizes the place. The landscape is so changed.

Patricia and Amadia are still asleep after sitting up all night. He would love to join them. Yesterday's defeat and the silence that followed, peppered with awkward small talk between Božo and Vidar, who forced out an apology, left their mark—he's exhausted, almost brittle.

Božo and Darko Miljanovic didn't take Lovisa Markström's life. When he thinks about the only direct link he could find between them—Billy Oredsson's cautious allegation that Lovisa might have mentioned them once—he's almost ashamed. That was in 1993. Why would they have known one another for so long? Why would someone like Lovisa have had anything to do with Božo and Darko? Surely Billy had just misremembered. It happens. Maybe Vidar had asked too many leading questions.

He realizes it now. He let himself be controlled in a way he hasn't before. He let it get too personal. He goes inside and sits down at the kitchen table, where he takes out the copies of the threatening letters that he is still carrying in his inner pocket. He compares them to Božo's shopping list, which he asked if he could take with him before he left. Božo just shrugged.

"Hi," says a sleepy voice behind him. "How are you doing?"

"Fine," Vidar lies.

Patricia puts her arms around him, kisses his neck and his throat, his cheeks.

"I was worried about you," she mumbles.

"Me too, for a while." He laughs cheerlessly. "But it's all okay now. Hey. Can I ask you something?"

"Yeah, sure."

He holds one of the letters next to the shopping list. "Is it just me, or are these awfully similar?"

Patricia raises her eyebrows.

"They're not very similar at all, honey. Come to bed. She's still asleep."

Vidar looks at the pieces of paper one more time. She's right. It's a figment of his imagination. You see what you want to see. Shit.

"I'll be right there," he says. "You go on up."

She leaves him alone at the kitchen table. An emptiness is growing inside Vidar. He gazes out the window. Someone is walking out there, a lone figure with their hands stuffed in the pockets of a heavy coat.

Vidar rises and goes out. The woman is patiently picking her way through the fallen landscape, over trees and branches, looking out for uprooted trees and the pits they leave behind.

"I had to leave the car a ways back," she says. "You, too, I noticed. Wasn't that your car back there?"

It's Chief Inspector Aronsson.

"It was. Good morning."

"Good morning, Jörgensson."

Aronsson takes his hand and gazes out at Marbäck. "It's terrible."

"How are things in Åled?"

"The same. But I just came from town. At least they've got power there." Aronsson takes in the landscape. "They're already calling it a natural disaster. But parts of this must be salvageable, right? I mean, the forest owners will chop it up. Of course, they'll have to plant new forests and those probably won't be usable for quite some time."

"Did you come here to look at the mess?"

"Unfortunately, no. I need to talk to you."

Aronsson doesn't like to move. She prefers to be left alone, at her desk or in her easy chair, engaged with problems that you get paid good money to solve. The fact that she came all the way out here on a Sunday, hours after the storm, no less, is saying something.

"Edvard Christensson died last night."

"He did?"

Aronsson nods grimly.

"How?"

"Pills. They found quite a few painkillers in a hollowed-out part of his bed frame. And he hadn't been feeling well."

"Physically, you mean?"

"Apparently he'd been complaining of migraines. He probably took too many pills and didn't get help in time. Or maybe he didn't want help, if you know what I mean. I'm still not sure—it seems they're not sure at the prison or the hospital, either. I suppose we'll see."

In time, this image will clear up a bit—if you can call it an image. In the first few years of his imprisonment, Christensson had regular access to a painkiller that contained codeine; he had become addicted to it during his time in jail. He used it to self-medicate—as they say about men when they drink too much. Then he quit, they thought. Maybe not.

He didn't get help in time. Or maybe he didn't want help. Does it matter which? Yes. It matters a lot. A guilty man might take his own life. An innocent man wouldn't.

"But," Aronsson continues with a certain measure of reluctance, as if someone had made a dubious play in a game of bridge and she was forced to address it, "I understand you've been involved in this case recently."

"Oh?" Vidar says. "What makes you think that?"

Aronsson looks askance at him. "That trick won't work on me, Jörgensson. I want you to drop this now, not least in light of the fact that the perpetrator is deceased. And if, in the future, you have your doubts about one of our cases, I would appreciate it if you came to me instead."

"I just thought that wasn't how we worked."

Aronsson raises a thin, neatly plucked eyebrow. "How do you mean?"

"I didn't think we would allow someone to spend ten years in prison for a crime he may not have committed, even as we also refuse to consider other perpetrators. As if that's not enough, I never would have imagined that there would be nervous bosses running around hallways and trying to put a lid on it."

"Put a lid on it?"

Dark clouds gather on Aronsson's face. She turns to Vidar and takes a step toward him, cracking her neck side to side. She smells strongly of perfume and coffee.

"Do you have any other suggestion of who might have done it, then? If my sources are correct, your only other hypothesis just went up in smoke."

A stab of pain in Vidar's chest. The only one who knew about that was Nashwan. Vidar had called him on the way home.

"That's right," Aronsson goes on, a hint of enjoyment in her eyes.

"Even your own partner is angry about what you've been up to. What did you expect? Why would two burglars from Skåne have sent threatening letters to *her*? They didn't know one another. It was a delusion, Jörgensson. You've let delusions and wishful thinking control you. You weren't working based off facts; you let something else get in the way. I don't know what the hell that 'something' is, nor do I care, but it's not seemly for a law enforcement officer."

Like he doesn't know that.

"I realized that last night," Vidar says slowly. "And I apologize. But the fact that it wasn't the Miljanovic brothers doesn't mean it was—"

"Edvard Christensson killed Lovisa Markström," Aronsson interrupts him, "and that is a fact the rest of us accepted ten years ago. Honestly, if you ask me, the guy killed himself yesterday. It's unlikely that he took too many painkillers by mistake. He committed suicide, and you and I both know what that indicates. Don't we? *Don't we*, Jörgensson?"

Vidar blinks. "Yes."

"As long as you work for me, you will behave yourself. If you can't do that, don't bother coming in tomorrow."

Aronsson's words fling saliva into Vidar's face.

Behave. As soon as he hears her utter that phrase, he knows he will never forget it.

She turns on her heel.

An ending is drawing near.

60

Finally, a sign. But what kind?

Something sweeps through the well like an even darker shadow. Isak doesn't know what it is, but he has a suspicion. They say that's how it starts when death comes for you. First there's a shadow you can only just make out, a shadow that grows until you're embraced and taken, as if scooped up in a sack.

A voice up above is calling his name. Someone is lowered in, a man in a harness. He has the kind of helmet firemen wear, and he's wearing heavy outerwear, protective gear. He has calm, kind eyes and a gentle voice.

He asks Isak his name, how old he is, how he ended up down here. Isak tells him the truth: His name is Isak Nyqvist, he's eighteen years old, and it's all Lovisa Markström's fault.

"Lovisa Markström?" the man repeats, surprised. "Did you know her?"

"Edvard."

"What did you say? Edvard?"

"My uncle."

"What about him?"

"He knew her. But he's dead now."

The man doesn't blink. Isak wonders if he's a fireman. He says he's part of the volunteer emergency response team, which helps the authorities search for the missing.

"My arm," Isak says. "My arm is . . ."

"I see."

The man is very calm. He tells Isak what he's going to do. Together they will get out of the well.

"Help me as much as you can, but don't worry, everything will be fine either way. You're okay now. Everything is okay."

Isak is so grateful. A steady, warm hand hoists him out of the well. On the surface, other people take hold of him, helping him the last little bit over the edge. They lay Isak on the ground and wrap him in a blanket. The wind is still blowing, but it's not as bad as before. They talk about him, saying *hypothermia* and *disoriented*, *a fracture*; they say *This one got lucky.*

He didn't give his name, the man down there in the well. It doesn't matter. Isak is so grateful that he came down there and helped him up. As Isak's still lying on the ground, the man breathlessly takes off his harness and walks off a ways to stand and stare, gasping, straight into the fallen forest.

This one got lucky. So strange, given the context, to have been fortunate that night.

TWELVE YEARS LATER

Summer 2017

61

The thing with the horse is hard to explain, but according to Ernst Hedman this was more or less what happened.

His vision isn't so good. For almost the last decade, just about all of the work on the old farm has been handled by his children and grandchildren, but when you've been doing something for more than seventy years it can be hard to stop. He wakes up as early now as he did when he was fifteen and started working alongside his father, old farmer Hedman, as a farmhand.

He opens his eyes, shuffles out of bed, and reaches for the reassuring handles of his Rollator. With creaky knees and quiet grunts, he makes his way to the bathroom and sinks onto the toilet in relief. It should have grab bars, according to his kids. You can buy those, but the ridiculousness has to stop somewhere. The Rollator is plenty.

Out in the kitchen, he drinks a glass of water as he observes the land that spreads out beyond the window. The large meadow, the young-growth forest in the near distance; the barn and the stable. It's bright, early on this summer morning. Everything is blurry, but Ernst Hedman can still see it; the images are imprinted in his mind. He feels them as much as he sees them.

It's been an unusually cool summer so far. Usually the weather in Marbäck is full of contrasts: Winter is white and cold; the summer is pulsating and hot, humid and stuffy.

The heat hasn't arrived yet, but it will soon.

Yes, something is coming.

Hedvig is out. The old mare walks slowly across the meadow. She probably doesn't have many years left, but she moves through the pasture with quiet dignity. She stops at the edge, her usual spot, and looks around.

Well. Ernst Hedman places the empty glass next to the sink. *Where are you? Are you coming today?*

All spring and summer, a dark figure has arrived around this time. Maybe it's even been going on longer than that.

Three or four times a week, Ernst Hedman stands at the sink and witnesses the encounter. It's a man—a woman would never walk with such a lumbering gait. He arrives at the edge of the pasture and extends a hand toward Hedvig, who steps forward. Sugar? Maybe.

He pets her for a moment, and they appear to stand there in conversation for a little while, until the figure continues his walk down the path. He rounds the bend toward the Göranssons' farm and is gone.

The last time he was here, it ended differently than usual. He walked up to Hedvig, spoke to her for a moment, and then kept going—but he stopped at one of the village bulletin boards. They are mounted at a few points throughout Marbäck, and on them are maps of the area and the farms, information about the next meeting of the Local Heritage Federation, notices of Christmas markets, information about soccer practice for kids in Breared, things like that.

The figure stood at the bulletin board on his way to the bend in the road and gazed at it for a while. Then he suddenly turned around and went back the same way he had come.

And that was it. A—what's it called—deviation. This was almost a week ago now.

Hedvig stands at the edge of the pasture, curiously turning her big, clever head, scraping one hoof on the ground, shaking herself impatiently.

No, Ernst Hedman thinks. *I'm sorry, but he's not coming today, either.*

62

This summer, a sudden oppressive heat wave. It arrived a week ago and has since settled on the village, making it slow and sleepy. The grass is starting to yellow; water must be rationed. Several of the farmers have gone to town to get more. The heat has snuck in everywhere: the kitchen and the bedrooms, the basement and the garage, into people's brains. It's like everything is pulsing.

Right now, it's intruding on Vidar Jörgensson's sleep. Bright white sunlight is shining into the stuffy bedroom. He reluctantly sits up, squinting. The sweat is a layer of damp and salt on his face, his chest, thighs, back.

It's eight-thirty in the morning and the doorbell is ringing insistently.

Vidar opens a window, turns on the tabletop fan, and wraps himself in his robe, then heads to open the door.

There's a woman on the front steps. Her arms are crossed and resting on her stomach as if she's freezing despite the heat. She takes in his half-open robe, his messy hair, the sweat, the fact that he's barefoot.

"Sorry to bother you. I don't know if we've met." She holds out a cool hand. "Karin."

"How can I help you?"

"May I come in?"

Vidar recognizes her, but at the moment he can't remember where from.

"Is something wrong?"

"It's about Isak. You know each other, don't you?"

"Isak Nyqvist?" Right. Now he knows who she is. "No, I can't say that I do."

"Can I . . . Is it okay if I come in for a little bit?"

Preferably not. Still, he steps aside. Karin takes off her sandals and rubs her belly.

"Okay." Vidar is at a loss. What is he supposed to do now? "Do you want . . . do you want anything? Coffee?"

"No thanks, I'm fine."

He plods into the kitchen and starts making coffee. "Remind me, can you have coffee when you're—"

"Three cups a day," she says and changes her mind. "And I will have one."

"It was a long time ago that my wife was pregnant, so I forget." The coffee maker begins to sputter and hiss from the counter. "When are you due?"

"In October."

He manages a smile. "That's great. Congratulations."

"Thanks."

Vidar crosses his arms and watches her as she stands with her hands on her big belly and her eyes fixed on a spot on the floor.

"You knock on the door to find a worn-out fifty-year-old wearing nothing but a robe, and yet you don't ask if you should come back later."

Karin looks confused.

"It must be important, I mean."

"Isak's been talking about you."

"He has? I haven't seen him since . . . Well, it must have been at the funeral. His uncle's. So that would have been . . . let's see now, more than twelve years ago. I've seen him around the village a few times, of course. But we haven't exactly *seen* each other."

"You're a policeman, right?"

"No."

"But you used to be?"

"Yes, I guess I did."

A few gulps' worth of strong black coffee has trickled into the coffeepot.

He waits, then pours two mugs and sits down at the table, placing one before Karin.

Karin takes a sip and makes a face.

"Strong." She adds some milk. The coffee is the shade of leather now. "Isak is . . ." She hesitates, as if it won't be true until she says the word out loud. "He's missing."

"Since when?"

"July tenth." She clears her throat. "Four days ago."

"When did you last see him?"

"In the morning that day, when I left for work."

Everything was normal then. When she got home, he was gone. "Have you gone to the police?"

"They say there's no reason to suspect foul play. And," she continues, "Missing People doesn't have enough volunteers to organize a search out here this time of year. I asked."

Vidar leans back in his chair. It creaks.

Her nails are bitten to the quick, her fingertips pink. He can sense where this is going. *Can't she just leave?*

"And what do you think?"

"I think something happened." She drinks more of the coffee. "He had . . ." Karin changes course. "It was a turbulent time, that last time you saw him, the funeral in 2005. He had a few wild years after that. I thought about leaving him more than once. But after that, about when we turned twenty-five, he calmed down. So I stayed. And now . . ." She rubs her belly. "Well. But it hasn't exactly been smooth sailing."

"But what do you think happened?"

Karin gazes down at the table. When she looks up at Vidar, her eyes are shiny.

"He's been acting strange recently. We've been talking about kids a lot. This little guy wasn't exactly planned, or whatever. And I guess Isak didn't react the way I was expecting, he got really . . ." She hesitates to say the word, as if it's very important to use the right one and she's not sure this is it. "I don't know what I had been expecting, but he got all worried. It felt *kymigt*, he said, and I never really understood what he meant by that. And then he started . . . Well, he disappeared."

"Disappeared?"

"But that time he came back," she is quick to add. "I mean, he was only gone for a day. He stayed at Karl's place, apparently, one of his old friends. When he got home, he smelled like whiskey." She takes a deep breath. "It's happened several times, but he's never been gone this long."

Vidar rests his arms on the table. "So it's happened before."

"Yeah, but not—"

"How long was he gone, at most?"

"Before this time? Two days."

"So if you ignore the fact that he's been gone a little longer than before . . ."

"It's been almost a whole workweek."

That doesn't matter. Loved ones never understand. All at once, the distress settles on Vidar's shoulders, heavy as a cloak. He wants nothing to do with Isak Nyqvist.

"But beyond that, would you say there's anything different about this time? When it comes to how he seemed, stuff he did, how he was acting, what he talked about, people he saw?"

"He's been anxious and low, kind of, keeps waking up in the middle of the night or early in the morning and he can't go back to sleep and so on. Maybe it doesn't sound like much but I know something is wrong. I . . ."

He knows exactly where this is heading. She can feel it.

". . . can feel it."

Everyone does. That's the problem. They're usually wrong.

Whoever is in charge of dealing with missing-person reports at the station now, he or she has presumably acted reasonably and properly.

People go missing. By the thousands each year. The vast majority of them reappear within a day or two; almost all of them are found sooner or later. Most of the time, the missing person left voluntarily. There's nothing anyone can do about it.

Please. Just leave now.

"This is a tough situation for you. Both of you. I understand that. But I don't know what I can contribute here. I'm sure the police have done what they could—nowadays they work according to international standards anytime someone goes missing."

"I just want you to . . . I don't know. I'm just trying to find him. His parents are so worried; they think something's wrong, too."

Beyond the window, summer is in bloom. Just a few weeks ago it was Midsummer. Vidar wore a wreath in his hair; Amadia and Patricia had made him one. It was a warm but cloudy evening down at the old factory buildings, where the Midsummer pole was erected. He touched Patricia and—as if time were circular—for an instant her hair smelled just like in 1995. They had talked, sharing twenty-year-old memories. It felt nice, but also a little melancholic.

Everything is still. The branches of the trees aren't moving. The sun refuses to blink. These are the days when you imagine summer will last forever.

People go up in smoke. It's a good way to get rid of some troubles. Most storm clouds are figments of the imagination.

Not all of them, but most of them.

63

It was no surprise that a person who decided to make a life with Isak Nyqvist would need help one day. Anyone who so much as touched him would soon find themselves in a big mess of trouble. It was like he was a beacon for problems.

These days, Vidar tends to his own affairs. He goes to work. He comes home again. There and back, he avoids the road past the police station.

When he gets home for the day, he goes to the garage and props the lawn mower up so he can change the blade.

The first day he didn't go in was strange. He stood there with his coat on, a mug of coffee in hand, ready to head into the cold and go to the police station. Then he remembered.

He looked out the window, taking in the mangled landscape Gudrun had left behind; just standing there. Slowly he drained his mug. After that—he's not sure how much time had passed—he took off his scarf, hung his coat on the hook in the hall, and stepped out of his boots.

Everyone in the village knew he was a policeman. That was how they talked about Vidar; that was how they received him. The first time it happened after he had left the force, it hurt, and he didn't know quite how to react. They hadn't heard yet, of course.

"Sure, sure," old man Backlund said when he explained. "But isn't it like they say? Once a farmer, always a farmer."

An empty space, like loss. A calling, even though he hadn't experienced it as such, but *still*, a calling abandoned. He felt an odd pressure in his chest, and his hands got shaky.

Vidar leaves the garage and goes out behind the house, looking at the field that spreads out beyond the property line. It's still very hot. The young forest's silhouette is grayish blue in the gentle evening light.

Isak Nyqvist is probably passed out unconscious somewhere; maybe he escaped to a friend's place to avoid a pregnant, hormonal wife. Who the hell knows, and who cares.

That was probably why it turned out as badly as it eventually did. *Enough of this,* he thinks. *Enough, have to look forward.*

A creaking window opens from inside the house. Patricia is home. His phone rings in his pocket.

"Hello?"

It's Karin again. She's sobbing and apologizing, saying that she didn't want to call and bother him, but she has no one else to turn to. Vidar looks at the phone and his thumb hovers over the red button, but then he hears her say something. He brings the phone to his ear.

"What did you say?"

"He was down by the falls," she repeats. "What was he doing there? I'm so confused. And I'm so scared that—"

"Is that the last place anyone saw him?" Correct term: LKP. Last known position.

"I think so."

Karin collects herself. Vidar says, without really meaning it, that he will get back to her tomorrow. They hang up. He takes a deep breath. History has linked their names together, building a chain. *Isak Nyqvist. Edvard Christensson. Lovisa Markström.* What doesn't kill you makes you stronger. According to conventional wisdom. If that case hadn't broken him, he probably would have come out of it with renewed strength and energy. But it did break him.

The phone rings again. "Yes?"

"Are you gonna just stand around out there?"

"I was on the phone, Patricia."

"Who with?"

"Isak Nyqvist's wife."

"Why?"

"I'll be right in."

He ends the call and lingers in the pightle.

64

The hulking addition is nine stories high, resting in the afternoon sunlight. Its façade is black and shiny.

"According to the architects, it's supposed to look *curious* and *attentive*," Markus says.

Vidar squints. "Seems more like *threatening* to me."

"I know."

"Where's your unit?"

"Third floor. We've got the prosecutors right above us."

From a sun-warmed wooden bench on the other side of the street, the older brick building looks shrunken, as if the newly built glass façade is about to gobble it up.

"It must get warm in there when the sun is shining."

"It's a sauna. They're already being bombarded with complaints. But at least we all fit inside." He looks curiously at his old patrol partner. "How are you doing?"

Vidar rests a palm against the bench, feeling the warmth rise into his fingers as he touches the wood. "Fine."

"Are you still with the city?"

"Ticketing cars wasn't really my thing, I mostly just wanted something to do. I'm working part-time at the airport now."

"In security?"

"Hell no." Vidar smiles wanly. "I do a little of everything. Fuel the aircraft, load and unload baggage, take care of the ground crew's machines, make sure the runways are in good shape, and so on."

"And you like it there?"

"Sure, I guess so."

He doesn't *dislike* it, anyway. He did dislike working for the city. And the sheet metal workshop. The only job he stuck with for more than a year was driving a cab. It was a good job, maybe the best one Vidar's ever had. He was always in motion, meeting new people, most of them pleasant, easy passengers. Then came hard times, with Uber and the new app-based services, and the taxi business was bleeding money.

"How about you?" Vidar asks. "You're in the violent crimes unit, right?"

"Yep. It's going. But the restructuring has taken a toll on us; last year we left for vacation at Midsummer without having any idea where we would be when we got back in August. But we got to stay, almost all of us." He looks at Vidar inquiringly. "What did you want to talk about?"

"Isak Nyqvist."

Markus raises an eyebrow. "Okay . . . ?"

"His wife contacted me. I mostly just wanted to get rid of her, so I promised to get in touch and see how it was going. But I didn't know that the third-floor crew was in charge of missing persons."

"We're not, really, but we've been taking on certain cases to ease the load elsewhere. I'm not assigned to this particular case, but I know they've followed the missing-persons protocol as usual. We've been doing what we can, as far as I can tell, but it's not illegal to hide out somewhere."

"Okay. Now I know, at least."

Markus tilts his head. "What?"

"I was just thinking," Vidar says, "his LKP, was it down by the falls?"

Markus nods slowly. "I seem to recall he was down there around lunchtime on July tenth, according to his cellphone. He had come from home. When he arrived, the signal disappeared."

Down by the falls, Dane Falls. Vidar can hear the roar. The long waterway empties into the sea near Trönninge a little south of Halmstad.

"We think he might have thrown his phone in the water," Markus adds. "Or maybe he turned it off. We followed the water all the way downstream but didn't find anything."

"Right. I'm sure that's it."

"You can't . . ." Markus clears his throat. "I can't give you the material. But you can take a look at it." He looks at his watch. "Come in tomorrow at ten."

"No, thanks. That's not necessary."

"No, you should come. There's still no one around on Saturdays. If nothing else, just to take a tour and admire the big new conference rooms. Which share walls with the way-too-small offices."

"I don't know if I really have the time."

"Come on. I'll buy you a beer for lunch after."

Vidar raises his eyes to the sky. It's the time of day when everything is still. "Two."

"Two?"

"Two beers."

Markus laughs.

65

The next morning Vidar is taking in the bright, spacious lobby, the sleek furniture, the openness. It still smells new. "Nice."

"Yeah," says Markus. "And expensive."

The elevator is silent and smooth; the conference rooms bright and empty, almost untouched. Several of the instrument panels that run the electronics are still covered in the plastic they came in.

They walk through the old offices of the property crimes unit on the way to the Criminal Investigation Department. It still feels familiar. Vidar peers into his old office and can almost sense his own shadow there, from his last days on the force.

Younger, but paler and thinner than he is now. Only later did he realize what bad shape he'd been in that winter. Maybe that's the way of it: No matter how bad off you are, you don't realize it until later, when it's already too late.

On the desk in Markus's office is a pile of documents on top of a blue plastic folder. It all concerns the man from Marbäck.

"Not much, as you can see."

Vidar looks at the material. There's a humming inside his temples.

Markus sits down at his desk. Vidar pulls over the initial report and reads through the first interview with Karin. Then come the efforts of the emergency services, the missing-persons protocol, the last known position, maps and search areas, a cellphone analysis, photographs from his home, the usual.

"What's this?"

"A map. We had one made."

Markus unfolds it on the table. A few marks of color here and there, drawn-in circles. From above, Marbäck looks more isolated than it actually is. Vidar rests his finger on one of the colored marks.

"Is this the LKP?"

"Like I said yesterday, he was down there at lunchtime that day. Then the signal died."

Vidar takes in the meandering water, the way it moves like an ancient snake through the even more ancient landscape.

"And you searched downstream?"

Markus taps the map. "All the way to here."

Fair enough. Vidar puts the map aside and looks through the rest of the material. Nothing stands out. The wall clock ticks slowly.

"Satisfied now?" Markus asks at last.

"More than satisfied."

Vidar is holding photographs taken by a young dog handler who came to the site. They're almost always the ones to perform an initial probe in the case of a possible missing person, since dogs are an effective resource. They can find just about anything; they're obedient and they work quickly. The handler asks questions, documents the scene with pictures and notes, and lets the dog sniff around.

No luck this time, it seems. Vidar flips through the photos. "Nice place they've got, anyway."

The area had a rough time after Gudrun, and during the financial crisis a few years later, a lot of people moved. Property values crashed. Isak and Karin Nyqvist moved to the small house across from the old factory a year or so ago. It could use some renovations, but they likely haven't had the money.

The house is squat but rather cozy and warm. A nursery is ready and waiting. Bright curtains tied with bows. An old wooden crib with a colorful mobile. A white rug with balloons on it. A dresser. A sampler is hung on the wall like a painting; it reads MY HOME MAY BE HUMBLE, MY QUARTERS SO MEAN, BUT A LOVELIER DWELLING I NEVER HAVE SEEN.

Vidar's stomach clenches; a lump forms in his throat.

He wipes a bead of sweat from his forehead. Markus was right. Headquarters turns into a sauna in the sunshine.

"Is the dog handler around?"

Markus shakes his head. "Vacation."

Of course. Vidar puts the photographs aside. Why is he concerning himself with stuff that makes him sad, that only reminds him of . . .

But hold on. He picks up the photographs from the kitchen. No, not there. He selects another but can't find what he's looking for and turns to Markus.

The kitchen photos were taken from various angles. In one of them, the handler has captured the objects on the kitchen counter: keys, Post-its, a stack of bills, the headset for a cellphone, a charger, a small jar of iron tablets, an ultrasound of a tiny bundle. A boy.

"They don't have a table in the front hall," Markus says. "According to Karin they keep their keys, bills, and so forth on the kitchen counter."

"What's that underneath the ultrasound?" Markus raises his eyebrows.

"No idea."

"There's something under it. Didn't she move the pictures?"

"Maybe she didn't see it." Markus leans forward. "It looks like another picture. Is it another ultrasound?"

Vidar can make out a date stamp, tiny orange-red dashes that form numbers. His stomach clenches. Not again. Not this again.

"No, it's not," Vidar says.

And his mind goes perfectly silent.

It says *13 11 94*. The day Lovisa Markström died.

66

His inheritance doesn't disappear with time, but it can change shape and make itself harder to spot.

Throughout the years, the physical tokens he located in himself as a boy have transformed to a maxim. Something to live by. *Considering how badly it could have turned out, it's actually turned out okay.* Something like that. And if things did go badly, he could just say *Well, what did anyone expect?* That's its own sort of reaction.

His time in Hedman's old well in the early hours of January 9, 2005, wasn't long, but afterward, when Isak had the energy to think back on it all, it stood out as a pivotal moment. A transformation had occurred. He had fallen as one person but had been lifted out as someone else.

It took some time to see exactly what was different.

There was the obvious part, of course: Something happened that seriously shook him up that spring. It must have been in March because it wasn't long after Edvard's funeral. He was at school. Isak had accidentally spilled a cup of coffee on the floor, and the fascist who worked in the café, a man who went by the name Coffee Hitler, forced him to clean up after himself. If one of Isak's teachers hadn't been sitting nearby eating a Danish, Isak probably would have thrown the coffee cup at Coffee Hitler's ugly face.

Instead he ended up in the janitor's closet looking for something to clean up with.

Tiny and dark, cramped and chilly. The door was heavy and almost closed behind him; the crack of light got smaller and smaller. He grabbed a mop and bucket, sticking his foot in the door to prop it open. Then, grumpy, he went back out to mop up his spill. It felt degrading. He started to sweat. His recently healed arm began to ache. When he was done he went back to the closet and tossed everything back inside.

"The likes of you belong in here," came Coffee Hitler's voice from the hallway, an instant before the door slammed shut, and Isak was plunged into darkness.

The room closed in on him. His heart was pounding, and he couldn't breathe. He was blind. The chill seeped through his clothes and made him stiff and shaky. He couldn't move. *Oh my God, I'm going to die. I'm dying.* He knew it was absurd, but that didn't make it any less real, or any less convincing.

He began to fall.

The door opened from the outside.

Isak staggered out, dizzy with fear. Small spaces, dark places, cramped corners. He couldn't handle them anymore. He gasped for breath as if he had been underwater for too long and had finally broken through the surface.

Coffee Hitler laughed. Isak was on his knees, the dirty floor blurry and swaying beneath him.

His arm had stopped aching. To get rid of the fear, Isak threw himself at the man. At last, he was giving in again.

Two months later he received his first real conviction. The assault and battery resulted in fines. In the only interrogation he faced, he said he had gotten mad and hadn't been able to rein in his anger. Everyone believed him. Their eyes said, *Well, what did anyone expect?* It was easier that way, easier than admitting that he had been scared.

:::

The people around him disappeared. Theo, Karl, Anton, almost every-one. Summer had come and gone, and Isak had barely seen them. They were doing their military service now; Theo was somewhere in Stockholm; Karl and Anton in Gävle. Isak didn't pass muster, partially because of the Coffee Hitler incident. He wasn't considered fit to serve. The psychologist had looked at him for a long time and said, *It sounds like you're in the middle of a chaotic period,* or something along those lines.

Chaotic? Edvard was dead, everyone was gone, Isak had been convicted of assault and battery. A black mark on his record that would show up when he applied for a job, if he ever got it into his head to do that.

Everything was chaos.

There was an abundance of time in the gap that followed. What should he do? He hung out at bars in town. He tried to keep out of trouble, but it found him in the end: An argument at Ida's Pub spi-raled out of control and became a fight. Isak tried to step in. Someone pulled a knife. Isak was convicted of a second assault and battery, got fines and probation this time, and made a new friend who made a liv-ing selling alcohol to sixteen-year-olds out of the back of a car.

The only one who stuck around, in the end, was Karin. She never left him, but she came close. During the worst months, when he was drinking a lot and sleeping and eating very little, he almost wished she would just get it over with and leave him alone.

The token was so visible now. At night he dreamed of his grand-father August's gray dog, walking at his side, faithful and quiet, as he strode up the gravel road to the white house in Skärkered. A hand opening and closing, three dots on the skin between index finger and thumb. They appeared and disappeared like signals.

Isak was a hot topic in the village—he'd been spotted in a parking lot behind the scrapyard in town, lifting a flat of beer out of an open car trunk.

He knew about the gossip but didn't care.

Theo did call now and then. He sounded different, and worried. Isak missed him and looked forward to his return.

"I'm doing fine," Isak said.

Theo was silent, waiting. "Are you?" he asked.

"What, did you talk to Karin or something?"

"Huh? No . . . ?"

"I'm okay," he assured Theo. "Things are just a little complicated."

But Theo *had* talked to Karin. Isak found out a week later, when he noticed Theo's number on the list of calls made to and from her phone. He never mentioned it to either of them. Maybe he should have known from Theo's voice after all, from his tone: "Okay. Because you know, if anything's wrong, you can, I mean, you can tell me."

"I will. You know that."

"Good." Theo took a deep breath, an *Okay, now what do we talk about?* "Are you working right now, by the way?"

"I'm starting in a week, at the sheet metal place in Getinge."

Isak had, after pressure from Karin and lengthy visits to the employment office, been given the chance to work a few hours a week there, to start.

The money from the black-market alcohol sales didn't go very far, and at least it was something to do until Theo came home.

"How are things up there?"

"It's going really well, actually. I've been thinking, maybe, I don't know, I'm considering . . . they've got continuing training up here. To become an officer. My command thinks I would be a good fit."

"Okay?"

"If it happens, I'll come home, of course, to get my stuff on Svanåsvägen and everything. But starting next fall I'll be living up here."

Isak's mind went blank. "Okay. For how long?"

"For a few years, at least. I don't exactly know."

"That's great."

"Thanks."

"I have to go now," Isak said.

"But I—"

"I guess I'll see you when I see you," Isak interrupted, ending the call.

Afterward he stood there looking at his reflection in the mirror.

They disappeared. That was it, wasn't it?

Because surely it wasn't him.

And now, when he opens his eyes, it's dark all around him. He's lying down; he knows that much.

He's thirty-one years old and back again. He has feared this, of course, that he would be forced to return. It's finally happening. But where's the water? The cold, dirty water is missing. And the roar of the storm isn't there. Instead it's perfectly quiet, and he's lying on something hard and cool.

Suddenly he understands: He's not back there at all. Isak is somewhere else, on a floor surrounded by dense darkness. He tries to move but can't. He starts to pull his arms and legs in toward his body, but nothing happens.

Someone has tied him up.

The nausea hits him in the car. Maybe it's the stuffy air. Vidar rolls down a window and pulls air in through his nose, breathes out through his mouth.

"Is everything okay?" Markus asks curiously from the passenger seat.

"Yes, fine. Hey, by the way, how's Nashwan? Is he still around?"

"He works on burglaries. We ended up colleagues for a while after I left patrol. He seemed to be doing well there."

"Better than I did, anyway."

"How are things between the two of you these days?"

"I haven't seen him in—what would it be?—ten years."

"But you saw each other afterwards, didn't you? After you . . . you know."

"We went out for a beer. He wanted to clear the air and explain. I didn't feel all that inclined to listen."

"Why not?"

"I had already quit. There wasn't much to say."

Vidar's eyes dart around; he keeps breathing. His nausea slowly subsides.

"Listen, are you sure everything's okay?"

"I mean, did it have to be that particular date on the picture? That fucking day. I just . . . you know. But yeah, everything's fine."

"It *was* an awful story. You lived up there, you knew everyone . . . and for Christensson to die in the midst of it all, too. I'm just saying it's understandable that you wanted it to be someone other than him. And that it feels crappy to be reminded of it."

Vidar had needed to see the perpetrator's face. Instead of a question mark, a shadowy being, instead of a blank space—a face. That was all he was after. Only then could Vidar and, he imagined, the rest of the village be released from the hold the case had on them.

That was more or less what he had told himself. Instead of a void, a face. Vidar needed that.

In reality, he'd had a face before him the whole time, ever since the night it all began. After all, Vidar was the first one to spot Christensson.

"No one really blamed you, you know," Markus continues. "No matter what they said."

"Except Beate Aronsson."

"Aronsson." Markus snorts. "She was a sorry excuse for a police officer."

"She was a sorry excuse for a *boss*. She wasn't a bad officer."

"You weren't either. Totally the opposite."

Vidar looks down at his hands, suddenly dejected. To think that it still doesn't take much. What had Beate Aronsson said that time?

A figment of his imagination.

Vidar parks on the street up in Marbäck. The house is shabby and white, with some algae and discoloration along the gutters and the gray foundation, but otherwise it seems to be in decent shape. Two stories, plain windows, light brown roofing tiles, a lawn so green it almost glows.

"Are you sure this is okay?" Vidar asks.

"Hell yes. You're the one she talked to. It's good that you're here."

The door is open. Vidar and Markus exchange puzzled looks before they cautiously step into the front hall. It smells like old wood, and the floor creaks pleasantly under their feet.

"Hello?"

Karin is on the phone with her mother-in-law and waves at them to come in.

"Yes, I know. No, they're here now. Of course, I'll call later." She puts down the phone. "Sorry. Eva's been calling nonstop."

"That's understandable."

Vidar walks into the kitchen, observing the white counter with the bills, phone charger, ultrasound. He approaches it as you might a strange animal.

"Have you touched anything?" he asks, wiping the sweat from his forehead.

Karin shakes her head. "Not since you called."

Vidar looks around, still feeling vaguely ill. "You don't have a tabletop fan or anything, do you?"

"It's on the fritz. We haven't had time to buy another one."

Of course. Vidar takes out the photo for comparison. The keys and the chargers aren't in exactly the same spots, but that's only to be expected.

They're everyday objects. The bills are untouched, and so are the pictures.

And there it is: the photograph and *13 11 94.*

He pushes the ultrasound image aside and cautiously picks up the photograph underneath, observing it closely. He turns it over. There is the time, as well: *11:34.*

A flutter in his chest.

"What is this picture?" he asks.

"I don't know," Karin says. "It's been lying here for a while. I assumed it was just one of Isak's photos."

"And it didn't seem important?" Markus asks.

"Not given the situation, no."

Vidar looks at her. "What situation is that?"

"For a while he collected stuff like this. From back then, I mean. It's all in a box in the basement, but he goes down there to look at it sometimes."

"Had he done that recently?"

"Not that I know of."

Vidar considers the photograph. "And yet here it is."

"Yeah, but he's always leaving things out. Clothes, tools, his things, all of it. It drives me nuts."

Karin chuckles, but it gets caught in her throat and turns into something else. She rushes out of the room. Vidar is left standing there with the photograph in his hand.

It shows a car captured almost exactly in profile, possibly from just slightly behind, as if the car is about to take a gentle curve in the road. The taillights are two red dots, one larger and one smaller due to the angle, and they're glowing in the darkness. The photograph is quite sharp; the photographer must have been moving the camera at the same speed as the car. The only person inside is the driver; you can make out two lower arms and hands at the wheel, and there's the hint of a nose and chin before the body of the car hides the rest of the face.

It's impossible to make out a license plate, or even tell what kind of car it is, or what color.

Mumbling in the background. Markus's voice seems distant.

"What?" Vidar asks. "I'm sorry, what did you say?"

"I said this doesn't necessarily have anything to do with why he's gone or where he is. But to be on the safe side, perhaps we should take over."

He nods pointedly at the photo in Vidar's hand, a pained look on his face.

"Oh. Right, of course. Can I just take a picture of it?"

Vidar gets out his phone and places the photograph on the kitchen table, where the light shines bright and clear through large windows. He takes two pictures and studies the results. His nausea is gone; it has made way for something else, something he can't quite put his finger on.

"Wonder where it was taken?" Vidar says.

"In the forest."

"Yes, but where in the forest?"

"It's all just forest to me."

"Aren't you from Laholm?"

"The *city* of Laholm."

Vidar wants to laugh. Somewhere nearby, Karin is sobbing loudly.

Markus looks at the picture again. "Is that something in the camera? A technical issue or something?"

His finger is on a shining red dot that's visible between the trees, past the car.

"Maybe."

"Guess we're going to have to hold off on those beers," Markus says.

68

One single night: A house burned down in Tolarp. There was someone inside, on the kitchen floor. One instant, a before and after: the
stillness before the spark appeared, and the inferno that followed.

One single event. That was all it took to redirect the path of a life.
Like the filament of a root moving through time.

It's 2004. Everything is different: He's sitting in front of Isak
Nyqvist in an interrogation room. He's standing at a memorial service
with a lump in his throat. He's holding a list of the missing in his
hand. It never ends. His thoughts are elsewhere, causing him to
neglect the victims of the tsunami. This will cause him agony, but not
until later. When it's all over. He's meeting with Clara Nikander. He's
sitting in a car in Ängelholm. A burglar clicks a lighter in the darkness.
An end is drawing near.

And maybe a beginning too. You leave one place behind in order
to go *to* another place. That's why running away can never be anything but a temporary solution. As his old man used to say: *A punch in
the face solves a conflict. For a few minutes.*

Something like that. Vidar had nothing but the force. Sure, Patricia and Amadia, but they weren't enough. He needed something
more.

Vidar is standing on the side of a gravel road in some out-of-the-
way part of the district, surrounded by strong young-growth forest.

Twelve years ago, tree trunks lay like pick-up sticks around here. Hard times followed, but the farms and forest owners fought to stay afloat, and they cleared and cleared the destruction. It never ended. Gudrun had felled two hundred and fifty million trees.

Many operations went under. One of the foresters, old man Backlund, worked day and night for months to save what he could. When he finally had his land back in order, he planted new trees. *Once a farmer, always a farmer.*

He meticulously planted hundreds of tiny trees. About ten minutes later, as he was sitting in his camping chair, exhausted, drinking coffee from his thermos and gazing out at his land, he had a stroke and collapsed.

Backlund was called home, but his young trees have grown into a strong, thick, healthy forest. Their tall trunks reach for the sky. A stuffy July breeze moves across the gravel road. It smells musty and heavy. Heat rises from the road. Vidar stops, takes out his phone, and looks at the photograph.

The front tires aren't perfectly straight. He moves back, stepping out into the grass. The road curves here.

In the photo, a small red dot shines in the distance, through the trees. It wasn't something wrong with the camera. It's a radio tower.

He turns around, backs up, and holds up the photo again, moving to the left, no, too far, a little to the right, *there.*

Right here.

It's November 1994. Midnight is approaching; darkness fell long ago. The photographer is standing about a yard from the gravel road, which sweeps by and on through the trees. A car comes zooming up. The photographer captures it in motion, the car sharp against a blurry background. But where did the photographer come from?

Through the forest? Behind Vidar, a path runs through the bushes and up the slope. And way up there is the top of a roof. Vidar's eyes trace the path.

There.

That's where you came from.

:::

A small house with a flat roof, cracked gutters, and a single black cat sitting on pale wooden steps and following Vidar with alert green eyes. An old moped is leaning against the house. Vidar places his hand on a cool engine. The cat meows, stretches, and looks at him curiously. Then she lovingly rubs against Vidar's shin.

Someone chuckles.

"She's not much of a burglar alarm, that one."

A woman is standing on the steps with a chain saw in hand. She has big, brown hair, sharp features, dirty jeans, and a fleece pullover full of wood chips and sawdust.

"Animals usually like me."

"Don't flatter yourself. That one likes everybody."

She steps down. Vidar offers his hand. Her grip is gentler than he'd expected.

"Anneli."

"Vidar."

"Jörgen, my husband, isn't home yet. But he should be here soon. You're from around here, aren't you? I feel like I recognize you."

Vidar nods and explains. The cat rubs his legs. He holds out his phone to show her the picture, but he's cautious—as if he's trying out a role he abandoned long ago.

"Oh, sure. I'm the one that took that."

He's surprised. For once, something is actually *simple*.

"Come in." She steps aside and picks up the cat. "This is Maja, by the way."

Vidar scratches Maja's belly. The cat looks at him in surprise. Then she yawns and looks bored. No shadows, but heat, and everything is very still.

69

"I was only eleven," she says. "But I wanted to go to a dance up in Simlångsdalen. Dad said no. And I'll tell you, I could be a really mean little cuss, and I held a grudge, too. After I had refused to speak to him for a week, he came home with a little camera. He knew I loved taking pictures, and I'd asked for one for my birthday that same summer but didn't get one."

"What kind of camera?"

"A nice little compact one, which I'm sure was very expensive at the time. It wasn't a plastic disposable one or anything. I had read in the user manual that it could take nighttime photographs even without a flash, which I thought was super cool, so I wanted to try it out right away. But they, my parents, they told me to wait until the next day." She laughs. "I never listened as a kid. I did whatever I wanted. So I snuck out once they fell asleep. That's why it was so late; I think it was almost midnight."

"So that was here? You still live in your childhood home?"

"Not too great, is it? But it was the only way I could afford to own a house. I bought it from my mom for a symbolic sum after Dad died and she got too old to stay here. She's at the senior living place up in Simlångsdalen now."

They're sitting on a leather sofa in the living room. It squeaks as Vidar crosses his legs.

She went down to the road, she says. Didn't dare go any farther; it was so dark and cold and, after all, she was only eleven.

"What were you planning to take pictures of down there?"

"Can I see the picture again?"

Vidar shows it to her. Anneli zooms in and points at the red dot. "Exactly. That's what I originally wanted to take a picture of. I guess I thought it would be cool, a pitch-black background, almost, with just that red dot shining. I hoped it would look like an alien or something. I suppose I took three or four pictures and, you know, nowadays with digital cameras you can see right away on the display how they turn out. But this one didn't have that. So after a while I was heading back up. That's when I saw the car. It was all so fast. I only had time to take the picture as it was flying past, sort of. But it turned out to be a good picture, I think, you can see here." Anneli runs her finger along the edge of the car. "It's pretty sharp, but the background is really blurry because of the movement."

It turns out she didn't get the film developed for a long time. Only a week after she took the picture, she dropped the camera on the floor, and some part of its inner workings broke. She was so ashamed that she was afraid to tell her dad, and it was another decade before she found the camera again, at the back of her closet.

"By then, of course, I had forgotten all about it and the pictures. But I got them developed anyway. There were several pictures of a red dot and one of the car, and then some of flowers and Nancy Drew books—you know, girl stuff. I put them in my photo album, not because they were so great but mostly just to keep them."

Anneli strokes the cat's back and looks like she's about to say something else, but then she changes her mind.

"Is something wrong?"

"No, I was thinking, I'm just sitting here yakking your ear off. But what's going on? You said it had something to do with Isak Nyqvist?"

Vidar leans forward, resting his elbows on his thighs. The cat opens one eye but soon closes it again; she sighs contentedly and goes back to sleep.

"Well, how did he end up with the photo?"

Anneli shifts in her seat, uncertain. "What is this all about?"

"I'm trying to understand why he was interested in this picture. It reminds me of an old case."

"Oh. You mean Edvard Christensson." Anneli crosses her arms, eyeing him as if to decide whether he's telling the truth. "Sure, okay. It's a long story. You probably ought to talk to Jörgen; he jumped in as a temp at the rubber factory earlier this summer. We've both had to, him and me, to make ends meet." Anneli nods at the land beyond the window. "It's impossible to make a living on this anymore. So he and Isak were coworkers for a while. He came over for coffee one evening a week or so ago. We were talking old memories and stuff, all three of us are from here, and of course everyone's heard of Isak. And it's not all good. But it turned out we have a few friends in common, and when I said I took a lot of pictures until about fifteen years ago, he wanted to see them."

She'd pulled out the album. They drank coffee, ate Danishes, and looked at pictures, chatting: *What's so-and-so up to these days? Oh, he got saved? Never would have guessed that. What about so-and-so, did she marry that guy?* And so on.

Isak lingered at the picture of the car, and at first Anneli didn't understand why.

"It was so dumb of me. I can be really thoughtless sometimes. But it wasn't on purpose; I just didn't link the date with what happened then, you know?"

"I understand."

"Anyway, he asked about the photo. I told him the same story I told you, and when I was done he asked if he could borrow it. Sure, I said. So he took it with him when he left."

"Did he say why he wanted to borrow it?"

"No. But I didn't ask, either, you know . . . I didn't want to pry."

Vidar scratches his cheek as he thinks. "You said you'd heard things about him. What kind of things?"

"Oh, well, you know." Anneli squirms. "Everyone remembers his dad's brother and so on."

"You mean his mom's brother? Edvard?"

"Oh right, it was on his mom's side. Exactly. Just like, you know, my dad had some run-ins with Edvard's dad, August, in the eighties. August had brought home a batch of oak logs and Dad wanted to buy it to redo the attic here. He got it for cheap from August but when he got home it was full of bugs. It wasn't even fit to be firewood, and Dad had to toss the whole lot. He wasn't exactly a big fan of August's after that. And that wasn't even in the ballpark of what Edvard did later on. So when Jörgen came home and said he was working at the same place as Isak Nyqvist, I was a little surprised, to say the least. I mean," she adds, "back to what you asked, I've heard stuff about him, too. He seems to have calmed down now and so forth, but a few years ago I guess there was a lot of gambling and drinking. I heard he sold drugs, too, but I don't know if it's true."

Vidar drifts away on his thoughts. On the walls in here: wedding pictures, paintings in copper-colored frames, a bookcase with books about animals, nature conservation, a series of publications by the Local Heritage Foundation in Marbäck. An old crystal chandelier hangs from the ceiling.

"Do you know?" Anneli asks.

"Sorry, what did you say?"

"Do you know if it's true?"

"That he was dealing drugs? No, no idea. I was wondering, did he say anything about the picture? Back then, when he was here."

"He asked if I knew who it was. The driver."

"Did you?"

"No. I mean, this was more than twenty years ago, but I don't even think I saw his face. I noticed the headlights right when I was about to head back, like I said, and then I was focusing on the camera to try to get a shot of it. So I have no idea who was driving."

"Had you ever seen that car before?"

"No, I don't think so."

"But it must be mostly people who live nearby who would use that road. It's not exactly a thoroughfare."

"Isak said the same thing. But actually, that road meets up with the old Oskarströmsvägen, which goes all the way up to Oskarström, obviously. And it's not like we all know everyone's business."

He should have been taking notes. He has to remember to jot some down later. His sense of unease is growing.

"When was he here?"

For the first time Anneli is uncertain. "I think it was the seventh or eighth of July."

"So, two or three days before."

"Before what?" Anneli raises an eyebrow.

"Before he went missing," Vidar says, distracted.

Anneli's jaw drops. Her bottom teeth are discolored and uneven. "He's missing?"

Vidar blinks. "You didn't know."

Anneli slowly shakes her head.

70

Once upon a time, everything came close to coming apart.

That was two years ago now, during his time with the city. There was a party, and the staff of Carlsson and Ericsson was invited since their new offices were right next door to the City of Halmstad's. Clara Nikander was there. She and Vidar hit it off and spent most of the night standing next to each other.

They ate lunch together increasingly often. They talked about how things had been, and how they were now. Only rarely did they mention the Edvard Christensson case, but it was still the link that bound them together. She lived alone; he didn't. She loved her job. He was bored.

Perhaps it looked a little odd, the two of them sitting there, her and him, Clara in a very proper suit on the days she had to appear in court, and Vidar in his workman's overalls, a simple laborer in those days. She asked if he missed being a police officer. He lied.

A staff party led to a night out at the lounge in Tylösand. She was there with a few colleagues. It was summer, and he felt so lonely that he didn't know where to put himself.

He had developed problems eating during the spring; he was often nauseated and slept poorly. He and Patricia no longer had much in common and, aside from Amadia, they had almost nothing to talk about. Vidar slowly realized he didn't even really want to talk to her. She was working in correctional care, which only reminded Vidar of the career he'd left behind. So silence was more pleasant.

They were living the same life within the same walls—but not really. Sometimes he felt like a stranger in his own home, in his own bed.

He didn't understand why it was happening; it had just come over him. It was like existing permanently in twilight, where the light was very weak.

Patricia liked to say that his big green eyes were expressive enough to convey what his lips couldn't manage. It was one of the reasons she'd fallen for him. He might not have been much of a talker, but he didn't need to be.

"But now," she said one night when the situation was starting to seem dire. "I can't see it anymore."

"What *do* you see?"

"Nothing."

It was so straightforward that he didn't know how to respond. And this, the silence, was the problem.

"You thought if you could solve it you would solve some bigger issue as well. Something more important. But it didn't happen. You just ran away. And now—"

"Wait, what are you talking about? Solve what?"

"Don't *even*, you know what I mean. You haven't been yourself since." They were sitting in the kitchen. He hoped Amadia had fallen asleep. Once upon a time, he had traced the Miljanovic brothers' spree through Sweden with purple crayon on his daughter's coloring paper. That on its own wasn't the end of the world, but it wasn't about the action; it was about what it *meant*. That's what he thought. Patricia had said something along those lines, and maybe she was right.

"You seem so far away sometimes," she said at last.

"So do you."

Vidar walked out of the house. That was his solution for most problems, at the time. If it could be called a solution.

Beyond the picture windows of the lounge was a view of the sea expanding toward the horizon. It looked welcoming. Clara had a cocktail; Vidar was holding a beer. She had uneven dimples, he noted.

"You know," she said suddenly, "your life could have been much simpler."

He took a sip of his beer and gazed at her in amusement. "Okay. How so?"

"You're a good person. You want to do what's right. You believe in good values. Police headquarters is a not a good workplace for that sort of person. Or, no," she contradicted herself, waving her hand, interrupting the protest Vidar was about to launch into. "No, I'm exaggerating. I do that when I'm drunk. But this case in particular was not good for you."

He was startled by her choice of words. She said *this case* as if it were still ongoing, still current. And he supposed it was, in some sense. But it didn't make any difference.

"If you hadn't been the man you are, you could have let it go. If you had been more pragmatic, you could have lived a much happier life. You would still be on the force, probably a chief of some sort. If you hadn't . . ." She swayed. "I don't know what I'm trying to say. It's just something I was thinking about. Do you know what I mean?"

"Yeah."

He did, after all.

"Maybe you don't agree, what do I know? That's just how I see you."

She wasn't really saying anything he didn't already know; it had all been said before, either by Patricia or by Vidar himself, but he liked the way Clara saw him. That was what was chafing at him.

"Don't get me wrong." She took a step toward him. She placed her hand on his chest, with a pleasant, gentle pressure. "I like that you're the man you are."

She didn't move her hand. Beyond the window, the sea expanded, infinite. A human is a tiny thing.

He went home with her. She was dominant and brusque, but tender. She stroked his cheeks and ordered him to come inside her. When he finally let himself do it—that was the last line to be crossed—she smiled and closed her eyes.

Vidar welcomed the feeling of submission, as if it implied that what was happening was beyond his control.

Afterward he lay there staring at the ceiling, then left her satisfied and asleep in the bed and took off.

She called him the next day. He didn't answer.

He could handle the shame for only a little more than twenty-four hours. Then he broke down and confessed. Patricia didn't hit him, although he deserved it. Instead she just stared at him and sank into silence.

Her anger grew slowly, toward him and toward Clara. She became paranoid and mean. She asked for the passwords to his phone and email, his Facebook account. She got them.

This was the real reason he quit his job with the city. It became impossible to be near Clara Nikander.

He looked in the mirror and stared at someone he didn't recognize.

Someone who had failed a basic task in life.

71

Each summer he has a recurring dream. With a gray dog at his side, Isak is on his way to the white house in Skärkered. Edvard is waiting inside; he's sure of it. His steps are quick and impatient. He can feel the longing all the way out to his fingertips. He's grown, but when he looks at his hands, they belong to a child: soft, smooth palms, small knuckles.

Isak never arrives at the house. All that's left is an empty space among the trees. Somehow it has been moved, even though that's impossible. He doesn't let himself be discouraged. He walks on, deeper into the forest. Often he makes it very far before he wakes up; sometimes he only goes a few steps.

In his dream, he's never afraid.

It comes only in the summer. The first time was a few months after the funeral. When it happened again a few weeks later, he tried to interpret it as if it were a riddle and contained a solution that would clear everything up if only he could find it.

He has the dream a few times each year. As the years go by, he has started to welcome it, see it more as a sign than a riddle, more a message than a question. An indication that he is close to something bigger.

As if someone wants to make themselves known.

Now it comes again. It's all familiar: the gravel crunching under his soles, the cool air, his impatient steps, the house waiting up ahead, far beyond view.

A noise breaks through the background of the dream. There's a bang as a door closes somewhere above him. Isak opens his eyes.

A moment of disorientation when he can't move, and then he recalls the sharp, strong zip ties that cut into his skin the last time he tried to get free.

It's not dark this time. Daylight filters in through a narrow, dusty window in the ceiling. A cellar. He's in a cellar.

Tool cabinets and shelves loaded with heavy work implements line the walls, and there are two rows of fluorescent lights on the ceiling. It smells like oil and earth, metal and rubber.

The floor makes his joints and muscles ache. His face hurts; a jolt goes through his cheek and brings tears to his eyes.

There's something in his mouth. Something hard, scraping at his tongue. Isak spits.

A tooth falls out in a little puddle of saliva and blood.

Right. That's right, someone punched him and he felt the tooth come loose. The last thing he heard was the sound of the falls. Then everything went black.

There are narrow windows up along the edge of the low ceiling. He tries to move, to stand up. He can't. He tenses his arms and legs but nothing happens. The effort makes his head throb and grate.

He tries to crawl instead. It's slow going, but he does move. He makes his way forward.

Below the windows is a wooden workbench. It looks heavy, sturdy, with massive drawers. *I can do it. I can do it. I think I can stand up.*

The room sways and he tries to steady himself. He looks around for something to break the window with. He tries a shovel, but it's too heavy to lift with his hands tied behind him. Instead: a broom. He gets hold of it and aims the shaft over the workbench, toward the window, and starts tapping on the glass. Harder and harder. The effort makes him tip over.

The glass won't give way. He tries to swing harder. There's a loud sound. He doesn't even know why, but when he blinks the room sways again, and his temples are pounding and his vision goes black and he falls to the floor like a bowling pin, into the collection of shovels, brooms, and other equipment that's leaning against the wall in the corner.

The crash echoes loud and cold and sharp through the cellar.

He lies still, panting.

Steps above him. They're quick, heavy. A door opens.

He heard. He's coming.

Isak tries to hide, but he doesn't get anywhere, He must look pathetic, blood trickling from his mouth, down on the floor.

A man comes down the stairs like something is chasing him. He's sweaty; his clothes are disheveled. There's something black and oblong in his hands. Isak squints.

Then he hears himself crying for help.

The man stops in front of him. Gray sneakers. The pitch-black barrel of a gun trembles violently before Isak's eyes. The man shouts at him to be quiet. In the warm cellar, sweat runs down his temples and into his eyes.

"Quiet, I said!"

Isak roars.

The barrel trembles, trembles, trembles. Is yanked away. In its place comes a kick that knocks the wind out of Isak and cracks his ribs. He opens his mouth again and gasps for breath but can't keep going. It hurts too much.

"I told you to be quiet," the man hisses, almost reproachingly.

"Just shoot me, then," Isak growls.

Tears spring into his eyes. He can't stop them. What an idiot he's been, to let himself be tricked like this. How did it end up this way? There are many outcomes he could have imagined, but this isn't one of them.

"Shoot me!"

The barrel is the length of an arm. Its mouth is round and steadier now.

Isak looks past it, at his eyes. They're wide and blue, bloodshot.

Their eyes meet, like electricity. Time stands still. Isak's head crackles.

The man's gaze is nearly vacant.

Slowly, the gun is lowered. Everything is muddled, but the man seems almost demoralized. Isak looks at his legs, at the gray sneakers. They back away, head up the stairs. Only once Isak is alone does he exhale and notice the stench of piss. His pants are wet. A sick feeling grows in his mouth.

He doesn't know where to put himself, so he starts to laugh.

The world had shown what it was truly capable of. As if a lifeline were suddenly severed, it could take your loved ones away. The world watched without blinking as you fell.

Maybe it could also bring back those you'd lost. It almost seemed like it, even though that was impossible.

One night, a week or so before Edvard's funeral, Isak was crossing a back street in Halmstad. A slushy, cold rain was falling, and the streets were empty. He walked. That was all he did these days; he kept moving. If he stopped he would disappear, he was sure of it. He was grieving for someone he hadn't really known, someone who had destroyed so much, who had been a cruel and cowardly person. Whom he loved. How was anyone supposed to make sense of all that? So he walked.

Then he spotted him. A lone figure, hands in pockets, was passing on the other side of the street; he walked fast and jerkily as you do when you're afraid of being spotted.

Isak froze mid-step. He watched the figure go; it quickly turned a corner.

It was all so familiar: the shoulders, the neck, even the way he moved. It was Edvard.

Who to call? Mom?

He fumbled for his phone. There wasn't time. His heart pounding, he ran after his uncle. It was him, but how? He hadn't seen Edvard's dead body. None of them had, when he thought about it. Somehow, something had gone wrong.

Isak turned the corner. There he was. Isak tried to say his name, but his voice gave out and the man didn't react.

"Edvard," Isak called, louder.

The man quickly turned his head and sped up. Isak rushed after him.

The cold rain was hard and sharp on his face.

"Edvard!" he exclaimed, grabbing the man by the lower arm— a grasp so familiar and comforting that only then, as he touched his uncle, did he understand how dreadful it would have been to have to live without him.

In the blink of an eye, Isak was seven years old again and it was Midsummer and everything was warm and lovely. Edvard helped him with the wreath that rubbed. Everything was fine, there was nothing to worry about, and Edvard said *The best days are the ones we spend with the people we care about the most.*

"What are you doing? Let me go."

The man tried to free himself. Isak held on. "I—"

"Let me go, dammit."

Isak stared at him, dumbfounded. The man shoved him abruptly. Isak let go, paralyzed, and watched the stranger's back vanish in the rain.

He was reeling. His senses had betrayed him. Everything betrayed you, sooner or later.

Edvard didn't exist. Isak's legs couldn't hold him and when he caught himself with his hands he felt the wet, uneven asphalt, the cold, so sharp and terrible. He gasped for air, hoarse, but it wasn't panic tearing at him; it was his memories and sorrow.

He's in his uncle's house in Skärkered. He's holding Edvard's hand through the forest, down to King's Rock. He gets a wreath in his hair, and he's so happy. That's before all the horrible stuff happens; Mom and Dad are happy and he and Theo will be best friends forever, and you just have to look out for the highway, and that's easy, and as long as his uncle is holding his hand nothing bad can happen, and *all the other days we're just sort of waiting.*

Isak cried that night, cried until his chest hurt for an uncle he almost hadn't had but who had once been his, his very own, *his only.* The world's best Edvard, who was gone forever.

That was the way of the world. It tore people away from each other. Isak was alone.

There hadn't been many people there to say goodbye. *There will be a private service,* they had written in the obituary. It sounded nice, almost reassuring. Isak had worn the graduation suit he'd bought the same day that Edvard died. He hadn't had time to purchase another.

The pastor's name was Olof. He had baptized Isak once upon a time. He had a low, pleasant voice, and he spoke about Edvard, but it wasn't true, what he said. Not all of it, anyway. Or, the problem was more what he *didn't* say. He left out almost all the bad stuff. And the bad stuff is part of people, too. This was something Isak had learned.

It's true, a story almost always has to leave out something in order to make sense. You can't include everything; that would be impossible. You have to sift, prioritize. Olof, too, had done so.

We don't know exactly how Edvard died, he had said. *That is one of the hardest things to realize, that we have to live with uncertainty. But we know where he is now. We know he can see us, and that he especially watches over those he loved. This is how we take comfort from those who have left us.*

He had spoken about Edvard's upbringing in an insecure, sometimes tumultuous home, and how he had been blessed with an older sister who loved and protected him, and who was loved and protected in return.

About how Edvard had once, as a little boy, stolen a living budgie for her, since she had been assigned to draw one for school but hadn't been able to find a bird book in the bookmobile and didn't know what to do to keep from getting a failing grade. The bird flapped its wings wildly in the siblings' room, confused, as Edvard hid under the bed and his sister sat with her paper and pen, her brow furrowed, trying to render it.

He had spoken about Isak, too. How Edvard had been overjoyed when Isak was born. "*In those first pictures,*" Olof said, "*it's plain to see how proud he is to hold his nephew.*

"*Spending his Sundays with Isak brought him great joy. He never had children of his own, but we know he wanted them. He felt a great affinity for childhood. Perhaps that is another trait that set Edvard apart. He never forgot how the world appears to a child.*

"*How mysterious and strange, how magnificent and fantastic it can be. How books felt, how love felt, and perhaps also how the divine felt.*

"*He would remember his days with Isak as the best of his life.*"

Then it was time for a psalm. It hurt so much. Why did he have to die; what was the point of it? Isak had loved him so terribly. Despite what he'd done.

72

He used to read books. He could picture himself standing before the rows of spines at Edvard's house, reaching out his hand, taking one out, opening it. He could hear the sound of dishes clinking in the sink, the water running. Ten years later, he slipped a lovely Byzantine chain around his wrist and wore it with warmth in his heart. He took it off before the funeral—he doesn't remember why—and when the service was over he saw it on the nightstand, waiting for him. He left it there.

He hasn't worn it since.

He doesn't read books anymore; he doesn't have the time, energy, or desire to. Reading only brought his mind back to things he didn't want to be reminded of. There aren't always many choices, and trying to forget the past was the only way he could see to move forward.

That was why he moved. He lived outside the village for the first time when he was twenty-four, in one of the apartment buildings on Maraton near the Andersberg neighborhood in town. Andersberg was 85 percent immigrants and 40 percent unemployed. Car alarms went off at night, mixed with laughter and shouts. Isak got by on odd jobs. He drove a delivery truck part-time, a moving truck a day or two each week, and sometimes he filled in on one of the paper machines at Nordiskafilt.

He lived in limbo, a convicted criminal with a partner who

threatened to leave him more than once. He actually fit in pretty well in Andersberg, but it took some time for him to realize it.

That was the strange part. Theo, Karl, Anton, and everyone else—even though Isak's story was different from theirs, hadn't he looked at his friends and hoped that he was probably actually like them? That his life would turn out okay after all? His fear of carrying the token inside him had initially taken the shape of a child's fear, and later a teenager's rage and frustration. Some part of him had still been hoping that his path in life wouldn't look noticeably different from the others'. He never did military service, but he would work. He would buy a house. He would have a family with Karin. He tried to persuade himself of that.

But that wasn't what happened. As the others moved forward along the same path most people on Svanåsvägen and the area had traveled before him, Isak lagged behind. His path diverged. It took some time to realize. It had started down in the well. *That* was the difference; noticing it had been a long time coming.

His life *was* marked by the token. What could he do?

Considering how badly it could have gone, his life had actually gone pretty well. That was the sort of stuff you had to tell yourself.

One morning he woke up with a strange feeling in his stomach. By then he hadn't been to Marbäck for almost six months.

He went there alone, with the sense that something was waiting for him up there. When he arrived, he was met with odors that didn't exist in Andersberg: the scents of nature and trees and old land. It smelled eternal.

In God's Field up in Breared lay Lovisa Markström and now, too, his uncle Edvard Christensson, at opposite ends of the graveyard. When he stood before the gravestone, it struck him that he hadn't visited since the funeral. More than five years ago.

Suddenly he felt very shy. What was he doing there?

Isak stood alone in God's Field, at least in an earthly sense. He took in his uncle's name and squatted down, picking out wilted leaves.

He took a small candle from his pocket, a lighter. The flame burned clear and warm. He opened his mouth.

"I . . ."

The words stuck in his throat.

"I should have come sooner. I'm sorry. It's . . . I don't live out here anymore."

He stared at the birthdate, the date of death. A thin thread bound them together. It didn't feel right to say that he seldom visited Marbäck, as if it might hurt Edvard's feelings.

"I still don't know . . ."

He faltered. He looked around. Still alone. What should he say? He got only eight years with his uncle. It almost felt like another life.

"I still haven't decided whether you did it to yourself or whether it was an accident."

Not even the investigation, which he'd actually read all the way through even though he'd feared it would be too difficult, had been able to give him an answer. When there are no answers, you have to make up your own mind sooner or later. If it wasn't on purpose, it was so pointless. Just like when you were a kid and heard about how death could appear at the edge of the forest. You had been selected without having a clue why. And if he had done it to himself, if he took those pills deliberately, then of course he had wanted to put an end to it all. In that case he had consciously left everything behind, unfinished and open.

How could anyone decide which it was?

"I think my car is stolen. I mean, I didn't steal it; I bought it from a guy on Maraton. But I think *he* had . . ."

He looked at the grave. A large, heavy stone at the edge of the field was all that was left.

"This feels weird."

He gazed at his uncle's name, the lines carved in the stone, the birth year of 1969. At twenty-five years old Edvard had taken the life of the girl he loved. Isak was twenty-four. *One year left,* he thought, *before I'm the same age you were then.*

"It was you, wasn't it?"

Isak waited. No response was forthcoming. Vidar Jörgensson must have had his doubts. He never did anything about it; instead he'd apparently quit the police. Maybe it was just as well. The whole thing was like a curse. Isak had also had his doubts, but they had more or less subsided.

It was probably him.

"I'm going to come here more often" was the last thing he said before he turned around and left, and at the moment it felt true.

It was a warm afternoon. He took the car to Marbäck and visited his parents. They wondered how he was doing, whether he was working and so on. He lied.

"You're not here very often these days," said Mom.

"I'll try to come more often."

"That would make your dad happy."

"And you too, I assume."

"Yes, of course. And you, I hope."

What was he supposed to say? Marbäck filled him with pangs of loss and regret. It made him want to drink something. He took a walk through the village, across the bridge, and down to Tolarp. His steps brought him there; his head was strangely empty.

He arrived at the spot. Only history knew that Hans and Erika Markström's house had once stood here. The lot was almost overgrown now. The weeds grew to his waist. Even so, you could still sense the violence and the smoke in the air, somehow. Maybe they would always linger. He turned his head and could almost see himself there, eight years old, standing next to his best friend, two bikes and two pairs of wide eyes taking in the wreckage of the Markström house.

Isak stepped onto the lot. It was the first time. It felt forbidden, as if he had crossed a line. The weeds opened for him and closed behind him, stroking his hands and lower arms. He stepped toward the center of the lot, where the house had once been.

When he got there he stopped. The weeds were shorter here, but it wasn't just that. He took a step back, then forward. Strange.

It looked flattened. As if someone had recently been sitting there.

73

The questions didn't come until later. Vidar couldn't tell if Patricia asked them to hurt him or to torture herself out of some absurd sense of inadequacy. *What did you say to each other beforehand? What did you say to each other during? After? Did she give you a blow job? Did it feel good? What positions did you have sex in? In what order? Did she come? Did you come? Does she have nice breasts? Do you want to fuck her again?*

Vidar responded until he could no longer muster the strength. He felt he owed her answers, even when he didn't have any. It was clear to him that he'd gone through some sort of crisis, but he didn't realize it until later, once he was already on the other side.

He never moved out, not even temporarily, but it had become very quiet in their house. Amadia wasn't unscathed. She spent more and more time out of the house.

Or was that the reason? She was a teenager, after all. Wasn't this just a natural development? He told himself it was. Patricia maintained that he should stop being so blind to his own role in what was happening to their daughter.

He wasn't unhappy, just empty. He visited his father's grave once a week and stayed longer and longer. Clara Nikander called. He didn't answer. He started driving a cab.

There are few constants in life, he's learned. Everything changes, if slowly.

And sometimes, during those years he spent in the taxi, on his way to or from a fare, he pictured himself as a child.

He's ten years old and outdoors, playing somewhere near his house up in Marbäck. He's thirteen and kissing Tilda in his same grade behind the gym. He's fifteen, on a moped with his buddy on the luggage rack. Later that year he's at a party and sees Edvard Christensson smoking indoors. He turns eighteen and graduates, he's twenty and applying to the police academy. It's easy to breathe. Life awaits. He's twenty-eight and dancing with Patricia. Her eyes meet his.

But then? What happens then?

Somewhere along the way, he almost turned into someone else.

Patricia made him see a therapist. He had things he needed to work through, and if he didn't do it this would happen again and she would be forced to leave him.

That was what she said. Then she cried.

He went once a week. After six months they began to go together. After nine months she held his hand as they sat next to each other on the sofa. It was a big step.

She seldom touches him, but when she does it means that much more. It's impossible to go back; moving forward is the only option.

There are few constants in life, but they do exist. One of them is the roar of the falls. There's something timeless and eternal about the light. Vidar is standing down there now, looking around.

He comes down here on July tenth. Then something happens. His phone stops sending a signal. What happened? Where did he go?

Vidar picks up a rock. It's sun-warmed in his palm. He flings it at King's Rock. *Clack.*

He inspects the ground thoroughly. As his senses search for signs of conflict, violence, a sudden attack, old nerves begin to twitch. It's been a long time, but where his gaze should move next, where he should and shouldn't set his foot, how to read the ground—none of this takes any effort. A sense of calm settles over his shoulders.

He moves along the edge of the water, then up between the trees.

He stops and considers something on the ground before putting on a fresh latex glove. He took a few from Markus before they went their separate ways.

Vidar picks up a crumpled cigarette butt. Yellow Blend.

He's waiting for someone. Right? Who is he waiting for?

When he closes his eyes it's like everything is pulsing, a rhythmic pressure against his eardrums.

The list of phone calls. The last number Isak called was Karin's, on the night of the ninth. No out-of-the-ordinary numbers on the list, he remembers that much: The police have a color-coding system and mark such calls with a pink highlighter. The list didn't contain any pink numbers, just the usual green ones. Text messages? Unclear. They hadn't gotten that information. Nor had he been active on Facebook; Karin said he'd made an account a few years ago but hardly ever used it.

So who is he waiting for? How did they get in touch?

The water roars. Foam flies up at the rocks. He goes down to the water again and moves along the edge, heading upstream, approaching the falls itself. A faint breeze comes through the trees, ruffles his hair.

It makes something else move, too; something flutters at the edge of his vision. He turns his head. A flock of birds goes by, their shadows unnaturally large on the ground. Vidar lifts it carefully. It's caught on a branch, that must be why it hasn't been blown away.

He takes out his phone again and calls Markus. "Yes?"

"Hi, it's me. Listen, something occurred to me. Isak Nyqvist is a smoker, right?"

"Yellow Blend. Why?"

"I found a butt down by the falls. The search was only performed downstream, that's what you said, right?"

"Are you down there by yourself?"

He probably doesn't mean to sound accusatory, but that's still how Vidar takes it.

"Yeah, I just had some extra time, so I thought I would come down and have a look around. I didn't have anything particular in mind, or whatever."

"Okay." Markus is slow to respond. "I suppose that the searches were mostly focused in that direction, yes. Why?"

"I went the other direction for a ways, and I found something. Either they missed it, or else it showed up here later."

"Hold on, what did you find?"

It's a tiny piece of paper, hardly bigger than a stamp, but it's torn and rough at the edges. You can see black numbers that have begun to fade: *5 60*.

"Probably nothing," he says.

74

The fact that Edvard Christensson had killed Lovisa Markström didn't change just because he was dead. Quite the opposite. In some sense his death was a confirmation and felt like justice, finally—to a great degree, this was thanks to the Borås prison facility.

When it became clear that Christensson had had illicit access to Panocod—acetaminophen with codeine—they were forced to open an investigation. The source was located: a guard who occasionally supplied the inmates with the medication they thought they needed but which the prison refused them. The guard thought he was doing a good deed, since the drugs numbed them from the pain of being deprived of freedom. This is what he said during interrogations.

But Christensson had had a migraine in the days leading up to his death. Considering that his medical records stated he had previously been addicted to Citodon, which also contained codeine, the staff were hesitant to give him any medication at all. In the end he was given over-the-counter acetaminophen, which couldn't have helped much. Maybe he took the smuggled Panocod to ease the pain. Or had he simply had enough, after the recent emotional turbulence in his life—as the investigation termed it—and couldn't deal with it anymore? After all, he had recently seen his nephew for the first time in a decade. This, and the fact that ten years had passed, and that he was presumably guilty and had lived with that guilt in his heart for so long, refusing to confess, and that his two petitions for a new trial had been rejected . . . well. Wasn't that enough to make anyone give up? But there was no letter.

A chemical analysis of Christensson's blood didn't say anything one way or the other, just that the overdose had caused his body to fail. The Borås prison fired the guard and saw to it that he was convicted of his drug-related crime, but that was the end of it.

Aronsson believed it was suicide, Vidar recalls, and that a person who takes their own life is seldom innocent.

This has stuck with Vidar, the movement out of the corner of his eye when he was about to leave Tolarp. Strange how it can move through time like a whisper. When he closes his eyes, it's November 1994.

Hey. Hello. There's someone in here.

It came from the edge of the forest. He strode into the darkness and there he was, Edvard Christensson. Vidar crouched down beside him and touched him. His forehead was shiny, his clothes bloody.

It's okay, he said. *Everything's okay. Just wait here, help is on the way.*

Christensson's wide-open eyes. His breaths, like faint smoke from his gasping mouth. He was shaking.

I couldn't, he said. And fainted.

Was he the one who did it? Maybe he was, after all. He had it inside him, and there really wasn't any other candidate, now that the Miljanovic brothers were out of the running.

It didn't matter anymore. He was dead.

This is how he's been thinking: in circles. Everything sank and settled in the part of his soul where you keep stuff that's on its way to losing significance. Then he started working for the city and met Clara again and life nearly shattered into a thousand pieces. If it hadn't been for the murder in Marbäck, their paths never would have crossed.

Vidar has returned to the little house. The front door is closed.

Breathless, he presses his index finger to the doorbell and a dull *ding-dong* sounds on the other side. Karin opens up, her eyes full of questions. Vidar catches his breath. The heat makes his shirt stick to his back.

"You said he had a collection. Can I see it?"

A moving box—that's all it is. It's on a shelf in the basement and it looks heavy. As Vidar carefully pulls it out, Karin stands there watching him.

"What's going on?"

"I don't know."

"But it's something. You're different now."

"Am I?"

Vidar opens the box.

"Do you think he's dead?"

The question catches him off guard.

"No, I don't. It's just . . ." Yes. He does. "I just want to check something. I'll let you know if I find anything."

She takes this for what it is, a subtle request to leave him alone. He watches as she heads up the stairs, Isak Nyqvist's great love.

That's still how it goes for most people: They make out with a classmate or someone at a party and, almost imperceptibly, a link forms between them and causes them to stay together as love grows. It's not a compromise, but nor is it just about love or lust. It's about being able to say *There, that aspect of life is taken care of now. There may not be enough jobs around here, the farms aren't doing well, my grades aren't good enough for any sort of higher ed worth the name, and I have no desire to move, but at least I don't have to worry about this part.* To spend your time alongside someone else is the least you can ask. Successes big and small are made better; tragedies of any scope are easier to endure.

This is probably true even in Vidar's own case. Otherwise he'd probably be living alone by this point. No matter how bad it gets, it's still better than being on his own.

Once he's alone in the dim light of the basement, he peers into the box. Old calendars, the first newspaper clippings about the Marbäck murder, a lovely old bracelet of the sort Vidar hasn't seen since visits to the prison back when he was a police officer. The inmates make these themselves, in the workshops. Photo albums, old toys, more newspaper clippings about the case against Edvard Christensson. A child's T-shirt with Superman's face on it, a framed photograph of a group of boys on the ice, in skates and helmets. Vidar recognizes them. He sees little Isak, his friend Theo Bengtsson, a few others.

Something is bothering him.

That's it. On the floor is an old TV, and on top of it is a VCR. He follows the cords to the wall. Plugged in, as if they've recently been used. He turns on the TV, presses PLAY.

It flickers in white, black, gray. Then: a scene. It's Midsummer's Eve in the Nyqvist pightle. Eva goes by with a cake platter in hand and a wreath of flowers in her hair. She looks young and very beautiful.

Out on the grass, little Isak and his uncle. So strange to see Edvard Christensson alive. He lifts a wreath from the boy's head and starts to adjust one of the twigs. They're talking.

Christensson: "*But mostly I'm happy that I get to see you. And later tonight I'm going to see someone else I like.*"

"*Lovisa?*" the boy asks.

They laugh. Soon the wreath is ready. Christensson places it gently on Isak's head.

The clip ends.

Flickering. Vidar blinks. The picture returns, shaky at first. It's later that same evening but the setting is different. They're at the sports fields in Simlångsdalen. The shadows have grown and the image is grainier; everything is unnaturally blue and gray in the strange color balance of the TV.

Lots of people, they're sitting and standing in groups, holding glasses and food. Vidar recognizes several of them. He was on duty that night, otherwise he can picture himself having been there, too. Eva must have been holding the camera; you can hear her laughter at close range when the dancing around the Midsummer pole begins.

A drunken orchestra performs Midsummer songs. They're off-key but no one cares. They laugh at one another and keep going, louder and clangier: "*See what I have here in my hand, see what I have to carry! A little fellow, so fair and oh so fine, so pretty all in his garments.*"

Lots of people are dancing, but even more are watching, clapping in rhythm, laughing and shouting with glasses and bottles in hand. They turn blurry in the background. It's probably still rather light out; lots of them are wearing sunglasses. Or maybe they've just forgotten to take them off.

The circle breaks out into pairs. There they are, Edvard Christensson and Lovisa Markström, almost like an illusion. In spite of the grainy image, you can tell it's them. They're facing each other and holding out their hands. Laughing and smiling. She places a hand on his shoulder; he puts a tender arm around her back.

"*To me you are so dear, I want to have you near, I tell you my beauty, you're lovely without peer . . .* "

Eva follows them for a moment, then lets the camera move on.

Vidar waits for them to return to the shot. They don't. The clip ends shortly thereafter when someone—maybe her husband—calls out for her cheerfully. She puts down the camera, and the image is once again black and still.

Vidar rewinds. *You sat here. You watched the tape. You were looking for something.* He presses PLAY again. Eva slowly pans the camera across the dancers. They enter the picture from the right. He watches the sequence from beginning to end, then rewinds again.

What were you looking for?

Play one more time. The musicians playing, the groups of men, women, young people and old dancing together, everyone looking on, Eva Nyqvist laughing, her husband calling for her. "*Eva. Eva, come on!*"

Something is niggling at him.

He rewinds and watches the same thing again. But that's not all.

Vidar stands up, staring at the picture. Once he spots it, it will be the only thing he sees.

Show me your face.

He takes out his phone and brings up the picture of the car that drove through the Marbäck forest late at night. He compares what little he can see of the driver's chin and nose.

Maybe. Maybe not. Impossible to tell.

Someone is standing there on the tape, in the distance. He's far enough away that it's impossible to identify him, but he's not singing along, or clapping, or smiling; he doesn't even seem to be talking to anyone. He stands there with his arms crossed, his head tilted slightly— that's all.

It was him. He's the one you saw.

From behind a pair of narrow sunglasses he's staring at Edvard Christensson and Lovisa Markström, following their movements as if he were monitoring them.

75

The house on Svanåsvägen has aged. It needs a new coat of paint and new pavement on the driveway, and the roof could use a wash.

As Vidar steps over the threshold with the tape in hand he is transported back in time. The muggy, humid air is replaced by a crisp, cold fall. The incident is only a few days old; the wounds still gaping wide. K-G Öberg's broad back is before him. The chief inspector shakes Eva Nyqvist's hand, nodding to her husband. Vidar lingers in the hall. *The boy,* he thinks. *Where's the boy?*

"I'm wondering if you remember this."

"The videotape?"

"Well, more like what's on it. Do you have a way to play it?"

Eva shows him an old DVD player that's gathering dust under the TV in the living room. It looks more dead than alive, but it works—and a closer inspection shows that it takes VHS tapes, too.

"Where's Peter, by the way?" Vidar asks, sinking to his knees before it.

"At work."

"He's still working?"

"Until fall. Then he can be done, with one year's salary."

She says it mechanically, almost absently. Vidar feeds in the tape. It begins to play. Eva goes by, the cake in her hands.

"Oh my God, look at me," she says, shaking her head. Then she goes stiff. "Oh."

It's Isak and Edvard with their wreaths. "We're all so happy."

"This is what I was curious about," Vidar says cautiously as the scene changes on screen, moving to the Midsummer celebration at the sports fields.

Laughter and shouts. People. There are Edvard Christensson and Lovisa Markström. And there. There he is. Vidar freezes the image.

In the foreground, Eva's brother and his girlfriend have stopped as well, as if prisoners of time.

"They look so happy," she whispers.

Vidar looks at the man in the sunglasses. Dammit, he should recognize him, considering how small Marbäck is. It's 1994 and this man was an adult then; you can tell by the build of his body, he's between maybe twenty and forty. There can't be that many candidates, assuming he's actually from here. But God, it's so grainy, it's starting to get dark, everything is tinged with dim, blue light, and he's wearing sunglasses, and the tape is twenty-three years old and you can't even fucking tell who it is.

"What I'm wondering is—"

"You know," she interrupts, as if she didn't hear him, "I haven't mentioned this to anyone before, but Peter was gone a lot when Isak was little. I think he was considering leaving me. We had really become *parents*, you know? We didn't have much of a life beyond parenthood, and that was tough. It's why Isak spent so much time with Edvard. Which actually didn't help much. Peter was still gone an awful lot, working overtime all the time, and going to the racetrack with Bernt and everyone and all that. I don't know if he . . . I don't think he had anyone on the side. But I'm not sure. I've never asked, either."

"Why not?"

Eva smiles mildly.

"There are some questions you might not want to hear the answers to. But if we hadn't had those days to ourselves, I mean, if we hadn't had Edvard, then it probably all would have gone to hell. So he saved us. Oddly enough. Isn't that funny?"

Vidar points at the TV.

"What I'm wondering about is this man. Do you recognize him?"

She leans forward.

"The picture's so bad."

"I know."

"I can't tell who it is."

"So you . . ." He falters. "I know this is unreasonable to expect, but I don't suppose you remember him?"

The man watching Edvard Christensson and Lovisa Markström is wearing a light-colored, short-sleeved shirt, buttoned up all the way. His arms are crossed. In the moment he's caught on tape, he appears to be alone, with no company; those moving around near him are busy with one another.

"No, I'm sorry, I don't."

"What about the people around him?"

She shakes her head.

"There were lots of people at those parties back then, you know. People came from the village, of course, but also from Oskarström and Skedala." She looks at Vidar. "Who is it?"

"I don't know."

"Do you think *he* was the one who . . ." Eva doesn't finish her sentence. She looks from him to the TV, then back to him. "What *happened*? Why is my son missing?"

"I don't know," Vidar says again.

"I know he was kind of a mess for a while. But he's been doing pretty well these past few years. I can't imagine that . . ." Her expression is harsh, her jaws clenched. "But you all had seen this back then? I mean, back then as in during the investigation? You knew about the tape, or what?"

The force leaves its traces so deep inside that even now, years later, it's still hard to admit. Vidar observes the man on the screen. *I need to see your face.*

"No. I expect we didn't."

:::

He calls on the way to his car, the tape in hand. Insects are buzzing listlessly from bushes and trees. The sound comes and goes in waves, like hypnotic vibrations.

"I'm sorry to call again," he says as soon as Karin picks up.

"Every time I think something has happened."

"I know."

He continues to apologize as he gets in the car and backs down the driveway. The evening sun sparkles off the asphalt of the road, washing everything out to white. It's been a long day.

"When we first spoke, at my house, you mentioned that he's been waking up early recently, and can't get back to sleep. Right?"

"Yes."

"Do you know what he did when that happened?"

"Nothing in particular, I don't think. He said he takes walks sometimes."

"Where to?"

"I don't know." Silence on the other end. "No, wait, down towards Hedman's farm. I know he's walked that way before."

A face on an old Midsummer video, a car speeding through the dark. A piece of paper, three numbers. "*To me you are so dear, I want to have you near, I tell you, my beauty, you're lovely beyond peer . . .*"

Restlessness tugs at him. He calls Markus again, to ask where everyone is.

"I know, we've been held up" is the first thing Markus says. "But we're about to organize a search now. It took some time to arrange the helicopter."

Soon, dog handlers are walking through the village. There's a racket from the sky and the residents leave their houses, squinting at the evening sun and spotting the police helicopter hovering above the fields. Police officers stand in clumps, maps in hand; they confer and point, give orders. Then they begin to move.

Can't help but fear the worst.

76

Some time before his departure, Theo said he didn't know where it was.

He came back for one last Christmas with his parents. He brought the girlfriend he had found in Stockholm.

Isak and Theo saw each other on Svanåsvägen, just like they always used to. He had just parked the car when Theo stepped out of the front door to take out the trash. Marbäck was white with a thin layer of snow; there were Advent candelabras in the windows and Christmas ornaments dangling from the curtains, like memories of a time when life was easier, more open.

They stopped as if both had been caught. Theo looked taller than Isak remembered. At first he couldn't say why that was—sure, his shoulders were broader and his hair was shorter, but there was something else too.

His posture had changed. Theo moved the way you do once you've found your place in life. You wait for the world to shift a little and make a little space for you. For some people it happens, while others wait in vain. He'd learned this over the years. It had happened for Theo; it was like he was glowing.

They smiled and walked to meet each other. Isak hugged him. He smelled almost the same.

"Merry Christmas," Isak said.

"Merry Christmas."

"It's been a while."

"I should have come down more, but I haven't had the time. It's . . ." Theo hesitated. "I've been busy."

They talked for a while, chatting about the little stuff. It was a bit stiff, but eventually it felt almost like normal, for a brief moment, until a strange look came into Theo's eyes.

"Are you doing okay and everything?"

"What do you mean?"

"No, I was just thinking . . . I know things have been, like, a little rough for you."

"Oh. Yeah. But I'm fine."

"You got your license back, obviously." He smiled. "Right?"

"Yup."

"How fast were you going?"

"Way too fast."

Theo laughed.

"But you know," Isak went on, feeling the need to explain himself, "that's not really why they pulled me over. They did it because they know my car and they don't like me."

His friend looked puzzled but didn't ask any more questions. Isak was grateful. Instead, Theo's eyes swept over the old houses and fences, the asphalt and the cars, the small potholes in the road.

"I'm going away in February," he said. "I've been accepted into the foreign deployment regiment."

"Where are you going?"

"Afghanistan. We—or, the Swedish military—have a base there. Northern Lights."

Isak blinked. Afghanistan was desert and sand, automatic weapons, men stoning women to death under the broiling sun. War. Bombs: in cars, turbans, and stores; on streets and bodies; under the ground and under clothing. Tanks, crazy terrorists screaming nonsense.

"How long will you be gone?"

"Six months, maybe. You're not allowed to be gone for too long."

"Okay. I mean, I've heard on the news and stuff, about—"

"Yeah," Theo interrupted calmly. "But it's good money. We need it." He glanced toward his childhood home. "Mom and Dad probably won't be able to work that much longer, but they don't have much of a pension. Which means they'll have to sell the house. So I was thinking . . ."

"Have you told them that? That it's why you're going?"

"That's not the only reason I'm going."

"Okay." Isak looked at the strip of asphalt between his own worn shoes and Theo's shiny, clean boots. "Just be careful."

"I think I better go inside now," Theo said. "But let's try to meet up before I head back, okay?"

"Definitely. And if we don't, bring me something from Afghanistan. Like a shirt or something."

Theo laughed.

"I don't even know where it is yet," he said with a playful wink. "But I'll find out."

Maybe he was joking. It was always hard to tell with Theo.

"Take care of yourself, anyway."

"You too, Isak." Theo looked strange again, almost like he was scared. "You only have one life, you know? Remember that."

There. There it is again. Steps above Isak's head. Everything around him stinks. He had no choice but to piss and shit where he lay. Everything hurts, his stomach, head, mouth, hands, legs. His eyes burn. For long stretches it's just dark. But there: Here he comes.

The cellar door opens. Steps again, and those gray sneakers. The adrenaline starts to pump through Isak's body and he curls into a ball, trying to make himself small. The man comes down. Unarmed, it seems.

He stands there staring at Isak. He has a small book in his hand. Suddenly he tosses it at Isak.

"You said you wanted it. Here it is."

It's landed on the floor in front of Isak's face. Isak's voice is scratchy.

"But why—"

"Shut up. I said you could have it, and there it is. I keep my word."

Why is he giving me this? What's going on? Maybe he doesn't even know.

Yes, that could be it. Maybe the man, now on his way back toward the cellar door, is just as broken as Isak.

"Hey," Isak croaks. "Hello."

The man turns.

"Why did you want to go down by the falls?"

A cold gaze stares back.

"I was planning to throw you in the water."

He was planning to, but couldn't. Then he tried to shoot him. That should have been simpler. Guns are impersonal; they allow for distance. Isak recalls Theo having said that once. *He was planning to kill me. He couldn't.*

"What are you going to do with me? Am I just supposed to lie here forever, or what?"

"I don't know."

That's all he says.

"They're going to find me," Isak calls at his back. "They're looking for me now. You can just let me go, I won't—"

"Be quiet," the man says, sounding strangely detached. Then he leaves.

"Hey! Hey!" Isak swallows. "I'm thirsty."

The man opens the cellar door and walks out, closing the door without a sound. The lock turns with a click, and Isak is alone again.

On April 7, 2011, Lieutenant Theo Bengtsson from Marbäck, as well as Sergeant Rickard Sund from Helsingborg and Captain David Åberg, Bollnäs, had been stationed in Mazar-e-Sharif, Afghanistan, for two months.

On that day, west of the city, a Swedish Combat Vehicle 90 was fired upon with small-bore ammunition. Fire was returned and backup summoned to the area in the form of, among other things, a Patria Pasi armored personnel carrier operated by Bengtsson, Sund, and Åberg. In the vicinity of the firefight, the APC ran over an IED. It blew the vehicle to bits. All three perished.

When the news reached Marbäck, Isak thought of the last time he had seen Theo. His posture and smile, his *Merry Christmas*. The way he had smelled. One minute he was there, right in front of him on the path in the cold, and the deserted fields spread out around them, and Isak had just arrived, hadn't he, yes, he had just parked his car at his childhood home and there was Theo with a bag of trash in hand, and for once everything felt pretty good and a new year was about to start, and then Isak never saw him again.

The loss sliced him in two. It was true that they had hardly been in touch recently, but losing Theo was like losing an element, water or fire. Something he'd always taken for granted was gone. He couldn't wrap his head around it.

He went out to Svanåsvägen alone one Tuesday. It was raining. No one was out but the magpies. Theo's parents had asked if he could bring himself to go through the wardrobes in Theo's old room.

Isak had wanted to say no, but he couldn't do it, so suddenly there he was, on the floor in Theo's room. Theo's parents had turned it into a home office. He opened one wardrobe door and pulled out a box. On top was the T-shirt with Superman's face, the one Theo had worn in their second-grade class photo up in Breared. Isak had worn one with Batman. That was before all the bad stuff happened. He lifted it and placed it gently to the side. Underneath: a wall calendar from 2005, turned to May.

The spring they graduated. Theo's handwriting: *Macke's party! Cap day! DANCE! Jonna's party.* Isak paged back. January 8, 2005: *Buy suits with Isak. Play GTA with Isak and Karl.*

The next few days: *Visit Isak at the hospital. Isak comes home! Party at Isak's.*

Isak didn't remember the party. Maybe that was just as well.

A framed photo from 1994. They're on the ice, Isak, Theo, Karl, Anton, all of them. They're wearing skates and helmets, arms around one another's shoulders. Everyone is smiling at the photographer, who must be Theo's mom.

A spark of something, at the very back of his mind. He didn't recall that anyone had taken pictures.

He set the picture on top of the Superman shirt. He cried until his eyes hurt.

That was the start of it. Soon he was collecting items. It was probably a way to remember. He stored it all in a box: photographs and videotapes, newspapers, calendars. A bunch of crap, but not to him. They weren't talismans or amulets, more like portals. When he was there, surrounded by all the objects, he felt a little bit closer to a different, better time. A time that was less ruined.

Theo's funeral was Isak's first since Edvard's. He sat there unsure of where to put himself. Theo's big brother, Jacke, was at his side; their parents were beside themselves with sorrow. Karin squeezed his hand, but he didn't feel it. All he felt was *Not again. I can't handle any more.*

It was a military service with an artillery salute and everything. The large hall was full of people he didn't know. They were in uniform. It felt so strange, not Theo at all. But it *was* Theo. That was who he had become.

Afterward he stood in the bathroom in the church, looking at his own reflection. He was sober and almost twenty-five, but he looked remarkably old, as if he had aged prematurely.

Well, what did you expect?

What was the last thing Theo had said to him?

You only have one life. Remember that.

Right. That was it.

Maybe it was time for a change.

77

Patricia notices it as soon as Vidar closes the door behind him and steps out of his shoes. He gives her a cautious *hi,* and she responds in kind. Then she just stands there looking at him.

"What's wrong?" she asks.

"With me? Nothing."

She crosses her arms. "Weren't you supposed to work today?"

"No, tomorrow."

"Then where have you been?"

He walks past her. "Nowhere."

Suspicion rises from her like wreaths of smoke, burning his back. "What have you been doing?"

"Is Amadia home?"

"Vidar!"

It's an order. He stops. Hard to say how many times it's been like this. You stop counting. If you don't, you'll go nuts.

"Yes?"

She's breathless. "Where have you been?"

He brings up the photo on his phone. Shows her the videotape, the little scrap of paper with numbers on it. Patricia's shoulders relax. He asks if she's heard the helicopter, seen the dog handlers, the police. She shakes her head, mumbles that she's been in the house since she got back from work.

"And you don't have to shout," she says.

"I'm not shouting."

"Yes you are."

"Isak Nyqvist is missing. I think something happened."

"Why didn't you just tell me that?"

"Why don't you trust me?"

"Well, what do you think?"

"That was two years ago, Patricia."

"Doesn't feel like it. Don't you understand that every day is a new day in which I choose to trust you? In which I actively choose not to be suspicious?"

"It was *one time*. It was *two years ago*. I haven't even seen her since. I even changed jobs."

"But that's one time more than me," she exclaims. "You did something I would never do. If I wanted to sleep with someone else, I would tell you."

"You would?"

"We've talked about this."

"*Do* you want to sleep with someone else?"

Patricia rolls her eyes.

"Jesus, you're so primitive." Her dark eyes are angry. "We've talked about this in therapy more than once. Don't you remember?"

"Yes."

"I thought you cared."

"I do care." He cautiously steps toward her, attempting to touch her for the first time since Midsummer. "Is Amadia home?"

"No. I'm going to take a bath, I'm tired."

Vidar says her name, softly, pleading.

She turns around. "This isn't working. You're about to get caught up in something again. I can see it on you. I can feel it."

"I'm not."

"You can't keep running away, Vidar."

"But I'm not running away."

"Yes, you are."

"From what?"

She stares at him. "This. Your family. Our life. *Your* life. You think if you run straight back into this it's going to solve something, but it won't. Don't you see that?"

"But what do you think I'm—"

"You know, I have a fucking life, too. Not our life, but my own. And I'm so goddamned tired of always having to be the one who thinks about us; it's so freaking typical. I have friends, too. I have interests, too. But I have to prioritize us, because apparently you don't give a shit. I'm the one who has to point out and apparently solve *your* goddamn problems, so that we can stick together and solve *our* problems, even though I actually have plenty of my own to deal with. Don't you see how unfair that is? I never fucking asked for that role. I'm not some goddamn housewife who puts my husband's needs before everything else. And I hate that you've turned me into that person."

The therapist likes to encourage him and Patricia to be *specific*, so they understand each other. What she has just gotten off her chest is not particularly concrete, but something tells him it would be a bad idea to point this out.

"I'm not running away from anything, Patricia," he tries. "I just want to—"

"What?" she interrupts him. "What *do* you want from all of this?"

She probably wants him to say something, but he's out of words. As she walks away, he feels once again that he has failed, done something wrong.

It will never again be the way it was before.

Even so, she comes to Vidar that night. She lies down next to him and with a serious expression, possibly deep in concentration, she places two warm palms against his thighs, pulls off his underthings. He's surprised.

It's been such a long time. They tried, at first. He supposes they both wanted to save whatever was salvageable, but he no longer got hard; she was unable to get wet. It was hopeless. So they gave up.

Something is different now. Vidar notices it when she settles onto him. It's silent and brief, because Amadia is home, but intense and wired, as if there's a current running through them. He doesn't quite know why it happens. Maybe she needs it, or thinks he does.

Afterward he's out of breath and confused. The little dip in Patricia's spine reflects the evening light from the window. She's warm and shiny.

"Hey," she says in a low voice.

"Yeah?"

She turns around.

"What you showed me earlier today. The videotape and the photograph, I mean."

"What about it?"

She hesitates, like she's not quite sure. "Is Isak Nyqvist missing?"

He leans away from her. Not again. "I told you that before."

"That's not what I mean." She places a hand on his chest. "Does it have to do with her? Lovisa."

"I think so. I don't know."

"But what are *you* supposed to do about it?"

"You don't need to worry."

"It's not that. But you just . . . I mean, I . . ."

Patricia sits up, but she's still touching him. She runs her fingertips over his collarbones, exploring, gentle, as if she's trying to find out if he's really the same person.

"When you talk about this," she says quietly, "you act just like you said you never wanted to, when you described your dad. Remember that? Can't you tell that you're doing it? It's like you go totally mute."

It was a long time before he realized this. After all, as a child, he had been so fond of his father. His mother, too, of course, but it was different. He couldn't identify with her job as a secretary for a construction company in Fyllinge in the same way, and her personality was withdrawn and cautious compared to her husband's. Vidar recalls spring and summer nights when Dad came home late, hardly saying a word to her or to Vidar himself, only to sit alone on the porch in the dark, chain-smoking in silence. He kept a box in the attic. It contained unsolved cases he couldn't let go of, and sometimes he sat out there paging through them.

This was hardly any help to Mom. They'd had a good relationship at first; you could see their contentment in the old photos. They looked happy. But Vidar could see that the silence was painful to Mom.

Vidar hadn't understood back then, but later he figured out what was going on. There were certain things you experienced on the job, he learned, that marked you the way an animal is marked with a branding iron. That sort of thing is impossible to share with anyone else. It's not just about the terrible things you see. It goes deeper than that.

"I think I feel guilty," he says, visibly weak. "Because he . . . it might not have been him. But I'm the one who found him. I was the one who . . . I just want to know that . . ."

Words aren't enough. He closes his eyes.

Show me your face. I just want to see your face.

"What do you want to know? Whether you did the right thing or the wrong thing?"

"Yes. I think so."

"But it doesn't matter, Vidar. Not to him. Edvard Christensson will never experience it. He's dead. But *we're* alive. Amadia and I. And you. You can't disappear into this case again. If you do, you'll never come back out. And if you do come back out, Amadia and I might not be here." Patricia doesn't say anything for a long time. "Do you even think he's alive?"

"Who, Isak Nyqvist?"

"Yes."

Vidar opens his eyes. "No."

78

It started in April.

He had been clean for a long time. He didn't drink anymore; he'd stopped messing shit up. He'd gone to the employment office. He got a job and was able to stop living off welfare. He and Karin had moved into a fixer-upper in Marbäck. It was weird, but nice to be back. He had realized where home was and finally accepted it. He had been pretty bad off for a while, but at last he was saved. His grief over Theo's death had been such a heavy burden, but it also forced him to focus.

On this April evening he was hurrying across the fields, into the deep Marbäck forest. There was something behind him, chasing him, grabbing at his legs and arms.

Sounds. Sounds in the forest; they were everywhere. Possibly not real.

It was cold and raw out. He was going to be a dad.

When Karin showed him the stick with its double lines, his first impulse had been unbridled joy. This was hardly planned, but it didn't matter.

He had hugged her so hard, kissing her hair and laughing, his face pressed to her neck. Only several hours later, when the first wave of feelings slowly began to ebb away, did he go to the bathroom to sit on the lid of the toilet and bury his face in his hands and take a deep breath.

Then came the fear.

"I . . . I'm just going to go out and get some exercise."

That was the best he could come up with. Breathlessness was taking over him.

"Now?" Karin looked surprised. "Is everything . . . are you okay?"

"Yeah. I'll be back soon." He managed a smile. "Hope I don't run into Mom or Dad. I don't think I could keep it to myself."

Karin laughed.

Now he was rushing through the forest, his heart pounding.

What is happening to me?

The forest opened onto a field, billowing and cold, and there, in the background: the steeple of the old church. He had come all the way to God's Field in Breared. Isak bent double, panting, his palms on his thighs. A wave of nausea rose through his chest.

It was unavoidable for the boys in the Christensson family. Some people just have something inside them that makes them destroy everything they touch. What happened to them just happened. He had experienced it himself. Really, it didn't mean much that things had calmed down for him recently. Maybe it wasn't even over for him yet. *Well, what did anyone expect?*

He wandered aimlessly among the heavy headstones. What you cannot escape, you must learn to live with. He'd heard that somewhere.

At last there she was, right in front of him.

Lovisa Vilhelmina
Markström

1974-04-12
1994-11-13

The work of your mind,
The love of your heart,
The beauty you dreamed,
Time cannot destroy

He sank down before her, unsure of where to go next. A gray dog slunk around nearby, beyond sight, just like before. Once upon a time, a house burned down. He could still smell the smoke.

Time cannot destroy.

Some things refused to stop their workings.

He rose. Standing in the April darkness, he squinted through the night, toward the place where his uncle rested. It was far away. God's Field is large. He was forced to return home.

He placed his hand on Karin's belly, terrified of what awaited.

He was standing in the driveway, covered in sweat, about to unload a crib from the trunk, when old man Antonsson came walking down the street. He stared at Isak as though he were a stranger.

"Are you back?" the old man asked with something like distaste in his voice.

"Have been for a few months. We bought this old place."

"Aha. I missed that. Well. I suppose I should have guessed."

"What?"

"Well, you know, that you would be back one day. I mean, lots of you do that."

"I don't think I follow," Isak said, closing the trunk. Antonsson cleared his throat and leaned forward.

"Everyone knows who you are and where you're from. If you're going to live here in the village, you better conduct yourself like someone in the village, too. Otherwise, we don't want you here."

Isak stood there, taken aback, with a good mind to punch the old man in the face. And he probably would have, too, if he hadn't been holding a crib.

"You mean people don't have babies in the village?"

"You know what I mean," Antonsson muttered, going on his way.

Isak was used to this by now, but it still stung. He was home alone. He set up the old crib and took in the baby's room. *I have no idea what I'm doing.*

He fled to the basement. Surrounded by the old clothes, the newspaper clippings, the photographs, he just sat there and breathed. *I think I need help.* At the very bottom of the box was the VHS tape from a long-ago Midsummer's Eve. He rolled out the old TV that had once been in his boyhood room and inserted the tape into the mouth of the VCR.

Everyone knows who you are and where you come from.

The tape began to roll. Isak saw himself and Edvard. It hurt. If he tried, he could still feel the wreath on his head—or maybe it was just his imagination—how annoying that poky twig had been.

The scene changed. They were at the sports fields. He heard his mom's voice behind the camera; he saw Edvard and Lovisa and all the others. He watched it over and over again. The images were entrancing.

Then something happened.

Isak moved closer to the screen.

Who is that in the background there?

When Isak finally tracked him down, he'd said he had something to show him. He remembers that much.

To keep from setting off warning bells, Isak had decided not to call. Instead he went over there with an uncomfortable sense of anticipation in his chest. It was like finally reaching an endpoint, beyond which only a fog awaited. He knocked on the door and waited.

The man who greeted him was in bad shape; you could tell from miles away. He was worn out and pale, as if an invisible force were eating him from the inside out. He looked, Isak thought, a little like Isak himself. This confused him.

"I'm here about the lawn mower."

He let Isak look at it. He asked questions but didn't hear the answers. If he had, he might have noticed how absent-minded, how almost incoherent those words were, more like fragments than responses.

He hadn't brought anything but a pocketknife to get what he wanted, or to defend himself if it became necessary. Now, glancing around, he regretted that choice.

The man was looking at him. He was strangely familiar, somehow. They had met before. Isak just couldn't tell where. There was something about his voice. He tried to remember, but everything was too muddled, too tense. His thoughts refused to fall in line.

"I'm not really here for the lawn mower," he said at last.

"No," the man said. "I figured that out."

"I just want to know what happened."

The man looked like he was of two minds.

"Should we . . . I can show you. If you come with me."

"Where to?"

"It's not far. Down by the falls."

Isak had his hands in his pockets. He squeezed the pocketknife. "Why?"

"I've got . . ." the man cleared his throat. "I have something down there."

He was about to yank out the knife and shove the fucker up against the wall. *We're going to work this out right now. Talk.* He had no intention of calling the police; that was a way out he had given up on a long time ago. They knew who he was now. They wouldn't believe him.

After such a long time, there was also no reason to drag it out. Rage began to ring through him like a dull, vibrating tone. He was surprised to find he was so calm and collected as he adjusted his grip on the knife.

"Her diary, I mean," the man clarified. "I thought maybe you would want to see it."

A tremor ran through Isak's chest. The diary. Lovisa Markström's diary.

The one Edvard had mentioned. At first Isak hadn't been sure if it even existed for real, or was just something his uncle had come up with in an attempt to confuse the police, to confuse everyone. Later on it became clear that she had indeed owned a diary, and she wrote in it now and then. He had wondered many times what it contained. Far too many times.

It could be a lie. Isak's eyes went to the man's large, rough hands. They were trembling wildly. Just like his own.

"It's down by the falls?"

"That's where I keep it."

"Why?"

The man's eyes darted here and there. "It's hard to explain. I don't want it near me." The man raised his eyebrows. "Look, I'm telling you the truth: It's down there."

It might not be true. But if it was, then Isak could sort of understand where the man was coming from. He, too, kept most of what mattered at a comfortable distance. Isak studied him again. The man looked shaken, but it didn't seem like he was trying to hide anything.

This wasn't what he had come for. On the other hand, it was hard to figure out what he'd expected to happen. Isak was moving through a fog now, beyond the end point.

The man locked the door. He was unarmed. They set off on foot.

Around them, the summer was so incredibly green. They didn't say much. From a distance they might have been mistaken for two friends on a walk through the outskirts of the village. Rage was still ringing through Isak; the feeling of injustice forceful as a nightmare, but it was like the moment had rendered him weak and docile.

When they got to the falls, Isak stood once more with his hands in his pockets, one hand around the knife. It had become slippery with sweat. They were alone down there; the only sound was the roar of the powerful water and a fainter, softer rustle from the trees.

For a long time the man gazed at the current sweeping by them, the foaming surface, the sharp, wet rocks. He seemed uncertain. Isak squeezed the knife.

"Where is it?"

The man nodded at a rock. "Under there."

Isak took a step forward. "You're lying."

"No."

Isak yanked out the knife but lost his grip as the man took a quick step toward him, his eyes wide open and blank, and hit him in the face. Isak didn't have time to duck. The blow was so hard that he fell backward.

From the corner of his eye he watched the man grab his arm. *Did I get him? Where's the knife?*

He was no longer holding it. Instead he saw the man take it from the ground and place it in his pocket. Then a cruel kick came flying at him and his head sang for a split second, but after that came nothing but a dark, dark silence.

Isak doesn't have the strength to read very much; it's too difficult in the darkness and with his hands bound behind him. But as he comes to understand, during an hour or two when the light is shining through the small windows near the ceiling, it's Lovisa's diary. Was it down by the falls? No. He must have had it somewhere in the house. It's hard to think; everything is bleeding together. Impossible to say how much time has passed, and in which order the events occurred. *First I went to his house. He took me to the falls. When I came to I was down here, all tied up. Now what? What's going to happen?* He thinks about the man, his gaze sunken into madness.

Maybe he doesn't even know it himself. The unpredictability frightens Isak. Anything might happen.

He touches the diary with reverence, like it's a part of her. *Lovisa . . . you were so lovely, I remember. I liked you. And Edvard, he . . .*

He interrupts the thought. It hurts too much. He manages to open to one page and he suddenly sees himself through time, a boy in proximity to the words, just beyond reach.

26 October 1994: We were supposed to meet up today. I was standing at the edge of the forest behind one of the farms, watching some kids play hockey on the ice. He must have followed me there. He came up and wanted to talk. I didn't want to. He said he still loved me. I left.

It was Isak's secret once upon a time; it was just that he didn't understand it. He recalls Edvard asking him about it. Yes, Isak had seen Lovisa standing there. And he had thought it was Edvard who came over and scared her.

It wasn't. He wasn't the one she was afraid of.

Isak gazed in their direction. Then he called someone's name. A pass came flying by. Karl took a puck to the mouth. Blood all over the white ice.

At last the confusion hits him. The chaos and panic temporarily draw back, making room for realization. Somehow it was easier to believe that Edvard had done what everyone said he did than to be forced to see his history and himself in a fresh light. Surely it can't be true that he's lived for more than twenty years with a fake history. The boy with the token inside him, the teenager full of rage that eventually let loose, and the twenty-five-year-old who looked at himself in the mirror and thought, *Well, what did anyone expect?*—they've all been shaped by something that wasn't true. He feels duped.

During his walks earlier that summer he had spent a lot of time thinking about it. And about the baby, and Karin. About whether he would be able to cope with everything that awaited. And what would happen to him if he couldn't. He talked about it with the old mare. She still looked wise.

Edvard was dead. Nothing could change that fact. You are not laid to rest in God's Field only to return one day. But he—

Isak's thoughts are suddenly interrupted. Here he comes again.

"We're leaving," he says, standing in front of Isak.

Isak squints. And he finally realizes why the man is so familiar. "It was you."

"What?"

"During Gudrun."

"What?"

"The storm. You're the one who helped me out of the well."

The man is knocked off guard.

"No."

"Yes." A spark of hope ignites in Isak's heart. "You saved me once. You—"

"Shut up. We're leaving."

"Where are we going?"

The gray sneaker comes sailing toward his face again. Isak tries to shield himself, but he's too slow. The heavy kick lands at his temple, and a gong sounds in his ears.

"I just want you to be quiet," the man says, his voice trembling, almost pleading.

He comes to as tall grass brushes his palms. He's being carried down a path in the forest. The trees smell just like they usually do after the hottest days of summer, but the evening is cool.

That's right.

In that moment the panic hits him, bringing with it the pain in his legs, ribs, head, mouth. Everywhere.

Isak tries to wrench himself free, but to little effect. His arms are bound, and his legs, too. A strong arm is carrying him over the man's shoulder as if he were a sack of dirt.

The man carrying him stops, turns to the left, the right, hesitant. The motion nauseates Isak. He wants to throw up, but his body can't comply. You can manage a lot more than you think, but there are limits. Anything else would be inhuman.

Maybe that's what it means to be human: being unable to manage.

And then he's dropped. He isn't set down. That will turn out to be crucial.

The man leans forward and lets Isak's heavy body slide off him.

Isak falls to the ground neck first and hits a rock, and the last thing he sees before everything ends is the clear night sky, the stars watching over Marbäck, way up high.

79

Vidar's phone rings early—only quarter to seven. It's Amadia.

"Dad?" she says. "You have to come get me."

She wants to be a lawyer or an architect. This fall she'll be starting her last year at Sannarp secondary, in the sociology program. In the meantime she's got a summer job at one of the tourist spots along the Tylösand beach. Each morning at seven she catches the bus. She's saving her money for a trip to Tunisia with Rebecca and Evelina this winter.

Something is wrong this morning. She sounds scared.

"Are you okay?" he asks.

"I already called the police, but I—"

"Amadia, where are you?"

Across from him at the breakfast table, Patricia raises an eyebrow.

"I don't know what happened," their daughter mumbles, "but someone has to come."

"Amadia."

Vidar's heart is pounding. Patricia rises from the table as if she can see it on him.

"Amadia, just tell me where you are, and Mom and I will be there right away."

:::

Blood. There's blood on her hands. And her clothes.

His stomach clenches. He moves faster.

She's crouching on the ground next to a body, has a hand on its chest but isn't looking at it. When she hears Vidar, she startles and turns her head.

In the air, far away, he hears rotors.

Vidar dashes up and embraces her, Patricia at his heels.

"He was just lying here," Amadia whispers. "I didn't know what to do. I'm okay, I'm just shocked."

Vidar inhales the scent of Amadia's hair. She's as stiff as a board. Over her shoulder, he peers down at Isak Nyqvist. Or what's left of him. Shit.

Patricia puts an arm around her daughter and kisses her hair.

"Amadia," Vidar says gently. "Did you touch him?"

"To see if he was breathing. I put my hand on him to feel whether his chest was moving."

"He's alive?"

"Yeah. And I'm okay." She's beginning to collect herself; she wiggles free. "It was so fucking creepy, is all. He was just lying here."

"Did you touch him anywhere else?"

"On his neck. To see if he had a pulse. He was pretty cold. And so freaking pale."

"Good, Amadia. You did a good job."

"Fuck, he stinks so bad."

Patricia and Vidar gaze at each other for a long moment. The rotors are getting closer, chopping at the air. Sirens howl.

"I'll catch up with you," he says. "Is that okay?"

She nods silently and puts an arm around Amadia. They walk off together. Vidar watches them go, then squats down next to the body and holds a hand in front of the nose and mouth.

Yes, he's breathing. Very shallowly.

It's a popular walking path; it runs between the fields and toward the nearby forest. People walk their dogs here; Hedman's sons bring the horses here sometimes, and on occasion people use this path to get to the bus stop instead of going the other way. It's more overgrown, but shorter. Just a coincidence that Amadia was the one who found him.

He's wearing jeans and a thin, long-sleeved gray shirt, black Converse. He's dressed for a cool summer day. Dirty and bloody, fingernails edged with brown, his skin unnaturally pale. He smells terrible; he has pissed and shit himself both. More than once, it seems. His face is swollen, the skin broken in several spots, purplish blue and bloody. Hard to say whether those are his only injuries. The worst of it might be internal.

The back of his neck is resting against a stone, and Vidar realizes now that the stone is discolored and sticky. Blood covers the grass around it like a halo.

His skull has been crushed.

Vidar gently pats the pockets of Isak's pants. Nothing unusual, as far as he can tell, but he's afraid to move him to check the back pockets.

The sirens are getting louder. An unnaturally strong breeze kicks up. The paramedics come running.

The sun warms the ground.

80

Karin Nyqvist is sitting at his side when he says it.

Tubes and wires trail from the body in the bed to machines that beep, count, and record. She's holding his hand.

It's no longer a missing-person case; it's kidnapping and attempted murder. Maybe, soon, murder full stop. Judging from Isak's condition, his odds aren't very good.

He's undernourished and hypothermic, dehydrated, with bruises and sores around his wrists and ankles, a broken collarbone, and multiple wounds on his face. He's missing at least one tooth, has a fractured jaw, and his tongue is huge and swollen like a bloated fish.

It's hard to hear what he's saying.

"What happened, honey?" Karin asks, squeezing his hand.

A long silence. Then: "Mouth for stop."

That's how she interprets it. It sounds like *muhfuhstob*.

"What?"

"Get . . ." he starts.

He squeezes her hand. Then he goes perfectly limp.

"Get what? Get who?"

But Isak is no longer responsive.

:::

The doctor is a dark-haired woman in her forties. She has smooth features, alert eyes; she's too busy to chat but is patient and kind when she answers Karin's questions.

The bleeding and swelling are forcing his brain into a coma, so it can try to heal and recover. *Try*, that's the doctor's term. That is to say, it might not succeed.

"Does he know I'm here?"

"It's hard to say. Some people know; others don't. But we always assume they're aware of our presence and can even hear everything we're saying. So we act just as if he were awake. You can do the same thing. Come in here with me so we can talk a little more."

She sits down in the doctor's consulting room. Moves like she's in a torpor. In her belly is their son. In less than four months he will be here with them, in their arms. With Mom and Dad.

Muhfuhstob. Get . . .

Get what?

That's the first thing Vidar asks too, when he hears the story a few hours later. He's sitting in his car at the time.

"I don't know," Karin says in his ear. "I think he was trying to say more, but couldn't quite . . ." She gathers herself. "Manage."

"And what did you say, *mouth for stop*?"

"That's what it sounded like. I asked what had happened, and he said *mouth for stop*. I think he had something in his mouth before. Or maybe he meant something about his tooth, I'm realizing now, I don't know. One got knocked out, after all. Maybe it was a dumb question, to ask what had happened, I should have asked something else, but I just sat there looking at him and how injured he was, and—"

"Karin," Vidar cuts in calmly. "Have you told the police?"

"Yes, they were right outside."

"Good."

"Oh my God, I just keep talking." She collects herself. Vidar climbs out of the car, closing the door behind him. "I really just wanted to thank you for being so kind to him this morning. You and your family. But I'm so, I don't know, it's just so terrible. I just keep talking."

"You need to," Vidar says. "It's no trouble."

There's no natural end to this conversation. Karin just waits. Vidar understands. At last he brings it to a close and calls Patricia instead; she answers after a few rings.

"How is Amadia?" he asks.

"She's okay. Weren't you coming home?"

"Yes. I'm coming. It just took longer than I thought, is all, I had to go to Oskarström."

"Oskarström?"

"I'll explain later; I just need to do this before I come home."

He hears her sigh.

"Do whatever the fuck you want."

Click.

The sun warms his back as he walks toward the car dealer's house.

Oskarström is home to about four thousand people, and it's situated along the Nissan River, just over twenty minutes from downtown Halmstad. It's an old settlement, like Marbäck. The oldest villages in the area go back to the Iron Age. On one out-of-the-way road lives the old car dealer Birgersson.

They've met before. A little more than twenty years ago, two hooligans broke into his store and stole a Volvo each. Vidar hadn't been on the case from the start; he'd been brought in later when it was time to question witnesses. He also spoke to Birgersson himself during that time, and the man had turned out to be something of an original.

He was, he claimed, one of the few people in the country who could tell the difference between an oncoming Morris Minor and a Renault 4CV in the dark. From the back or from the side was no big accomplishment, but from the front—apparently that took a practiced and careful eye.

He had been approaching sixty at the time, and this time he

informs Vidar, with a firm and energetic handshake, that he turned eighty this summer.

"But having coffee and chatting with police officers," he says, gazing at the bag of pastries in Vidar's other hand, "are still two of my favorite pastimes."

"Yes, I thought so."

"It must have been twenty years ago that we met after that break-in. What a shenanigan."

"But we caught them, didn't we?"

"Sure, but I was talking about time. It just flies. And Christ, if it isn't hot out. Yesterday the lady next door got heat stroke. I had to call the ambulance and the whole nine yards. She's fine, but it makes a body nervous."

Birgersson is a wiry man with a potbelly, frizzy white hair, and deep-set eyes. Narrow steel-rimmed glasses perch on his considerable hook of a nose. He sits down on his old kitchen bench with a sigh. Coffee is waiting on the table.

"I'm not actually a police officer anymore. But that break-in did turn out to be an important moment in my life. I met my wife because of it."

"Imagine that," Birgersson says. "Imagine that. Are you still married?"

"Yes."

"And you've stuck together all this time?"

"More or less."

"Not even one tiny slip-up?"

Vidar raises his eyebrows. "Why do you ask?"

Birgersson sips his coffee. "I was married for fifty years. I'm no better or worse than anyone else, so of course I messed up a few times. Once she left and I was so afraid she wouldn't come back."

"Did she?"

"After I called her, drunk and miserable, and said I was going to kill myself. Then she came home."

"That sounds drastic. But effective, maybe."

"And nasty." Birgersson shakes his head. "Very nasty. It was wrong. I'm ashamed of it now. But love can sometimes make a person loony. Here, there's more."

He picks up the pot of coffee and refills Vidar's mug. Slipups. Loony. Yeah, you could say that again.

"To what do I owe the honor of your visit?" Birgersson asks.

"Your eyes."

The old man looks surprised. "What did you say?"

"Your eyes." Vidar brings up the photo on his phone. "I'm wondering what kind of car this is."

Birgersson takes the phone with a trembly hand. His crook of a nose almost touches the screen.

"It's a Ford Sierra sedan. Likely from the late eighties, I'd say 'eighty-eight or 'eighty-nine."

Vidar lets this sink in. "How sure are you?"

The old man looks at him. "*How* sure?" Birgersson pushes the phone back over to Vidar. "I'm sure."

"How many cars like this were there here in town in the fall of 1994?"

"You mean in Halmstad?" Birgersson leans back. "That's a completely different sort of question. Hard to say, but twenty-five? At most."

A large but not unmanageable number. Vidar looks at the car once more, how it slices through the darkness, fragments of a face.

81

Vidar contacted Clara once. It was a mistake. He knew that, but he did it anyway.

It happened about a year ago, when his relationship was at its worst.

Patricia had no idea. He had started taking late-night drives. When Amadia was asleep and the silence of the house became too claustrophobic, he took off in the car, never with any destination in mind. *Just get away. For a little while.* He drove through the village, out onto the highway, and into town, sailing down streets with the night-time radio on low. He thought about everything and nothing.

Vidar had recently run into Dennis Götmark, his old schoolmate, at work. Dennis had come out to the airport to pick up a load of construction materials. Vidar had had some spare time and helped him load the items onto his truck, and then they had coffee in the departures hall.

Dennis had some tough years behind him, with his kid and wife, a divorce, and hard times finding work.

"But it's looking up now," he said. "I'm starting to get my life back under control. You just have to tie up loose ends."

That sounded nice. It was probably why he did it. Vidar had his phone to his ear and one hand on the wheel, drifting slowly across Slottsbron, which sparkled in the lights of Halmstad City, the place where he'd spent his whole life aside from the years at the academy, and where he would probably remain until the day he kicked the bucket.

"Yes, hello."

She sounded sleepy. She knew it was him. She had his number. And yet she had picked up. Or maybe she had deleted it?

"Hello?" she said.

"Why . . ." he began, surprised at how thick his voice had become. "Why . . ."

"Vidar? Is that you?"

"You shouldn't have . . . I was married. I am married."

"Excuse me?"

"We shouldn't have done it."

"What, so it's *my* fault?"

Yes. No. Not just . . . he didn't know. He couldn't produce a single sound, either.

"Jesus Christ," she muttered. "Have you been drinking or something?"

"No. I'm in the car."

"What do you even want? We fuck once and you don't answer when I call to make sure you're okay. I don't hear from you for a year, and then you call in the middle of the night to hurl accusations at me?"

Vidar didn't say anything. He headed down by the Victoria Viaduct. Streetlights flashed in the dark.

"I never want to see you again," he said.

She snorted. "I got a new job; I'm moving in a month."

She hung up.

He was ashamed.

That was the last time he spoke with her.

A sudden shadow has settled over this summer. The village is full of unrest. People are out talking about the discovery that morning.

Yeah, it was Jörgensson's daughter who found him. So awful. Sure hope he makes it, that Isak.

But heck, the guy's never exactly been on the straight and narrow. You remember his uncle, of course.

An invisible hand has, once again, set something in motion.

Vidar has returned to Marbäck. It's almost lunchtime. Patricia is out getting groceries; Amadia is at work. She wanted to go, according to Patricia, because it felt better to have something to do.

"When this is over," Vidar tried, "things will be different."

"You're not even a cop anymore. Don't you get it? I thought we . . . yesterday it felt like you finally *got* it. But today, it's just . . ."

The last straw. He shouted: "Our daughter found a man who was beaten half to death, Patricia. What the *fuck* do you want me to do?"

She looked at him for a long time. He was breathing hard. He wanted to apologize.

"When this is over," she repeated slowly, "we'll figure out what we're going to do."

She stroked his cheek. He touched hers. Neither of them was smiling, but it felt like atonement.

It's back again. The case is winding around him like smoke, encapsulating him. He needs to leave for the airport soon. The afternoon flight from Stockholm arrives at three-fifteen, and his shift starts two hours before that.

Sitting in the car, he leans back against the headrest and closes his eyes, trying to think. *Isak Nyqvist. Edvard Christensson. Lovisa Markström. Again. What the hell is going on?* It is soon way too warm in the car, and he opens the door for some cooler air.

"Whoops—dammit," someone says.

Vidar opens his eyes and glances out in confusion.

"Did I wake you up?" Markus asks, squinting. "Sorry, the door almost hit me."

"I didn't mean to, it's just so damn hot."

"Do you have a minute?"

"I have to head to work soon."

"And I'm going to town."

Vidar starts the car. "I can leave now. It's fine. Hop in."

It's almost like before. The two men in the car, heading for the station, Vidar at the wheel and Markus in the passenger seat, surrounded by question marks. This time, with a creeping sense of danger in their bodies.

"It doesn't feel right," Vidar says.

"Not right at all," Markus agrees, opening his bag and taking out a laptop.

He opens it and clicks between documents and brand-new evidentiary photographs. They're uncomfortable to look at: Isak Nyqvist, lying in his hospital bed. Images of his body, technical evidence, his clothes, bruises, and wounds.

"The car in the photograph is a Ford Sierra sedan, from 1988 or 1989," Vidar says. "Birgersson wasn't sure on that point. According to him, there were twenty-five of them, tops, in the area in 1994. Can you access the National Vehicle Registry on that thing?"

"No. But I'll call it in. Which years, did you say?"

As Vidar repeats them, Markus puts his phone to his ear. Beyond the windshield, the world rushes by.

Markus relays the information and listens.

"Great." He turns to Vidar. "They're going to perform the search as soon as possible. But, listen." He hesitates. "I'm not quite sure . . . I mean, this is so strange, all of this, but when we were at Karin's place yesterday and I said *We'll take over now*, or whatever I said, I meant—"

"I understand," Vidar says.

That's the real reason Markus has sought him out. Vidar really can't blame him, in the end.

"You live out there. This affects you, Amadia . . . I know that. And you were one of us, once. You know what we always used to say, once a cop, always a cop. I just want you to remember that you're not a police officer anymore. You need to turn to us if anything comes up. And what's more, you figure into this investigation now, as a witness and as Amadia's dad."

A word returns to him from the past. *Behave. You will behave yourself.* That's not what Markus is saying, but the implication is the same.

"I understand," he says again. "It's fine."

"Are you sure?"

Vidar brakes for a red light at Sannarp. Tourist cars are lined up all around them, full of luggage, children, and grumpy moods.

"Can I just ask what you think happened?"

"Well, look . . ." Markus shifts in his seat, eyes on his computer. Probably weighing what he can and can't share. "Best guess is he went down to the falls, where we've got the LKP. He was waiting for someone; they'd arranged to meet there. The person arrives." He clicks on the computer, bringing up a picture of a footprint on the ground. "This is from the site. A sneaker, Lejon brand. We found identical ones near the body, and they don't belong to Isak. So they met up down there. Then something happened. I imagine he took Isak somewhere. And . . ." Markus clicks through pictures of clothing, fingernails, a hairline, Isak's shoes, and lands on his wrists. "We found these marks on his wrists. I suspect he was held against his will."

Vidar studies the image. "For almost a week?"

"He had received hydration, but not much. So it's possible."

"Jesus."

"Yeah." Markus shakes his head slowly and gazes out the window. "Like, who does that? And why?"

Vidar shifts gears and continues toward the station.

"Someone desperate, maybe. Someone who doesn't know where to put himself. Or someone who just likes dragging things out. How many people have you got on this now?"

"We're waiting for regional reinforcement. It will arrive tomorrow. But it's not exactly crowded, if that's what you mean. People are on vacation."

Too slowly. It's moving too slowly. He wants to say so to Markus, but he can't. Soon he's parking in front of the police station. Markus stays put, as if he's hesitant to leave, and turns to Vidar again.

"I—"

"According to Karin," Vidar interrupts, "he took morning walks down to Hedman's farm. Isak, I mean. I borrowed an impact driver from him last spring, and I was planning to talk to him while I was there, but . . ."

"We can do that. Talk to him, I mean. We can try to squeeze it in today, but we're swamped with the crime scene and questioning potential witnesses."

"Could you stop by my place and grab the impact driver, in that case?"

Markus laughs and steps out of the car, then disappears into the station.

82

He's working. The loud roar of the aircraft drowns out his thoughts. It's almost pleasant. During his break he stands in the bathroom, looking into his own eyes: absent, verging on empty. The lights are on but no one's home. He goes back out again. The heat is shimmering off the taxiways. Passengers are boarding and deplaning in sweaty lines. When the work before one departure is over, the preparations for the next arrival begin, followed by another departure. It goes round and round.

Vidar doesn't belong here. That's clear to him—he feels the same strange distance as when he had spent too long as a civilian during a vacation and started to feel like a stranger to himself. When he leaves the airport, he's restless. As if time has been unnecessarily wasted.

Vidar drives with his windows down to Marbäck and picks up the impact driver, then keeps driving and parks on a grassy flat near Isak and Karin's house.

He's only checking. Nothing more. He's going to keep his distance.

With the impact driver in hand, he walks toward Hedman's farm, the same way Isak supposedly went for his morning walks. It's evening, and the shadows are long but the air is still oppressive, muggy. The young forest rises around him, tall and dark, thicker than it looks in the daytime. It sighs and creaks, rustles and buzzes.

Muhfuhstob.

Get . . .

Wonder what he meant? Maybe Markus and his colleagues have already gotten to the bottom of that. A pang in Vidar's chest.

Down by Hedman's farm, one of the horses is out. She's moving slowly and gracefully on the other side of the pasture, but she raises her large head when she hears Vidar coming.

Vidar stops. He puts down the impact driver and extends his hand. The horse has deep brown eyes. She looks old and lets Vidar rest his palm on her muzzle. They stand there looking at each other for a moment, and something tells him she's very wise.

She gazes at something past Vidar's shoulder. He turns around. There's the old man, walking toward them and chuckling. He's got a cane for support.

"I can't walk so good anymore" is the first thing he says. "But no way in hell I'm bringing that Rollator outside." He waves a hand. "Don't let me interfere. I just wondered who it was visiting Hedvig."

"I came to return the impact driver. Have the police been by?"

"They called. Supposed to come tomorrow. What's it all about, do you know, son?"

"I think it's best for them to explain. Here." He hands over the impact driver. "She's a nice horse. Her name is Hedvig, you said?"

"Yes," says the old man. "But it ain't the first time you've met, of course."

"No?"

Hedman looks concerned. "So it's not you."

"Sorry?"

"Well, the fellow who's come around in the mornings. Then again, it ain't morning right now. And you were going to drop off the impact driver, you said." Hedman looks a little comical, sort of a caricature of a farmer, with a serious underbite, crooked teeth, silvery hair peeking out from under his cap, puzzled eyes. "What time is it?"

"Almost ten," Vidar says. "At night."

"I'm a little old now, so I get confused sometimes. More than ninety, you know, sure as shit never expected a fellow would make it this long." The old man walks over to Hedvig and reaches over the fence. She butts his hand gently, as if she wants him to pet her. "But look at this old bugger. I made it to a ripe old age after all, ain't that right, Hedvig? Hell, you've managed pretty well yourself. But I suppose time is running out."

"Did you say someone has been here, mornings?"

And Hedman tells him about the figure he'd seen earlier in the summer—not every morning, but almost. The last time, he says, was July tenth. He remembers that day in particular because the man stopped down here. Hedman points the impact driver at the big bulletin board. He stood there for a moment and then took off again, but in the other direction. It wasn't his usual routine.

"And that was the last time you saw him?"

"Yep."

"That was July tenth, you said?"

"Sure was."

Vidar looks at the bulletin board. In his mind, the gears turn slowly.

Hedman goes back to chatting with the horse.

"Thanks a lot. I'm going to keep moving."

"Good idea." Hedman raises his half-blind eyes to the sky. "It's too hot. Right, Hedvig? Way too hot."

The horse rubs against his hand.

The bulletin board waits, just a stone's throw down the path. These still exist here and there in the village. They used to be gathering places; meetings were even held around them. The dark, oiled wood structure looks heavy in the summer night. On it: an old farm map of the area, information about a meeting of the Local Heritage Foundation, a notice about a missing cat, a handwritten "for sale" poster for a lawn mower, a notice about a flea market, an ad for some sort of healing course, and a poster for *Summer Night Music* up in Simlångsdalen.

He stood here, and then he turned around and hurried back.

What did you see?

Vidar takes a step forward.

Show me your face.

He studies one of the ads up close, meticulously, for a long time. At the bottom of it, the paper is cut into strips with a phone number on them. It ends in 560. One of the strips is missing. *For Sale: Riding mower. Call for more info.* Above his head, a large, black bird is circling silently.

Then he sees it.

He yanks the notice down and starts to run back to his car.

83

Vidar, too, keeps the past up in the attic. It's all in a box. He pulls down the ladder and climbs up into the humid darkness, takes the box from its shelf and opens it, shining his phone flashlight inside. Papers, documents, preliminary investigation files, old photos of colleagues, diplomas and distinctions that once meant something.

There. There it is. Vidar opens the thick, brown folder and skims the contents. It's quiet around him; he can hear himself breathing.

He hasn't seen these for a long time. He both does and doesn't remember them, somehow. When he finds the old photocopies he holds his breath.

Sitting in the attic, surrounded by the remains of a lost criminal investigation, he shines his cellphone flashlight on them, comparing.

Call for more info.

Yes . . .

Right?

This is what you were looking at.

Whoever wrote the words has handwriting almost identical to that of whoever wrote the threatening letters to Lovisa Markström.

It *can't* be his imagination. Not after so much time has passed, after everything that's water under the bridge. After all he's lost. He doesn't even want to see the similarities. He doesn't want to have to deal with this again.

:::

How similar are they, really? Certain letters in the ad are too round; others are sharper than they should be. It could be the pen. It could be the passage of time; a person's handwriting isn't static, but nor is it likely to transform completely. It could be the paper he wrote on. It could have been written by someone else. And what can you even get from old handwriting?

Not as much as you'd hope.

Vidar throws the papers down.

He closes his eyes. In the darkness of the attic, it almost doesn't make a difference. Although night has fallen, the heat of the day lingers within the walls, making the attic hot and stuffy. Leo always had a particularly tough time in the heat. In the summer he often lay in the shade between Vidar's legs and refused to move. Strange to think of the old dog now.

He opens his eyes. Tension in his temples. He calls Markus to tell him what he's found, but there's no answer. Maybe it's too late at night, or maybe he's got his hands full with something else.

Picking up the papers again, he takes a deep breath and looks at the phone number on the ad. He brings the phone to his ear and waits for it to ring. Five, six, seven times. No voicemail, either. Shit.

He sits there for a long time. Through the floor he can hear Patricia on the phone. "*Yes,*" she's saying. "*Yes, I guess she's been okay today. No, she's going to work tomorrow, too. I suppose it was just . . . Yes. I don't actually know, I think he's in the attic. But yes, of course he was shaken, too. I could tell just by looking at him.*"

A brief silence.

"*I don't know. We had a talk yesterday and it felt like I got him to understand, but I don't know, today it was . . . No, exactly. I'm so goddamn tired of this. I love him, obviously, but the question is whether that's enough.*"

And I love you, he thinks. *But I don't know, either.*

He puts the phone to his ear again. Ringing. Two, three, four times.

"Yes, hello, this is Dennis."

Vidar breathes, listens. He doesn't move.

"Hello?"

Vidar has heard his voice before. He sounds uncertain but not scared.

Vidar hangs up and hurries down the stairs. It's his old school-mate, Dennis Götmark.

84

The oppressive heat of the day has given way to a warm, comfortable summer night. A pair of headlights, brights on, flashes in the dark. A car approaches, passes him on the narrow road, and Vidar almost loses control when the back of the car starts to slew. He's driving way too fast; he slows down and tries to rack his brains.

Dennis Götmark. Shit. *I only checked out his friend. Never him.*

The tires are spitting pebbles and dust. The gravel road winds upward, between the trees and into the forest. Dennis Götmark lives in the same place now as he did twenty-three years ago, in the house his father once built. Vidar parks in the shelter of the trees a ways off, afraid he may have frightened Dennis with the phone call. When he steps out of the car, he wishes he had some way to defend himself.

The lights in the window glow through the trees. The colder light of a TV flickers on the walls inside. Dennis is nowhere to be seen, but his car is in the driveway. Vidar presses the doorbell and stares at the handle.

Waiting. A gentle breeze rustles the branches of the trees.

The door opens. There stands Dennis in jeans and a T-shirt that says DON'T TALK TO ME WHEN I'M WATCHING THE GAME in capital letters. He's a heavyset man with large hands and thick lips, broad shoulders, skin that looks hard and rough.

"Vidar?"

"Hi, Dennis. May I come in?"

"What's going on?"

Rain strikes Vidar's face.

"Can I come in? I won't be long."

His old schoolmate moves to the side and Vidar steps onto the hall rug. "Do you want, uh . . ." Dennis is at a loss. "Do you want anything?"

"No, thanks, I'm fine."

Vidar closes the door behind him.

Dennis's shape is altered. When you find what you've spent so much time looking for, when someone transforms into a perpetrator, it's like a shadow settles over him. His gaze becomes darker, his movements threatening; everything he says is charged with an undertone even though he's not doing anything out of the ordinary. It makes it hard to act normal. You must not hesitate or let your hands tremble, just act natural.

"It's about the lawn mower."

Dennis looks confused. "Okay?"

Vidar steps forward.

"I was wondering if it's still available."

"How should I know?"

"I'm the one who called before."

Long seconds tick by between them. Dennis doesn't know where to focus his gaze.

"Oh." He scratches his cheek. "You were the one who hung up."

More time, Vidar thinks. *I need more time. I need to get a good look at him.* They knew each other once, that's true, but that won't help now.

"Where is the lawn mower?"

"Listen," Dennis says. "You probably came to the wrong place."

From his pocket Vidar takes the ad he ripped down.

"This is your number, isn't it?"

Dennis shakes his head. "It's Billy's. He's the one selling the lawn mower."

"Why would you answer his phone?"

Too tough, too antagonistic. Fuck. Now Dennis's arms are crossed; he's backing up, looking skeptical.

"He was here when you called, but he was in the bathroom. You called twice, right?"

"Yes."

"I let it ring once, since it wasn't for me. But when it rang again, I answered for him. I thought it might be important."

Vidar looks at the ad for a long time.

"Billy," he says. "Billy Oredsson. This is his number."

"Yeah," Dennis says, perplexed, even though it's not a question. "Dammit, explain yourself. What's going on, what are you doing?"

"Figuring out what happened. That's all." He slowly folds the piece of paper and puts it in his pocket. "You lied to me. Once, a long time ago."

85

They've taken a seat on the sofa in the den. On the table in front of them are a drooping houseplant, empty glasses, and beer cans.

"You said you and Billy were at your house all night when the Markströms' house burned down. Did he ask you to lie for him?"

Dennis looks at Vidar, his lips tense. "You're still a cop, right?"

"I work at the airport, you know that. I quit the force more than a decade ago."

"Why?"

"I wasn't happy there anymore."

Dennis leans across the table and picks up one of the cans. It's empty. He heaves a mild sigh and sinks back onto the sofa. He doesn't seem to know what to do with his hands, so he laces his fingers and rests them on his belly.

"If you're not a cop, then what is this all about?"

"Dennis." Vidar stares at him. "You need to answer me. Did he ask you to lie?"

Something happens with Dennis's face. He looks pained.

"I didn't even understand that it's not allowed. I know now, of course, but back then I didn't. Or else I just didn't think of it like that. He was my buddy. And my coworker, at the time, back then we worked as roofers for a small company up in Breared. Of course I had his back. It was no big deal."

Vidar leans forward. He's calm now, his pulse ticking steadily beneath his temples.

"What did he say to you?"

"It's weird, this was more than twenty years ago, and it's not like I have the world's best memory, but I actually remember. He called and said maybe I'd heard what had happened, and of course I had, everyone had by then. So fucking awful. Maybe that's why I remember it. Like when the *Estonia* sank or when Palme was shot, but different at the same time. Do you know what I mean? A great tragedy in miniature, kind of."

"I understand."

"I remember I could smell the fire all the way here," he continues. "Considering how Billy felt about Lovisa, his name was sure to come up, that's what he said, I mean, and the cops would come talk to him, too. He'd been feeling crappy all weekend and had stayed home. Hadn't seen or spoken to anyone. But of course no one could vouch for him. So he asked if I could say he had been with me, just to avoid a lot of hassle. And I didn't think much of it, you know, maybe I didn't really understand what he was asking of me. He probably didn't, either. I wanted to help him out. So when you came around later that day, that's what I told you. And, sure, okay. Maybe it was wrong, I can see that now. But he was my friend, and no way in hell was I about to let him take the fall for something everyone knew Edvard Christensson had done. And I feel the same today."

"I can understand that." Not all truths are good, and not all lies are bad. Vidar blinks. He wants to ask more questions than he has time for. It's all about keeping the searchlights pointed the right direction. "But I was thinking, you said *considering how he felt about Lovisa*."

"Hmm?"

"You just said that. How did he feel about her?"

"Well, you know . . ." His cheeks are red now. "I don't actually know. They met at a party in town somewhere, and after that he kind of fell for her. It sounded like they had something going for a while, but nothing ever came of it. I seem to recall Billy saying that she kissed him at some party during the spring sometime, but that it just fizzled after that. He was really torn up over it. He didn't say so, of course, probably too macho for that, you know? But I thought I could see it on him."

"A party in the spring. Could it have been in 1994?"

"Could have, sure."

From the pocket of his jeans Vidar takes the copies of the old letters. He hands them to Dennis, who takes them, curious, and reads. His eyes grow large and uncertain.

"What are these?"

"The handwriting is very similar to that on the ad." Vidar hands him the lawn mower ad. "Isn't it?"

The ceiling creaks. Once, twice, three times. Then a soft dragging sound. Vidar goes stiff. Just below the surface of his skin, his nerves are on full alert.

"What was that?"

He tries to play it cool. Dennis doesn't seem to have noticed how on edge he is.

"That's Johan. He'll be nine this fall, and he's started sleepwalking. Didn't I mention him when we ran into each other out at the airport?"

"You did."

Sleepy footsteps come down the stairs.

"Best day of my life, when he was born. But after that . . ." Dennis smiles wanly. "It went downhill after that. Now I've got him every other week. His mom lives in town."

"Is she from around here? His mom?"

He shakes his head. A little boy is standing there, holding on to the railing. He's got pajamas and big eyes, and thick blond hair.

"Dad?"

"Are you awake, Johan?"

The boy nods.

"I'm just going to take him back up," Dennis mumbles, putting down the ad.

"Who is that, Dad?"

"It's just my friend Vidar," Dennis says on his way to the stairs, one hand reaching for the boy. "He and I used to go to school together."

Johan places his small hand in his dad's larger one. Together they walk up the stairs. Vidar stays on the sofa; he retrieves the lawn mower ad from the table, folds it, and puts it back in his pocket.

He perches on the edge of the sofa, very still, his back ramrod straight. The threatening letters are still on the table. He thinks about the videotape, the dim light of the Midsummer sky, the grainy image. The man in the sunglasses. It could have been him.

The murder of Lovisa Markström, and Edvard Christensson's guilt, have wound through the years like a common thread. At such a great cost.

Heavier steps down the stairs. Dennis returns, apparently still lost in thought. He sits back down on the sofa. The large man fixes his empty gaze on an invisible point somewhere in the air above the table.

I have to reach him. I have to make him understand.

"Do you remember whether he had a car?"

"What?"

"Back then, in the fall of 1994. Do you remember whether Billy owned a car?"

"He did. A Ford."

"Are you sure of that?"

"It was a real piece of shit." Dennis laughs, but it's devoid of humor. "When he got to work in the morning we would sing that old song, you know, *I'm a little pile of tin, nobody knows what shape I'm in, I'm no Chevy, I'm a Ford* . . . You know that one?"

"Vaguely," Vidar says. "Where does he work these days?"

"At a construction site up in Simlångsdalen. He's installing the electrical up there, as an independent contractor."

Vidar leans forward. "Dennis."

"What?"

Vidar struggles to keep his voice calm.

"It never occurred to you that he might have been the one who . . .

well." He nods at the threatening letters. "You can see it as well as I can. How similar they are to Billy's ad."

"Sure, but that doesn't mean it was him. I can't imagine . . . no, he never would have . . . it's too dang bizarre to even think of. Like, not Billy. He's the nicest guy in the world."

"But that can happen. It's not so strange, really. Sometimes, good people do things they shouldn't."

"Sure. I just . . ."

"Dennis. Did you just contact him? While you were upstairs?"

Something happens in Dennis's eyes.

"No, for God's sake. If it was him, he got me to cover for him when he'd . . . I mean, he got *me* to . . . Shit. I'm not about to do that again." He blinks. His eyes are still oddly blank. "It was because of me, wasn't it? That it was . . . I remember people talking afterwards, about Christensson. That he claimed he was innocent until he died. Is that true?"

Dennis is a fifty-year-old man who, for an instant, looks a lot like a little boy who's been bad. Vidar rises from the sofa.

"Yes. It's true." What can he say? "When did you last see him? Besides today, I mean."

Dennis's broad shoulders are sagging.

"We don't see each other very often anymore. I have Johan and stuff, like I said. A week or two ago, maybe."

"What was he doing here tonight?"

"Nothing. He said he needed company. I think he lives a pretty lonely life, you know, without a family or kids. He's been on his own for basically his whole life, now that I think about it. I suppose I feel sorry for him sometimes, or whatever, and when he calls I usually just answer because I feel like I should. So I told him if he wanted to he could come over once Johan was asleep; he's usually out by seven-thirty or eight. So he came by around eight and we drank these and then chatted for a while, and then he left about fifteen minutes ago. I got the . . ."

"What?"

"Oh, I just got a feeling, is all, the way you do sometimes. You know?"

"What kind of feeling?"

"That there was actually something more he wanted. But he didn't say anything. And I didn't ask, either." He looks at his hands. "Maybe I should have."

Two headlights in the dark on the way here, brights on, it must have been him. Vidar passed him on the road.

"I'm glad you told me this, Dennis."

Vidar wants to do something, pat his arm maybe; Dennis could probably use the comfort. But something stops him, so he just stands there looking at the man he once went to school with. Dennis meets his gaze.

"What's wrong?" Dennis asks.

"I just realized I need a UV light."

"Oh," Dennis says tonelessly. "I have one, actually. I use it at work sometimes to look for leaks in old pipes. It's probably in the cabinet in the hall."

"Can I borrow it?"

"Yeah, sure."

Vidar heads for the hall.

"Hey," Dennis says, behind him.

"Yes?"

"I think he was scared. When I told him his phone had been ringing, he seemed caught off guard. Stiff, kind of. I could tell by looking at him."

86

Through a dim, still summer night, Vidar drives back through the village. The lovely fields bow slightly in the warm breeze.

He knows so little about Billy Oredsson. He was born and raised on the outskirts of the village, two years older than Lovisa Markström. Vidar noticed him at school on occasion, a bony little guy in a cap and jeans that he had to keep hiking up because they were too big. He looked a little goofy, but there really wasn't anything goofy about him. He became a tradesman and later, in the late nineties, he occasionally took part in the civilian rescue corps, mostly due, perhaps, to the fact that his father had done so before him. Vidar remembers it; they ran into each other one winter day during his time with the patrol unit after a bad traffic accident down on the highway.

After the murder of Lovisa Markström, his name showed up on a police list, since he had apparently shown interest in her. *Shown interest,* that was the phrase. That's all.

That, and the fact that he lives in an old shack of a place over by the lake called Toftasjön. Vidar checks the address on his phone. No phone number pops up this time either.

The highway is black and deserted. Vidar follows it for a while, then turns off at the rest area, down the gravel road toward the area surrounding Toftasjön, a place as old as the village. The lake is small but deep. People used to fish for perch here.

That's why, they say, things went badly for fishermen Jansson, Bengtsson, and Gabrielsson in the early 1900s. They took off to go fishing on the lake and never came home. No one knows what happened to them, but it's said that bandits were lurking in the lake. They yanked the men into the water and sold the fish out at the harbor.

A forest of fir trees surrounds the lake, a tall, black silhouette. Vidar parks near the small picnic area and steps out, walks up into the forest.

The house is old and painted Falu red, the siding dotted with algae and mold. It's isolated, squeezed among the trees on a rise above the lake; everything is dark. No car outside, and no garage either, but there are fresh tire tracks in the gravel.

Vidar sweeps the perimeter of the house. An old rake, a crowbar, a rusty bike, weedy flower beds with drooping sunflowers and lilacs. Old leaves and fir needles in the gutters. The windows are closed. A familiar yellow-and-black riding mower stands in back, looking abandoned.

He walks up to the front door and cautiously tests the handle. Locked.

Of course. But this is a house with an aging door, worn bolts, weak windows. He gets the crowbar and sets to work on the closest window. Old paint and insulation rain over his hands, legs, shoes. The wooden molding gives way with a protracted creaking and cracking.

Vidar peers into a living room. And old flat-screen TV on a white stand, a well-used leather sofa. A dusty coffee table. Vidar climbs in.

A person really ought to be armed for this. What if he's home?

He left the crowbar outside; all he has with him is Dennis's UV light. He turns it on and trains the beam on the walls, the floor, the sofa. Small spots here and there, nothing out of the ordinary. Dishes on the counter, grease on the stove, reminder notes on the door of the fridge. A few photographs on the walls: the oldest ones depict two parents and a small child; the parents wear thin smiles but the child's face is extremely serious. In the more recent pictures, the mother is missing. Did she die? Vidar tries to recall, but can't. No smiles in those pictures, in any case.

A basement door. The glow of the UV light turns it cold and blue.

There. Stains, maybe paint, on the handle. Smeary handprints. Could be blood.

He cautiously nudges the door open and goes down the stairs. They're narrow and creak under his weight. Along the walls hang cords, lights, tools, work clothes. Nails for hooks. Two of them are empty. Vidar considers them carefully. Something used to be hanging there. *Could it be . . . yes. Maybe.*

It smells like mold. And paint.

He's no longer trying to disguise his presence. At the bottom of the stairs, he sweeps the UV light across the basement. Small and damp like any old cellar; old boxes and bags full of all kinds of crap. Everything is grouped in the center of the space, along with paint cans and brushes.

It's been freshly painted.

Vidar runs his hand over the wall in one corner. It was a sloppy job, far from the quality you'd expect from a tradesman. The floor has been painted as well. He lowers the UV light, takes out a key, and gently starts to scrape away the paint.

Stains. Lots of them.

The more he scrapes, the more he finds. Traces of blood and saliva, and maybe sweat. Pretty fresh, too; they haven't had time to fade.

This is where you kept him. You arranged to meet Isak down at King's Rock, then overpowered him and brought him here. But why?

When Isak is reported missing and a coordinated search begins, he's worried but keeps a cool head. Not until the sound of helicopters and barking dogs flood the village does he realize that sooner or later they'll find their way to the house down by Toftasjön. He loses control and tries to get rid of the body. That's when he crushes Isak's skull on the rock. He's trying to silence him.

Right? But why wouldn't he do it here and bury the body? It doesn't add up.

Vidar turns around. He can almost see them there, a silhouette on the floor, one man cowering before the other. They move. They speak. Maybe they shout. Isak is kicked in the stomach; his ribs crack.

You want to get rid of him here. But you can't do it. You're not really a murderer. Everything's just gotten out of hand. You don't know where to put yourself. You drop him on the ground on the path, where Amadia finds him later. His skull is crushed against the rock, but it's an accident. You probably want to but can't kill Isak Nyqvist.

He was just trying to get rid of him.

Vidar leaves the basement and inspects the hall. A rack of shoes, hooks on the wall, a mirror. An empty hanger. On the floor is a half-packed bag that contains an overnight kit and pants, underwear.

As if he'd been planning to leave for a time but stopped in the middle of his preparations.

Vidar blinds himself as the beam of the UV light is reflected in the mirror, white as lightning, and he closes his eyes hard, blinking rapidly. His vision swims with white spots.

A thin envelope is wedged into the old wooden frame of the mirror.

It says *Dennis* on it. Vidar pulls the envelope loose and places it in his pocket.

At that moment, his phone rings.

87

"I think I know."

Vidar gets in the car and closes the door behind him.

"Know what?" Markus asks.

"Where he is."

"But where are *you*?"

Vidar tells him. By the time he's done explaining he's back to the highway, and he turns onto it, too fast, the car fishtailing.

"Oh my God," Markus says. "Okay. Have you called it in?"

"Didn't have time," Vidar mutters, shifting up.

"I'll call right now."

"What did you want?"

"There were nineteen Ford Sierras in the Halmstad region in October of 1994. One of them was owned by a Billy Oredsson. But never mind that, I'm calling this in. Just be careful. And wait for us."

Vidar places the phone on the passenger seat and swerves off the highway again, heading down toward Årnarp. The dark road winds through the fields and pastures. It slopes down steeply; it almost looks like a cliff. As a kid they would ride bikes here, their hearts in their throats and their bodies euphoric.

There is, at the narrowest point of the road, a nameless bridge. Once upon a time it was made of wood; now it's concrete. It's the bridge where the Old Man sleeps. Vidar speeds across it as fast as he dares and continues through Årnarp and back up toward Tolarp with his heart beating hard in his chest. As he approaches he turns off the engine and the headlights, rolling silently between the farms until the car stops near the place where the house once stood.

He takes the last little bit on foot, under the big Marbäck sky, through the outskirts of a village that has settled down for the night, peaceful and green.

The place where the Markströms' house once stood has remained untouched. Weeds and bushes grow high on the old property. If you didn't know there used to be something here, it would never occur to you.

Still no sirens, just silence and the pulsating, almost electrical buzz of innumerable insects. Vidar looks up at the grove of trees. The new forest has recovered well after Gudrun.

He had come walking out of there one night. He had smelled the smoke.

The dogs were barking. That was how it all began.

He steps into the tall weeds and hopes it's not already too late. High steps. Branches and blades of grass brush his arms.

The ground at the center of the lot, where the house had stood and where the worst of the fire had raged, is no longer dead but the weeds there are sparser, lower. There's a sheltered clearing in there. In the middle of it, a figure is on its knees, hunched over, apparently inspecting something on the ground.

Finally. A face.

Vidar pushes a branch aside. It creaks. The figure quickly turns its head, as if startled. His eyes are impossible to see in the dark.

"I thought you might be here," Vidar says.

"I can't."

He's trembling. He lowers his head again. Vidar slows down and squints to make out the shape of the man, to see what he's looking at.

"You can't what?"

"Stay there." Still trembling, but firm. "Stay there, don't come any closer."

Then he sees. The nails on the wall in the basement; something had been missing. He was right.

On the ground in front of Billy is a rifle. "It was Dad's. He used it to hunt moose."

"Billy. Take it easy, now."

When Vidar says his name, something happens. It's like a fog lifts from around the man.

"You're a cop, right?"

It's unfortunate that Vidar's standing while Billy is crouching down. The difference in level is bad. It only makes the man more unstable.

"I'm not a cop, no. But I was last time we met. At the café in Åled, if you recall. We had coffee there. My name is Vidar."

"You called me tonight, but Dennis answered."

"I know."

"I was in the bathroom."

Vidar slowly kneels down, keeping his distance. "It's okay. I'm here now."

"I didn't mean to . . ." He coughs. "He made it, right?"

"Isak? He's not feeling very well, but yes, he made it."

Alone, narrow-shouldered, freezing. That's Billy. There are wrinkles around his eyes and mouth; he has a receding hairline.

"I was trying to put him down, but he was so heavy. I didn't mean to . . . I mean, I helped him once. In the well."

Something clicks in Vidar's mind. The cards turn face up.

Muhfuhstob.

Billy was part of the civilian rescue corps. They were out during Gudrun, the night Isak Nyqvist was found in the old well on Hedman's property. It was a story that made the rounds of the village for days afterward.

Isak wasn't trying to say *mouth for stop*.

He was saying *man from storm*.

Vidar cautiously approaches Billy. Billy notices and moves a hand to the rifle, a big old Mauser with deep scratches in the wood. Under it is something else. It looks like a small book.

"Take it easy, Billy."

Sirens. He should be able to hear sirens by now. It seems like the insects and crickets are buzzing louder and louder around them; you could almost imagine that they're starting to coordinate, organize themselves. That they have teeth.

"You *are* a cop."

"I haven't been a cop for twelve years. What are you doing here?"

Billy looks around, as if he's hoping the answer is waiting somewhere in the weeds.

"I come here sometimes. Just at night, is all. I like sitting here. Well, no, no I don't. I hate it. But I feel better afterwards."

"As if you deserve to suffer." Vidar nods slowly. "I understand, Billy."

A sudden vibration right next to them. Billy starts and lunges, as if to grab the rifle, but he stops when he hears the ringtone.

"Your phone is ringing," he says.

"Yes."

"Aren't you going to answer it?"

Vidar shakes his head. "But I am going to put it on silent. I need to put my hand in my pocket. I'll do it slowly."

The sound echoes between them. Billy's eyes follow Vidar's hand. He silences the phone and takes his hand back out again. Hope it wasn't Patricia. God, Patricia. And Amadia. If something were to happen . . .

"Can you go away?" Billy says, interrupting Vidar's thoughts.

"Do you want me to?"

"Yes."

"What would you do if I did?"

Silence. The man gnaws at his lower lip.

"I can't leave, Billy. Not now. I was at your house tonight. I saw what was on the mirror, but you don't have to worry. Dennis doesn't know yet."

"He told me that even if you feel awful it will stop eventually. But it never does."

"Did you want to tell him?"

"I couldn't."

"He'll probably need to know, eventually. Do you want me to tell him?"

Billy avoids his gaze. He doesn't say anything.

"What's under there, Billy? Under the rifle?"

"It's hers."

"Lovisa's?"

He nods slowly, unsure of the consequences the admission will have.

"It must have been terrible to carry this around all on your own for so many years. How did you manage?"

Billy doesn't say anything for a long time. His eyes are still on the ground. He takes his hand from the rifle, a broken man realizing it's not supposed to end this way. He's not going to die tonight, either.

"I didn't mean to," he says. "I was just so mad. Because she had . . . I thought she wanted to be with me. I just got so mad."

"Sometimes you feel mad," Vidar concurs. "That's only human."

Then he waits. They're breathing in rhythm now, sitting in similar positions. The sound of the crickets and insects is still moving like an electrical pulse, but they seem to have decided to wait.

"She kissed me at a party. By then I'd been in love with her for a year or so. And then, just . . . I heard she had started dating him. The same night. *That same night.* I guess now I understand it wasn't that out of the ordinary, but at the time . . ." Billy wipes something from his face with the back of his hand. "*Who would want to be with someone like you?* That's what they used to say. I thought she was different. But then she wasn't. And I just got so mad."

"And maybe sad, too?"

"Really sad. I *loved* . . ." He shakes his head and doesn't finish his sentence. "I suppose it sounds weird, but it was true. I tried to tell her, to make her leave him."

"In the letters?"

Billy nods weakly.

"But she wouldn't listen. So I got in the car and went to her house. I wanted to talk. Then *he* showed up. I didn't mean to . . . I hit him before he could see me, but *she* saw it. And then she attacked me. *Me.* I only wanted to . . . I had to defend myself, I just . . . I was so mad at her. I didn't want to hurt her. I didn't know where to put myself."

"I understand."

Sometimes, that's the only explanation you can give.

Well done. Good job, Billy. Keep talking. No sirens yet, but they'll be here soon.

He slowly lays his hand on the object under the rifle. A small, hardback book.

"You have a daughter, don't you?"

"That's right."

"The Black girl."

"Her name is Amadia."

Billy nods slowly.

"It must be fantastic to have kids."

A slight tremble in Vidar's hand. He tries not to let it show.

"It is."

"I never had kids of my own. I really wanted to, though. I suppose I didn't deserve them. I've lived a lonely life. So I've been punished, too."

"I'm glad you're telling me this, Billy. I know it must have been incredibly hard to carry this burden. Have you talked to anyone else about this? Ever?"

He shakes his head.

"Not even Isak?"

"I didn't know what to do with him," he whispers. "When he rang my doorbell and wanted to ask questions."

"He came over to your house, just like that?"

"Yes."

"With no advance warning? I understand why that would startle you."

"He said he didn't want to call first and scare me. But I've been scared all this time. I panicked when I saw him. Then it occurred to me that we could take a walk. Down to the falls. I thought I could throw him in the water. I just wanted to get rid of him, but I couldn't do it." His eyes gleam in the darkness as he looks at Vidar, almost pleading. "I've never . . . I didn't want to hurt anyone. I just didn't want to . . . I wanted him to stop asking questions. I've always been bad at figuring this sort of thing out. So I made him be quiet. I had to bring him home. It was hard. I had to drag him through the forest. I was going to shoot him, but it . . ."

"You couldn't. I understand. But you kept him for almost a week, Billy. That's a long time."

Billy looks confused. "Was it that long?"

"Did you talk to him?"

"Not much. It's all blending together. I don't know . . . I haven't been sleeping very good."

"Isak recognized you, didn't he? You must have known it was all over when you dropped him in the grass. As soon as he was found, he would tell what had happened and who was responsible."

Billy is shivering now; it's coming from the inside. A broken man. Vidar glances at the rifle. If he's quick enough, he could grab it. If he just . . .

"I didn't mean for his head to hit the rock," Billy says, louder now. "I didn't mean to."

"That's not what I'm saying, Billy. You must have known it was over. You must have realized you wanted it to end. Didn't you?"

"I . . . I don't know. I just wanted to get rid of him."

Vidar waits. Breathing in time with the man. *Soon, now. Soon.*

"I was so ashamed," Billy says. "When you all arrested him and stuff. Edvard Christensson, I mean. There were a bunch of times when I was about to turn myself in. I even sat in my car in the parking lot outside. But I couldn't do it."

"But when we met at the café in Åled years later, you didn't say anything then, either."

"You asked me about two brothers."

"Do you remember telling me that their names sounded familiar? Were you misleading me?"

He looks at the sky, blinking.

"Yes, I was."

Vidar studies his shoulders, his posture. It's like he's collapsing into a pile. *Now,* Vidar thinks.

"Okay," Billy says, more to himself than to Vidar. "Okay."

"Good."

And then Billy's going to carefully hand over the rifle and stand up. Vidar will help him. He looks almost grateful, as if it's Vidar's turn now to take over the burden that Billy's been carrying around for so long. Vidar wants to say something, but he doesn't know what, and maybe it's better to remain silent anyway.

It's over. A lot has been lost, but not Billy. Vidar has managed to hold on to him, at least. Now they will leave the property, together.

Vidar pictures it, how Billy hands over the rifle, his hands and his expression; he can feel the weight of the weapon in his hands and the relief in his body, their calm steps as they walk through the weeds.

Even though it hasn't happened yet.

Sitting in the grass, Billy is all at once very quick and assured in his movements, as if he has practiced this many times.

The song of the insects rises, becoming deafening. The barrel of the rifle under his chin. His eyes almost empty. The shot is a bolt of lightning, loud and sharp and over in an instant. A crater in his head. His eyes swell and bulge out of their sockets. He falls with the rifle beneath him.

88

At last the first responders arrive on scene. They stand around, empty-handed and pale, looking at a dead man in the midst of all the silence. The officers speak to Vidar, but he doesn't notice them, doesn't hear them. He can only see their lips moving.

The little book that was under the rifle is spattered with blood. He thinks of how tenderly Billy had touched it.

He picks it up and opens it.

4 April 1994. *Nothing much happened today. I was at work and did a round through town after, then went home. It was cold. I was bored all day. Patricia from work called. We talked for a while. She asked if I wanted to meet up but I didn't feel like it.*

One of the officers cautiously removes the rifle and puts it in a heavy plastic bag. Vidar looks at his phone. Markus was the one who called. He's tried to reach Vidar several times since.

Vidar doesn't call back.

Most of the entries are brief. Some days she writes longer ones; other days she writes nothing at all. She mentions Billy on occasion, during the first few months of 1994. By May, he's almost completely absent from the diary. She has met Edvard by then. She's in love *for real*. That's what she writes.

Before that point, she was of two minds.

26 January 1994: *I know Billy likes me. I think he has for a long time. But I don't know if I can be with someone like him.*

4 March 1994: *Billy is so sweet! He sent me flowers today. A huge, pretty bouquet. I put them in the window so he'll see them if he walks by.*

15 March 1994: *Had coffee with Billy. He came to work and hung around until my shift was over. We had coffee and he ate a cookie. It was nice! But I don't know how much we have in common. He's not very good-looking, either. I told him I liked the flowers. He had movie tickets and asked if I wanted to go see something. I said yes, even though I'm not really sure. We'll see.*

17 March 1994: *Went to a movie at Röda Kvarn with Billy. He tried to hold my hand. I let him, but when he tried to kiss me I leaned away. I was ashamed, because it felt so mean. But he said it was fine, that we can take it slow. But you can't just take it slow forever! I know what he wants, I'm not stupid, I see what he's trying to say with his flowers and movie tickets and stuff.*

And then it happens.

10 May 1994: *Party at Lina's! 7:00.* Then, a longer entry: *I went to the spring party at Lina's. Drank wine, I don't really like it though. But it tasted good. Billy was there. We talked in the kitchen and I was pretty drunk and he tried to kiss me again. I guess I wanted to too, at the time. It was a nice kiss. We made out and I think he wanted more, but I had to use the bathroom. Then I felt so weird, so I told Lina I was going to go home and go to bed. I left without saying goodbye to Billy, maybe that was stupid? On the bus I met Edvard.*

That's all.

The magnitude of what had happened only becomes clear later on:

25 May 1994: *Worked 8–4. When I got home, Mom said Billy had called again. I feel like a bad person, but I don't want to call back. All I can think about is Edvard. What would he say if he found out I had been making out with another guy just like an hour before we met? What would he think of me? I don't want it to be like with J-E.*

She's referring to Jon-Erik, her ex. A minor thing has turned into a major incident, and she's afraid Edvard will leave her. *I've never been this in love before!* she writes in July. *Everything felt so pointless before. Now I wonder if I was depressed. But then he came into my life, this guy who lives here, he was right here all along. Life is so weird!*

She doesn't mention their arguments until they've been going on for some time. The first mention is in early September: *I get so tired of him sometimes! If I tell him so, he gets mean. It always ends in a shouting match. And then it gets worse.*

So she writes. She never uses the word *violence*. Maybe you can't blame her.

Sometimes you don't understand how much you've been shaped by something until it's gone. You see yourself in the mirror, unsure of who you're really looking at, who you've become.

Vidar takes the small envelope from his inner pocket. *Dennis*, it says in an uneven, scrawling hand.

An old photograph. That's all: Billy and Dennis, sitting in go-karts up in Simlångsdalen. They're wearing identical coveralls, holding helmets, their hair mussed. They look happy.

Billy, Edvard, and Vidar. They're all from Marbäck. How many years between them? Not many. Now only Vidar is left.

Vidar puts the photo back. He had been expecting more.

Isn't there always a distance between what you've learned and what you desperately want to believe, a chasm that separates what you've become from what you wish you were? It can take time to realize this. Almost half a life, if worse comes to worst.

The cards are face up, but it doesn't feel like it. He stands, the envelope in hand, and only now does he hear it: The insects and crickets have gone silent.

89

Tiny ruptures appear in the blackness. Cracks and sparks. The dark curtain turns dull red, then orange. When he blinks, the light is too bright; it's all blurry, and he squeezes his eyes shut. They tear up. A wave of nausea washes over him, and his head is pounding. His own pulse is thumping at the back of his skull.

"Basically not at all," he hears someone say. "In the spring of 1996, he checked himself into the psychiatric urgent care unit down here because he felt upset about something and wanted to talk. He never actually said anything. He was discharged a week later with a prescription for antidepressants. Which he never refilled."

The voice is familiar. It's Vidar Jörgensson. He sounds tired.

"I met him once up in Åled. I wanted to ask him about his relationship with Lovisa. We had coffee. But there was nothing to suggest . . . or, well, maybe there was. I just didn't see it at the time."

"Anything else?" *Karin*. Karin is here.

"No, that's all."

Karin starts to say something, but she cuts herself off. It's probably because of Isak. He's moving, trying to lift his arm. It works, even though it feels heavy. He tries to open his eyes again. It's still very, very bright, but with a lot of effort he can make out shapes, movements.

Karin takes his hand. She's warm.

"Isak? Isak, can you hear me? Call the doctor."

He can't move his head; it hurts too much. Hard to talk, too, his tongue is swollen. *Oh right. I bit my tongue.*

"Aah," he manages.

The sound is strange, as if it had come from someone else, but Karin sighs with relief.

"I missed you," she whispers.

Isak reaches for her. His hand touches her belly, and he can feel movement inside.

Maybe it's not impossible to become free after you die.

Free. That seems like the right word. But it feels strange.

90

Summer is still in full bloom, and everything looks so beautiful as Vidar walks through the village one evening, down toward Hedman's farm. And there he is, Isak Nyqvist, waiting by the pasture. He's tan and has grown out his hair; he's wearing the Byzantine chain around his wrist and he smiles as they meet.

"Didn't she come?" Vidar asks.

"Not yet. But I'm sure she will."

"So you still come down here."

"On occasion," Isak says. "But not very often. It just feels nice sometimes. How about you? Where are you headed?"

"Nowhere," Vidar says. "Home. Just thought I would take a walk down here."

"But don't you live up the other way? Isn't this way longer?"

One night, a house burned to the ground. There was someone inside, on the floor, someone who couldn't move. Something began; something ended. It took a long time to clear up.

It had probably been meant to be, what happened. So they'd said, to comfort one another, even though the whole series of events was *kymig*. People want to find a deeper meaning in everything. But maybe there isn't one.

"Yes," Vidar says. "This way is longer. But it still leads home."

ABOUT THE AUTHOR

CHRISTOFFER CARLSSON was born in 1986 in Marbäck, Sweden. He holds a PhD in criminology from the University of Stockholm, where he continues to teach, and is one of Sweden's leading crime experts. His awards include the International European Society of Criminology's Young Criminologist Award, and he's the youngest winner of the Best Swedish Crime Novel of the Year.

ABOUT THE TRANSLATOR

RACHEL WILLSON-BROYLES is a freelance translator specializing in translating contemporary literature from Swedish to English. She received her BA in Scandinavian studies from Gustavus Adolphus College in 2002 and her PhD in Scandinavian studies from the University of Wisconsin-Madison in 2013. She lives in Saint Paul, Minnesota.